The

Hero

was

Handsome

A Triple Threat Novel

Kristen Casey

The Hero Was Handsome

©2020 by Kristen Casey

This book is a work of fiction. All characters, situations, and dialogue are a product of the author's imagination and are not real. Actual locations and organizations are used only in a fictitious capacity. Any resemblance to actual events or persons, living or dead, is entirely coincidental.

ISBN-13: 978-1-949529-13-5

Cover Design ©2020 Tugboat Design

Author Photo ©2016 Kathleen Oristian Photography

EST 2016

GALLANT FOX
PRESS

The Triple Threat Series

The Titan Was Tall

The Doctor Was Dark

The Hero Was Handsome

The Triple Threat Box Set

About This Book

Lead the way...

Yeah, right. All *leading the way* had gotten Tate was a seat too close to a roadside bomb and a psych eval gone sideways. He was benched from the Army for months while he healed, but he wasn't going to mope around about one unlucky incident. He was going to get better and return to active duty in just a few more weeks.

In the meantime, he needs to keep busy so he can stop climbing the walls. Tate agrees to pick up a couple extra bucks and hit the road, working security for a hot little author his buddy wants protected. What could go wrong with a cake job like that? After all, Lyla is a writer, not a terrorist.

However, Tate's little temp job soon turns all kinds of complicated. When a mysterious fan starts getting too close for comfort on her book tour, he begins to suspect that he's not the only one who's fallen for Lyla's charms. It looks like some of the pretty bookworm's gritty research has followed her into the real world—and it's none too happy to find Tate barring the door.

Can he find the person scaring Lyla out of her wits before something truly bad happens? Or will his inconvenient crush keep him from completing the one mission more important than any other?

Suddenly, this job's about more than guarding an asset...

Tate's protecting the woman who holds his heart in her hands.

One

T ATE AWOKE, AS he often did these days, with the white-hot bang that came at the end of his dream. Sadly, it wasn't the sort of bang that had him balls-deep in a good-hearted woman. Instead, it was the kind that knocked him flat on his can if he was lucky—and sent him straight to his maker if he wasn't.

He sat up and blinked away the lingering fog of the recurrent nightmare and did a quick assessment. By all accounts, he was luckier than most. Tate was alive and whole, for one thing, and back home in the States, for another.

He'd been born to a nice, solid set of parents who'd been coddling him for months and, courtesy of his kick-ass best friends, he'd spent the night on a posh hotel mattress instead of on the rocky ground of the Middle East.

On the other hand, Tate's career would soon be swirling down the toilet like a college kid's bar-binge piss if he couldn't get his shit together today, and his current condition didn't make that look terribly promising.

It wasn't like he had a ton to do—no mountains to scale, no insurgents to neutralize, no wounded teammates to hump out of the desert on his back. No, by his count, Tate only needed to accomplish three small, non-life-threatening tasks in the immediate future.

One, move through his day as calmly as possible, so his dumb-ass brain would keep healing. Two, nail the job interview his buddy Red had set up for him this morning—and three, act like an upstanding civilian convincingly enough for the next few months that the Army finally let him go back to being a soldier.

Where life made sense.

True, it was a peculiar sort of sense, but it was what Tate knew and what he was good at. Fuck if he was any good at being normal anymore—these last few months he'd discovered the hard way that he was too far gone for that.

Tate groaned and scrubbed his hands over his face. In the Army, he didn't have to confront the fact that his two best friends were both killing it in their careers and personal lives while Tate was just killing.

He didn't have to face that Red and Luca would soon be settling down with the loves of their lives, while he was stuck in a bizarre pseudo-adult stasis—responsible enough to carry firearms capable of grisly destruction, but completely oblivious when it came to, say, shopping for groceries.

It shouldn't be okay that a 99-cent cheeseburger from the drive-through had taken on all the ambrosia-like qualities of a once-in-a-lifetime five-star meal. It definitely wasn't okay that Tate had ended up at said drive-through last week because sitting at his mom's table for a holiday meal had made him want to claw his way out of his own skin.

He pushed to his feet and shuffled over to the hotel room desk, where he'd left his list the night before. It was crumpled and messy, and he'd scrawled it on the hotel stationery before he'd crawled into bed, but it still seemed to be accurate.

A while back, Tate's doctors had suggested he make lists to help himself stay on top of the things he needed to do while his memory remained unreliable. Lately, it felt like Tate's whole life revolved around these goddamned lists.

Wake up. Shave and shower. Take a cab to Red's office for the interview.

Tate's eyes hitched on what he'd written in parentheses after that: "*Uber?!?*" His old friend had suggested he take one of those, and while Tate knew very well *what* an Uber was, he didn't have the faintest idea *how* a dude went about securing one.

But maybe that was more of a city-versus-country thing, instead of a soldier-versus-civilian thing. He decided a taxi would get the job done old-school this morning, and later—if he remembered—Tate could google the whole Uber issue to death for next time.

On the nightstand, his phone dinged out a reminder, and he went over to check it. *Ten a.m. appointment. Don't be late, Fucktard.*

Tate huffed out a laugh. His prior-day self had clearly left nothing to chance. Yesterday's Tate had probably also asked Red to text this morning—not that he'd needed to.

Ever since Red and Luca had shown up at Landstuhl with a company jet and world-revolves-around-them demeanors, they'd been all over Tate like white on rice. If they had their way, they weren't going to let him forget his own name, much less today's interview.

The idiots had always had his six, right from day one of freshman year at college. You couldn't pay for that kind of loyalty with blood, and that was another reason why Tate couldn't screw up today. He absolutely refused to let Red and Luca down.

One more glance at his list, a hasty line drawn through the words *Wake up*, and Tate headed for the fancy marble bathroom attached to his suite. When he showed up at Red's office later this morning, there'd be no trace of the sweating, blood-stained, barely human thing that had played the starring role in his dream this morning.

Tate was going in spit-shined and tight, and there'd be no way on earth anyone could refuse him.

NO TWO WAYS about it, the chick was an absolute babe. And sure, Tate knew you couldn't say that kind of thing about a woman you were trying to work for. He knew he had no business whatsoever noticing the looks of a stranger on the street right now, much less one of Red's most important employees.

But facts were facts, and Ms. Lyla Lawson's shiny brown hair and hot secretary glasses were totally doing it for him. She had a sweet ass and pretty hazel eyes and a soft, husky voice that was so sexy it ought to be criminal.

His buddy appeared to be utterly immune to her charms, but then again, Red had always had a ferocious poker face. Tate listened to his former roommate define terms and kept his eyes on Ms. Lawson's back while he surreptitiously readjusted himself in his pants.

No use having her bust him rearranging his junk. Nothing in the world said *Not Qualified* quite like sporting untimely wood in your dress slacks.

While he sat there trying to rein shit in, Tate attempted to convince himself that Lyla had breath like festering sewage or a nasally, cackling laugh. He hadn't gotten close enough to determine either of those things for certain, however.

Since Tate had retreated to the chair Red offered him once he'd shaken Lyla's hand, and she had immediately paced over to the big windows overlooking downtown Manhattan, his dick still knew there was doubt.

She was keeping her distance and keeping quiet, while Tate attempted mightily to ignore her charms and Red talked.

He talked a hell of a lot. Once Tate was sure his ill-advised condition had gotten a little less obvious, he checked his buddy's face to see what was up—and met Red's narrow-eyed glare of death. *Shit.*

Red gave him a tiny shake of his head, delivering the most subtle and dangerous *Back Off* in history. Tate widened his eyes and shrugged, one-hundred-percent the innocent boy scout.

The glare got darker and more threatening. Clearly, his old roommate had seen him on the prowl one too many times to buy the whole *Who me?* charade. Tate would have to remember that. He wasn't with his unit anymore.

People knew him better here—knew his habits and his history. Plus, they were peers instead of subordinates. They didn't have to accept his bullshit just because he told them to.

Tate wanted to believe that he might have one or two new tricks up his sleeve that his friends hadn't seen yet, but that might be wishful thinking. Like so many other things were, these days.

"Here's the thing," Lyla said suddenly, spinning around and placing her back to those precarious-looking windows.

Tate took a moment to admire the way she'd cut off Red's big-man bluster so handily. It diverted him from obsessing about how any fuckface with a decent scope out there could so easily get a bead on them.

"I'm supposed to be going on a book tour next week to drum up buzz for Red Devil and my new series with them. I've been telling Red that we ought to just cancel it, but he's…"

"An over-bearing ass who doesn't want you to be in danger," Red supplied. He pulled out his chair and sat down heavily.

Tate snapped to attention. While he'd been dwelling on shades of hotness and degrees of unsafe exposure, the real reason he'd been summoned here had somehow dropped into the room without him noticing.

When Red had broached this idea to him last week—indeed, while his buddy had been expounding on it for the last ten minutes—the job had not, in fact, been about some cake security guard position, as Tate had assumed.

All this time, he'd been envisioning a geeky gray uniform with a stupid patch on the breast pocket. Tate had been thinking he would fritter away his days sitting at some desk in an office lobby, with Lyla working upstairs getting Red Devil, the new publishing imprint, up and running.

He'd been entertaining fantasies of telling her, "*Morning, Ms. Lawson*," and "*Evening, Ms. Lawson*," when she walked by his station. Five seconds ago, Tate had every intention of flirting with her for the next few months like his pants were on fire.

But that kind of job involved no *danger* whatsoever.

Tate cleared his throat, and inquired, "What kind of danger are we talking here?"

"It's no big deal," Lyla scoffed, at the same time Red explained, "Unfortunately, Lyla's acquired a stalker."

Holy *crap*. This woman didn't need a security guard—she needed a *body*guard. For her very female and attractive *body*.

"I see," Tate said, so he wouldn't blurt out his thoughts on *that* subject.

Lyla looked troubled. She pivoted around again and returned to her post near the windows.

He asked, "Could you, uh…"

She peered over her shoulder at him and bit one of those full, peach-glossed lips of hers.

Tate swallowed and looked to Red, instead. "Can we close the blinds, maybe? There's an awful lot of open space…there."

Red blinked and sat back, studying him. In an undertone, he murmured, "Light hurting your eyes?"

Tate sat back, too. Injuries sucked, but they were better than letting people know how freaking paranoid he'd apparently become. "Yeah. Little bit," he said.

Red hit a button near his desk phone, and a thin, tinted screen began its slow descent from the hidden niche near the ceiling. As Tate had hoped, Lyla came and sat safely beside him once she was deprived of her view.

She smelled like a meadow of wildflowers, damn it. Not even a hint of sewage wafted his way.

Once she was settled, he continued, "Are the police involved?"

Red muttered pissily, "Those guys."

Lyla sighed, "I didn't want to call them. And when the letters stopped coming to Trident, I thought whoever it was had moved on. But then…" She stopped. Paused and took a big breath. "Then one came to my house."

Tate looked at Red. The man stared back at him, six-and-a-half feet of bristling fury. Lyla might be trying to downplay the situation, but whatever was going on had his friend plenty worked up.

"You insisted she go to the cops?" Tate confirmed.

"You bet I did."

"And they said?"

"Without any fingerprints or overt threats, they can't do anything," Lyla told him.

Tate couldn't read her expression. Was she scared—or embarrassed? Hard to say.

He zeroed in on the most obvious issue. "Guys, what makes you think I can help here? I have no experience whatsoever with this kind of thing. I don't do investigative stuff in the Army. I just shoot things."

"Tate's right," Lyla told her boss. "The last thing this mess needs is a gun."

"I disagree," Red countered. "I think the last thing it needs is for some deranged punk to show up at one of your signings *with* a gun, and all anyone has to protect you are a stack of paperbacks and some permanent markers."

"We should just let the police handle it," she tried again.

"Lyla, we've been over this," Red said. "NYPD does not have the manpower to assign someone to you day and night, and they're not going to send a cop on the road with you, either. I am, however. I think it should be Tate."

Tate's gaze pinged back to Lyla to see her return salvo.

"This is overkill," she countered.

"I wish you'd chosen any word but that one," Red retorted.

Tate held up his hands. "Okay, kids, let's back things up a step." He pointed at Lyla. "How long have you been getting freaky letters from this person?"

"About six months, as far as we know," Red replied.

"Not talking to you," Tate fired back. This time, he emphasized the author's name, "*Lyla*, what do they usually say?"

"They're angry and they get personal. They talk about my books and they always tell me I 'got it wrong,' whatever that means."

"How angry are we talking?"

Lyla opened her mouth to reply, then shut it again when Red drummed his fingers loudly on his desk. She ran an unsteady hand through her silky-looking hair and tucked it behind one ear.

"Okay, fine—they *are* pretty creepy. And the person seems like they're getting madder. Or more frustrated, maybe? I don't know. But the last few letters have come to my apartment, and now, once or twice they even…"

"…mentioned what she was wearing," Red finished for her, unable to keep silent any longer.

Suddenly, Tate had a good idea why his buddy was taking the steps he was. The thought of some crackpot watching Lyla had Tate steamed, too, and he'd only met the woman a little while ago. He couldn't imagine how much worse he'd feel if the fucker managed to lay hands on her.

"What makes you think the person is going to up their game for the book tour? Maybe they can't follow Lyla out of town. Maybe they're just some house-bound looney-tune with too much time on their hands and not enough meds."

Red stared Tate down. "Lyla is not some chess piece we're moving around on a game board, dipshit. She's a very prominent mystery author that I lured to Red Devil using highly refined and specialized business world techniques."

"He pays really well," Lyla interjected.

"Lyla is also my future wife's friend," Red barked back, "And, therefore, *my* friend. Ergo…"

Tate had never much cared for mathematics—he was more of a history buff, himself. But even he could follow the simple A+B=C equation being presented to him now.

"Ergo, you are now *my* friend," Tate informed Lyla. "And no friend of mine is going to be out swinging in the wind for a sociopath on her upcoming book tour."

Lyla groaned and slumped back in her plush armchair. "Oh, for the love of—the fix is in, isn't it? You two really aren't going to let this go?"

Tate scoffed, "Do we look like the kind of guys who would let a threat to our friends go?"

"*Jesus*," Lyla muttered.

In her slim black jeans and slinky polka-dotted blouse, she looked like a model straight out of the pages of *Hot for Teacher Weekly*. And Tate had to commend his friend Red on his taste in office furniture—the dark leather of the chair Lyla was perched on highlighted her looks perfectly. It made Tate want to grab a scotch and then *her*.

Probably not in that order, though.

"So, am I hired?" he wondered.

He might not have experience, but Tate could ask around and probably look up the rest of what he needed to know. He had heart and he had drive, and he had quite a few weeks of involuntary leave left that he wanted to spend productively.

Red set his big hands carefully on the sides of his pristine desk blotter. "I'll call you later and let you know."

"I'm sorry, what?" After all that bickering with Lyla, his buddy was pulling back *now*? "What's that supposed to mean?"

"It *means*, I am now going to get Ms. Lawson's thoughts on the subject before she and I make a final decision on whether you are a good fit for the position." There was no wiggle room in that statement—only the sky-high brick wall of Red MacLellan's indomitable will.

Fuck if Tate hadn't found himself *here* a time or two before. And he'd learned that if he couldn't scale the wall, he had to find a way around it. His gaze swung to Lyla's, but she was focused on her hands, knitted together in her lap. He couldn't read a thing there.

What was more, her profile was a smooth, impossibly-pretty mask and gave him absolutely nothing to go on.

Tate forced himself not to chew out Red in front in Lyla. He simply said, "I look forward to hearing from you," and got to his feet.

Then, because he couldn't quite help himself—this was *Red*, for crying out loud—he clicked his heels together and snapped off the world's most sarcastic salute before he stalked out of that posh office door.

Behind him, Tate heard Lyla giggle, and he grinned. Score one for the good guys.

Two

ONCE TATE WAS gone, Red asked Lyla, "Well, what do you think?"

"He's definitely…militaristic," she said.

Even lounging in his chair like he was bored in geometry class, Tate Monroe had had the unmistakable bearing of a soldier.

Lyla had no doubt that if Red's assistant Wayne had suddenly decided to stage a coup, Tate would've been up and over that freighter-sized desk in a heartbeat, wielding Red's fountain pen like a deadly weapon to put down the insurgency.

He'd been kind of breathtaking, come to think of it. Lyla only wished she'd been able to meet the man under different circumstances. At one of their group's happy hours, for instance, instead of discussing her…*situation.*

"I hope you'll pardon my French," Red said, "But I didn't pick Tate for his charm, dubious as it is—he's just the most tenacious fucker I know. If we hire him, he will stick to you like glue or die trying."

"Yes, but the question remains," Lyla countered. "Is that really necessary?"

"You know that I think so." Red leaned way back in his desk chair and contemplated her. "Lyla…we don't know what we're dealing with here. I told you before that Tate is an old friend, but I have to be clear about this—he's as loyal as they come. I chose him, instead of some professional we don't know, because I know we can trust him implicitly. Injured or not, Tate is clever and resourceful, and he's got a sixth sense about trouble like nothing I've ever seen."

Red sighed heavily, then added, "We're in the dark about how serious this thing is. I think Tate's exactly what we need."

This thing. Her situation. So many ways to say what Lyla refused to give a name to. Because, once she labeled it, once she put on her writer hat and assigned words to the amorphous entity out in the world that had her in its sights, then the ghost became real. It took on substance as an actual human, with actual malicious intent.

She shied away from the thought. "Then that's good, right?"

"It is," Red agreed. "But before we go ahead, I need you to be one-thousand-percent sure you're on board. Once we put this bone between Tate's teeth, those jaws are going to clamp down like a bulldog's and not let go until you're safe or he's dead in the ground."

"I mean, when you put it like that…do we really want to put this on his plate? If Tate's going to take it so seriously? Because I'm reasonably sure my superfan is only some lonely person with nothing better to do. Eventually, they'll get tired of me and move on to someone more interesting, and Tate will have wasted all his leave on me."

Lyla thought about the cops she and Red had talked to. They'd had no qualms whatsoever about using nouns—they'd called the person hounding her a *stalker* without one second thought.

She wrote about people like that all the time in her mysteries, but somehow the term had never seemed quite so chilling before. Except, who was she kidding? Lyla wrote about stalkers and their ilk precisely *because* they were chilling.

Even the word sent tremors down the spine. *Stalk*—like a predator hunting prey.

Red wrenched her attention back to him. "Are you positive about that?" he demanded. "If you were so sure this was nothing to worry about, why bring it to me in the first place? Why agree to go to the cops?"

Because Lyla was good and scared, that was why—and her boss knew it.

"That's exactly what I'm talking about," Red went on, looking at her face. "At some point, you have to acknowledge the seriousness of this. And, if we hire Tate, you'll have to trust him. I can't have you two battling about whether he's being too heavy-handed or whatever. You have to let him do his job."

"Heavy-handed?" Lyla snorted. "Come on. He seemed nice."

Red rolled his eyes and countered, "Don't be fooled. Tate is bossy as shit. He's a complete prick when he doesn't get his way."

Lyla raised her eyebrows at him. Whether he was her boss or not, Red had to see the irony in that statement.

He chuckled, seeing her point immediately. "Why do you think we're such good friends?"

ONCE THEY'D FINALIZED the details of the arrangement, Red walked Lyla out—but they both stopped short when they hit the elegant waiting area outside his office.

Tate was still there, sitting on the loveseat in his impeccable navy-blue blazer, leafing through an old issue of *City Style*.

"Oh," Lyla blurted out, as she took in her future bodyguard's attributes once more—all the way from his sandy-blond hair down to his perfectly-shined shoes.

"You're still here," Red announced.

Tate put down the magazine and got slowly to his feet. "I am."

"And you are here because..." Lyla's boss trailed off with a perplexed frown.

"You clearly forgot we were going to have lunch," Tate replied.

Red nodded and kept nodding, as if that announcement didn't quite clear things up. "Yes. That did slip my mind. Completely."

Tate shrugged and leveled a boyish smile at Lyla. "Busy guy," he told her.

Something wasn't adding up. Lyla glanced at Red's assistant, Wayne, whose fingers had flown into sudden activity on his computer keyboard, and whose face now bore a distinctly panicked expression that hadn't been there moments before.

"I should get going," Lyla said into the pregnant pause that descended on the room. She gestured vaguely toward the elevators to underline the sentiment, but didn't move quite yet.

Red nodded again, but he didn't take his laser-like gaze off Tate.

"You should join us," Tate told Lyla cheerfully.

If Red's eyebrows could've shot any higher, they'd be on the ceiling. "Yes. That's true," he agreed warily.

Lyla rolled her eyes at their antics. "It's obviously not even a little true. You two go on and figure out—" She waved her hands between them, "—whatever this is. We can all talk later."

"Can't wait," Tate said, leaning forward to shake her hand another time.

His grip was strong and firm, but not crushing, and Lyla's appreciation of him ratcheted up another notch.

Her dad had given her plenty of pointers over the years on how to evaluate the males of the species, and a man's handshake was right up there at the top of the list. Tate's was *perfect*.

Lyla smiled at them once more and walked away, but not quickly enough, it seemed. She'd barely rounded the corner when she heard Red murmur, "What the fuck was that all about?"

She froze in place.

"Sorry, dude. I think I stood up too fast before," Tate grumbled. "I'm tight now, though. I'll get out of your hair. Don't worry about lunch."

"No, it's fine. If you can hang out for another fifteen minutes or so, I think it's actually doable. Are you up to it?"

"Yeah, sure. Sounds good."

Just like that, Lyla remembered the one distinctive thing she knew about Tate Monroe—four months earlier, he'd been flown from the Middle East to Landstuhl, Germany, with a combat injury and he still hadn't been cleared to return to active duty. That was why he was available to act as her bodyguard in the first place.

Lyla had been there on the evening Red and their friend Luca had gotten the news. In fact, she still had a silly cartoon that Luca's fiancée had drawn that night, stuck to her fridge with a Red Devil magnet.

She had no idea why Tate had captured her imagination back then, but suspected it was because all the stories his friends had told about him had made quite an impression. That was months ago, though.

Tate looked like he was in perfect health, now. In fact, *more* than perfect health. The man was a specimen, for sure—an exemplary prototype of the classic, red-blooded American male.

Sadly, that was exactly the kind of guy that seemed to be in somewhat short supply here in Manhattan. Lyla had no trouble meeting metrosexuals and hipsters. But strapping hunks from some farm in the middle of the country were decidedly thin on the ground. Unfortunately, those were the kind of men that just happened to be Lyla's weakness.

She was going to have to be very, very careful if this was going to work the way it was supposed to. Given her body's all over reaction to sitting three feet away from Tate, going on a road trip could end up being a ridiculous test of willpower. Her recent dry spell when it came to dating was only going to make the problem worse.

Just her luck.

ON HER WAY home from Red's office in the financial district, Lyla stopped in at the Trident Publishing building to check in with the PR department there. They were making progress on the new Red Devil imprint swag she was going to be carting to her signings and readings, and assured her everything would be done in plenty of time.

From there, it was only a short walk to the print shop she normally used for her own materials. Lyla picked up part of her order—a variety of bookmarks and postcards showcasing some of her backlist titles—and confirmed when the rest of the stuff was going to be done.

All routine and unremarkable tasks. For good measure, she picked up her dry cleaning at the end of the block, then headed home.

In the lobby, Lyla spent a few minutes with her building's longtime doorman, Joe, hearing about how his grandkids did in their soccer games over the weekend. She got her mail and managed to dodge what would undoubtedly have been a drawn-out conversation with Mrs. Meecham from 4B.

By the time she reached the elevators, everything in Lyla's world seemed so ridiculously *normal* that the very idea of having to be saddled with a bodyguard for the foreseeable future seemed like total nonsense.

She didn't need an off-duty soldier trailing along with her on this publicity tour. Lyla was perfectly capable of driving herself to all the events, and it wasn't like she was going to be alone that much, anyway.

During the days, she'd be interacting with fans or on the road, and in the evenings, she'd be locked safely in hotel rooms, surrounded on all sides by hotel employees and other guests.

How hard could it possibly be to stay safe in those conditions? Lyla had lived in the city for years. She knew perfectly well how to stay alert and aware of her surroundings.

By the time the elevator reached her floor, she'd all but decided to call Red back and tell him she wouldn't be needing Tate's services after all. He'd been kind to offer, but she was going to pass this time.

On her way down the hall, Lyla thought about how it had been weeks since her superfan had contacted her, anyway. As she'd predicted, they had no doubt gotten bored with her, and moved on to their next obsession. Good riddance, too.

But as she approached her door, Lyla's steps slowed and then came to a faltering stop. Her drycleaning drooped in her hand, and the box from the printer nearly slipped to the floor.

There was a dirty, dog-eared envelope taped to the center of her front door, a ragged "D" scrawled so awkwardly on the face of it, that it was almost certain the writer had altered their handwriting on purpose.

Lyla shifted the box she was holding to one arm and ripped the note free with trembling fingers. She glanced nervously around, but the hallway was still empty.

The only sound was Mrs. Meecham's television, still broadcasting her usual late-afternoon soap operas at top volume, even though the woman herself had gone on a little jaunt to the lobby.

Lyla fumbled her key a few times before she was able to fit it into the lock and get herself inside her apartment. She piled her dry cleaning, printing, and mail-stuffed purse on her dinner table and tried to calm her galloping pulse.

She forced herself to take a couple of deep breaths as she stared at the envelope in her hands.

She shouldn't open it. Lyla should just call the police.

Except—what if it was nothing? What if it was only a note from the super, or a message from the doorman? Joe hadn't mentioned anything just now, but he'd been so excited by the grandkid discussion, he could've simply forgotten.

Lyla must be letting all of Red's nonsense go to her head. So, she turned the envelope over, slid a finger under the flap, and pulled the note free.

Oh, no. Like something out of a bad movie, the paper was a messy hodge-podge of glued-on letters and words.

You silly fool, it read. *Do you really think that leaving town will keep you safe from me?*

I can always find you. I'm going to be there.

I'm going to be everywhere you are until you learn your lesson.

Lyla pulled out the chair next to her and collapsed into it. She dropped the letter on the table and kept a wary eye on it while she pulled her purse close and dug through it for her phone.

It took a little effort to find the NYPD detective's business card among all the rewards cards and coupons tucked into her wallet, but within a few minutes the receptionist at the station had patched her through to the guy's voicemail, and Lyla had left a message letting him know what had happened.

She debated making her second call for another minute or two, but in the end, Lyla knew she had no choice now. It was time to face facts.

Her boss answered on the third ring, "This is Red."

"Red, hi. It's Lyla."

"Well, that didn't take long. What's up?"

Lyla tried to make her mouth say the words, she really did. But for some reason, all the ones she was supposed to say got stuck in her throat when she looked down at that letter once more.

"Lyla? What's going on? You okay?"

She blinked and sprang from the chair, backing away from the offending missive so she could think straight. "I'm, uh…I'm fine. But I got another letter. When I got home. It was on my front door."

"Did you call the cops?" Red barked.

"Of course. I left a message for Detective Scarletti. I'm sure he'll—"

"Hold that thought. I'm sending you Tate's contact info right now. Text him your address so he can find you."

"Red…"

Her phone dinged with an incoming text, and sure enough, there was Tate's contact.

"Lyla, we hired Tate to do this job, so let him do it, okay? He's not far away, and he'll get to you soon. Just tell him where you are."

The thought of having all six-foot-two, two-hundred pounds of Tate keeping her safe was definitely appealing at the moment. Lyla was scared to even peek behind her bathroom door, much less spend the rest of the night here alone.

"Okay," she capitulated. "I'll text him right now."

"Good. I'm heading into a meeting but once I get out, I'll let Trident PR know to add him to your tour. Piper and I will check in with you later, and Lyla—one last thing."

"What?"

"Be careful. Call 911 if anything strange happens."

Lyla flinched. "Will do," she said, and then the line went quiet.

How close was *close*, anyway? Was Tate five minutes away or thirty? Only one way to find out. Lyla added his information to her list of contacts and sent him the damn text.

While she waited for a response, she tried to envision the next few weeks with him, strong and handsome and close enough to touch.

No! No touching! Under no circumstances could Lyla even think about jumping her new bodyguard, even if it had been way too long since she'd even been on a date. To avoid temptation, however, she was going to have to keep busy—really busy. Busier than Trident's reasonable tour schedule had any prayer of making her.

Lyla edged around her table, giving the evil letter as wide a berth as she could manage in her dinky apartment, then beelined for her laptop. It would take no more than a couple of clicks to put the word out to her readers. There would be book clubs she could visit in between signings, and maybe—if she was lucky—a local book festival or two she could drop in on.

She dove into her social media accounts with a vengeance, and when her cell phone and the door buzzer sounded at the same time twenty minutes later, it was startling enough that Lyla let out a very humiliating, but very heartfelt, scream.

Oh, yeah. This was going to work out great.

Three

S O, THAT'S THE deal," Red said, pushing aside his plate and leaning back. "Trident's PR department is working with Marketing to line up the last few tour stops, and I'll let them know this afternoon that you're coming on board. Otherwise, you two should be good to go."

"Sounds like it," Tate agreed. He and Lyla would stay in side-by-side rooms in a string of nice hotels, and Red had even told him he could have his pick of vehicles for the trip.

"Just a nice, easy loop through the Northeast," his friend added, for the hundredth time.

"Yup. Got it."

"And all you have to do is keep any psycho motherfuckers away from my new author."

"So…basically everyone," Tate joked. Because honestly— who was Red kidding? They both knew this was a charity case assignment that Tate wasn't the least bit qualified for.

Red signaled for the check, then slapped his credit card on the waitress's little plastic clipboard so fast, Tate couldn't even draw breath, much less offer to go halfsies on their overpriced cheeseburgers.

"You can do this," Red assured him. "I wouldn't have called you, otherwise."

"Your faith in me is heartwarming, but it's complete bullshit. You get that, right?"

His friend stared him down with an expression that probably terrified lesser men. "No fucking around, Tate. This is the real deal. Lyla's scared, and I've…"

Tate frowned when Red trailed off. "You're…what?"

"I've got a bad feeling about this. I don't know why. I just do."

Soldiers could be a superstitious group and Tate didn't question Red's hunch, or ask him to explain. He just took it as fact and trusted the supporting evidence would show itself in due time.

"Don't sweat it, brother. I'll look out for your girl."

"Piper's my girl. But Lyla is a friend, in addition to an employee. I'm worried about her."

"I know. I'll do my best. I promise."

"That's what I'm counting on."

OUTSIDE THE RESTAURANT, Red immediately ducked into a sleek black town car that was idling at the curb, waiting for him. He rolled down his window and offered Tate a ride to the hotel, but Tate declined.

For crying out loud, Tate had once lived here for years. Even if he'd been gone for a while, he could still find his way around—it wasn't like taxis or the subway had changed so much since he'd been gone.

The only problem was, after Red pulled away, it didn't take more than five minutes of fumbling before Tate was thoroughly flustered by the midday chaos. He and Red and Luca had gone to school in the Village, and Tate couldn't seem to get his bearings here in the financial district.

He couldn't even remember which subway stop was close by, and so he stood there like a dolt, kicking himself for turning down that swanky ride.

Once, he'd found New York energizing—a playground full of possibility, new ideas and experiences around every corner. At age eighteen, he'd taken to Manhattan like a duck to water.

Now, though…now it felt more like an assault on his senses. Tate wanted to make a break for it, not dive right in. When he finally spotted an open cab, he flagged it down and hopped gratefully in the back.

Then, instead of going sightseeing or something, like a normal guy on leave, he just barked out the name of his hotel and hunkered down. What a crying shame.

Tate had to admit—he wasn't terribly disappointed that the job would take him out of town for a few weeks. And he was even less disappointed that it would be in the company of the lovely Lyla Lawson. Hazard duty, it was not.

He sighed and watched the streets of Midtown streak by. He might not be able to keep the job if Lyla hadn't liked him. And the truth was, he had no idea if she had or not. He'd never had an interview that was harder to interpret than the one he'd just sat through. Tate had always been good with people and could always tell how he was being received, but Lyla—Lyla had thrown him for a loop from the very start.

Back at the hotel, Tate barely managed to kick off his dress shoes and hang up his blazer before his phone went vibrating across the nightstand, where he'd plugged it in to charge.

It only took a quick glance to see the 216 area code and the Cleveland Clinic name on the caller ID, but given how fucked up this day was turning out to be, Tate was half tempted to let the call roll over into voicemail.

That'd be a pussy move, though.

He accepted the call with an all-business, "Captain Monroe."

"Hey Tate, it's Dr. Ross. How are you doing?"

Tate exhaled, somewhat relieved. Dr. Ross had been in charge of his care from the moment he'd been transferred from Landstuhl to the States, and he was a good dude. A straight shooter.

However, it wasn't like him to call out of the blue, so this call had to have a reason—and Tate wasn't terribly keen on hearing what that was.

"I'm good, thanks," he told the man. "How about you?" Like they were buddies passing each other in the park, for crying out loud.

Ross sighed. "Oh, you know. Same old, same old."

Tate did know. "I hear ya," he sympathized, then perched on the edge of the hotel mattress, waiting for the first bomb to drop.

It didn't take long. "Hey, listen," Ross began. "I got your message about you maybe heading out of town. I figured I'd better touch base today, so we aren't keeping you in suspense any longer than necessary."

"I appreciate that."

The doctor hesitated. "Going anywhere special?"

"Not really," Tate told him. What he had planned was straight need-to-know, and the Army did *not* need to know. "A friend's taking a road trip around the Northeast for a couple of weeks. I might tag along."

"Sounds fun."

"Should be. I haven't decided if I'm going to go, though."

"All right, well…I'll cut to the chase. I have good news and bad news and you get to pick which you hear first."

Oh, they were going to play this game, were they? Tate rolled his eyes and barked, "I'll take the bad, first."

"Of course, you will. Okay, here it is—based on the results of your last evaluation, the Med Board is not going to recommend that you return to active duty at this time. They're going to mail you their findings, but I wanted to give you a heads up myself, first."

Fuck. Fuck, fuck, *fuck*. That was bad news, all right. Tate kept quiet until he was sure he could speak civilly.

When he pulled himself together, he asked, "*At this time*? What does that mean?"

"Well, that's where the good news comes in. They do believe that your condition hasn't fully stabilized yet. They think you might still be improving, so they'd like to schedule you for another evaluation in a week."

"*Next* week?" Okay, that had come out loud. Tate took a deep breath before adding more quietly, "That seems…soon." Even he knew he hadn't improved enough to pass an evaluation so close to the first one.

"Yeah, that's on me," Ross told him. "I know how much you want to get back in the mix, so I figured you'd want to shoehorn this in before you left on your trip."

Which made perfect sense, if you weren't a paranoid mess with basically your whole life riding on the outcome. "What if I screw it up again? Is this my last chance?" Tate wondered.

"Not necessarily. Some guys go through this part of the process five or six times before the Board makes a final decision."

"I see." And he did, sort of. Tate understood that his career might stay in limbo for many more months if he couldn't convince those Army assholes he was right and tight again. However, that might be easier to do if he believed it himself.

"Is there a problem I am unaware of?" Dr. Ross inquired. Which seemed like a very classy way of asking, *What're you hiding, you cagey little shit?*

God, there were so many problems frying Tate's circuits right about now, he didn't even know where to begin. He tackled the easiest first—logistics.

"Not a problem, per se," he explained, "But I am in New York right now, visiting that friend. Any chance I could do the eval here? I'll be cutting it close trying to get home and back again if I end up going on that trip."

"Right. Sure. If you're okay with me not being there, that shouldn't be an issue."

Tate *wasn't* okay with that, but beggars couldn't be choosers.

Ross took his silence as agreement. He mumbled, "Okay, what've we got? Uhhhh…looks like there're some folks at Weill Cornell who can handle the tests you need. How's that sound?"

"Not there." *Anywhere but there.*

"Why not?"

Because his best friend Luca was a prominent physician at Weill Cornell, and if he caught even the slightest wind of what Tate was going through, he'd never be able to resist sticking his prying Italian nose in it.

"Because I'm staying clear across town," Tate hedged. It was a matter of blocks, but whatever. "How about Presbyterian?"

"That probably works, too. Mind if I make a few calls and get back to you?"

"Not at all." And especially not if it kept Tate flying under the radar where his friends were concerned.

"All right, chief. Hang tight and I'll let you know as soon as I have something set up for you."

After Dr. Ross signed off, Tate sat there and contemplated his situation. By now, his head was probably as healed as it was going to get. He still got migraines occasionally, if he spent too much time out in the bright sun. Or, as he'd discovered the hard way, in bars with too much neon and loud music.

The Army didn't need to know about that shit, though.

The times in the field that replicated those conditions were few and far between. Mostly, Tate was hanging out under cover, waiting for someone to show who never arrived, or something to happen that never did.

And frankly, when the whole world was exploding all around you, no one really cared if your head hurt or you felt a little queasy. For Christ's sake, *everyone* wanted to toss their cookies when they were being shot at. Tate was no different than anyone when it came to that.

The bigger issue, as Tate saw it, was that his survivor's guilt was not going away. *That* motherfucker had dug a trench and installed ramparts in his soul, clearly settling in for the long haul.

The Army wouldn't know about *that*, either, if Tate hadn't been such a touchy-feely blabbermouth in those first few weeks in the hospital.

It'd been a classic case of entrapment. He'd been shell-shocked and hurt and they'd sent in a chick therapist with the biggest, warmest, most understanding pair of brown eyes Tate had ever seen outside of the family dog. How was a dude supposed to guard against those? He'd been conditioned to trust puppy-dog eyes since the day he'd been born.

Without even intending to, he'd stupidly spilled his guts and then some, and he'd been paying for his rash mistake ever since.

People weren't joking when they said that loose lips sank ships—talking about every negative thought that had grown roots in his gray matter could very well be the mistake that ended Tate's career.

In retrospect, he guessed it wasn't so surprising that he'd failed his first Med Board evaluation. Tate had waltzed into it blind, having no idea the Army would come back at him with all the sad-sack crap he'd spewed months earlier.

Now he knew better. When Tate checked in next week, he'd say all the right things, and he would pass their mysterious tests with flying colors.

He had to. The Army was his life, and the sooner he could complete this side mission and get back to it, the better.

Tate loosened his tie, swung his legs up and laid back against the pile of fancy pillows. Between the interview with Lyla, the huge burger he'd wolfed down at lunch, and the Med Board landmine that had just gone off in the middle of his day, he was suddenly inexpressibly exhausted.

INSTEAD OF JUST closing his eyes for a few minutes like he'd intended, Tate must have fallen out cold. When his cell starting ringing for the second time that day, he was so groggy, he felt like he had to claw his way up out of a well just to answer it.

Naturally, it was Red again, the world's least warm-and-fuzzy person to wake up to.

"Were you fucking *asleep?*" his friend demanded.

"Small siesta," Tate mumbled. "Perfectly normal."

"Christ. What must it be like, to be you?"

Tate scrubbed his face. At least he hadn't had the nightmare. "Basically, it's a long, straight road of sunshine and roses, dude. Some honeys throwing themselves at me along the way. You know."

And Red probably did. Ever since Tate had been back in town, he'd been confronted with the rather inescapable evidence that his old college buddy had grown up to be a bazillionaire—which didn't make Tate feel like a late bloomer *at all*.

Red groaned. "All right. Wake up, you tool. The job starts now. Lyla's going to text you her address any minute now, and you need to get over there ASAP."

Tate sat up straight, and the room took a long, lazy spin around his cranium before it settled back into place again. "What happened?"

"She found another letter on her door when she got home. I'm heading into a meeting, but if you can get over there and hang with her while she waits for the cops to get there, that would be grand."

Tate was already tying his shoes and looking around for his wallet. "Anything for you, my love."

"Save it. I'm out of pocket for at least the next hour, but keep me posted later, okay?"

"Roger that," Tate told him, pulling on his jacket and finding his wallet still tucked in the pocket.

The hotel keycard was on the dresser, next to his list. He grabbed them both, just in case. With a quick tug to tighten up his tie and a hasty gargle of mouthwash, Tate was out the door and heading for the elevators.

Downstairs, he asked the bellhop to get him a cab, then watched his phone like it held all the answers to the universe.

Sure enough, Lyla's text came through a minute later—and damn if it wasn't an address no more than five minutes away. Red *had* to have planned that, but there was no time to delve into the whys.

Tate was too busy feeling piqued that Lyla's text had contained nothing more than an address—like Tate was only a robot, instead of a man who thought she was extra cute.

It wasn't like he'd expected her to beg him for salvation, or anything…but a simple thank you might've been nice.

No time like the present to start working on that little misfire. Tate was hired, and he was going to do his job—but he was also going to give Miss Lyla a big old dose of *bright-eyed and bushy-tailed* to go with it.

Four

THINGS WITH TATE got off to a rousing start from the moment he crossed her threshold. Detective Scarletti had beat him to Lyla's by all of three minutes, but her new bodyguard had a way of filling a room with his presence and immediately trying to take charge.

The officer eyed Tate for a long moment, and dismissed him with a few careless words. "You the boyfriend?" he asked, then turned away to snap on his latex gloves and slip the offensive letter into a large plastic sleeve.

Tate slouched and fired back with, "Nah. Just the hired help."

Lyla stared at him. Since Tate apparently didn't plan on being forthcoming with Scarletti, she felt compelled to elaborate.

"Detective, Captain Monroe is my new bodyguard. My publisher is taking this business pretty seriously, so they hired him to accompany me on my book tour."

Implicit in that, of course, was that the NYPD might try getting a bit more serious about *their* end of things, too. If Lyla had to hear one more time about how many murders they had to deal with, she was liable to blow a gasket.

"That so?" Scarletti looked Tate over once more. Lyla wondered if maybe the "Captain" she'd thrown in there had caught his attention.

In answer, Tate only shrugged and smirked, insouciant as could be. Lyla scowled at him. He'd been on the job five minutes and he already couldn't play nice?

"Captain of what?" the officer demanded, just like she'd hoped he would. Scarletti could try to brush off this soldier, Lyla thought—but she had to bet he wouldn't get far.

Her bodyguard snapped to attention and belted out, "United States Army. *Sir.*"

"If that's true, what're you doing working security?"

"I'm Ms. Lawson's *bodyguard*, not some random mall cop. And, if you must know, I'm on leave right now."

"For what reason?"

Lyla could tell Scarletti was pushing his little impromptu interrogation too hard, but Tate only muttered, "Medical," and left it at that.

Then the two men simply stood there, facing off and oozing suffocating clouds of testosterone into the atmosphere of her apartment.

Lyla was about to intervene before things got even further out of hand, when Tate suddenly blurted out, "Listen, I don't want to tell you how to do your job, but shouldn't you be more worried about that letter in your hands, than you are about me?"

"I don't know, Captain. You tell me. How do I know you're not the one behind all this crap? It seems awfully convenient that you showed up here, right on the same day Ms. Lawson received another note. Maybe you get off on this kind of thing—maybe you enjoy seeing women upset by your little art projects."

"You've got to be kidding me," Tate objected. "If this is how you investigate, no wonder you're not getting very far."

"Is that right. You wanna get mouthy with me? Go ahead and keep it up. See how well it works out for you."

"*Jesus*," Lyla muttered.

Scarletti was all puffed up with righteous fury, but for the life of her, she had no idea why he'd taken such an instant dislike to Tate.

Louder, she pointed out, "Detective Scarletti, Captain Monroe is a very old friend of my boss's. I do not consider him a suspect, and neither should you—he was deployed *overseas* when most of the letters were sent."

"So? He could still have mailed them. Or had someone else deliver them."

"Yeah, now we're cooking with gas," Tate sneered.

"Not helping," Lyla hissed at him. To the officer, she argued hotly, "No, he could *not* have done those things because A, he had no idea I even existed back then, and B, he's been in the hospital for months, recovering from a combat injury. Tate wasn't even mailing letters to his own mother."

She'd gone out on a limb with that last part, but Lyla really, really hoped Tate wouldn't deny what she'd said. He looked like he wanted to.

Instead, he only spun around and stomped off, going to stare sullenly out of her living room window without another word.

Scarletti frowned after him.

"Detective," Lyla continued, hoping to move this party along, "When do you think Forensics might get here? It's been a long day, and I haven't had a chance to eat dinner yet."

"Join the club," he sighed. "For what it's worth, I did call this in, but the Forensics guys said they can't make it out this time. Bigger fish to fry at the moment."

Across the room, Tate snorted.

The officer pressed his lips together and closed his eyes, and somehow managed to restrain himself. "Anyway, I'll send this little love letter of yours out to the lab when I get back to the station. I'll be honest, though—I'm not expecting much. The lab's as backed up as the rest of us, and if this paper is like all the others, they won't find anything once they get to it."

That caught Tate's attention. "You didn't pull any prints off the others, either?"

"Not a one," Scarletti said. "And even if we had, the chances of them popping up in IAFIS are slim. Besides, if we were dealing with a repeat offender, we'd know it."

Tate rubbed his chin thoughtfully. "Huh. Interesting."

"You get any bright ideas, Captain, feel free to share them. God knows I'm fresh out." With that, the detective packed up the rest of his things and took his leave.

Tate stared at Lyla's door for a full minute after Scarletti's departure, deep in thought. Soon, though, he was swinging toward her with a sardonic grin on his face, apparently recovered.

"I think that went very well. Don't you?"

"No, I do not," Lyla disagreed. "It *never* goes well."

"Yeah, but I'm pretty sure somewhere in there you mentioned dinner, so there's that," Tate said. "What do you feel like?"

Now he wanted to go out to dinner? "I feel like crawling into bed with a bowl of cereal, if you must know."

"We can do way better than cereal, sweetheart. Let's bug out of here and see what we can find."

Lyla took a deep breath and evaluated the situation. She categorically did *not* want to be alone in this place right now, and she had no idea if Tate would simply ditch her if she shot down his dinner idea. They hadn't even had a chance to hash out the details of their arrangement yet.

There really wasn't any question about what she had to do. With a huff of frustration, she told him, "Fine, you win. There's a diner down the street we can go to. If I'm remembering correctly, they serve boozy milkshakes after 4 p.m."

"All right, Slick. Lead the way. I'll hang back and look studly while I bring up the rear."

There were so many things wrong with that statement, Lyla barely knew where to begin. However, since kicking things off with Tate's *wink-wink* tone of voice when he said *rear* was probably akin to waving a red scarf in front of a bull's face, she decided to tackle the more overt offense.

"I am many things, Tate—but I am not your *sweetheart*," she declared, once they got in the elevator.

"True enough," he chuckled. "For starters, I don't believe I've ever been sweet on someone so damn contrary."

"Then, for the love of God, don't call me that!"

"Yes, *ma'am*."

Hell. Tate had managed to make *that* sound even more cheeky.

Lyla blew out a long breath and said, "Tate, tell the truth. You're just going to find some other nickname for me, aren't you?"

He shrugged, and everything from his smirk to the way he jammed his hands in the pockets of his dress pants told her she was right.

"And, it's probably going to be something even more inappropriate," she muttered to herself.

"Can't say that for sure," Tate mused. "With nicknames, you really have to bide your time until the perfect one presents itself."

He eyed her in amusement while he extracted a stick of gum from his jacket pocket—and of course, it was that green spearmint stuff she despised.

Lyla was a cinnamon aficionado, herself. "How many nicknames would you say you've handed out in your day?"

"Quite a few," Tate acknowledged, holding the elevator door open so she could exit at the lobby.

"You probably have a snarky name for every person you know," she sighed.

His grin got wider, and he shrugged once more, saying, "Lyla, I'm from the Midwest. When someone there calls you an endearment, like 'hon,' it's meant to be friendly, not disrespectful."

Lyla was no dummy. It was looking like she might have to cede this small battle if she wanted to win the overall war.

"Okay," she groaned. "*Sweetheart* is fine. But I swear to God— if you let anyone else hear you call me that, I'm going to kill you."

Tate crossed his heart and told her, "You got it, Slick."

Crap. She'd forgotten about that one.

Lyla spun on her heel and marched down the sidewalk, determined to concentrate on eating, and not on the hulking, sassy piece of man-candy who'd be following her around for the next few weeks.

What the hell had she gotten herself into? And why on earth did Tate have to be so darn cute while he pushed her buttons?

AFTER DINNER, TATE convinced Lyla to stay out a little longer, so she strolled down the block with him, eventually stopping at a funky little bookstore that she liked to visit sometimes.

Since the shop specialized in secondhand literary fiction, Lyla was almost never recognized there by any but the most hardcore mystery fans, and she could enjoy a cup of tea at the café in the back without being interrupted.

Tate settled into an open booth in the far corner and eyed her quizzically.

"So…" he said after a while. "*Lyla.* That's an unusual name."

"Is it?" she asked idly.

She was trying to decide whether she wanted to have some tea now, or just wait and drink a cup at home later, before bed.

She couldn't remember whether she'd finished off that box of decaf Earl Grey that'd been in her pantry, though—and the thought of running out alone to get more after Tate left was not appealing.

"Yeah, it is," Tate prodded. "Is it short for something?"

"My full name is Delilah, but no one except my mother ever calls me that," she explained. "Besides, 'Lyla' looks good on book covers, so why mess with it, right?"

Tate cleared his throat and opened his mouth, and Lyla instantly knew what was coming next. She held up a hand to stop him before he could sing a note.

"No, no," she instructed, "Don't do that."

"What? How do you know what I was going to do?"

"You were about to sing Tom Jones," Lyla accused him.

Tate flushed an adorable shade of pale pink, and would no doubt be appalled if she pointed it out. "I...no I wasn't," he stuttered.

"*My, my, my Delilah,*" she sang. "Yes, you were. Do you have any idea how many people have sung that song to me in my life?"

"Not too many, I'd have to think. That song must've come out fifty years ago."

Lyla thought about it and grudgingly admitted, "Okay, you might be right. It was really only my Uncle Gene. But he did it a lot."

"Huh," Tate said.

"He also can't carry a tune to save his life," Lyla elaborated. "And he's super loud."

"I don't have either of those problems."

"Still. One can never be too careful."

Tate sat back and toyed with his mug in amusement. "Have it your way."

It was clearly time to change the subject. After the waiter took their orders, Lyla nibbled on her lip and fished around for a good conversational topic. She didn't have much to go on, though.

She finally settled on the obvious. "So...the Army. Do you like it? Is it your avocation as well as your vocation?"

"Yeah," Tate said, smoothly shifting gears. "I guess I was like a lot of little boys, playing with Army guys and screwing around with war games outside with my buddies. And in college," he added, "I liked all the military history and current events classes. It was decent preparation. I guess."

"So, you always planned to make it your career?"

Lyla knew she was shamelessly digging, but if it meant she didn't have to go back to her dark apartment yet, she didn't much care.

"Actually, no. Back in school, I thought I'd just do my tour and then be done."

"Let me guess. You fell in love with it, right?"

Tate rubbed his jaw and looked away. "No, I was just really freaking good at it."

"So, you stayed."

"Yeah. I stayed."

"And now?" Lyla prodded.

Tate sighed and shifted in his seat. He looked distinctly uncomfortable, and she wished she could take all her prying questions back.

"And now I'm not much good for anything else," he told her.

Every cell in Lyla's body wanted to deny the impossibility of those words She barely knew the guy, and it was already clear he was the type that was good at everything.

She said, "That can't be true. There's a ton of stuff you'd probably be successful at. And you could settle down one day. Start a family, or whatever."

Tate scoffed outright at that. "Nice try, but I'm not exactly the settling down type."

"Oh. Why? You don't like kids?"

He reared back with a frown. "I...no. That's...not why."

"Oh."

He didn't elaborate, and Lyla was forced to retreat or die of embarrassment. "Sorry. I guess it's none of my business."

"No, it's just—I'm not good at relationships and stuff," Tate explained. "Never have been. It's probably better that you know, anyway, in case..."

Lyla gaped at him. He couldn't be serious.

"In case *what*? I can't help falling into bed with you?"

"Something like that," Tate laughed.

"I think I can control myself," Lyla drawled, rolling her eyes. *Look at her, acting all confident.*

"I am curious, though. Did you decide all on your own that you were bad at relationships, or did you have help?"

Tate squinted at her over his coffee mug. "You ask a lot of questions, don't you?"

"Correct. Care to answer?"

"Do I have a choice?"

He looked so wary, Lyla figured she might have better luck focusing on the narrower topic at hand, instead of the broader picture.

"What I'm wondering is if—perhaps—someone *else* told you that you were bad at relationships, and you believed them."

Tate was clearly taken aback by that idea. "I guess…when you hear something often enough, it has a tendency to come true?" he tried.

"Oh, please," Lyla scoffed at him. "Who was the doofus who told you that, Tate? Because based on what I've heard from Red about your family, I can't believe it was one of them. Although— if it was my damn *boss* who said it, I'd like the chance to strangle him with my bare hands."

"And they say I'm bloodthirsty," Tate smiled. "No, it wasn't Red."

"Do you remember who it *was*?"

"Yeah, I do," he admitted. "It was my girlfriend in sophomore year of college. Happy now?"

Lyla could've predicted that. "And she dropped this science on you when you broke up with her, presumably."

"Naturally."

"You must have been…what? All of nineteen?"

Tate raised his eyebrows and nodded.

"So how come you still feel like the opinion of a kid with hurt feelings, from ten years ago, fits you now?"

Tate gestured lazily. "Like I said, there's been plenty of subsequent reinforcement."

"How delightful for you."

"I've made my peace with it."

Tate didn't look like he'd made his peace with it. He looked unhappy as hell, but perhaps that was because he was sitting through an inquisition when they were just supposed to be having coffee.

Lyla winced. Once again, her rampant curiosity had gotten away from her.

"I'm sorry," she told him. "I'm really nosy about why people do the things they do. Sometimes I get carried away and offend them with my questions."

"No, it's cool." Tate waved her off, as if a virtual stranger prying into his inner thoughts was no big deal. "That's probably what makes you a good writer, though. Cataloging all that motivation, right?"

"Sure. Let's go with that."

Tate's grin was charming and handsome, and completely irresistible. But now, Lyla was the one feeling uncomfortable. How was she supposed to *work* with this kind of specimen underfoot all day?

"Well, what do you think?" Tate inquired. "You about ready to head home?"

"Yes, I think I'd better," Lyla said. Much more of this, and she'd be staying out all night with him, trying to learn more.

On the short walk back to her place, Tate was agreeable, making small talk and sticking close beside her, but careful to avoid any awkward brushing of hands or anything.

Not that Lyla was thinking about holding hands with him— she just didn't want *him* to think that she was thinking it.

Even without that possibility, however, it was already feeling like the best non-date date she'd been on in ages.

Back at home, Tate combed methodically through every inch of her place, looking under and behind any possible thing that might hide a human being, then checking to be sure all her windows were locked tight before he made a move to go.

"That should do it," he told her, lingering on the threshold. "Lock your door behind me and call if you need anything."

"I will. And I'll email you my schedule for the next few days later, okay?"

"Sounds good. Good night, Lyla."

Yes, it was.

Five

INSOMNIA WAS A bitch. Seriously. To fill the time until he could either fall back asleep or start the following day, Tate knocked out a couple hundred sit-ups and the same number of push-ups, then took his second shower in twenty-four hours.

Finally, he settled in with his laptop to see what Lyla's schedule looked like in the coming days.

Reading it over, Tate saw that her book tour kicked off with a few small events in town this week, before they were due in Newark next Monday. In addition, Lyla had noted the blocks of time when she'd be working at home, some meetings at Trident and PKM headquarters, plus a few vague references to "errands."

Tate supposed he'd find out what *those* entailed soon enough. In the meantime, he probably ought to determine what the hell a bodyguard was expected to wear out in the real world. Somehow, he suspected it wasn't BDUs or workout gear.

After some debate, he decided that the safest course of action would be to simply follow Lyla's lead. With a couple of taps on his keyboard, Tate did a search on her name and pulled up a bunch of images right away. Lyla at readings and signings, Lyla at conferences—even publicity shots of Lyla at an award event of some kind, looking sexy as sin in a long red dress that showed off every one of her curves.

He could dwell on that little number later. For now, all Tate needed to know was that Lyla favored a sharp, business-casual look most of the time. Luckily, that was simple enough to match.

The downside of spending the majority of his adulthood in the military, however, was that the bulk of his dress clothes were comprised of the green uniform variety.

If Tate didn't want to wear the same jacket, pants, and dress shirt every day for the next month, he was going to have to drop some cash on new clothes—and fast.

Even if he bought stuff online tonight and picked it up in the store tomorrow, he still probably wouldn't have time to get it tailored, though. That pained him, but at least he wasn't Red's height and had a prayer of fitting into some off-the-rack things. He also wouldn't have to worry about any surprise inspections from superiors, so he had some leeway.

Another quick glance at Lyla's schedule confirmed that she intended to stay at home for the first half of the day tomorrow. Tate would have plenty of time to run out and buy another blazer, and a few more shirts and pants that he could rotate through.

Hell, with the amount of coin Red's company was throwing at him for this gig, Tate could afford a whole new wardrobe—and maybe he should. After everything his friends had done for him this year, he didn't want to make them look bad. Red was putting a lot of stock into this new imprint he was starting, and Tate hated the thought of doing anything to jeopardize that.

Even more than that, though, he didn't want his appearance to reflect badly on Lyla. Based on what he'd seen online and what she had going on for the next few weeks, making a personal connection with her readers was important to the bottom line.

No way was Tate going to be the weakest link in that chain. And, if a certain gorgeous mystery author happened to take a shine to her new bodyguard's fashion sense, then who was he to complain?

With that in mind, Tate was sorely tempted to shoot for the whole badass g-man aesthetic, complete with dark sunglasses and a tough-looking earpiece. Sadly, that was probably overkill—and he suspected Lyla would only laugh at him, anyway.

Okay, so…he had his marching orders. Now all Tate had to do was find a freaking menswear employee who knew their way around a six-foot-two, 200-hundred-pound killing machine. This was Manhattan, though—if he couldn't find it here, it didn't exist, and maybe Red or Luca would know where to start.

Tate grabbed a pen and added *shopping* to his list for the next day, then relaxed back into his pile of pillows to begin learning everything he could about being a bodyguard, courtesy of the loose-lipped internet.

BY THE FOLLOWING afternoon, Tate had learned a number of things about the woman he was shepherding around town. Acting as Lyla's bodyguard felt sort of like taking a crash course in *getting-to-know-you*—so many details about her presented themselves, courtesy of their peculiar arrangement.

Hell, in a matter of hours, Tate had found out more about Lyla's wants and needs than he'd ever known about any of his ex-girlfriends, even after months of dating them.

For example, where Tate was particular about his coffee, Lyla was fussy about the tea she drank (honey and milk, and hold the lemon or creamer, *thank you very much*).

She claimed to be allergic to making beds, but was meticulous with her laptop and notebooks, as well as her appearance.

Perhaps the most interesting thing about Lyla, however, was that she was apparently a vegetarian. And not a vegetarian as in, *let me tell you all the ways you're ruining the planet, you savage*—but a no-fanfare, quietly never-ate-meat kind of person.

Tate hadn't realized it at first, because she'd never made a big announcement of the fact like a lot of people would have. As far as he could tell, if there weren't acceptable things on hand for Lyla to eat, she simply went without.

And normally, that wouldn't be the least bit interesting, he knew. It was what Lyla did for a living that turned her food choices into something fascinating for him.

That was because, while Tate had never actually read any of her books, he *had* browsed through several of their descriptions online last night. He'd also read some of her customer reviews, and there was no mistaking that Lyla wrote some really gritty stuff. The disconnect between that kind of imagination and Lyla's real-life, wouldn't-hurt-a-fly demeanor stuck out to Tate like a sore thumb.

How had it happened? While he trailed around after her, waiting patiently while she went about her business, his brain couldn't seem to let it go. Here Lyla was, kindhearted and gentle as a lamb. If Tate had met her out of the blue and been told what she did for a living, he probably would've bet good money that she wrote something cozy and heartwarming.

Instead, she spent her days penning dark and twisty books that her readers devoured. She was an enigma, and Tate was inconveniently fond of those.

Even if he had no business dwelling on it, the puzzle of Lyla wasn't dangerous, at least. The riddle of her overwrought "fan" *was*, however—and fortunately, Tate was on solid ground there. Unlike speculating about his new boss's considerable assets, trying to figure out the stalker business was a good and helpful use of his time.

Tate would figure it out, too—he felt it in his bones. The more time he spent with Lyla, shadowing her through her daily life and author-y pursuits, the better sense Tate had of how normal civilians were supposed to interact with her.

When or if someone behaved abnormally, Tate was sure he'd be able to spot it. He could report it to the cops, Lyla would be safe, and Tate could go back to his unit with a clear conscience.

He could resume keeping the world safe from asshole insurgents like he'd never missed a step.

Easy as breathing.

LYLA WAS ON the move again a couple of days later, completing chore after chore with the efficiency of a military operation. Tate was impressed, and not a little daunted.

These days, he could barely stay on task with the help of a list—but Lyla knew exactly where she had to be, and when, and she made it all look easy.

On the way to her afternoon appointment at her publisher, Tate had a minute to breathe in the back of their cab. He seized the opportunity to ask Lyla something that had occurred to him around three a.m. that morning.

"So, the other day, when that detective came by," he began, "He mentioned the other letters you've received from that nutcase."

Lyla dropped her head back on the cracked black pleather of the cab's seat. "Don't remind me," she groaned.

"I was just wondering if you have copies of them, though. I wouldn't mind taking a look to see if anything jumps out at me."

"Sorry, but no," she said. She didn't sound one bit sorry, and Tate could hardly blame her.

"If you want to look at them," she went on, "I'm afraid you'll have to ask Detective Scarletti. He's got everything at the station, as far as I know."

"*Pass*. What do you remember off the top of your head?" Tate asked. "Can you give me an idea of what they sounded like? Or if they all said the same thing?"

"*You've got it wrong*," Lyla sighed.

Tate paused. "How so?"

"No, I mean that's what they always say. Whoever it is totally has a screw loose. They complain about something I've done or said and then tell me I got it wrong. It's like they're keeping track of everything I do and measuring it against some rule book only they know about. No matter what, though, I don't get anything right as far as they're concerned."

"That's weird."

"Tell me about it."

"Have the cops looked at other authors? Maybe failed ones who write the same kind of books you do? Or…what about some rabid fan of a different writer—someone who leaves you bad reviews because they think you're in competition with their hero, or whatever."

"You'll have to ask Scarletti that, too. All I know is that he can't figure out who the person is, and he can't do much else unless the freak decides to up their game. He's stuck, I'm stuck, we're all stuck."

"Not me," Tate said, and hoped Lyla would believe it.

LYLA'S CELL BEGAN ringing the minute their cab pulled up outside Trident Publishing, so Tate waved her off to answer it, while he took care of paying the fare.

By the time he'd figured out the whole card-swiping apparatus and reached her side, Lyla was pacing on the sidewalk with a decidedly pained expression on her face.

"Mom? Mom!" she cried. And then, "Oh, hi Dad."

Tate smiled, enjoying the glimpse of normalcy. Lyla wasn't nearly as enthralled.

"No, not until next week," she told her parents. "About three weeks, but…no. Mom, no—I'm not going to Mars. You can call me anytime. If I'm tied up, I'll just call you back later."

Tate's dick twitched a bit at that image—approving immediately of tying Lyla to a bed wearing only her cute secretary glasses. He coughed and sent a stern *settle-down* to the idiot, then unabashedly eavesdropped some more.

"Guys, it's not that far," Lyla groaned. "I think the farthest we're going is only Cleveland. I will be home before you know it."

Tate stuck his hands in his pockets and chuckled. Lyla's parents sounded like nervous nellies—no wonder their daughter had grown up into such an independent woman. She'd probably done it just to spite them.

"Well, yeah. I can try," she was saying. "I'll let you know, though."

Lyla listened for a long moment, and then practically yelled, "No! Do not—Mom, please do *not* do that!"

Well, that sounded weird. Tate swiveled toward her and caught her eye.

Lyla mouthed, *I'm so sorry*, then stared up at the little patch of sky, just visible between the tops of the buildings, like she was searching for deliverance.

"Because I don't *want* to have dinner with them, that's why," she groaned. Lyla shook her head and gave Tate a look that said, loud and clear, *What in the actual fuck?*

"Because I can't stand them! Dad…Mom! Guys, will you *stop?* For crying out loud, we've been over this a thousand times."

Tate had no idea what "this" was, but maybe he could still lend a hand. He walked closer and met Lyla's beseeching gaze, then murmured, "Everything okay?"

"Oh my God, they're insane," she whispered back.

Tate tapped his watch and raised his eyebrows. "Need an out?"

That earned him a grateful squeeze on his bicep, and he'd be lying if he said he didn't preen a little at the way Lyla's hand lingered there. He might've even flexed a tiny bit, but come on— these things happened.

"Listen, I love you two, but I've got to hang up now," Lyla said, taking care of things herself. "I'm going into a building. I'm going to lose you. Okay! I love you, too. Okay, bye!"

She stabbed ferociously at her phone screen, making extra sure she'd hung up, and then moaned loud enough to catch the eyes of a few people walking by them on the sidewalk.

"I am so sorry," she said again. "My parents are super nice people, but sometimes they just do not get it."

Tate was dying to know what all the fuss had been about, but it felt weird to come right out and ask. He certainly didn't have the excuse of being professionally invested in people's motivations like Lyla did.

So, he only smiled and told her, "That is the way of parents. I'm sure they're trying their best."

"Yeah, I know. They just have really bad taste in friends, that's all. Whenever I visit them, they want me to get together with the neighbors, and I kid you not—those people are the *worst.*"

That answered Tate's primary question. "I'm sorry. That sucks," he commiserated.

As they headed into the Trident lobby, Lyla told him, "I feel so guilty arguing with them like that, though. I haven't had a lot of time to go visit them much, and I know they mean well." She blew a piece of hair out of her face. "And they're getting older, you know? I miss them sometimes."

"Of course, you do. And they're probably being overbearing because they miss you, too."

Lyla sighed and changed the subject. "You're away from home for way longer stretches than me. What do you miss when you're gone?"

That wasn't hard at all. "My parents and my little brother, obviously. Home stuff, like food my mom makes and the way my dad keeps the fireplace going every evening in the winter. I miss having a dog."

"Do you miss your Army friends now that you're here?" Lyla prodded curiously.

"Sure." Though oddly, not as much as he'd expected to. It was like there were two Tates—one for home and one for over there.

Home Tate was perfectly happy to take the field right now, and he suspected the guy wouldn't want to give it up once the time came for him to fade gracefully back into the woodwork.

Lyla wasn't *quite* satisfied with Tate's answer, however. She had one more bullet in the chamber, and as soon as they were alone in the elevator she let it fly. "You must miss your girlfriend, right?" she asked, then watched Tate's face to see what he would say.

Well, well, well. What did they have here?

Tate tried very hard not to pump his fist in triumph. Miss Lyla Lawson wanted to know if he was single, and he was happy to oblige.

"As it turns out, I do not have a girlfriend to miss," he told her.

"How is that possible?"

Another compliment. *How sweet.*

"I don't do the long-distance thing," Tate explained casually. "It just doesn't seem fair to anyone."

Lyla's pretty lips turned down at the corners, and she pivoted on her heel to study the buttons for the floors. "I see."

The crack she'd made at that coffeeshop the first night—about old ideas not fitting his current life—bounced around in Tate's brain like a drunk, knocking shit over and generally being disorderly.

Why was that, though? The way Tate did things had always made perfect sense before now—so there was absolutely no reason why he should feel guilty telling Lyla about it. Still, Tate could feel the heat climbing up from his collar and the walls of the elevator closing in.

It must be all her questions that were making him uncomfortable—it had to be. However, Lyla would eventually have to realize that Tate was about as interesting as a box of rocks. Then she'd leave him be.

If only that idea didn't sound worse.

Six

A S THEY USUALLY did, Trident's public relations team had scheduled the first events of Lyla's book tour there in town, and today's was at a big chain bookstore in Midtown where she'd made a number of appearances over the last few years.

At first, this event seemed as routine as all the others. Things got started on time, there was a decent crowd gathered, and the mood was good.

With Tate stationed quietly behind her, serious and squared-away in his immaculate jacket and tie, Lyla felt like she could relax and act normal, and not spend the whole time worrying about whether her superfan would show up.

But then, about a quarter of the way into the line of people waiting to have their books signed, a young woman sat down who changed everything.

When she handed over a hardcover of one of Lyla's backlist titles, Lyla happily told her, "Oh, I've always loved this one."

The woman only smiled vaguely and nodded.

"Who should I make it out to?"

"Um, I'm Kim," she replied, distracted and fidgety. "And thank you so much."

"You got it, Kim."

Kim's attention was fixed over Lyla's shoulder, however, and she didn't respond.

Lyla waited her out with the signed book in her hands, and eventually Kim worked up the nerve to ask, "So, um…Who's that guy?"

Lyla glanced back, even though she had a pretty good idea who the lady meant—and she had to smirk at what she saw there. Tate was in position, all right, his hands clasped loosely in front of him while he tried to look tough in his jacket and tie.

He wasn't half bad at it, either.

"Oh, that's just Captain Monroe," Lyla chuckled.

Kim's eyes got round and she stammered, "Who is…what does he…I mean…"

"Tate?" Lyla called over her shoulder, "You wanna tell Miss Kim why you're here?"

He sprang forward immediately and stuck out his hand, giving Lyla's fan a firm shake. "Ma'am, I work security for Ms. Lawson. How do you do?"

Kim gaped at him for a long beat. "I do fine," she breathed. Then she turned back to Lyla and fanned herself dramatically. "Omigod, this is so cool. I've never gotten to meet a cover model before. Please tell me he's in the new series!"

Lyla blinked. "Uh…"

After that, the book signing went completely haywire. Several other women wanted introductions and handshakes, and eventually, a pair of blogger sisters even scampered around the table to take selfies with Tate for their social media feeds.

Lyla was going to have to get things under control if she ever wanted to be invited back—or to make it out of there, to begin with. She got to her feet and signaled for the people still waiting in line to quiet down so she could make an announcement.

"People, can I have your attention, please? We have a long line today, and not a lot of time left to get your books signed. So, in the interest of keeping things moving, I'd like you all to meet someone."

She turned and waved Tate forward. "This is Captain Monroe. He really does work security for me and, despite appearances to the contrary, he is not a cover model or the inspiration for a new book."

"Why *not?*" called someone in the back.

Lyla grinned at her. "Alright, settle down back there. If we want everyone to get their turn, we need to have some ground rules in place. First, you may look, but not touch."

"*Awwwww,*" they complained in unison.

Lyla checked on Tate's reaction and, of course, he made things worse by winking at her.

"Not helping," she hissed under her breath, but the collective sigh that wafted out from the crowd was so ridiculous, even she had to laugh.

"As I said," she continued, "you can admire Captain Monroe from afar, to your heart's content. He doesn't appear to mind. But let's allow him to do his job, okay? No more handshakes or selfies, please."

They booed her. They actually *booed* her. Lyla stood there in shock, without a clue as to what she should do next.

But then, the clutch of giggling moms at the front of the line stepped forward with their strollers and books, and the signing finally rolled on with a minimum amount of good-natured whining.

Lyla breathed a sigh of relief and got gratefully back to work.

WHEN IT WAS all over, Lyla expected Tate to simply escort her home and be done with it. For one thing, he couldn't possibly have expected to be the center of attention like he'd ended up—though he'd handled it good-naturedly.

For another, he *had* to be tired. Lyla was exhausted, and she hadn't been the one standing at attention for hours.

But instead, Tate surprised her once more, and somehow convinced her to stop for a dinner out again.

Which didn't indicate that he was dying to spend more time with her, she reminded herself. It only meant that Tate was staying in a hotel and didn't have a kitchen to cook in. She was reading too much into it, she knew.

Since it was still on the early side, they didn't have to wait long to be seated at the restaurant they picked. The hostess walked Lyla and Tate back to a booth near the kitchen, handed them a couple of menus, and took her own sweet time in leaving.

Surprise, surprise—the girl couldn't peel her eyes off Tate. However, despite the fact that the hostess was about twenty-five years old and pretty—with long black hair and painted-on jeans—Tate didn't even acknowledge her attempts to flirt with him, much less try to flirt back.

Lyla looked him over, impressed with his restraint. "So, that was a scene, today, huh? What did you think?"

He looked up from his menu. "It was cool."

"You sure got a lot of attention."

"Maybe a little," Tate hedged.

"More than a little," Lyla corrected, shaking her head. "What are we going to do with you?"

"What?" he protested. "They liked me, didn't they?"

"Too much, Tate. They liked you *too much*."

"I…apologize." He looked thoroughly confused, the poor thing.

Lyla sighed. It was hardly Tate's fault that he was freaking adorable—or that a room full of female bookworms was particularly inclined to notice that fact. But he and Lyla had a whole book tour to get through, and he had no idea how much worse it could get if he kept being cute and charming.

"Don't be sorry," she told him. "But we might have to make some adjustments going forward."

Tate set down his menu, all business. "Okay. Like what?"

"I suppose staying out of sight won't work."

"I mean…it could be fun," he mused, "but I probably need to stay close if you expect me to leap into action at the first hint of trouble."

Lyla rolled her eyes. *Men.* "What about…" *Donning an ugly-suit?* Hell, Tate's inveterate charm could probably overcome that. "Maybe you could lose the blazer."

He'd been taking this conversation with reasonably good grace so far, but now Tate looked thoroughly piqued. "What? But it's brand new!"

"You bought a new jacket just to be my bodyguard?"

"I didn't want to make you look bad."

"I think it's fair to say you're not going to do that. But maybe you could just wear regular street clothes going forward." Lyla frowned. "Try to blend in, if you can."

With Tate's height and muscles, that seemed unlikely, but Lyla supposed she had to work with what she had.

Fortunately, he'd perked up at her suggestion. "So, no ties?"

"I really don't think they're necessary."

"Oh, thank Christ." Tate immediately yanked the one he was wearing loose and unbuttoned his shirt collar with a groan of happiness.

Lyla laughed. "Let me guess—not a fan of suits?"

"That's a negative, Ghostrider."

"I'd think you would love them, given the amount of adulation they seem to garner you."

Tate snorted. "That's because you haven't ever been choked by a tie for hours on end."

Talk about a softball over home plate. As much as Tate seemed to enjoy teasing her, Lyla couldn't resist the chance to toy with him a little, now. "You don't know that," she smirked, making it sound as dirty as possible.

He froze, blinking owlishly at her. "Uh…excuse me?"

A waiter stopped by to take their order, but once he was gone, she relented. "Just kidding," she said, "But hey—fair's fair. You have to wear ties, and I have to wear pantyhose and heels. So, we're kind of even."

"Ugh. *Touché.*"

Tate took a long sip of his water, then asked, "Other than your poorly-hidden jealousy of me stealing the show, that went well, though. Right?"

"Right. Good turnout, invested fans, lots of excitement. I think this book tour is going to be a big success. At least, it will be if you can suppress your cheekiness."

Tate sneered at her, "*Ha, ha.*" Then he added, "Anyway, it's nice of you to lend your name to Red's new imprint."

"It was nice of Red's fiancée to pass my name along to him," she said.

"Come on. Piper can't be the only reason he hired you."

"Okay, then how about…it's nice of Red to put so much faith in my books," Lyla countered. "There are a lot of bigger name authors he could have picked to launch Red Devil. I'm honored he picked me and happy we could come to an agreement on the contract so easily."

"That's extremely diplomatic of you," Tate chuckled.

"Feel free to tell him that."

Their food arrived and they both dug in, but Tate kept eyeing her, laughing at her last comment. "*Man.* Red must be paying you a shitload of money to take this on, huh?"

Lyla laughed right back at him, "You're one to talk."

"I never cash checks and tell."

"You don't have to. But if I were you, I'd be hoarding that PKM gold like a leprechaun. Once this gig is up, you'll be back to taking Uncle Sam's money, and we all know how stingy he is."

Tate's smile faded and he got quiet. "Way to be a buzzkill, Lyla."

"But I thought you loved your real job and missed your buddies," she taunted.

"I do. But let a guy enjoy his vacation, why don't you."

He was actually serious. Lyla had no idea what she'd said to flip his switch from joking around to somberness, but she wished she could undo it and go back to how he'd been before.

"I'm sorry. I didn't think that was a sore subject."

"It's not," Tate claimed, but his entire demeanor said otherwise.

"Are you sure? Because—"

He brushed his hands together and dropped his napkin beside his plate. "Hey, you ready to get out of here? We pay up front, I think, and it's getting pretty crowded at the bar. I bet they want to turn this table over."

Well, that was sudden, and not a little disappointing. However, Lyla agreed, "Yeah, sure. You're probably right," and got to her feet.

"I don't think we don't need to grab a taxi, do you? Didn't you say your house was close?"

"Yeah, we can hoof it. It's only four blocks or so."

Tate kept a hand on her back as he ushered her out, and Lyla tried to view it as protectiveness, instead of him just hustling her along.

When he dropped his hand to his side once they were out on the sidewalk, Lyla reminded herself that ladies only got to lament stuff like that when they were on actual dates with people they were allowed to like.

They could not get angsty about hands and touching when they were at a business dinner with a coworker—someone who also happened to be BFFs with their boss, and who was only in the city on a very temporary, involuntary basis.

Ah, romance. How did people ever freaking survive it?

BACK AT HOME, Lyla hung back a step once they reached her floor and fought the nearly overwhelming urge to bury her face in Tate's sleeve while he looked to see if there was another note on her door.

But Tate wasn't there in a boyfriend capacity, and he wouldn't be sticking around for anything even approaching the long term. So, Lyla let him move a step ahead, but she kept pace and tried not to let her fear show.

Until Lyla's shoe caught on Mrs. Meecham's oversized welcome mat, making her stumble ten feet from her front door, that was.

Tate's reflexes were lightning fast. His arm shot out and tucked Lyla behind him before either one of them could take a breath—and so there she was, after all, eyes squeezed tight against fine black gabardine, her hands wrapped around his large, hard bicep as she held on for dear life.

If she'd had any concerns about his lack of experience, they evaporated instantly in that one, fraught second.

"Lyla, no one's here," Tate said finally. "And there's nothing on your door. What happened?"

"I tripped," she whimpered, embarrassed, but not quite ready to let go.

Tate chuckled, and it sounded even deeper filtered through his chest and clothes. That sound was kind and familiar, and for some reason Lyla would rather not look at too closely, it steadied her.

"Why don't you give me your key, and I'll take a look inside?" he asked.

"Okay."

Tate went through her apartment the same way as last time, sifting through every corner and checking every lock to make sure the place was safe and secure, and clear of any threats.

Lyla trailed after him as he worked, trying to see her house through his eyes. Maybe…she needed to make more time to straighten up once in a while.

She had begun packing for their trip, and there were clothes strewn all over her room. At the very least Lyla should try to make her bed and get her laundry in the hamper more often, and perhaps she should invest in more shelves, to help with the stacks of books everywhere.

Tate probably thought she was a total slob, but he was too nice to even make a joke about it.

Lyla frantically kicked a bra under her bed when his back was turned and plastered an unconcerned expression on her face, figuring that if she acted like her lack of neatness was no big deal, he might, too.

At last, Tate completed his loop and they arrived back at her front door once more. He lingered in the doorway, and Lyla wished that meant he was as reluctant to leave as she was to let him go.

Once he left, she'd be alone in this place, and she'd never noticed before how many dark corners there were.

"Lock the door as soon as I leave, so you don't forget," Tate instructed. "And leave your windows closed tight and locked, too, okay?"

"I will."

"And…" he shifted on his feet, hesitating. "If the phone rings, don't pick up unless you know who it is. You have caller ID, right?"

"Yes, Tate," Lyla smiled. "And voicemail, too." He was being so cute, she had to forgive him for his abrupt flight from dinner.

"Good." He looked over her shoulder and scanned her living room yet again. "Don't be shy about calling me if you hear or see anything strange. I'll come right over, I promise."

"Tate, we're in Manhattan. If *strange* is the barometer we're using, you may as well just stay the night here."

There was no mistaking the way his brows winged up and his eyes twinkled at that suggestion, and Lyla's heart skipped a beat or two in response. *Bad, bad heart*, she scolded.

Tate told her, "Believe me, I'm tempted. But remember—there's normal strange and weird strange. Trust your gut to know the difference."

"What if my gut's wrong?"

"Then I'll have come running over here for no reason, and I won't even care because we'll all know you're safe. Until then, you're going to have to settle for me picking you up tomorrow at nine for your hair appointment."

Lyla flushed with gratitude—for her friend Piper, who'd so kindly passed Lyla's name to her publisher fiancé, Red, when he'd wanted to start a new mystery imprint. And also for Red himself, for thinking that his old friend might make the perfect bodyguard for Lyla.

She was also thankful for Tate, who was cheeky and funny and strong and protective, and who would've had her stupid heart singing arias if Lyla had met him under any other circumstance but this one.

Regret for the missed chance flooded her, and Lyla had to turn away so Tate wouldn't see. On impulse, she dug around in the small drawer of the console beside her, finding what she wanted almost immediately.

"Here," she told Tate when she'd pulled herself together. "You probably ought to have this. It's my spare key."

Tate nodded, looked her over one last time, and stepped back into the hall. "Good night," he said.

"Night, Tate. And thanks—for everything."

"My pleasure," he told her.

If only that were true.

Seven

I T WAS TOO warm in this damn hotel room, Tate thought. He wondered if Lyla was having the same issue.

They'd landed at this midrange chain, which didn't even have a full restaurant downstairs, after Lyla's second event in Newark earlier that day. Without any excuse to hang out together, they'd both retired to their rooms and called it a night.

Tate had already called the front desk twice, but it had yielded no measurable results on the temperature front, and a quick glance at his watch confirmed that it was too late to knock on Lyla's door to check on her.

He was stuck here, hot and alone with his fucking insomnia, watching the worst television show in history. Yet somehow, it still felt better than being in the desert, staking out some asshole zealot camped out with his homies in a fucking cave.

Would wonders never cease.

As he gazed at the lingerie fashion show unfolding on the TV screen, Tate decided—as long as he was here—that he had a bone to pick with the person in charge of supermodels these days.

The poor women stalking that runway looked like storks—all long skinny limbs, pale feathers stuck everywhere, and awkward gaits.

The dry ice swirling clouds around their feet only added to the odd effect.

He knew his complete lack of arousal probably put him in the minority among men, but those lacy outfits on the stick-thin models did nothing for him. They only made him uncomfortable—and not in a *my-pants-just-got-too-tight* kind of way.

Tate supposed all the ribbons and buckles crisscrossing their bodies were supposed to look seductive, to compensate for the ladies' lack of female curves. But those ribbons could not make them look like something a man might actually want to touch.

Not this man, anyway.

As TV specials went, this one was about the least erotic thing Tate had ever seen. If the guys in his unit could see him now, they'd probably want to kill him. He turned the show off and heaved a long sigh.

He'd ordered a couple of sodas and some snacks from room service as soon as they'd checked in, then made sure Lyla was squared away in her room before settling in here.

She was no doubt writing or sleeping now, or whatever it was that she did on her own time—all of which was decidedly none of his damn business.

Tate had merely stripped to his undershirt and boxers as soon as he realized he was stuck in a sauna for the next twelve hours, and then attempted to find something worth watching on TV. But now, the TV was a lost cause, the sodas were soaked in condensation, and his damp t-shirt was sticking uncomfortably to his back.

Tate drained the dregs in the second bottle of pop and began tearing the sodden label off in strips as his mind wandered. He'd had a lot of time to consider what he wanted in a woman in his last several years in the Army, as had many of the soldiers.

All that time waiting for shit to happen gave a guy plenty of time to think, it seemed. So now Tate knew, without a shadow of a doubt, that if he ever got the chance to pick his perfect woman, she wouldn't be a beanpole like those models had been.

He liked women who were fit, sure—but gaunt and wiry gym rats did nothing for him. Tate wanted a healthy-looking woman, one with actual breasts and hips and thighs. An ass that filled his hands. He wanted someone he could hold close at night without getting jabbed by her elbows or hip bones.

Tate liked when a woman's stomach had that slight, enticing curve to it, just below her navel. The sunken abdomens of the women on TV had only made him want to feed them—not to get busy plastering them in kisses.

Maybe that was the root of his dislike, though. When you loved to eat, it sucked to be with a woman who viewed food as the enemy. Luckily, Tate did not currently have that problem. He had no woman, and his body still required a hell of a lot of calories to perform his job. He got to eat whatever he wanted, and he did.

Someday, though, he hoped to find someone who approached food the way his mom and grandma did. They were people who enjoyed the whole process of a meal—they liked shopping for special ingredients, the prep work and the cooking, and the savoring of the end product with loved ones. They had taught him to enjoy all the phases, too: the appetizers and sides, the entrees and desserts.

Because, with that kind of attention, the meal became something more than fuel. It became community, and love. Was it so wrong to want to share that with someone special, someday? It was as good an example of home, and the kind of thing Tate missed, as anything he could think of.

Lyla, for example, was a woman who might get that. She had a normal relationship with food, as far as he could tell.

They'd gotten dinner together a few times now, and even if she didn't eat meat, she still seemed to savor reading menus and trying new things.

Tate could picture her finding funky new restaurants to try in the city and making special trips to discover the best places to get good produce.

He immediately shook off those treacherous thoughts. What Lyla liked did *not* matter. She was only someone he was being paid to keep safe, not a new flame to evaluate for her wife potential.

Jesus. This heat was fucking with his brain.

Tate stomped into the bathroom to rinse off, but his thoughts started roaming again. In some ways, he was like a lot of other guys—he'd played football and joined a fraternity, then went into the Army, for crying out loud.

In other ways, though, he'd never been into the same things as other dudes. Maybe he was just old-fashioned.

But when his high school buddies had been drooling over actresses and supermodels, Tate had been nursing crushes on 1940s pin-ups and reading biographies of war heroes.

It had been a relief to find Red and Luca in college, who'd accepted him as he was and never made Tate feel like he was playing a role just to fit in with them.

Lyla was like that too, Tate reflected. She just had a way about her that put other people at ease. Without even thinking about it, Tate had simply acted like himself from the very beginning. It was incredibly relaxing, and kind of…addicting.

Again—*not that it mattered.*

In a frustrated snit, Tate slapped at the shower lever, turning off the icy spray and snatching a towel off the rack. He was already starting to sweat again. This room was a freaking cauldron and it was making him crazy.

At least he could take comfort in the fact that his career suited him perfectly. When things went according to plan, Tate got to swoop in and right the wrongs. He could wreak vengeance and serve justice on occasion, and rest easy in the knowledge that he and his brethren had made a difference in the world, even if it was a small one.

Tate was eager to get back to that. And someday, if he ever decided to leave the military, he might even give this whole bodyguard gig another try.

That brought him right back to the subject of Lyla, however, and women in general. Women weren't as easy to figure out as jobs were—no, chicks were going to be a whole other story.

These days, women were too smart, too independent, and too capable to require much saving, and the ones who still made a science of the damsel-in-distress schtick were better to avoid.

Tate was fine with that, though. He didn't need to be the dude on the white horse, as such—he just wanted to find a woman who actually engaged his heart. Tate wanted to find someone with fortitude and vulnerability, and a brain that could keep up with his.

He wanted her curvy body to fire up his. Tate wanted someone with a good sense of humor and figured, knowing him, she ought to have some patience. A lot of patience—probably all of it.

The fact that both of his best friends had already accomplished this feat had him feeling like a loser of the first order. Why couldn't he seem to manage it, too?

He flopped on top of the bed covers and tried not to move, so he wouldn't start sweating again.

Tate's mother liked to claim there was someone out there waiting for him, but he wasn't so sure. In the last fifteen years, he'd been all over the world and interacted with all kinds of people, but he'd never met a soul he'd consider marrying. That seemed like a bad sign.

He tried to look on the bright side, though. In all that time, he'd been lucky to date a string of mostly-nice ladies and they'd been kind enough to share their bodies and their beds with him.

If one were inclined to find a silver lining, then Tate supposed it would be that—when and if he ever found the woman of his dreams—he would damn well know what to do with her.

For the time being, he was quite alone, and was too hot and irritable to even consider jacking off to help himself fall asleep.

On that sorry note, Tate turned in for the night, and his dreams were a strange hodgepodge of TV models, Lyla, and his girlfriend from sophomore year of college—bitterly informing him, over and over, that he wouldn't know how to settle down with one woman if his life depended on it.

TATE WAS TIRED and out of sorts when a frantic knock on his door woke him the next morning. He could barely be bothered to throw on yesterday's dress slacks before he yanked it open and found Lyla quivering like a leaf out in the hallway.

She stood there in a thin t-shirt and a pair of pajama bottoms. Her eyes were wide, and she looked rumpled—like she'd just been woken up, too.

Tate's body snapped to attention. "Lyla? What happened? What's wrong?"

She shuddered and seemed like she was trying not to cry. "I don't know. There was a knock on my door. I—I thought it was you. I—"

When a door slammed down the hall, she jumped and searched warily over her shoulder. Tate pulled her into his room and locked the door behind her.

"It wasn't me," he pointed out. "I was asleep. I didn't think you wanted to take off until ten today."

"I want to leave right now," Lyla said miserably.

Tate's foggy brain abruptly registered the weird bundle she was holding. He pointed, "What's that?"

"I don't know. He shoved it into my hands when he pushed open the door."

"He…you…you opened your door?"

"I thought it was you," she repeated.

Tate realized that something was very wrong here. He led Lyla over to his messy bed and sat her down. "Why did you think it was me?" he asked.

"I did check the peephole first, but the guy was turned away. It seemed like it could be you. And then…and then—" she stammered.

Jesus, she was terrified. Tate sank down beside her and wrapped an arm around her shoulders. "Okay, sweetheart. Take a deep breath. Slow down and start from the beginning."

Lyla nodded, doing as he said. "I was asleep, too. But someone kept knocking, so I thought maybe I'd overslept. I got up to see who it was."

"Alright. I'm with you so far."

"Like I said, I looked out the peephole, but you know how weird they make everything look. I was half asleep. It looked like you." She halted.

"And then what?" Tate asked.

"Well…he must have been listening for the clicks or watching for movement or something. As soon as I had the door unlocked and started turning the knob, he pushed hard and forced it open."

"*Shit*. Really?" That was bad—really fucking bad.

"I wasn't ready for it," Lyla explained. "It pushed me back against the doorjamb of the bathroom, and I hit my head."

"Let me see." Tate cupped the back of her skull, feeling gently through her silky hair to find the bruise. "Yeah, you've got a pretty good knot back there," he told her.

"It hurts."

"I'll bet."

Lyla was still trembling, so he swallowed back his rage at the situation. Losing his shit here wouldn't help her, it would only make things worse—and she still hadn't told him what the hell she was holding.

"So…what's that?" Tate asked, pointing at the odd, lumpy bundle clutched in her hands.

"I don't know. The guy shoved it at me before he took off. I guess I took it by reflex."

"So, once you took it, the person ran. Then what'd you do?"

"I didn't want to get caught alone in my room with him if he came back. I thought, at least in the hallway, I could yell and maybe someone would hear me, right?"

Tate nodded. "Good thinking."

"I came over here and just started knocking until you heard me," she finished. "I'm sorry I woke you up."

Tate wasn't worried about that anymore. Lyla had said something else that was far more important.

"Lyla, you keep saying *he*. What made you think it was a man?"

She swallowed and closed her eyes, trying to think. "Uh, his size, maybe? His build? I'm not sure. He just seemed like a guy. Men hold themselves differently than women. They move differently, too."

"How big was he?"

"About your size."

"Did you see anything else?" Tate asked. "Hair, skin, clothes? Anything?"

"He had a hat on. A baseball cap, but it was too faded to see the logo. I saw his neck and cheek, and I'm pretty sure he was white. And, um…his clothes were just clothes. I'm sorry—it all happened too fast for me to notice much."

"Did he say anything?"

"No, he just made me take this." Lyla lifted her package grimly.

Tate rubbed a hand across the whiskers on his jaw and leaned over to get a closer look—and tried not to get distracted by Lyla's light, feminine scent in the process.

Whatever she was holding looked like a long tube of some sort, wrapped all around with a grimy, torn-up necktie. Seeing it, Tate went abruptly cold, and thought immediately of the conversation he and Lyla had had yesterday about his attire at her events.

He jumped up and went over to his bag, pulling out a pair of latex gloves and a large plastic bag like he'd seen Detective Scarletti use at Lyla's house. He brought them over to where she was sitting.

"You packed rubber gloves?" she squawked.

"Just in case," Tate said, glad he'd thought of it. "You know what they say—hope for the best and prepare for the worst."

"Who says that?"

"People." He snapped on the gloves and reached for the package. "Let me see it."

Once Lyla handed it over, she scrubbed her hands on Tate's sheets like she was trying to slough off any freaky residue that might be clinging to her skin.

Then Lyla grabbed his phone off the nightstand and told him, "I'll take pictures for Detective Scarletti while you open it."

"Good idea."

Tate carried the bundle over to the desk, found the knot holding it together, and worked it free. Lyla stood beside him, carefully aiming the camera.

After he'd unwound the tie, Tate found another one, as well as a rolled-up sheaf of papers inside. The top one had a message printed on it, in a nondescript computer font. *"A guard dog, Delilah?"* it read. *"You make me laugh. You're so wrong if you think your puppy can stop me now, but what else is new? You're always wrong."*

The rest of the papers, some ten or twenty of them, were all the same: just line after line of the word *wrong*.

"Wow, you weren't kidding," Tate said.

"I told you," Lyla groaned. "What do you think we should do?"

"We need to call Scarletti, clearly. We can text him the photos you took, and maybe find a place on our way out of town that can overnight this crap to him." Tate gathered up the pages and the ties and dropped them into the bag, then carefully slid the zipper closed.

"Do you think it was him? The superfan?" Lyla wondered. "I've never actually seen him before. He was big."

"I don't know, sweetheart. It might've been him—or it could've just been someone he hired to deliver his message. Hard to say without knowing more about who he is. Or if he's even a *he*, I suppose."

"But..."

Lyla trailed off, looking deeply troubled. Tate couldn't blame her. If she had even half as many questions as he did about how this had happened here in fucking *Newark*, then she was probably plenty upset.

"But what?" he asked.

"How did he find me here?" she wondered. "I haven't done an event in Jersey in a while, and I've never stayed at this hotel before. I've always just driven out and back again."

Tate shook his head. "I'd love to know the answer to that, myself."

Lyla wrapped her arms around her stomach and rocked forward. "Tate, I want to get out of here. This place is giving me the creeps."

"Of course. Let's call the detective real quick, and then I can be ready whenever you are."

"Okay, but…" She bit her lip, looking sheepish. "Can I just hang out over here for a bit? I know he's probably long gone, but the thought of going back to my room is kind of psyching me out right now."

"Totally understand," Tate assured her. "Give me ten minutes to hop in the shower and throw my stuff together. Then we'll go over together so you can get ready."

Lyla nodded and pulled herself up to snuggle into his bed, grabbing the TV remote and telling Tate, "Thanks. And take your time. I'm not going anywhere."

The sight of her hunkering down where he'd been sleeping less than an hour before was unnerving and endearing and hot, all at once.

It felt downright domestic, and as Tate stood there staring like an ape for far longer than he should have, he tried to permanently imprint the image on his brain. There was someone out there for everyone, his mom always said. What were the odds of Tate stumbling over his…here?

TWENTY MINUTES LATER, Tate had left a message for Scarletti and texted the detective the photos—and was now the person trying to watch morning television while Lyla showered and primped and whatever else chicks did for hours on end in the bathroom.

He had to believe he was far less sanguine about it than she'd been, however.

You could only turn up a TV so loud, after all, before the other hotel guests started complaining, and even then, it wouldn't drown out the sound of a beautiful woman splashing hot water all over her body, mere feet away.

Tate kept himself under control with one thought, something he'd decided he had to tell Lyla once she emerged. She wasn't going to like it, but honestly—he was going to be the one who was suffering.

He tried to keep his eyes on the sports highlights, instead of sneaking peeks at Lyla blow-drying her hair and applying her makeup. Tate also attempted not to bury his face in her pillows, so he could inhale that tantalizing, all-female scent they were emitting all around him.

Tate steeled himself in every way he knew how so that once Lyla was finally standing in front of him looking fresh as a daisy, her bags packed and her purse on her shoulder, he could drop his bomb with a clear conscience.

"Hey, Slick," he said calmly, "I gotta tell you. This separate room thing we have scheduled for the tour is making me really nervous, in light of what happened this morning."

Lyla didn't wig out, thank God—she merely blinked at him. "What do you suggest?"

Tate blazed ahead, "At minimum, I think we need to call ahead and arrange for suites or adjoining rooms, or something. I promise I won't invade your privacy," *much*, "But I don't want that prick to think he can just get to you whenever he feels like it. What's the point of me being here, otherwise?"

Then Tate held his breath and waited for the explosion.

Lyla only said, "I agree."

"You do?"

She nodded, eyes worried. "I'll call Trident from the car and see what they can set up from their end. Everything else, we'll just have to figure out when we get to each place."

"Alright, then." And *fuck*—her complete lack of objection meant Lyla must be *really* scared.

Tate had to figure this out for her, and he had to do it fast. Once he got his results back from his last Med Board evaluation, he was going to be headed back to the Middle East to rejoin his unit—and no way could he leave Lyla here to deal with this shit alone.

Why that was so all-fired important suddenly, was a question he'd leave for another day.

Eight

F ROM THE SMALL desk in her new hotel room, Lyla could just see Tate in his—sprawled on his couch with his knees spread wide, one arm thrown casually across the tops of the cushions.

He had headphones on but, ever vigilant, had left one ear free so he could hear her if she called.

The way his eyes were tracking across the tablet screen in his lap made it look like he might be watching a movie. She wondered what it was.

Lyla rolled her eyes and turned back to her computer, afraid that Tate would catch her staring at him again. His wide shoulders and long, muscular limbs might be ridiculously hard for her to ignore, but *he* didn't need to know that—his ego had enough to work with already.

However, when Tate's cell phone rang beside him, curiosity won out like it usually did. Lyla peeked through her lashes and watched him reach for it.

With one tap, he engaged the speakerphone and a sweet woman's voice sang out, "Happy Birthday! How are you, Tiger?"

"Hey, Mom," Tate smiled, slipping off his headphones and setting them aside.

"Grace is here, too," the woman added. "Say hi, honey."

"Hey, Tigger!" a young woman chirped excitedly. "I was just bringing your mom and dad some cookies we had leftover, and we got to talking about you. God, it's been ages."

His mother jumped back in quickly. "I can't believe we caught you, kiddo. I wasn't sure if you'd be working today or not. Where are you, anyway?"

Tate stabbed at the screen to take it off speakerphone, then told her, "Philly, right now," before he glanced nervously over at Lyla.

Just in time, she forced her gaze back to her laptop screen and made her fingers type a few words. A few seconds later, she heard the door to his small balcony slide open and shut again.

Through her own door, she could barely see him as he leaned on the railing and looked out at the hotel lot. Tate's deep voice filtered into her room, becoming nothing more than a muted rumble after passing through the thick glass.

Lyla exhaled, and her screen came slowly into focus. The words she'd typed blinked back at her: *It's his birthday?* She felt a little bit ashamed that she hadn't known, but how could she have? Tate had never said a word.

The girl on the phone had called him Tigger, and Lyla could see how Tate might end up with that nickname. It suited him, she thought. Even lounging on a hotel room couch, Tate was all latent energy, barely suppressed beneath the surface.

Like a tawny tiger lolling in the sun, his relaxation belied the play of muscles under his skin—and the sense Lyla always got that he could leap into a mayhem of violence at a moment's notice if the need arose.

Much like a real tiger, Tate's beauty was of a dangerous, ferocious sort, but God help her, if she ever tried to tell him that he'd probably make a joke about it. And while Lyla's nerves got busy prickling at *that* thought, a new one bubbled to the surface.

Who was Grace? A sister or neighbor—or someone else? An ex-girlfriend, perhaps? The one who got away?

Tate had told Lyla that relationships weren't exactly his thing, but that hardly prevented the women he dated from carrying torches for him long after he left.

In fact, it probably ensured it.

Lyla gnawed on her lip. She *had* to stop wondering about his private life. Tate was here to do a job, not to be ogled by her. The last thing she needed was to be accused of workplace harassment, but Lyla was losing her mind with these connecting rooms.

What was left of it after this morning's brush with her superfan, anyway.

Honestly, though—why did it feel like Tate's presence was seeping into every corner, demanding her notice? Why did she feel like she was breathing him in with every inhale? It couldn't just be because he'd put his arm around her earlier, and run his fingers through her hair.

That would be dumb.

Directly behind her, Tate cleared his throat and Lyla jumped so badly she was pretty sure she left part of her psyche on the ceiling.

"Sorry about that," he chuckled. "I hope I didn't interrupt your flow or whatever with that call."

"No, it's fine. I'm fine," Lyla stammered. "You should have told me it was your birthday, though."

"I was hoping you didn't hear that."

Lyla shrugged. "Come on. If I'd known, we could've tried to do something nice today, instead of you being bored out of your skull while I type in here."

Tate arched a dubious eyebrow at her. "Like what? You've got a signing in an hour."

"Well, it's too late now, obviously. But I could've at least gotten you a cupcake at the coffee shop this morning."

Tate smiled wide. "I like chocolate frosting. For future reference."

"Duly noted."

He scanned her room briefly, then backed toward the adjoining door. "It'll probably take us about twenty minutes to get to the bookstore. I should let you get ready."

"Right. Sure," Lyla said, fount of all things smooth and professional that she was.

"And still no suit, right?"

"Just keep being normal," she agreed. "Blend in."

Tate gave her a thumbs-up, stepped through the opening and swung the door mostly shut.

In her head, Lyla was screaming, *Who is Grace?* At least, she *thought* it was in her head.

But then Tate knocked and stuck his head back through the gap. "Hey, Lyla?"

"Yes?"

"Grace is my cousin. She and her fiancé run a café," he told her. "In case you were wondering."

"Oh," she nodded, "That's cool." She acted like it was all the same to her. *She hoped.*

Tate nodded back. "I just thought you'd…" He hesitated, then blurted out, "Anyway," before disappearing again.

Lyla waited, but he didn't pop back in with any other juicy tidbits. While she got changed and put on some makeup, she tried not to feel as happy as she did for the one measly crumb he'd given her.

She should not want to know any and all personal details about her bodyguard. It was wrong, wrong, *wrong*, just like her superfan liked to say—even if her heart kept singing that Tate was all kinds of right.

LYLA'S HANDS WERE shaking. As she stood in the back room of the indie bookstore on the outskirts of Philadelphia, waiting to be introduced for her book signing, she wasn't sure if she could do this tonight.

How could she paint a smile on her face, when she felt like her scary fan could pop up at any moment? How could she act like everything was normal? She had no idea how other people functioned like this.

That guy could be *here*, somewhere—his little gift this morning had made that fact eminently clear. And it was equally obvious that he wanted her to know it.

Out near the table piled with some of her more recent books, the bookstore manager was grinning and gesturing to her, a gaggle of people was standing and clapping nearby, and Lyla was frozen in place.

Tate's big hand dropped to her lower back, calm and steady.

"You need another minute?" he asked. His voice was low. Concerned.

Lyla squared her shoulders. "Nope. I'm good."

If she kept dropping the pen when she was signing books, then so be it. Most people understood about imperfect days, and Lyla had found out along the way that they only liked her better for having them. It helped them relate.

So, the whole "stars are just like us" effect would just have to work in her favor now. Lyla was a professional and she wasn't going to fight it or whine about it. She was simply going to go out there and do her job, no matter what she was feeling.

"You sure?" Tate asked.

"Yes."

His hand pressed on her back, urging her gently forward. Lyla took one step out, and then two—and then she was in full *fake-it-until-you-make-it* mode.

For three long-ass hours.

The thing was, Lyla did enjoy meeting her readers. She liked hearing what they thought of her characters and her plots, and she even liked to hear how they might have written the story differently.

She enjoyed the way people's different life experiences made them absorb her books in their own unique ways. And she especially loved hearing about how her books got people through their rough patches.

What she hated about this evening, though, was how she couldn't help looking into each of their faces with a kernel of suspicion and doubt. Lyla despised how defensive she felt, every time someone's eyes strayed over her shoulder and landed on Tate, quiet and solid as a monument behind her shoulder.

Could she trust their kind words, or was it all an act? Were their smiles fake? It felt like stepping into the pages of one of her own mysteries, and Lyla's busy brain couldn't help playing out each storyline.

The reader did it, in the bookstore, with a letter opener they pulled from the clearance gift table.

The author never stood a chance.

IN THEIR RENTED SUV afterward, Tate kept studying Lyla like she was a strange new snack that might be delicious—or might give him food poisoning.

"What," she muttered.

"You sure you're all right?" he wondered, keeping one eye on the road and one on her.

"I'm fine. Just tired," she said. Lyla leaned her head against the cool glass of the window and told him, "It's kind of a drag shuttling from town to town. We're only a couple of days in and I already want to go home."

"I can see that," he replied. "But you hide it well. Once you were out there, I bet no one could even tell how nervous you were."

"You noticed, huh?"

"I'm supposed to. But don't worry—I'm sure no one else did."

"Let's hope so."

"Does that happen a lot?"

"Getting nervous?"

"Yeah."

Lyla thought about it. "I guess I always have a few butterflies. That's normal, though, right? I want to do well, and I want people to like me enough to buy my books. And now, since Red is trusting me to help get the new imprint off the ground, I don't want to disappoint him."

"Today was different, though. Because of what happened at the hotel in Newark, right?"

Lyla blew out a long breath. "You're right. It was tough. I kept thinking…" Then the rest of the words wouldn't come out.

"I know," he said. "But you were really good with those people, Lyla. Walmart shoppers or high society—you could talk to all of them. It was really something."

"Thanks."

"Lyla…" Tate hesitated, then went on, "…it's exhausting to keep conquering your fears over and over in order to do your job. Take it from someone who knows. You have to give yourself some downtime, too, or you're going to flame out."

Lyla felt herself wilt even further into the seat. They'd barely begun, and here Tate was, already having to give her a pep talk. "It's only for a few weeks," she sighed.

"That's right. And I'm here too, Slick. I'm not going to let anything happen to you, okay?"

Lyla couldn't talk about this anymore, or she was going to break down for sure. She searched for a change in topic. "There were some real characters there today, weren't there?"

Thankfully, Tate accepted her 90-degree conversational veer readily. "There were. Did that one lady have a dog in that little stroller?"

"Two tiny teacup chihuahuas. Their names were Bing and Bong."

"Seriously?"

"Apparently, she reads my books to them every day. They are *big* fans."

"Uh—"

"Don't ask," Lyla laughed. "I liked the old couple toward the end, though. They were holding hands and wearing matching sweatshirts. Did you see them?"

"I did. They were cute, but the motorcycle logos kind of threw me. I would've pegged them for the shuffleboard courts, not the Harley circuit."

"You never know," Lyla smiled.

They'd been super sweet and polite, and if there hadn't been another ten people in line behind them, she might've gotten their contact information so she could send them something special.

She told Tate, "I like to put people like that into my books, did you know that?"

"What do you mean?"

"People I meet. Sometimes I stick them in stories as cameos or side characters. Just for fun. I like to think of them as the ones who got away, the survivors, the happily-ever-afters that come after my part of the story is over."

"Lyla, that kind of rocks," Tate grinned. "Do they know you do it?"

"I doubt it. It's just an inside thing for me, and they'd probably never recognize themselves, anyway. We never see ourselves how others see us, you know?"

"True."

He drove for a while, watching the GPS and checking street signs while he looked for their hotel. After a while, he got pensive, though.

"So…do I need to worry about showing up in one of your books one of these days?"

She smiled at him. "Maybe, Birthday Boy. Do you plan on doing anything really interesting this month?"

"I mean…look at me. I'm fascinating without even trying," Tate scoffed.

He had no idea. And Lyla could see just how she'd write him, too—tall, strong, capable, and studly. Hard where a woman was soft, tight and straight where she was curved…but who was she kidding?

Lyla didn't write biographies *or* odes. She wrote mysteries, and the only mystery here was whether Tate would catch on sooner or later that she was nursing the world's most inappropriate crush on him while he tried to keep her safe.

Nine

INSTEAD OF SENDING them directly on to Baltimore, the next stop on Lyla's book tour, Trident's publicists had booked them for a second night at the hotel in Philly.

That was fine. Tate was enjoying driving the tricked-out SUV they'd rented, but he was happy to have the break, too.

Lyla wasn't complaining either, that was for sure. As stressed-out as she was getting from all the stalker crap, she was probably thrilled to have the day off.

They'd both vegged out for most of the morning—Lyla working on her laptop on her side of the suite, and Tate watching movies and emailing his buddies overseas on his. Almost exactly like they'd done yesterday—and while it might not have been the most exciting birthday he'd ever spent, at least it'd been comfortable and relaxing.

That was probably why Tate was so startled to suddenly hear the blast of a ref's whistle blaring loudly from Lyla's TV now, followed almost immediately by a string of curses coming from Lyla.

He lunged for the door that connected their rooms, but Lyla wasn't working on her computer any longer—she was perched on the ugly hotel loveseat watching a hockey game, of all things, with a couple of beers on the coffee table in front of her and a bag of pretzels in her lap.

"What…" Tate hesitated and reviewed the scene a second time, just in case he'd missed something—but unfortunately, it was still weird on the re-run. "What's going on in here?" he inquired.

"*Bruh*," Lyla muttered darkly. "You told me I should have some downtime, and it's the freaking Stanley Cup playoffs. What do you *think* I'm doing?"

Tate rubbed the back of his neck. "Since when do girls watch hockey?"

No girls he'd ever known had—though admittedly, he hadn't been talking sports with the majority of them, and Lyla was no ordinary chick.

Added to that, Tate had realized, somewhat recently, that he was kind of a dumbass when it came to women's non-bedroom likes and dislikes.

Tate tried again, "What I meant was, since when do *you* like hockey? Or beer, for that matter?"

"Tate?" Lyla asked distractedly, never once peeling her eyeballs from that TV screen.

"Yes?"

"Fight me."

Okay, so maybe *some* women enjoyed hockey. Tate blinked, flabbergasted by the strange transformation Lyla had undergone before his very eyes.

He told her, "I don't think Red would care for that, actually."

"All right, have it your way," Lyla scoffed. "But if you're done talking, you may as well pull up a seat and watch. I'm not going anywhere until the Rangers have this baby in the bag."

Tate edged closer and kept a wary eye on her as he lowered himself slowly onto the side of the mattress. This was a new, completely unanticipated side of her, and he wasn't quite sure how to handle it.

"Beer?" she asked, offering him a bottle from the six-pack he hadn't noticed near her feet. He had no idea where she'd gotten it, but it was fair to say he was not on his game right now.

"No, thanks." And then, because Tate didn't want to come off like a total Puritan, he added, "I'm technically working here, Lyla."

Right—because that sounded so much less dickish than *alcohol fucks with my meds, babe.*

Lyla shrugged, then gestured to the television with her own bottle, sloshing some India pale ale onto the table in the process. "Who ya got?"

Tate looked around for a take-out napkin or something, so he could have her wipe up that spill before it wrecked the wood of the table. "Uh…"

"Don't be wrong, dude."

"Um, Rangers?" he offered, glancing quickly at the TV. It was hard to focus on the game in progress, while also keeping an eye on Lyla's rather sudden personality transplant.

For lack of a better option, he got up and found the tissue dispenser near the bathroom, grabbed a few, and brought them over to her.

"That's right. Thank you," she bellowed, banging her beer down on the table. "The Devils can suck it."

Lyla swiped the tissues from his hand and mopped haphazardly at the beer spill, then tossed the soggy mess across the room, hitting a perfect three-pointer in the trash can next to the desk.

"Yes. That," Tate agreed.

It seemed possible—no, it seemed *likely*—that someone had managed to sneak past him and drug his formerly-well-behaved charge, turning her from a mild-mannered writer into some kind of puck punk.

The *why* of that was a conundrum, of course, and he couldn't figure out how it had happened. He'd been here all afternoon.

"Don't think I didn't notice how you hesitated right there," Lyla accused him, following the fast-paced game with avid focus. "Much more of that, and I might have to kill you off in my next book."

Tate took a long pause before answering. There was no pressing need to set off a potentially volatile situation, but he should probably know the answer to this question: "Lyla…I hope you'll forgive me for asking this, but—are you *drunk*?"

Lyla snorted and finally turned to him. Her eyes *were* a bit too bright. She toasted him and knocked back the remainder of what appeared to be her third beer, then pushed her glasses up her nose. "Only a lot. Wish I could say the same for you."

"That makes two of us."

Tate couldn't remember the last time he'd had enough booze to even feel buzzed, but this chick was flying after only three beers. There was something bizarrely charming about that, but now clearly wasn't the time to dwell on it.

Instead, he said, "So, I've met mean drunks and I've met sentimental ones…"

"Don't forget horny."

God. Tate absolutely could not think about Lyla drunk and horny or he would lose what was left of his mind. "Right. And those. But I've never seen this. This is…you apparently turn *gangster* when drunk?"

Lyla grinned at him, and the megawatt beauty of it punched into Tate's chest with the force of a cannonball. "It's a thing, homie," she said proudly.

Fuck, fuck, fuck. She was so cute and he was so screwed. Why was this happening to him?

"No. It isn't," he managed to say.

The whistle blared from the television again, and Lyla swung back around before she could volley anything back at him. "Oh, come on!" she yelled at the screen. "You big baby. Get off your ass and go sit down so the big boys can skate."

The problem was, in his downtime, Tate had started concocting a mental list of fantasy dates—places he'd like to bring Lyla someday if he were a different guy, and their situation was different, and she somehow magically caught the feels for him.

However, he'd almost certainly have to scratch off *hockey game* now, because bringing the lunatic beside him to any live sports event was liable to get them both killed.

For the moment, Lyla was oblivious to him. With her bare feet parked on the table and the rest of her slumped back on the couch, she was keeping up a rambling commentary on each bit of action while she munched on her pretzels.

When he'd encouraged her to build some downtime into her book tour, he'd never envisioned *this*.

At least she wasn't cracking open another beer, though. Tate thought maybe he'd have to stop her if she did—for both of their sakes.

As it was, he was perilously close to asking her to try using her inside voice.

Oh, how the tables had turned. Red had probably set this whole thing up specifically to spite him.

Tate put his hand down to steady himself, and all at once, his position in the room hit him.

He was sitting on Lyla's messy, unmade bed. The heavenly scent that sometimes drifted off her was everywhere, surrounding him and filling his lungs with an essence so elementally Lyla, it was like he was merging with her somehow.

Worse still was that his hand wasn't resting on a crisp white hotel comforter. No, under his palm, to Tate's great dismay, was a filmy scrap of navy-blue silk and lace. Lyla's underwear was just *lying* there, out in the open. Under his hand. *Holy Christ.*

Tate swallowed and jerked his hand away, holding his arm across his stomach and trying to look anywhere but down. For the love of God, though—he was a red-blooded male, and the panties of the woman he was rapidly becoming hot for were inches away, in plain sight.

He *had* to look—of course, he had to look. It might as well be written out in plain black and white in the Dude Handbook.

So Tate snuck another peek, trying to determine in two-point-five seconds what type of underwear it might be. Thongs didn't seem like Lyla's style, but maybe some kind of low-cut bikini was? Perhaps those sexy things chicks called boy shorts?

Sadly, the lingerie was too crumpled to tell. If Tate had been at all alert this evening, he might have thought to spread them out a bit when he first pulled away, so at least his rabid curiosity could be satisfied, if not the sudden and uninvited stowaway behind his fly.

Lyla, the perfect noticer of all things inconvenient, suddenly announced, "Oh, *that's* where those went. I've been looking for them. Thanks!" She hooked the panties with a finger, then marched over to drop them into her open suitcase before plopping back down on the sofa again.

Tate sat paralyzed, willing himself to stop debating which situations, exactly, might cause Lyla to lose a pair of panties in her own bed. He commanded himself to cease inserting himself into said situations immediately.

He threatened grievous bodily harm to his own person, for even considering how fucking amazing it would be to sweet-talk Lyla into sliding a scant four feet to the left right now, so he could have her under him in this bed.

Fuck hockey. Fuck the Rangers and Lord Stanley. Tate would give his right eye to be able to fuck *Lyla* right now, but that was about the worst thing he could do, short of admitting to everyone what the Army really thought was wrong with him.

Tate clearly needed to beat a hasty retreat before this got even further out of hand. He stood up.

"Okay, Slick. I'm just going to—"

Lyla roared, leaping up and pointing at the television. "Yeah, baby! That's what I'm talkin' about!"

Jesus. He sank right back down again. He couldn't leave this room now, even if it was the right thing to do, and the smart thing. Tate had the distinct feeling he was seeing a side of Lyla very few people got to see, and there was no way he wanted to miss a single second of it.

He kicked off his shoes, settled back against the headboard, and focused on the television. Maybe getting busy with the hot chick wasn't in the cards tonight, but that didn't mean he couldn't still enjoy himself.

Watching the playoffs with Lyla promised to be as fun of a birthday party as he ever could've hoped for.

THE SIGNING IN Baltimore the next day wasn't nearly as good a time. Tate and Lyla hit traffic on the highway and arrived there late, the bookstore staff was disorganized, and the people waiting were getting testy.

Tate hadn't been able to find Lyla anything good to eat for lunch on the way, so she was running on fumes before they even got started, and it showed.

He couldn't leave to see if he could grab her a snack, either—not when her stalker would be looking for exactly that kind of opening to get to her.

If the asshole had even followed them this far.

Tate positioned himself behind Lyla, as he normally did, and mulled over what he'd learned about the stalker, so far. While Lyla worked, he sifted through possibilities and likelihoods, testing out how different theories might play out.

Because of that, it took him longer than it should have to realize the person sitting across from Lyla at her table was gripping her a little too maniacally.

The lady must have been sixty-five, with iron-gray hair sprayed into a cloud around her head, bifocals dangling from a beaded chain around her neck, and a lumpy sweater buttoned all the way up to her neck.

Her arthritic fingers were fastened around Lyla's forearm, and as Tate focused in on them, he saw Lyla subtly try to pull away without much luck. She listened to the woman some more, then tugged again.

Tate stepped closer to hear what she was saying.

"Now, I want you to listen to me, Mrs. Lawson. I counted fifteen instances where people were having unmarried S-E-X in this book. *Fifteen*. You're doing the work of the devil with writing like that," she said. "I bet you didn't know. But now that you do—"

Lyla interjected, "Mrs…uh…"

"Mulvaney, dear. It's Mrs. Mulvaney."

"You're hurting my arm, Mrs. Mulvaney. Can you please—"

"Oh, I know that I have a firm grip when I get worked up, dear. All my friends say so. But this is important, and you have to listen. Now that you know what you're doing—"

Tate leaned in and pried the woman's bony claws from Lyla's arm, then instructed her, "Ma'am, I'm going to have to ask you to refrain from touching Ms. Lawson again."

"Don't be ridiculous," she protested, "We're just having a nice discussion. Aren't we, Mrs. Lawson?"

Lyla was trying to rub some circulation back into her arm, but she still mustered up a smile for the wack-job. "I do thank you for sharing your thoughts with me. Here's your book, and I hope you enjoy it. Now, who's next?"

"Oh, but I'm not finished yet," Mrs. Mulvaney declared.

Tate rounded the corner of the table and held out his hand to help the crazy old broad up, and nodded at the next guy in line to step forward.

Lyla was already greeting him with a cheerful smile. "Hi! Thanks for waiting. How are you today?"

Huge surprise—Mulvaney didn't want to relinquish her seat.

"I'm sorry, ma'am," Tate told her. "But it's time to go now. Ms. Lawson has a lot of other people she has to sign books for."

The lady got really loud, really fast. "Just who do you think you are?" she cried.

"I work security for Ms. Lawson." Tate set a hand on her arm to steer her away from Lyla—who was studiously avoiding making eye contact—and toward the bookstore's security guard, who'd started over when he heard the raised voices.

When Tate touched her, the woman screeched like a scalded cat. "Let me go! Don't you touch me! Let me go!"

Tate held up both hands and stepped back, but he kept his eyes trained on her. The last thing he wanted to do today was drop a sixty-five-year-old crackpot, but he'd do it in a heartbeat if she made one move toward Lyla.

"I'm sorry I startled you," Tate said, as calmly as he could. "But let's let some other folks have a turn."

By now the store cop had arrived. "Hey, Mrs. Mulvaney," he said. "Fancy meeting you here."

She scowled and fixed Tate with the evil eye. "Hello, Paul."

"Just thought you'd want to know that your bus is stopped at the light out there. It's going to pulling up to the stop any minute now—and you don't want to miss your ride, do you?"

"No, no, no," Mrs. Mulvaney muttered, hustling away at top speed.

Tate and his new BFF watched her go, and sure enough, a city bus came rolling to a halt outside, not two minutes after she'd cleared the store's front door.

"You know her?" Tate asked the guy.

"Sure do. The old bat never misses an event here. She comes to every signing and reading, and even to the story hour for little kids on Saturday mornings."

"Lucky you."

"No shit. It took me two years before I figured out her schedule, but thankfully it hinges almost totally on the #9 bus."

Tate shook his head and checked on Lyla. She looked a little rattled but seemed to be powering on.

"Anyway, thanks for coming over. I appreciate the backup," Tate told the guy.

"No worries. Let me know if you need anything else. I'd keep an eye on those assholes in the back, there—I caught a whiff of them when they came in, and they've definitely been to happy hour already."

"Terrific."

"Welcome to my world." With that, Paul strolled away, and Tate went back to looming as intimidatingly as possible over Lyla's left shoulder.

Ten

W HO KNEW BALTIMORE had so many one-way streets?"
Tate complained under his breath for the third time.

They'd left the bookstore behind a while ago, but Lyla's bad luck appeared to be following them—they'd been circling the same set of streets for ages now, trying to find their hotel for the night without much luck.

At the corner, the GPS told them to make a left. Tate snorted and banged a right.

Lyla was tired and she was out of sorts after that whole thing with the strange old lady, but she still had to acknowledge that this trip was going a far sight better than they usually did.

Most of the time, she was trying to do all this stuff by herself. And while this afternoon hadn't been fun, exactly, it hadn't been as bad as it would have been if Tate hadn't been there.

Lyla broke the silence in the truck with what she hoped sounded like a joke. "So—having any second thoughts, yet?"

She studied Tate's focused profile and hoped to hell he'd stick this out, even if he was.

Tate smiled. "Well, if I'd known you were out there peddling devilish sex books all this time, I might've tried looking for work at a hardware store or something. But you know how it goes— *desperate times*, and all that."

Lyla shook her head. "Oh my God, Tate—you don't even know. The S-E-X that lady was complaining about is as vanilla as it gets, and it's all between consenting monogamous adults. How could she take exception to that, and not to all the murder and mayhem in the story?"

Tate glanced at her in amusement, saying, "I really need to start reading more." Once again, when the navigation system indicated a left, he turned right.

"Let me know when you're ready to get started," Lyla told him. "I've got some great recommendations."

Making their way up the busy street in the big SUV was a bit like trying to thread a needle with a corn cob, and Tate was taking it slow to avoid all the randomly stopped cars, sudden appearances of bicycles, and wandering pedestrians.

Eventually, he spoke again. "Lyla, listen—I'm sorry I didn't step in sooner before. I didn't realize what was going on at first. I thought she was just…emphatic, you know?"

"It's okay," she told him. "That kind of thing doesn't come up too often, so it didn't occur to me to warn you."

She sighed, remembering Mrs. Mulvaney's avid face. "I could tell as soon as she sat down that it was going to go off the rails, but I thought I could keep it from getting out of hand by myself. I should've asked for your help before she really got going, though. It might've made it easier."

Tate thought about that. "We should have a code word, so it doesn't happen again. Or some kind of signal."

He looked so excited about it, Lyla had to laugh. "You are *loving* that idea, aren't you?"

"What?" Tate squawked, affronted.

"Any time there's a chance for you to get all cloak and dagger, you jump on it. You do realize that?" she chuckled.

"I beg your pardon."

"Admit it—you probably loved Scooby-Doo when you were a kid. Didn't you?"

Tate paused, looking around at the street signs on the corners, then said grudgingly, "Maybe. But for what it's worth, I promise I won't ask you to split up so we can catch the villain."

"Amen to that."

He reached over to tap her on the knee. "So, how about it? What can you do, so I'll know it's time to jettison some knucklehead from your orbit?"

Lyla thought about that. It wasn't the worst idea in the world. It might even prove helpful, going forward.

"How about…I push up my glasses."

"No dice. You do that all the time."

"I do?"

"Affirmative," Tate said. "Pick something else."

"*Huh.* Okay, well—I could do something with my hair. Push it over my shoulder or something."

"Nope. That won't work either."

Lyla frowned at him. "Really?"

"Really."

"Then, I could shake my foot. Or crack my back."

"No. And…also no." Tate slammed on the brakes to avoid a couple of kids with backpacks who'd darted out between the parked cars to cross the street.

Lyla demanded, "How did I not know what a twitchy person I apparently am?"

"Beats me," he shrugged. "But sweetheart—you hardly ever sit still."

She crossed her arms over her chest in a huff. "And naturally, you just *had* to notice that."

"Lyla, it's literally my job to watch you all day long. I'd be an idiot *not* to notice it."

"I feel very exposed right now." Tate just laughed at her, but it did beg the question, "What else do you know about me, that I'm not aware of?"

"Nothing!" he answered quickly, and she could swear his neck flushed red. "Don't be paranoid."

Lyla threw up her hands. *Now* he told her.

"Okay, listen—" Tate continued, "for the signal to work, it has to be something you'd never do otherwise. Something that will stick out to me."

She blew out a long breath, trying to think, but her brain was completely fried. "I could break into song?"

"Something that *won't* stick out to other people, you dork," he groaned.

"Um…what about…"

"*Shh*. Let me think."

"You just shushed me!" Lyla balked, completely offended.

"Yes!" he fired back, "That means you're supposed to be quiet!"

Lyla just shook her head at him. "You get mean when you're lost."

"*I'm not lost*," he claimed, rather hotly given the circumstances.

"Tate, we've circled this block three times," she pointed out. "You're definitely lost. Stop ignoring the GPS."

"I'm *not*. Look—here's the parking garage for the hotel." He slapped on his blinker, then cut off a bakery truck to make the turn. "And now, I also know what your *save-me* signal should be."

"Please don't let it be something weird," Lyla begged.

"It's not. All you have to do when you need a bailout is crack your knuckles. You never do that, so I'll know right away to step in if I see it."

Lyla leaned back against her door and looked him up and down, impressed. "Wow, that *is* good. No one would even think it was strange—not if I've been signing books for hours."

"Exactly," Tate agreed, proud as a peacock. "And that's why they're paying me the big bucks."

"Awesome. I think I just felt your ego expand even more, all the way from over here."

"I mean…is there really any limit to how far it can grow?" he wondered. "*Should* there be?" He parked in a spot near the elevators, then turned off the truck.

Lyla shook her head yet again. "God, this day needs to be over sooner, rather than later."

Tate turned to her, instantly switching into caretaker mode. "You want to stop in the lobby bar and have a drink before we go upstairs? You had a rough day today."

It was tempting, but Lyla had figured out by now that she'd definitely be drinking alone, and that was far too depressing an end for today.

"Thanks, but…I think I had plenty last night. Let's just check in and find our rooms. I'm too whipped to even contemplate cocktails." Not to mention the fact that the memory of her hangover from that morning still loomed very fresh in her mind.

"You got it, Slick," Tate said, agreeable as ever.

Even as cocky as he was, Lyla didn't know how she would have made it this far without him. Too bad she couldn't tell him so.

ONCE THEY MADE it upstairs, Lyla swiped their keycard in the door, edged into their room—and then froze. Tate bumped into her back as the combination of his bulk, their combined baggage, and the heavy door swinging shut behind him jostled him forward.

"*Shoot*," Lyla said.

"What? Is everything okay?"

"Yeah, but…"

Tate dropped their stuff and shoved past her, placing his body in front of Lyla as he planted his feet and scanned the small room. In moments, he was turning back, though, utterly confused.

"What's wrong? Did you forget something in the truck?"

"No, nothing like that." Lyla gestured expansively since he clearly hadn't picked up on the glaring issue staring them in the face. "But look, Tate. There's only one king in here."

"Is it me?" he grinned.

"*Tate!*"

"Okay, okay. So…what's the problem?"

"There were *supposed* to be two queens," she explained.

"Even better," he teased.

"PR said they called ahead," Lyla moaned. "I'd better call the front desk and see what happened."

"Sweetheart…I'm not sure that will accomplish anything. Didn't you hear the lady at the front desk say we got the last room?"

Lyla thought back. *Crap.* She *had* heard that.

"It's okay," Tate told her, "I can just crash on the couch." He said it so casually, too—as if his oversized frame would easily fit on some dinky hotel loveseat.

"Are you blind?" Lyla inquired morosely. "There's no couch either."

Truly, this room was about as big as her living room at home and, given that she had a miniscule one-bedroom on the Upper East Side, that was not saying much.

"The chair, then," Tate offered, looking around with narrowed eyes and not finding one of those, either. "Or on the floor."

Lyla was tired, hungry, and beyond frustrated. The last thing she needed was a martyr on her hands. "Tate, don't be ridiculous. You can't sleep on the floor."

He stuck out his chest, looking capable and manly and not the least bit ruffled. "Sure, I can. I've done it for years."

Lyla rolled her eyes. *Freaking men.* "Yeah, except this isn't the Army," she reminded him.

"God, that's the truth," he sighed happily. "Here, we've got four solid walls, air conditioning, and carpeting. We have our own working bathroom, I assume. And, if we're lucky, we might even be bug-free, too."

He roamed around, checking the window and the curtains, the closet, and under the bed. Their predicament didn't seem to be denting his good cheer in the least, and that only irritated Lyla more.

"We've got no food and one bed for two grown adults," she countered, knowing she sounded petulant. "And at the moment, I don't know which I need more—a shower or sleep."

Tate exhaled and eyed her with sympathy. "It's been a long day, and I know it didn't go the way you wanted. Why don't you take a nice, hot shower, and I'll run out and find us some supper."

That sounded about perfect, but... "What, and leave me alone here? I thought that was against *the rules.*"

Tate smiled and came closer, his stupid dimples popping up on his cheeks and his dumb blue eyes twinkling. "This room has exactly one window that is welded shut, and one door with three locks on it. If you're a very good girl and promise not to open the door to anyone but me, I think I can bend the rules just this once."

"So magnanimous," Lyla muttered.

"What do you feel like eating?"

"Tate, you saw it out there. It's all tourist traps, coffee shops, and dive bars. You'll be lucky if you can find some stale chips at the minimart in the lobby."

She ought to have known he'd be undeterred by pesky things like simple facts, though. Tate only repeated in a singsong voice, "What do you feel like?"

The thing that dropped instantly into Lyla's head was *burritos.*

Her mom was a big believer in instinct—in hunches. She'd always told Lyla that the first idea you had was usually the one you wanted most, even if logic and rationality came next and muddied the field. Plus, there was no denying that cheese was Lyla's comfort food.

And so, even as unlikely and impractical as it was, she muttered, "I wish we could find some burritos." It was a hopeless idea, given that they both knew they'd probably be eating power bars for dinner. Lyla added quickly, "But please don't go out of your way. I'm serious."

Tate grinned. "You worry about your job. I'll take care of mine."

"Your job is not to feed me—it's to protect me. And that's going to be hard to do that from wherever you're going."

"Watch me."

With that, Tate grabbed his keys, made Lyla promise approximately seven-million times to lock up behind him and not open the door unless he specifically texted her that he was outside, then took off into the wilds of the Baltimore night.

Eleven

T ATE TOOK A few minutes in the lobby to do a search on his phone, then hit up the bellhop for his suggestions. Once he had a good idea of where to go, he took the elevator down to the garage to get the truck.

It figured there was nothing within walking distance—it was just that kind of day.

Still, he found the hole-in-the-wall Tex-Mex place after only a few wrong turns. They were doing brisk takeout business, so Tate ordered Lyla a vegetarian burrito platter and some fajitas for himself. Then he added chips, queso, guacamole, and bottled water to make sure she had a good selection of things to eat.

After only a second or two of debate—and several good looks at what other people were getting—Tate went back through the line and ordered them some churros for dessert. *Come on*, they came with chocolate sauce—what woman wouldn't like that?

Back outside, Tate was feeling like a boss when he tossed aside the odds and ends on the passenger seat and set the heavy bag of provisions down.

Lyla had been so sure she couldn't have what she wanted for dinner tonight, but the whole foray had gone about as seamlessly as Tate could've hoped for.

It only seemed fair that he'd caught a break, given how their afternoon had gone—but he ought to have known it'd been too easy.

Sure enough, when Tate rounded the hood and slid behind the wheel, he heard an ominous crunch beneath his feet, and realized his victory dance had been a bit premature.

When he leaned down to investigate, he found his sunglasses—or rather, the maimed remains of his sunglasses.

Shit. The shades hadn't come cheap and were pretty mission-critical these days—and Tate and Lyla had a two-hour drive to Pittsburgh in the morning.

Even worse, it was supposed to be a bright, clear day, and with Tate's light-sensitivity, the highway full of cars reflecting sun everywhere promised to be excruciating.

He sat there with the broken frames in his hands and tried to decide what to do. Tate had a ballcap he could wear, and the truck's sunshade he could use—but he doubted those things would be enough to cut the glare as much as he needed. And, given Lyla's upset mood, he didn't want to bellyache about it and worry her more.

Where could he find a pair of replacements tonight, though? Most of the retail stores had to be closing up by now, and he had to get the food back to Lyla before it got cold.

Tate turned on the truck, reflexively checked the fuel level, and realized he had his answer. No reason he couldn't gas up for their drive now instead of in the morning—and a gas station minimart was as likely a place as anywhere to have a rack of cheap sunglasses.

He texted Lyla his status, fooled around with his phone's mapping app until he found a filling station close by, and set off once more.

THE TINY SHOP attached to the gas station offered many things—ten brands of beef jerky, a selection of wiper fluid and propane tanks, fishing gear, and tourist t-shirts. They had stuffed-animal crabs, crab decals, and a variety of crab-flavored snacks.

They even had kid's sunglasses in the shape of crabs, arranged incongruously next to a rack of skeevy magazines.

Alas, the market did not appear to sell any *adult* sunglasses, crab-shaped or otherwise. Tate contemplated his options, cursed his clumsiness, and then sprung for a few sports bars and protein shakes, so the trip wasn't a complete waste of time.

His eyes kept snagging on the presence of those rods and reels back in the corner, though. Tate hadn't been fishing in years, but there weren't many activities he could think of that were as relaxing as spending an afternoon on a riverbank waiting for a bite.

Conveniently, Tate just happened to know someone who could use a few calm, lazy hours right about now.

On a whim, he went back and grabbed a couple of poles and some line, then dropped them on the counter with all his other stuff. He had no idea if he and Lyla would get a chance to use the things, but what was the harm?

Even if they never found a single creek on this tour, Tate could always stash the poles at his parents' place once it was over. His brother Tom could use them when he returned from the Peace Corps next year, or Tate and his dad could go out the next time Tate got leave.

He nestled the rods carefully in the back of the SUV, on the side where they wouldn't get broken by his and Lyla's luggage. And now that he had the things, he was feeling pretty determined to find an opportunity to use them.

However, right now he had to head back to the hotel and feed Lyla, before she went completely around the bend.

TATE STOPPED AT the front desk on his way upstairs to snag some extra blankets and sheets. Later, he could use them to make a pallet on the floor without having to deprive Lyla of any covers from the bed.

Tate hadn't considered how much that would be to carry, though, and found himself juggling the bedding and the food the whole ride up in the elevator.

He'd told Lyla he would knock and text her once he got back, so she'd know to let him in—but once he got there, he ended up having to set the food down in the hallway, just so he'd have a hand free to pull out his phone.

But as Tate stood outside their room waiting like the blue-ribbon ass he was, he wondered why he hadn't thought to bring the other room key with him in the first place.

Truly, he was beginning to wonder what the heck Red had been thinking, hiring a scattered dolt like him for such an important job. Probably, the decent thing to do was resign, but the thought of some other asshole trying to protect Lyla scrubbed that dumb plan right out of Tate's skull.

And, when Lyla opened the door and her face lit up like Christmas morning at the sight of Tate bearing food, he knew he'd see this job through—whether it was a good idea or not.

IT WAS A little amazing how something as simple as beans and rice could make a woman's day—but given how easy it had been to obtain the food, Tate was a little embarrassed by the conquering hero treatment Lyla was lavishing on him.

Not that he minded, exactly. Sitting cross-legged across from her on that bed, the fresh scent of her shampoo lingering all around him and weaving its bewitching spell, Tate was as happy as a pig in mud to be the object of Lyla's adulation.

He didn't deserve it, though—and it felt pretty lame to be basking in glory he hadn't really exerted himself for.

After Lyla's fourth, "You're the best human being on earth," Tate reluctantly made an effort to shut her down.

"For God's sake, Slick, all I did was run out and buy some fast food. It's not like I single-handedly vanquished the Visigoths or anything."

"I bet you could if you tried," she gushed, albeit around a mouthful of burrito.

With the way Lyla was twinkling over at him, Tate didn't have the heart to argue the point with her. "I mean, if I had enough duct tape…then maybe," he said.

She giggled, damn it. It was so natural and unvarnished—just sweet, happy, adorable woman—that it slayed Tate right where he sat. How was a guy supposed to resist it?

If women had any clue how cute they looked with their hair all soft and damp, their faces scrubbed clean of cosmetics, and their guards down—hell, men would never stand a chance.

But Tate wasn't here to enjoy a late-night picnic with a pretty woman, he reminded himself. He was here to work.

And that meant, when the food was demolished and the woman was yawning wide enough for him to hear her jaw crack, it was time for Tate to leave the bed.

He helped Lyla gather up the scattered containers, utensils, and napkins, and crammed them into the tiny trash can in the bathroom. Tate locked himself in that bathroom to change into a respectable t-shirt and pair of shorts to sleep in, and once he'd brushed his teeth and taken his medicine, Tate came back out to discover Lyla tucked daintily under the near side of the bedcovers.

"Mind if I just pop in there to brush my teeth?" she asked.

"It's all yours," Tate told her.

He grabbed the pile of bedding he'd gotten earlier and scoped out the best location for him to crash that night.

The largest square of space was on the floor near the bathroom, but he couldn't bed down there. If Lyla needed to hit the head in the middle of the night, she was liable to break her neck tripping over him.

That left the much narrower sliver of carpet between the bed and the A/C unit under the window. It would be a tight fit for his shoulders, but at least it looked long enough to accommodate Tate's height.

He began laying out some of the blankets to soften up the hard floor, and hoped that his spine wouldn't feel like complete shit the next day. Lyla came out of the bathroom and slipped right back under the covers again.

She kept to the far side of the mattress and eyed his arrangements quizzically.

A minute later, she inquired, "Tate, what on earth are you doing?"

"Making my bed." As if it wasn't obvious.

"You can't be serious."

Tate frowned. "Yeah. I am."

"But you can't sleep on the *floor!*"

He sighed, "Lyla, what else do you expect me to do? I'm sure as hell not going to make *you* sleep down here."

Lyla rolled her eyes. "If I wanted to sleep on the floor, I would've become a...uh..."

Sometimes it was just too easy. "A soldier?"

"Let's go with trail guide. I would've become a trail guide, instead of a writer."

"Okay, but I know for a fact that you've noticed we only have one bed. So, if you're not sleeping on the floor, that means I am."

"Tate, I realize that it's completely awkward and weird," she sighed, "but surely we are adult enough to share the bed for one night, without losing control and molesting each other."

"Speak for yourself," he smiled.

"*Ha, ha.* Would you please stop doing that and just lay down here?" Lyla patted the empty space beside her primly. "For crying out loud—that pile you're making looks like something a dog would sleep on."

"Lyla, I promise it's fine. I really don't care. Enjoy your big mattress and get some rest."

"I don't have cooties, you know."

"I believe you."

"I don't even bite."

"Well…I'd be lying if I said *that* wasn't disappointing," Tate cracked.

Lyla's exasperated tone was edging into something else, though—something less entertaining and far more concerning.

"*Tate*," she insisted.

He took a good long look at her face, registering the tightness around her eyes and the tension in her jaw. Something more was up here than who laid their head where.

"Hey, you okay, Slick?"

"I'm fine."

"*Lie*. What's going on?"

Lyla stared him down for a good long while before she caved. "Just…sit down, would you? I have to tell you something."

Did that sentence ever *not* sound ominous? Tate sat.

Lyla swallowed hard and told him, "Someone called while you were out getting the food."

"Who?"

"I don't know. It might've been—"

"The stalker?" he demanded.

"Possibly."

"Well, what'd they say?"

"Nothing. They only breathed—heavy breathing. I asked who it was a few times, but then they hung up."

"Could it have been a wrong number?"

"I don't think so. At first, I assumed that you'd butt-dialed me, but then I realized that you would've used my cell number, not the room phone."

Tate nodded and Lyla's eyes filled up. "I feel so stupid," she said.

"Why?"

"Because I stayed on the line for so long. I should've hung up right away, but it took me a while to realize what was happening."

"That's normal, sweetheart. Why should you have expected that fucker to call you here?"

"Because apparently, this is going to be my life now," Lyla blurted out. She began crying in earnest, then.

"Shh," Tate soothed, scooting closer so he could wrap an arm around her. "Don't cry. We're going to figure out who's doing this as soon as we can, okay? And then you won't have to worry anymore."

"I keep forgetting I'm supposed to be on guard," she admitted weepily. "And he always seems to sense the second I do it."

"I'm sure that's only a coincidence," Tate told her, and hoped like hell that was true.

Lyla snuggled down into the bed, so Tate reached over her head to turn off the light.

"Still. It's like he knew you were gone."

Tate had been considering that very thing, but he'd be damned if he let her know it. "No way," he said.

"Will you stay up here for another couple minutes?" Lyla asked him.

It was a terrible idea. But Tate said, "Of course," and rested a hand on her back, moving it slowly back and forth as she settled down.

"I'm so tired," she murmured.

"Go to sleep. I'm here. It's safe."

"Thank you, Tate."

"Anytime." In that moment, with Lyla's soft breath feathering over his skin in the semi-darkness, Tate meant that vow with every fiber of his being.

HE MUST HAVE fallen out. It was the only explanation for why Tate woke up with a start a few hours later, his body molded to Lyla's like he'd been welded into place.

His heart was racing, and his t-shirt was stuck to his back with the cold sweat that bathed him. Tate edged carefully back until he felt the side of the mattress, then pulled the sodden shirt over his head. He mopped off his face and tossed it on his bag, then took stock of his surroundings.

Dark hotel room. Unused pallet on the floor behind him. Lyla snoozing away peacefully, two feet in front of him. The A/C unit ticking under the window. No trace whatsoever of the nightmare that had awoken him.

It had been the same old thing, but with a frightening new twist. There was the usual impending sense of doom, and the utter conviction that the explosion was coming—but this time, Lyla had been there, too. Laughing happily, walking through the market, expecting Tate to catch up to her.

Except, he couldn't. He'd tried to make his legs work, but it was like running underwater, or through quicksand. Lyla only got farther away the harder he'd worked.

The road between them had stretched out, and the air between them had grown thick. Worst of all, he'd known the hellfire was coming with the vengeance of a hundred devils.

Tate gasped at the still-vivid memory and reached out a shaking hand to touch Lyla's hair, silky soft and spread against the stark white pillow.

She was safe. He was here next to her, and no one was trying to blow them up—tonight, at least. Tate desperately needed to pull himself together.

He focused on his breathing like they'd taught him in the hospital, pulling air in slowly through his nose, then letting it out on the count of ten through his mouth.

He thought about crickets chirping in the grass, water burbling over stones in a brook, and dogs with floppy ears, sound asleep in a patch of sun.

Tate dwelled on Lyla's giggle, the way it sounded when he made silly jokes.

Little by little, the fear dissipated, his pulse returned to normal, and his eyes got heavy again. Still, in case he had a repeat, it would be safer to move to the floor and let Lyla have the whole bed.

In a couple more minutes. Tate only wanted to steal one last taste of peace, before he went.

Twelve

W HEN LYLA AWOKE suddenly, in the most perfect cocoon of peace and safety, it seemed odd that the hairs on the back of her neck were standing on end. Stranger still, was her certainty that she'd heard something abnormal in the room.

What was it, though? A cough? A creak?

Lyla held herself as still as possible, but her heart was galloping a thousand miles per hour and her breath felt frozen in her throat.

She listened for the sound again, but only heard the hum of the air conditioning. Out in the hotel hallway, a door slammed.

And very nearby, another human being was breathing deeply—just like they'd done on the phone last night. Lyla squeezed her eyes shut and struggled not to whimper. Who was it? Who'd gotten in here?

Right behind her, the sheets rustled and a deep voice murmured. Then a heavy arm draped protectively across her stomach, pulling her back against a broad, hard chest.

A bare chest. A *warm* chest. From neck to toes, Lyla was surrounded by a big, brawny male, and she knew without even trying that struggling would only cinch his grip tighter.

Fear thrummed through her veins for a full minute before reality took hold. Lyla peered down at the arm and did the simple math.

Her snuggly companion *had* to be Tate. There was no mistaking the deliciously masculine scent enveloping her, and she'd recognize that hand, that wrist—those golden hairs on his tanned and muscular forearm—anywhere.

Even the arousal nestled against her rear seemed like typical Tate, and if he were awake, Lyla could envision him being characteristically cavalier about it.

First mystery solved, then.

Her memory of the night before returned in pieces. The one bed. Their picnic on a towel in the center of the bed, followed by them bickering over where Tate would sleep. After that, an hour of Lyla holding carefully still at the outside edge of the mattress, wide awake in the dark and listening to every sleepy sound Tate made.

And, while all that might explain Tate's presence behind Lyla to begin with, it did not explain how they'd ended up tangled in a cozy knot come morning.

Lyla had been so careful to hide how Tate affected her up till now. How could she have screwed up so badly while *asleep*?

Even worse was that the fear she'd woken with didn't seem to be going away completely. Lyla suspected it wouldn't until she saw—beyond a shadow of a doubt—that it *was* her hunky bodyguard wrapped around her like a friendly vine and not her creepy fan.

In order to do that, however, Lyla was going to have to roll over. She took a deep breath for courage, then slowly began wriggling around, pivoting on her axis under the weight of that steady arm, trying not to wake the man up.

On the flip side Lyla came face to face with—*huge shocker*—exactly who she'd expected to: Tate Monroe. She gazed at his face in stark relief.

He really was gorgeous. Tan and sandy blond, handsome without veering into pretty.

Since he was still asleep, she let herself study him for much longer than she normally did. Tate had a tiny scar that she'd never noticed before, high on his cheekbone under his left eye. His lashes were as long as a kid's, long dark fringes against his skin.

And his lips were…Lyla exhaled. His lips looked perfect. She wanted a kiss from those lips of his. A really good one.

Tate sighed and rolled to his back, and the arm that had been sheltering her fell casually across his stomach. He was sort-of clothed and not armed—but Lyla had to assume that his cuddling hadn't been social in nature.

Why would it be? It wasn't like Tate knew she was secretly lusting after him—and he probably wouldn't be inclined to do anything about it even if he did. Lyla needed to take the flicker of disappointment she felt and shove it down deep where it couldn't cause more trouble.

Speaking of which, if she *really* wanted to avoid trouble this morning, she had to get out of this bed before Tate woke up.

While she puzzled out how to accomplish that, however, her predicament got decidedly worse. Tate murmured something that sounded an awful lot like her name, and then, with an intense look of concentration on his face, the hand resting on his stomach began to drift lower.

Lyla peeked at the bulge in his gym shorts, and it looked far more pronounced than it had before. *Uh-oh.*

Panicking, Lyla blurted out, "Tate! Wake up!"

His eyes popped open and he turned his head, and Lyla came face-to-face with her sleepy, grinning, impossibly-devastating bodyguard.

Any remaining vestiges of her earlier unease flew clear away. *The rascal.*

"Good morning, Ms. Lawson," Tate rumbled, his voice so rusty and sexy she wondered why any other man ever bothered to speak at all.

To cover up her all-hands-on-deck reaction to it, Lyla snarked, "For a soldier, you sure have trouble respecting a demilitarized zone."

It was the best she could do given that she was waging an internal war, trying to prevent herself from pressing her whole treacherous body up against *his* mouth-watering frame.

Tate's eyes registered Lyla's proximity an instant later, and his entire demeanor changed. His morning-after face disappeared, and he wrenched himself back off that bed faster than Lyla would've thought possible—so fast, he might as well have been a bombing vaudeville act being yanked stage left with a cane.

"Are you okay?" he asked quickly.

Lyla nodded and glanced at the depression in the sheets he'd just vacated. Tate looked, too, and must have realized what she was wondering.

"I'm sorry. I must have fallen asleep." He rubbed at the scruff on his jaw. "Actually, I did wake up around three, but then you kept saying you were cold, and I forgot we had those other blankets, so…"

Oh, Jesus. Sleeping Lyla was even more hung up on Tate than Awake Lyla was. This was bad.

"So…you tried to warm me up?" she guessed.

"I didn't mean to stay that way. I'm sorry," he mumbled, blushing mightily.

Tate's gym shorts were riding low on his hips, and Lyla couldn't help taking another quick peek at the drool-worthy wings of his hipbones peeking out of the waistband.

He glanced down and immediately yanked the shorts higher— and then left his hands casually linked in front of his crotch for good measure.

"Hard to teach an old dog new tricks," he chuckled nervously.

And then Tate simply stood there, blinking down at Lyla like he expected her to *do* something. Abruptly, she became aware that he hadn't been the only one crossing lines in his sleep. She herself was lying rather obviously in the dead center of the mattress, as well.

She coughed and scrambled back, standing up to face off with him once she reached her assigned side of things. Tate's wide-eyed gaze flickered down, then came up to meet hers again. Lyla patted at her pajamas, making sure everything was where it was supposed to be.

Finally, when she was able to breathe like a normal adult, she said, "It's okay. No harm done. But I did warn you that sharing the bed was a bad idea."

Then she turned and began searching for the *de rigueur* coffee pot that had to be in the room somewhere.

"*Wait.* No, you didn't. You said we should share the bed like grownups," Tate argued. "*I* tried to crash on the floor, remember?"

Lyla squinted around the room. Was it a Monday? This day was starting off exactly like a goddamn Monday.

Tate relaxed from his paralysis, bent to grab a folded t-shirt off the top of his bag and pulled it on. Once his chest disappeared from view, she said a quick mental prayer of thanks, but left things vague as to whether the amen was for that too-brief view she'd gotten of Tate's delicious pecs and abs—or for the arrival of all that preshrunk gray cotton he was now sporting.

"Have you seen the coffee pot? I could really use some caffeine," she announced.

Lyla caught a glimpse of her hair in the mirror behind the TV and wanted to groan. Hot messes had nothing on her right now, and Tate looked like a freaking underwear model. How was that fair?

He was moving around, folding up the pallet on the floor, and making the bed as neatly as if he expected the room to be inspected by a drill sergeant soon. Lyla was amused by it, but at least his neatness quirk meant that she wouldn't end up leaving stray books or socks behind like she normally did.

"It might be over on that counter near the bathroom," Tate said. "But I wouldn't count on a big tea selection, Slick. This place is pretty basic."

"God, that's the truth."

At least they were back on nice, safe ground now. There was absolutely no way to spin this discussion into something raunchy. And that was especially true once Lyla realized that she'd been talking to Tate from mere inches away, only moments ago—and she almost certainly had morning breath. *So not sexy.*

Sure enough, the brewer was where he'd indicated, but it came equipped with only a single pod of decaf hazelnut coffee and a couple of packets of powdered creamer.

"Ugh," Lyla said, showing him.

Thankfully, she'd discovered early on this trip that Tate wasn't only a meticulous bed-maker—he was also a rabid caffeine addict and a ferocious coffee snob.

He'd been sheepish when she'd confronted him about it, but also unapologetic. *Let me tell you a little story about MREs*, he'd said, *and you tell me if I'm crazy.*

It worked in Lyla's favor, anyway—even though they were driving from town-to-town on the world's strangest book tour, every morning Tate still managed to find some kind of gourmet coffee purveyor to get his fix. And, as Lyla had learned, where there was gourmet coffee, there was almost always gourmet tea, too.

Knowing he'd find a way to caffeinate them somehow, she attempted to put the one-two punch of her waking terror and subsequent temptation by Tate behind her. Instead, she focused on their ultra-polite dance around the close quarters of the hotel room, as they showered and dressed and got ready to leave for Pittsburgh.

Trying not to come into contact with her titillating bodyguard, as it turned out, did nothing to dispel his allure. Tate's magnetic pull hung around in the air like the steam from his shower— enticingly fragrant, seductive and heavy with desire, whenever Lyla tried to breathe it in.

Thank God he was all business and didn't feel the same way. She didn't know how this arrangement was supposed to work if he did.

TATE GRABBED HER arm just as they were getting ready to leave and upended everything.

"Lyla, listen…" he sighed, looking conflicted. "I'm not a professional bodyguard, you know? I'm just a guy. I'm doing my best to look out for you, but…I don't really know how to avoid crossing some lines." He looked down in consternation. "I feel like I'm supposed to reassure you right now that *that*—" he gestured at the pristine bed behind him, "—will never happen again."

Lyla swallowed, but it did nothing to ease her abruptly dry throat. "Do you *want* to make that promise?"

Tate shook his head. "Actually, no. I don't," he admitted softly.

"Then don't." Lyla's heart jumped around in her chest like an overexcited squirrel.

"And you're okay with that?"

"Yeah." *And then some.*

"You're sure?"

"*Tate.*"

"Okay, okay. It's just—I keep wondering what on earth Red could've been thinking, sticking us together like this. He knows me, and presumably, he knows you." Tate frowned a bit, then tacked on, "But I hope to hell he doesn't know you as well as he knows me."

Lyla laughed, "Trust me, he doesn't."

"He had to be crazy to think nothing was going to happen between us."

"I don't know. Maybe he didn't think that. Maybe this was all one big fix-up," Lyla shrugged.

Tate growled, "Swear to God, if I find out that fucker made up this whole stalker thing, I am going to murder him, bring him back to life, then murder him again."

"Tate, Red would never—not in a million years—do something like *that*. Come on."

"You're probably right." He didn't look convinced, but he did relent. "Let's get out of here, sweet cheeks, and find you some English Breakfast before you turn into a toad."

"I think you have it backward. I'm a toad *before* the tea. After it, I turn sweet and kind and lovely."

Tate winked at her. "If you say so."

"Speaking of toads," she muttered, grabbing the handle of her suitcase and rolling it into the hall, "Just because we've established a détente doesn't mean you can start calling me things like *sweet cheeks*. I was barely okay with *sweetheart*."

"What if I only do it after you've had caffeine?"

"No."

"Only in private?"

"No."

"Only in bed?" he grinned.

"Tate! For crying out loud!"

He only laughed, pecked Lyla on the cheek, and hoisted the rest of their bags to follow her out.

FOR THE NEXT hour on the road, Tate was more fidgety than Lyla had ever seen him. He kept pulling on the brim of his baseball hat, readjusting the truck's sunshade, and holding up one hand to block the sun's glare. He'd shift in his seat, then do it all over again.

To make matters worse, traffic was terrible on their way out of Baltimore, and Lyla didn't know how long they'd have to plow through it before things eased up. She was a little worried she was going to be late for the first book club meeting she had scheduled later that morning.

"You know," she said to Tate after a while. "Working from home sure has its perks. I forget what rush hour looks like most of the time."

"Yeah, tell me about it. I should've thought about this when we were deciding what time to—"

Tate braked suddenly and honked at a white sedan that had cut him off. "*Dude*, seriously?" he griped.

After several more minutes of stop-and-go, Lyla wondered, "Do you think we'll be late getting to Pittsburgh? I should call those ladies and give them a heads-up, if so."

Tate squinted at her. "I wouldn't worry about it just yet. Unless we hit crazy construction or something, we should be good to go once we reach the Pennsylvania turnpike. We can make up time then."

Lyla watched him carefully weave the big SUV in and out of the cars. He'd insisted on taking the wheel today, as he normally did, and despite his obvious discomfort, Tate's driving skills were exemplary.

It just seemed like the bright sun was torturing his eyes. Lyla abruptly remembered Red asking Tate about it, back in that first meeting.

"Hey, Tate?" she asked. "Is the glare bugging you right now?"

"Yeah, a little," he admitted. "But it's okay. Pretty soon the sun will be high enough in the sky for it not to matter."

Lyla checked her watch. It was still really early—no wonder Tate didn't sound convinced.

"Where are your sunglasses?" she wondered. "You want me to find them for you?"

Tate's neck turned red. "Broke 'em by accident last night. I'll grab some more at a gas station or someplace, once we're out of this mess."

"You can borrow mine until then."

Lyla fished around in her purse until she found her sunglasses—her big, black, Hollywood-starlet-sized sunglasses. Tate would never accept them, but she held them out anyway.

He glanced over three times before he finally chuckled, turned his hat backward, and grabbed for the shades.

"All right, Slick, you win. Hand them over. And no photos, you got it?"

"Cross my heart."

Tate put them on, and the total effect was…comical, to say the least. But once the glasses were in place, the tension left his shoulders bit by bit, and his body relaxed back into the seat. Soon, he was turning on the radio and tapping his fingers along with the music.

Lyla managed to stifle her giggles, but she couldn't stop staring at the silly picture he presented. Tate noticed, of course.

"*God.* Red and Luca would have a field day if they could see me now," he muttered.

"Somehow, I think you'd have it coming to you."

"Lyla," Tate growled through his grin, "We will never speak of this again. You hear me?"

"Whatever you say, Marilyn. My lips are sealed."

He blew her a loud kiss, and Lyla smiled so hard her cheeks hurt.

Thirteen

AT THE FIRST rest stop they came to, Tate bought three pairs of manly shades from a tourist cart out front, cut the plastic ties off with the utility knife he had in his pocket, and returned Lyla's ridiculous oversized sunglasses to her—hopefully forever.

He stashed one of the spares in the center console of the truck, and the other in a special holder than unfolded from the ceiling of the SUV. He hadn't even known that was there before Lyla discovered it for him.

She ran in to use the ladies' room, and Tate walked around the truck, kicking tires and making sure everything still looked good to go.

By the time she got back, however, his butt was parked on the driver's seat and Tate was clutching his head in his hands, while the world looped sickeningly around his skull.

Fuck, it'd come on fast this time.

"Tate?"

He cracked an eye and saw Lyla's shoes come into view through his fingers.

"What's wrong?" she asked.

"Got a little light-headed for a minute," he explained. "Probably because I slept like shit last night." The simple act of speaking made him want to toss his cookies.

Tate slept like crap *most* nights, but the bigger problem was that he was not supposed to take his meds on an empty stomach. And even though he'd put those freaking protein shakes in the hotel fridge last night, they'd been warm and gross this morning and he'd had to toss them out.

He'd sacrificed the three sports bars to Lyla because she'd been hungry, and he wasn't a goddamn Neanderthal who would keep them for himself. She didn't need to know the extent of the sacrifice, however.

"I'm so sorry," Lyla said, contrite and obviously convinced that the sleeping issue had been her fault.

"Don't worry," Tate told her. "It'll pass in a minute, and then I'll be totally fine."

At least his voice sounded normal, even if the rest of him felt like it was on the world's worst carnival ride.

Lyla stood and watched him, and Tate choked back the overwhelming desire to retch at the dizziness swamping him. He couldn't give in—she'd never look at him the same way again if he did.

After a few more minutes, Lyla inquired again, "Tate? Are you okay?"

"Yup."

She waited patiently. Someday, she was going to make an absolutely perfect fucking mother with that kind of fortitude—and life would probably gift her with five rowdy sons just to screw with her in return.

In the face of her composure, Tate folded like a lawn chair. "*Damn it.* No, I'm not fine. I need a few more minutes. Maybe…more than a few. I'm sorry."

"We lost a lot of time back in Baltimore," Lyla pointed out.

"Believe me, I know."

"Then why don't you get into the passenger seat and let me drive for a while? You can rest. Take a nap."

"Do you even have a license?" It was a valid question—plenty of people in the city didn't.

"Yes, Tate. I am a grown-up with a driver's license."

"I should choke down some food first," Tate said, though the idea repulsed him almost as much as the thought of turning over control of the vehicle to a civilian.

What if there was something in the road they had to avoid, or what if they had an accident? What if—?

"Stay here," Lyla commanded.

Like Tate had any choice.

FIFTEEN MINUTES LATER, Lyla was installed behind the wheel and Tate was riding shotgun about as comfortably as a sullen teenager on his way to the dentist.

He forced himself to down the vanilla shake she'd gotten him in a few long gulps, then spent several interminable minutes trying to make the thick liquid stay in his stomach.

When he could trust his voice again, Tate told Lyla, "I'll be your spotter."

"I'm hoping we don't need one, but if you insist."

She gripped the wheel tightly and never moved her eyes from the road. For all her bravado before, Tate wondered when Lyla had last operated a motor vehicle. She was probably used to taking taxis and the subway back in the city, and as far as he knew, didn't even own a car.

She was trying so hard, though, and it melted Tate's heart.

"Lyla, for what it's worth I think you're being very brave about this whole stalker thing," he said, trying to throw her a bone.

"Brave?" she laughed sardonically, "Oh, you must mean the time I buried my face in your sleeve because I couldn't cope with whether there was a new note on my door. Or, I don't know, maybe you're talking about last night, when I broke down crying because of a two-minute phone call in which no one *said* anything."

Tate probably shouldn't have enjoyed taking care of Lyla on both those occasions as much as he had. But that was the male ego for you—always happy to be of service.

"Sweetheart, it takes courage to go out there every day and talk to your readers, especially when you don't know what might be coming at you next. Even if you can't see that, I do."

She peeked at him. "Well, thank you. I appreciate that."

"Don't mention it."

Grudgingly, Lyla added, "I take back what I said about you being mean yesterday."

Tate grinned, woozy as he was. "I'd rather you retract the part about me being lost."

"Let's not get crazy."

Tate chuckled. Truly, Lyla might be one of the best women he'd ever met. On impulse, he pried one of her hands from its death grip on the wheel, kissed the back of it, and laced his fingers through hers.

Her lips tilted up softly, and she didn't scream at him *or* let go.

A stupid smile was still plastered on his face a while later, when the warmth of the sun, the white noise of the tires rolling on the tarmac, and the sheer contentment Tate felt holding Lyla's hand lulled him into a deep, dreamless sleep.

BY THE TIME they hit the outskirts of Pittsburgh, Tate's catnap had recalibrated his synapses and restored him to fighting trim, so he reclaimed the wheel and ferried Lyla to her first two engagements—small meet-and-greets in private homes, with a couple of book clubs.

There was a signing at a library after lunch, but it was slow to get off the ground and had a small turnout. Tate could tell Lyla was worrying about it, until the head librarian informed them that a water main break that morning was keeping many people stranded in that part of town.

After an hour, it was clear the event was a bust, so they reluctantly packed up their stuff and shut the whole thing down. Tate and Lyla went out to sit in the SUV and ponder their next move.

She looked a little forlorn. "What do you think about pushing ahead to Cleveland tonight?" she asked him. "It's a nice town, and we have the time."

"Sure. Whatever you want."

"You don't mind the extra driving?"

Tate didn't mind anytime they got to be together, just the two of them. "Not at all," he said. "I promise, Lyla—I'm completely fine now."

She called the hotel to make sure they had room that night, and soon they were on their way. And, while Tate drove along yet another stretch of road, he thought about holding Lyla in his arms that morning, and about the conversation they'd had afterward.

He hadn't promised to keep his hands off her, and Lyla hadn't objected. Which basically told him it was *game on*.

TATE WAS HAPPY they'd decided to plow ahead. He knew Cleveland pretty well, since he'd grown up nearby, and the weather—for the moment, at least—was better than it'd been in Pittsburgh.

The lake effect could change that quickly, but hopefully by then, they'd be snug in their room, getting to know each other better.

Their hotel downtown turned out to be a historic building, updated beautifully for a conference the year before. The staff, too, were as nice and helpful as people tended to be in this part of the country. They gave Tate and Lyla a number of tempting options for dinner and after a short debate, the two of them ended up at a cozy Spanish place a few blocks away.

Tate hadn't eaten much more than a few muffins at one of those little book club things that morning, and he was famished.

The hostess sat them at a private table nestled in a dim corner, with a flickering candle on the table and some soft Spanish guitar music piped in overhead.

It was ridiculously romantic, and the fact clearly wasn't lost on Lyla. After they ordered an array of tapas, she led off with a conversational topic that must have been inspired by the date-like atmosphere.

"So…you said you don't have a girlfriend," she began, like a hotter real-life Lois Lane. "How is that even possible?"

Tate retorted, "Oh, it's possible. The last relationship I had fizzled out more than a year ago."

Lyla didn't even try to disguise her curiosity. "What happened?"

"Well, as it turns out," he told her, "I was terrible at communicating and keeping emotionally connected while deployed." Hannah's words, not his. "And *she* was terrible at not complaining about things I had no control over. She was also bad at not having an affair with the dentist who lived in her building."

Lyla's mouth dropped open. "She picked a dentist over you? Really?"

Tate nodded. "Really. She went to him to get her teeth whitened or some shit, and I guess sparks flew."

"Who knew having pearly whites could be so seductive?"

"Not me, that's for damn sure. At least she got out before I got hurt, though. She would've sucked at caretaking."

Lyla grimaced. "I'm sorry."

"It happens," Tate shrugged.

True, he might have been better at keeping the thrill alive if he'd been more than passably into Hannah. But what else was new? It was the story of his life these days—or rather, it had been until he'd laid eyes on Ms. Lawson over there.

Lyla paused, as she tended to do before she blurted out something that she thought was overstepping. She never could resist the awkward questions, though—bless her heart.

She said, "It's kind of hard to imagine *you* being bad at communication."

Tate had to chuckle at that. "Why? Because I talk so much?"

"I mean, there's that."

"Well, it's funny," he told her, "You can actually talk all the freaking time, I've found, and not say anything important at all." Tate had made something of a pet project of that lately.

He'd meant his comment to be funny, but instead of laughing, Lyla frowned. "I'm not sure that sounds like you, either."

Tate threw in another casual shrug, just to keep things light. "I'm evolving," he said. *Every second he spent in Lyla's presence, it seemed.* "It's a slow, painful process."

Hell, it had taken all the other cavemen eons to get to where they were on the male developmental scale. Tate could hardly be expected to pull it off in a matter of weeks—but he'd have to if he expected to ever have a chance with Lyla.

And after this morning, he really wanted that chance.

"So, if you're not saying anything important, what do you say?" she inquired.

She was toying with a piece of her hair thoughtfully, examining Tate like a perplexing specimen from behind a sweep of soft brown hair and those sexy glasses.

Suddenly, he wanted Lyla to recognize him as a goddamn *man* again, instead of just a character study—particularly after the way he'd choked on their drive that morning.

"Well, if you must know, I am a champion dirty talker. When I'm really into a woman, I never shut up about her." And, yup— that got the impenetrable Ms. Lawson's attention, all right.

She pointed at him, not backing down. "Examples, please."

It was almost too easy. But Tate didn't intend to kill this little kitty's curiosity—far from it. He was going to stoke it.

After discovering the feel of her body in his arms last night— no matter how accidentally—he wanted to make Lyla burn all over.

Tate leaned in like he was confiding a secret. "Let's see," he murmured. "I lead with how beautiful she is, how fucking hot. I talk about what she's doing to me and what I want to do to her." Tate sat back then, the perfect instructor. "I like to go into specific detail. Just to make sure things are crystal clear."

Behind her glasses, Lyla's eyes were wide and interested. The tip of her tongue darted out to wet her parted lips, and damn if Tate didn't want to lunge for her right there.

However, he wanted to enjoy playing this out even more.

She murmured, "That doesn't sound so bad."

Not yet, anyway. "Okay, so…then comes the running commentary on how I'm feeling and how she's doing and everything that's happening, but at some point, it becomes a little challenging to get the words out, you know? When I'm coming like a racehorse and she's begging for salvation, there're only so many things left to say."

Tate measured Lyla's reaction to that salvo. As far as he could tell, she was still all in, and then some.

She said, "Except for *Oh, God*, probably."

"Yeah, that works." Man, she was cute. "I still like to provide the play-by-play, even then," he told her. "Just in case. I can't help it."

Lyla swallowed, spastically picked up the wine list and held it near her face for a second, then threw it aside. Tate would've bet his left nut at that moment that she hadn't read a word.

She fanned her face, sat on her hand, then wrenched it up to grip the edge of the table. "It's too hot in here. Someone should say something."

"I feel fine," he lied—cheerfully, too. This was way more fun than worrying about some weirdo sending her notes they'd probably copped from a scary TV movie.

"You *always* feel fine."

"That's what they all say."

"*Argh!* Stop it!" Lyla cried, throwing her napkin in his direction. It floated harmlessly down halfway across the table, making her even crazier.

"Stop what?" he grinned.

"*Tate*," Lyla growled.

"Okay, fine. But you asked."

Sweet cheeks had no answer to that one.

Tate was feeling positively merry as he dug into the tapas that had finally arrived, so he let Lyla stew in her own juices over there across the table for a while.

If she wanted to ask him probing questions, then she was going to have to be prepared to deal with the answers.

Frankly, he was half hoping she'd come up with some more.

But also, if Tate didn't focus on eating now, he was bound to stand up, take Lyla by the hand, and lead her into an even-darker corner—so he could kiss that shell-shocked look right off her face.

There was leveling up…and *leveling up*, though. Tate figured he had done quite enough for the time being. Before long, they'd have to return to their hotel, and then he could worry about what came next.

Across the table from him, Lyla stole glances at him while she picked at her food. She fussed with her glass of sangria and kept checking her watch.

He prayed to the gods of flirtation that she was eager to get him alone, and not only because she thought he needed a good night's sleep after his little incident earlier.

Eventually, Lyla brushed her hands together and dropped them to the sides of her plate.

"Do you want dessert?" she demanded. "Because I don't. I'm stuffed. We should go."

Tate laughed out loud. "You're right. We totally should."

Fourteen

WHEN LYLA AND Tate came to a halt outside their hotel suite, they were all alone in the quiet hall. Neither of them made a move to go inside—maybe they both knew that once they did it was going to alter everything.

Tate leaned his shoulder against the wall, looking down at her with a small smile tugging at his lips. And just like at dinner, Lyla was completely unable to stop looking at his mouth.

It was a very normal mouth—not too big or too small, nothing strange about it in the least. It shouldn't be drawing her attention so much, but every little expression, every sardonic twitch and teasing smile and grumpy scowl, had her hot under the collar tonight.

And Lyla's shirt didn't even *have* a collar.

At some point, Tate's dancing eyes must have drifted down without her noticing, because when she checked, he was staring pretty openly at her mouth, too.

This dance they were doing had shifted into the ridiculous about an hour ago, and Lyla couldn't take it anymore. She was tired of being toyed with.

"Please just do it," she begged. She was so far beyond turned-on, that common sense was not only not in the building—it had moved on to a completely different stratosphere.

Tate obliged her without comment, bending forward to drop only a single, feather-light kiss on Lyla's lips before he pulled back to see her reaction.

It wasn't enough. Nothing short of total nuclear fission was going to be enough at this stage.

Lyla slid her hands up his broad, hard chest, then looped them around his neck to pull him closer. She kept her eyes open so she wouldn't miss a single flicker of those perfect eyelashes of his.

Thankfully, Tate didn't need any more hints than that. His smile disappeared and he ducked his head, diving in to launch a full-scale assault on her mouth and her senses that had them both groaning within minutes.

He broke off with a gasp, only to drag his lips down the hyper-sensitive skin of Lyla's throat to lick the hollow at the base. He flexed his hands on her hips, then slowly shifted them up her ribcage—on what she hoped was a direct course for her breasts.

Impatient and longing for his touch, Lyla finished the job for him, placing herself squarely in his palms with a breathless, "Oh. God."

Tate exhaled in another rush. "Look what I found, sweetheart," he commented. "Jesus, they're even more perfect than they look."

His big hands lifted and squeezed her gently, and his pretty blue eyes turned dark. Transfixed by the sight of himself touching her, he said, "Your breasts are beautiful, Lyla. You feel how well they fit in my hands? I'd do anything to see them bare right now."

They did feel seductively heavy in Tate's grasp. Lyla arched into his touch, wanting to get closer. In response, Tate ran his thumbs lightly over the tips, teasing her nipples into hard points beneath her shirt.

"You are killing me," she told him.

"Well, we wouldn't want that."

Lyla dropped her head back against the door with an ungainly thunk. "Don't stop, Mr. Monroe."

Tate did stop, though. "Slick, I'll act out any roleplay you want, except that one," he chuckled. "Mr. Monroe is my dad. He taught science to me and all of my friends in seventh grade—so, that is one place I will not go with you."

Lyla laughed, too, and moved his scintillating hands back to where she wanted them. "Okay, then who should we be? Doctor and nurse?"

"No good," he grouched. "Reminds me too much of Luca."

"All right, then how about…" Lyla cast around for something entertaining. "Soldier and spy?" she grinned.

"Great. As you know, I'm a captain," Tate announced, then dipped forward to nip at the shell of her ear.

He'd mentioned before that he liked her perfume, and Lyla trusted that it would do its job now. It would be tantalizingly easy for him to scent it this close, and she hoped that Tate would take the opportunity to fill his lungs with its supposedly *elusive, heady fragrance*. She'd spent a fortune on it—so it might as well live up to its ad copy for once.

Lyla dug up what she hoped was a passable Russian accent, and retorted, "Then tell me, Captain, why I leave you alone for five minutes and all my papers go missing?" She pronounced *missing* like it ended in a *k*, and tried for throaty and sexy on everything else.

Tate stopped kissing her neck, pulled back, and stared at her. Lyla pouted and blew him a kiss. After a long, loaded minute, they both burst out laughing.

When she could finally speak again, Lyla admitted, "So, clearly I'm not great at accents."

"Are you kidding? That was amazing," Tate gasped. "Straight out of *The Rocky and Bullwinkle Show*. Do it again."

Lyla shimmied lightly up and down the front of him like a lap dancer, but it was hard to suppress the giggles trying to fight free. "Do you even have a permit for this long-range missile, Captain?" she purred, as fake-serious as she could manage, under the circumstances. "Do you even know how to use it?"

"Lyla, how are you so fucking adorable and smoking hot all at the same time," Tate muttered darkly, before standing straight and wrestling himself back into character.

When he spoke again, he was every inch the silver-screen officer. "Natasha, I am a hardened soldier," he growled, "You'd better believe I know how to use my weapon."

At that double entendre, Lyla was pretty much ready to melt into a puddle at his feet, but she was saved from the embarrassment when Tate filled his hands with her ass and pinned her to the door with his own personal ICBM.

He took total possession of her mouth again, and Lyla couldn't do anything more than tag along and let him do what he clearly did best. If she'd had any idea how flipping good Tate Monroe was at kissing, she'd never have been able to hold out as long as she had.

Hell, he even tasted like cinnamon, courtesy of the flan he'd had for dessert. Her favorite flavor—imagine that.

LYLA HAD NO idea how long they stood there, making out against their suite's door like a couple of teenagers late for curfew. But at some point, the real world intruded in the form of a stairwell door crashing closed at the end of the hall.

Tate sprang back from her, scanning the area with an abruptly ferocious glare.

"Well, okay then," Lyla laughed.

"We shouldn't be out here," Tate told her.

"But it sure is fun."

He pecked her on the nose. "Lyla, you have no business being so cute and distracting. I'm supposed to be aware of our surroundings. *Protecting* you, not pawing at you."

"I happen to like your paws."

"And my paws like you. Let's get inside so I can put them back on you."

Despite his flirty words, though, it was obvious the moment was over. Tate positioned Lyla next to the open door so he could comb through the suite looking for anything out of place, and she tried not to mourn the loss of his lips.

He was all business as he sifted through the bathroom and the closet and the bedroom. Tate checked the locks on the windows and the sliding glass door, and he felt around for anything untoward stashed under the furniture.

Then, he moved Lyla's suitcase to the luggage rack, his duffel to an armchair, and slipped her purse off her shoulder to put it on the desk.

Tate pulled Lyla the rest of the way into the suite, closed the door behind her, and flipped the deadbolt.

When he finally turned to her once more, his gaze was incendiary again. He came to stand in front of her, but he didn't kiss her, and he didn't say a word. He only reached forward and brushed his fingertips down the inside of her wrist, then threaded his fingers through hers.

"Tate?" Lyla whispered, breathless with anticipation.

"Room's clear," he told her.

"So, I gathered." She tugged on his hand, but he didn't budge.

Tate swallowed, stared at her mouth, then met her eyes again. "Tell me you want me," he rasped.

"I want you."

"Tell me you need me."

"I do. So much."

"Say this is okay. That I'm not imagining this."

Lyla pulled her hand free and stepped forward, wrapping her arms around his neck and putting her lips against his. "I'm real," she told him, feeling his breath, hot and shaky, mingling with her own. "And I'm yours."

Tate crashed against her then, fusing his mouth to hers and walking Lyla backward to press her against the wall behind them. His hands were everywhere—molding to her hips and breasts and gripping her ass until they finally lifted her up against him.

Lyla wrapped her legs around his waist and held on for dear life, while Tate pushed his erection against her core and his tongue tangled mercilessly with hers.

He turned and headed for the bed, walking slowly until his knees hit the mattress. "You're so fucking gorgeous," he told her, wrenching away to lick a path down her neck. "God, Lyla. How are you so gorgeous? You make me crazy."

She whimpered when he nipped at the tendon between her neck and shoulder. In response, Tate smiled and dumped her on the bed, following her down and crawling over her.

He attacked the buttons on Lyla's skirt and tried to yank it down, but immediately got distracted by the triangle of skin that he'd ended up baring.

Lyla tried to help him get her skirt off by raising her hips and shimmying a bit, but that only elicited a growl and a hard suck just below her navel. She dropped back down and sighed.

Who knew belly buttons were so sensitive? It felt as if Tate had hot-wired hers directly to her nervous system—and each flick of his tongue was sending white-hot shocks along all the pathways.

He pressed her hips into the mattress to keep her still, covered Lyla's stomach in hot, wet kisses, and then proceeded to undo the rest of the buttons holding her skirt closed, one by one.

When Tate was done, he opened the two sides and spread them wide, staring down at Lyla's panties with a smug expression on his face.

"Freaking boy shorts," he gloated. "I *knew* it."

"Did you, now?" she asked. "And how much time have you spent, exactly, thinking about my underwear?"

"So much time," Tate told her. "You have no idea."

"I'm beginning to get *some* idea."

He braced himself over her and kissed her hard. "Hush, you. And kiss me back. I want your tongue. I want to feel your tongue all the fuck over me."

"That I can do," Lyla agreed.

"And your skin. Give me more skin. Give me all of it."

"You're pretty bossy for a guy who hasn't even taken off his shoes yet," she pointed out.

Immediately, there were two loud clunks, one after the other, as he toed off his loafers. "There, no more shoes," he mumbled, feeling around on her shirt, looking for how to get it off her. "Now this. Take this off."

"You first."

Tate stopped and chuckled, then sat back on his heels and smiled sexily down at her while he divested himself of his dress shirt and his belt.

He also did that move that some guys had mastered, whipping off his undershirt one-handed and throwing it aside. He even went one sexy step farther and unbuttoned his pants.

If Lyla could've pulled off drooling and had it look the least bit seductive, she totally would have. Instead, she ran her hands over the scorching-hot skin stretched across Tate's ripped abs and felt her body turn molten.

"You are…wow. Just…*wow*," she stuttered.

"Why thank you," Tate smiled. "Convenient side effect when you work out to burn off stress."

He bit his lip and worked Lyla's blouse up her torso, then urged her arms over her head so he could pull it off. And then, he gazed intently down at his fingertip as it traced a long line from her lower lip all the way down to her panties.

Lyla reached behind her back and released the clasp on her bra. Tate blinked, gently plucked the scrap of lace away, and rolled his eyes back in his head.

"You wreck me, woman. Everything you do. *Ruins* me."

He fell forward, kissing her long and slow and sexy, but grinding against her too gently to give her any real relief. He kept it up until Lyla thought she'd die if he didn't get on with things.

"Tate, *please*," she begged.

"What do you want, sweetheart?" He nibbled on her ear, his hot breath skating over her neck and making her shiver.

"You. I want *you*."

"You have me."

"Then, more of you." Lyla pushed his khakis and boxer briefs down his hips and reached for the part she wanted most. When she got ahold of it, Tate lost a little bit of his swagger and groaned loudly.

"*Oh my God*," he said, "When you do that—"

Lyla stroked him again, and his mouth clamped shut. Tate rolled his neck and looked like he was fighting for composure.

He was so hard and big, and she couldn't wait to feel him inside her. Her dating dry spell was looking like it had been one-hundred-percent worth every lonely minute if this was how it was going to end.

"I don't suppose Mr. *Always Prepared* brought any protection with him?" Lyla inquired.

"You bet your sweet ass I did," Tate told her. He immediately rolled aside and stood up, kicking off his pants and underwear while he dug through his bag, then returning a moment later with a strip of condoms in his hand.

"We probably only need the one," Lyla smiled, pulling him over her again.

"Shows what you know," Tate grinned back. He ripped a square off the strip and covered his magnificent length, and then hooked his index fingers into the waistband of her panties so he could drag them down her legs.

Lyla's breath was coming in erratic spurts, and she was salivating at the thought of all that broad, hard muscle being hers to enjoy for the next few hours.

"Last chance to back out," Tate warned.

Lyla snorted, "As if."

He smiled that mega-watt grin of his, kissed her deeply, and pushed into her in one commanding thrust.

"Jesus," Lyla moaned. "You're…"

"Feel me," Tate commanded, as he moved in and out in strong strokes. "Feel what we're like together."

"So good," Lyla told him.

"That's right. Even better than I dreamed."

When he brought Lyla up and over the edge, she could've sworn she saw stars.

LYLA WOKE UP before Tate the next morning and was immediately determined not to screw things up like she'd done the day before.

She slipped out of the bed they'd shared all night long, watched him sleep in the faint light bleeding through the blinds for a euphoric minute or two, and then went into the bathroom to pee and brush her teeth.

Tate hadn't been lying when he said he knew how to use his weapon—he knew how to use it better than any man she'd ever met. Lyla's body was singing in all the right places today, and she wanted to sing right along with it. She hoped they could add some more notes to the song, too—possibly in the next several minutes.

Tate was still face-down on his pillow when she crept out again. Before she crawled in next to him, Lyla bent to pick up the hotel check-out receipt that someone had stuck under the door during the night.

It would stink if she slipped on it and accidentally woke Tate before he was ready.

Yesterday, she had witnessed firsthand how badly the lack of sleep threw Tate off and she had no desire for a repeat performance.

However, once she straightened, Lyla noticed she'd picked up something else, too—a large manila envelope with her full name printed on the outside.

She frowned and pried it open, then slid out the contents.

The sheet on top had only two lines, but the simple computer font looked harsh against the white printer paper.

Delilah, you filthy whore, it read. *Don't you know it's wrong to sleep with the help?*

Lyla looked underneath it and fell to her knees. There were photos. *Oh, God*—there were so many photos.

That psychopath must have been in the hallway with them last night, she realized, and somehow, he'd managed to take pictures without either of them realizing it.

Across every one, he'd scrawled the word *Wrong* in thick black marker.

"Tate?" Lyla called, dropping the horrible images to the carpet like they might catch fire at any moment. When he didn't respond, she yelled louder, "Tate!"

Fifteen

I F IT WAS possible to wake up with one's blood already boiling, Tate had done it that morning. Just the panicked tone of Lyla's voice had made him want to strangle something with his bare hands, and that was before he'd even gotten a look at the photos.

Those photos—Tate was still absolutely furious that Lyla's jackass stalker had managed to take pictures of them without Tate knowing it.

He felt downright murderous that the fucker had ruined what should've been a blissful morning in bed for them.

Lyla had pulled herself together like she always did, insisting on getting cleaned up and trucking off to her reading on schedule, despite how hard Tate argued against it.

However, now that they were here, there was no denying she was flustered.

Usually, Lyla was a consummate professional, walking into her various appearances as poised and calm as anyone Tate had ever seen. She made pleasant conversation, projected a caring face to her readers, and smoothly deflected unwelcome prying or digs from the trolls.

He assumed that was one of the reasons Red had wanted her for this project.

Unfortunately, none of those stellar qualities were in evidence today. Lyla was distracted and restless at her table, and jittery and impatient with him. It'd been this way for two hours.

The fans waiting in line for her to sign their books did not appear to notice anything amiss, though, so maybe Tate was the only one seeing Lyla clearly—probably because he'd gotten so tuned into her frequency that it was almost like he could read her mind sometimes.

Under the fear and horror, she'd been really disappointed about their ruined morning, too.

And now, hours later, Tate couldn't think of anyone more in need of a change of scenery than Lyla. Luckily, he knew just how to give it to her.

While Lyla dealt with the last few stragglers in line and wrapped up things with the bookstore reps, Tate kept one eye on her and one on his phone.

It only took about five minutes of internet searching before he found what he was looking for—a state park that was only twenty minutes away. It would be perfect for what he wanted.

ONCE TATE TUCKED her safely back in the truck, Lyla exhaled heavily, but the tension in her shoulders didn't budge, and her hands didn't stop shaking, either.

"How we doin', Slick?" Tate asked her.

"I'm off," she admitted. "Really off. Do you think they could tell?"

"I doubt it. But it's not like you don't have good reason to be upset. That shit this morning was really troubling."

"I know. I just wish we could figure out who's doing this. And *why*."

"We will."

"How does he always seem to know where we're going to be, Tate? We weren't even supposed to be in Cleveland last night," Lyla said. "It's unnerving."

"Yeah, it is," he agreed. "And that's something I want to talk more about. But listen…I think it's time for you to take a little break from all this. Have a change of scenery."

Lyla sighed, "Believe me, I'd love to. But how am I supposed to accomplish that? We have to get to Erie by four-thirty. I have that interview with the woman from the Gazette, remember?"

"I know, and we'll get there in plenty of time. I just thought we could make a little pit stop on the way to clear our heads. What do you think?"

She shrugged. "Sounds good to me. It's not like this day could get much worse, right?"

Tate didn't want to touch that thought with a ten-foot pole. Of course it could get worse—things could *always* get worse. Still, he was going to try his damnedest to make sure that didn't happen today.

FORTY MINUTES LATER, he'd found the highway exit he was looking for, a drive-through with a good selection of sandwiches and salads that Lyla could eat, and the unassuming entrance to the park. It wasn't manned, but it did have a sturdy plexiglass case with helpful maps stashed inside.

Ten minutes after that, Lyla was changing out of her skirt and heels and ditching her cardigan, then trudging after Tate on the dirt path. She carried the bag with their lunch in it like she was planning to sacrifice it to the fishing gods.

Speaking of which—

"Where the heck did you acquire a pair of fishing rods, anyway?" she wondered. "I'm sure I would've noticed those being packed in the truck."

"I found them when I went out that night in Baltimore, and stashed them in the back," Tate told her. "I figured, even if we never got to use them, I could always give them to my dad or brother next time I visit."

"How convenient."

Tate grinned—he thought so. But first things first, "Have you ever fished before?"

"I'm a vegetarian, Tate. What do you think?"

"So that's a *no*. Don't worry, little camper. We won't hurt the fish today. We'll throw them back if we get any bites."

Glancing over his shoulder, Tate wasn't surprised that Lyla looked dubious. She even had that little divot between her eyebrows that told him she was considering things carefully before she weighed in again.

Soon, though, they reached the spot he'd scoped out on the map, and whatever Lyla had been thinking about got shuttled aside while they set up on the small hill over the water.

The river was more of a creek at this point, but it had a nice bend shaded by an overhanging willow, the fronds long and trailing into the water a couple of feet out.

Even better, when they'd gotten out of the truck before, Lyla had rummaged around in her bag after she'd put on her tennis shoes, and then done the *nothing-to-see-here* changing trick that every woman seemed to know. She'd slipped a pair of running shorts on under her skirt, and then the skirt came off without one glimpse of her ass or underwear—and wasn't that a shame.

Because right now, with those long, gorgeous legs stretched out in front of her on the grass, Lyla presented one hell of a beautiful view.

"What a beautiful view," she murmured, echoing Tate's thoughts with such eerie precision, he almost wondered if he'd spoken out loud. "How did you know this was here?"

"Just got lucky. Why don't you eat while I put the rods together? It won't take long."

Lyla pulled her legs in to sit cross-legged, then rummaged through the bag until she found her rabbit food and a plastic fork. She crunched away as she watched him, and Tate tried not to think about how it would feel to lay her out on this riverbank and make love to her with the warm sun on their skin.

He'd had her one damn time, and he was already dreaming about making it a habit.

Bug bites, Tate reminded himself. *Bug bites in bad places. Public indecency citations. Sunburned asses. Grassy nuts.*

In his mind, he listed any and every awkward and uncomfortable thing that could possibly befall them in this lovely, private, out-of-the-way place, lest his racing pulse got the better of him and he tried to kiss away that thoughtful look on Lyla's face.

As usual, she was completely oblivious to the furious battle Tate was waging behind the scenes. She sighed dreamily and told him, "You were right. This is exactly what I needed."

"I'm glad. Getting outside always helps me when I'm getting stressed, too." *He enjoyed other stress relievers as well, which he was not thinking about at all.*

"Don't you want your sandwich?"

"In a minute. I'm almost done." Tate had attached the reels and strung the lines, but he was trying to keep the hooks on the down-low for the time being. No doubt, Lyla would notice them at some point—her eagle eyes saw everything, it seemed—but he'd like to postpone that part of the fishing experience for later, if he could.

For the fortieth time, she piped up, "I think you're really going to like what I ordered you. You won't even miss the meat, I promise."

Tate smiled, but fuck if he didn't want to shudder. Between the list of odd vegetables and the promise of something called "soy cheese," he was not holding out much hope that his Veggie Explosion—or whatever it was—was going to be the least bit satisfying.

Still, it couldn't be much worse than an MRE, and Tate sure as shit didn't want to be the asshole tucking into a side of beef in front of a soft-hearted vegetarian, only twenty-four hours after he'd banged her.

"I'm sure it will be great," he replied, also for the fortieth time.

"Liar."

"Small lie. Well-intentioned."

"Just try it."

Tate set down the rods and crawled over to Lyla, settling beside her and accepting the paper-wrapped concoction she held out.

He offered her a cheerfully sardonic toast of, "Meat is murder!" then took his first bite.

Okay. So, the texture wasn't the worst, and there appeared to be some kind of tan spread on the roll that would probably work well on chips. The bread was pretty awesome, too, thick and garlicky and clearly homemade.

Lyla was tracking every last chew with avid interest. "Well, what do you think?"

Tate swallowed, then took another bite. Around the food in his mouth, he admitted grudgingly, "I don't think it will kill me."

Lyla's grin was so satisfied, you'd have thought she'd beat him at poker. Tate waited for her to start eating her salad again before he polished off the sandwich and went hunting for the second one he knew she'd gotten him.

It might not be pastrami, but at least it was good enough to distract him from all the female thigh action happening beside him. *That* was definitely capable of killing him.

The persistent visual of Lyla fake-undressing beside their car, followed by the sight of her skimpy-enough-to-be-illegal shorts mere inches away from his leg…those were deadly weapons that could easily enter through Tate's eyeballs and render him deceased.

"When we're done eating, I can teach you how to cast and everything," he said, by way of conversation.

"Won't the hooks hurt the fish?"

Yeah, so Tate was obviously not as sly as he'd thought. What else was new?

"I…can't say I've ever considered that aspect."

Lyla scanned the water of the creek for a minute, then announced, "It's okay. I'll just take the hook off mine."

"But how are you going to—"

"And I can tie a little piece of lettuce to the end!" she announced in triumph. "I bet the fish would like that. Some of them are probably vegetarians, too."

Tate blinked at her, not sure how to explain everything silly about that idea. "I'm not sure you'll be able to...you know. Reel one in." Tate scrubbed a hand over his jaw. "That way."

Lyla shrugged. "It's not like we were going to take any with us, anyway."

"True."

So, Tate taught the woman how to fish. Without her actually doing any fishing.

They sat there on the bank for a long time, listening to the buzzing insects and the birds in the trees. Every once in a while, Lyla would sigh happily when some geese flew by, or a heron picked its way across the opposite bank.

Fish would tug on Lyla's line and swim away, and then she'd reel it in so she could tie more greens on the end for them. Tate kept his hook in place, because *hello, Man Card*—but he made zero effort to catch anything.

He couldn't remember a sweeter day of fishing. Tate's brain settled and his earlier agitation drifted away, and after a while, his scattered thoughts began forming into an idea.

EVENTUALLY, LYLA BEGAN checking her watch again. "I guess we'd better get going soon," she said sadly.

"Maybe."

"We have to leave enough time to get to Erie, though. And I probably ought to clean up a little before the interview."

"Lyla, what if..." Tate was taking a risk, here, one that could potentially endanger her. It felt right, however, and he made a practice of never ignoring his gut. That's why he plowed on with,

"What if we ditched the public tour schedule and changed things up a bit?"

"Tate, I can't cancel these events," she said. "It would make me and Trident look really bad, and Red—for one—would probably be furious."

"No, I don't mean cancel the events themselves, though we might consider moving some of them around a bit. What I actually meant was, what if we change vehicles? Stay in places that no one would expect for the next few towns? We might be able to throw your whack-job off his game."

Lyla frowned, considering that.

Tate pressed her, "Who planned this tour, anyway?"

"Trident PR did. But I seriously doubt my stalker has anything to do with someone at work," she argued. "I know those people, Tate. They're friends of mine."

"Okay, but the schedule was publicized, right?"

"Yeah, of course. The coordinators at the places like to have a chance to hype things beforehand."

"So, whoever is tracking you knows exactly where you'll be and when. And I bet it wouldn't be too hard to figure out which routes we might take, and even where we might stay in each town."

If Tate were the one watching, he'd look at the fastest, most direct routes between points, and the nicest, brand-name hotels nearby. And he'd be right.

Lyla simply blinked at him, serious as a heart attack. "I broadcast some of it on my social media, too," she admitted softly. "Even…even the Cleveland thing. I feel so stupid."

"Okay, well—we're not going to do *that* anymore. And, what if we do the unexpected going forward?" Tate asked her.

"What are you suggesting?"

He checked the browser on his phone reflexively, but he already had a general sense of where they were. "If you were to reschedule your interview this afternoon to later in the evening— and do it over the phone, if you can, instead of in-person—then we could probably swing by my parents' house and still get to Erie in time."

Lyla's eyes popped wide. "Your parents? Tate, I don't want to drag them into this. If we put them in danger, I'd never be able to forgive myself."

"We won't stay. But we can pick up my little brother's truck while we're there. It's just sitting in the garage while he's away, and he won't care if we use it. And this way, maybe we can confuse anyone that's gotten used to looking for that fancy freaking rig we've got back there."

Tate threw a thumb over this shoulder, calling out the sleek black SUV they'd been tooling around in so far. Very large, very fine—very noticeable.

Lyla was nodding, but got sidetracked by the inconsequential details, as she sometimes did. "Where's your brother? And shouldn't we give your parents a heads-up?"

"Tom's in the Peace Corps in Jamaica, and he won't be back for ten more months," Tate informed her. "And my parents are on a cruise for their anniversary. I can text them afterward to let them know what we did."

"Are you just going to leave the rental truck at their house?"

Tate had considered that but decided it would make things too complicated later. "We can return it in Mentor. It's not too far from my folks, and we'll stick close together all the way there."

Lyla nodded. "You really think this will help?"

"Can't hurt to try, right?"

"I suppose not. Let me call that reporter and see if switching times is even an option. You find out how late the rental agency in Mentor is open."

A LITTLE WHILE later, flush with success and the promise of a new plan, they gathered their rods and the trash from lunch, and were just getting ready to head back to the car, when Lyla put a hand on Tate's arm.

She stood on her tiptoes and planted a faint kiss on his cheek. "Thank you," she whispered.

Tate could feel a blush creeping up his neck. "It's what I'm here for," he told her, keeping cool as one of the cucumbers in his no-meat sandwich.

"I don't mean the car suggestions and all the other stuff," Lyla told him, "Even though I appreciate those, too. I mean thank you for this." She swept her arm out to encompass the blue sky and the soft grass, the burbling river and the willow fronds swaying in the breeze. "I haven't had a day like this in a really long time. I needed it."

"I could tell. And you're welcome." Tate bent down and sealed his lips to hers, holding them there as long as he dared before things were in danger of spiraling out of hand. "I hope it helped."

"It really did."

"Good. Then hike up your booty shorts, Natasha. Operation Shuck-and-Jive is now underway."

Tate turned and quickly made for the wide dirt path, but he knew Lyla would never let that little jibe pass.

Sure enough, she squawked as soon as she marched after him, "*Booty shorts?* Are you nuts? These are completely normal running shorts, you freaking caveman. I've seen way worse things at the gym!"

So had he, but Tate had also spent a long time—quite recently—in a place where female legs were covered from head to toe in one of two things: bulky Army uniforms or the voluminous folds of an *abaya*. In contrast, Lyla's bare legs seemed like a revelation.

Frankly, anything beyond his mother's loose denim Bermuda shorts on Lyla was likely to get a rise out of Tate at this point—literally *and* figuratively.

"Settle down," Tate told her, chuckling, "It's just a joke."

Lyla huffed behind him, and he could almost feel the steam coming out of her ears. If she'd been a dragon, he had no doubt the skin on the back of his neck would have been singed clean off by now.

"Don't tell me to settle down, you troglodyte goon. Just because you can't control yourself doesn't mean—"

Tate spun and hooked an arm around Lyla's waist, yanking her in close. He'd been mostly successful in keeping things on the up and up so far today, but an incensed Lyla was just one of those delicacies he could not resist.

Her pupils dilated and she went soft all over in his arms.

Tate dropped his head to get nice and close to her mouth, and demanded, "What, sweetheart? What doesn't it mean?"

Sixteen

TATE'S MOUTH WAS millimeters from hers. Lyla could feel his hot breath wafting over her lips. She could almost taste the sweet lemonade he'd been drinking.

She swallowed, and to her ears, it sounded as loud as a gunshot. "It means…it only means that I have the right to wear whatever I want."

He smiled. "That you do. And conveniently, then I get to look at your pretty legs every time you exercise that right."

His hand dropped down and brushed clear up the outside of Lyla's thigh, coming to a stop at her hip, inches higher than the hem of her problematic shorts.

Lyla's breath shuddered right out of her lungs. Big hands. Such big hands.

"Promise me you'll take these off for me later," he murmured.

Lyla nodded, perhaps a bit too eagerly.

Tate grinned and dropped a quick peck on her mouth, then released her and tromped off once more, looking like an all-grown-up Huck Finn in his rolled-up khakis. The fishing poles and crumpled brown bag only added to the effect.

At that moment, Lyla doubted she would've refused him anything.

ON THE WAY to his parents' house, Tate tried once more to make contact with Detective Scarletti, back in New York. They'd left him a message before they departed the hotel that morning but hadn't heard back from him all day.

It was just as well. Heaven only knew what either of them might have said when they'd still been so upset. At least now, they had calmed down and were thinking more clearly.

Tate synced his phone with the truck's dashboard speakerphone, and he and Lyla listened to the call ringing for a bit before the officer finally answered, "Scarletti."

Tate said, "Detective, this is Captain Tate Monroe. I work security for Lyla Lawson. We met a couple of weeks ago."

"Sure, I remember. What can I do for you, Captain?"

"Well, first we wanted to make sure you received the package we overnighted you from Newark."

"I did. I'm sure Forensics hasn't had a chance to take a stab at it yet, but I appreciate you trying to keep it clean with the baggie and whatnot."

Scarletti's tone implied that he appreciated nothing of the sort—he obviously hadn't forgotten their contentious first encounter.

Lyla spoke up, "This is Lyla. I also emailed you some photos I took of the package before we opened it."

"I saw that. I'll be sure to take a good look at them soon."

Tate rolled his eyes at her, thoroughly unimpressed with how casually Scarletti seemed to view this whole mess.

There was some rustling over the line, and then the detective added, "I see that you also left a message about another phone call?"

"We did," Tate replied. "That was in Baltimore. Guy didn't say anything, but he did wait until I'd stepped out before he called Lyla."

"Yeah. Actually, it's not a guy we're dealing with," the officer informed them. "It's a woman."

"Pardon?" Tate asked.

"The stalker. She's a *she*—56 years old, has a long history of exactly this kind of thing. We've been looking at her for a while but couldn't find anything to tie her in until today."

Lyla and Tate shared a long look before she inquired, "She's threatened other authors, besides me?"

"Not only authors. She's got a hard-on for professional athletes, too. Friends them on social media, joins their fan clubs—the whole nine yards."

"And she *threatens* them?" Tate confirmed.

"Not right away," Scarletti explained. "It usually takes a few months before they do something to piss her off and she flips her lid. But her super called us yesterday to complain that she might be hoarding, so we went over this morning and had a look. Either of you wanna guess what she was stockpiling?"

"I'm going to assume it wasn't canned goods," Tate said dryly.

"Nope. Paperbacks. *Mystery* paperbacks, Ms. Lawson's among them. We brought the lady in and have her talking to someone right now. It seems she hasn't been checking in with her doctor or refilling her meds on schedule—shouldn't be long before we can wrap this case up with a nice big bow."

Lyla held up her hand before Tate could respond. "I guess Forensics is going to *have* to take a look at my stuff now," she said.

"They will. We'll have her connected to you six ways to Sunday. You wait and see."

"Detective," Tate interjected, "Can I ask what time you brought the woman in, by any chance?"

"Around nine. Why?"

"Because Lyla got another package from her stalker early this morning, which included photos that were definitely taken yesterday evening. That's actually why we were trying to reach you."

"No shit? Well, it certainly could've been her. The lady doesn't usually like to leave her house much, but when she's worked up, anything's possible."

"I guess," Lyla mused. "But does she…you said she joins fan clubs and stuff?"

The detective said, "Sure does. One time she even started the club herself. Got over a hundred members, too."

Tate understood what Lyla was getting at even if Scarletti didn't. "So, she makes herself *known* to her victims?" he asked.

"Captain, this gal thinks she's their BFF—you better believe she introduces herself. She also finds ways to accidentally bump into them at the gym, the coffee shop—you name it."

Lyla frowned and shook her head at Tate. He nodded but took a moment to change lanes, avoiding a semi merging onto the road in front of them.

Finally, he commented, "That doesn't sound like Lyla's stalker, though."

"Probably because we grabbed her up earlier than usual. She didn't have a chance to really get going yet."

Lyla said, "*Huh.*" Nothing about this felt right to her.

Scarletti told her, "Crazy world we live in, right? People are nuts."

"Yeah," Tate agreed, giving Lyla a speaking glance. "Hey, you want us to overnight you this new note? So you can test it with all the others?"

"Sure. The more stuff we've got to put this crackpot away, the better."

"Sounds good," Tate muttered.

"Well, Ms. Lawson," the detective said, "How's it feel, knowing you can sleep easy tonight?"

"I'm sure you won't be surprised to hear that I'll believe it when I see it," she told him.

"And here I thought I was the cynic in the family."

ONCE THEY DISCONNECTED the call, Lyla didn't have to wait long to hear Tate's thoughts on what Detective Scarletti had told them.

"I don't like it," he groused. "It feels all wrong."

Lyla asked, "I agree. How could she take those pictures, get them developed, and then deliver everything in time to return home for her arrest? How does a housebound hoarder do any of the things my stalker has done?"

"And you haven't had any contact with her either, right?"

"Not to my knowledge. I don't even have a fan club."

Tate blew out a long breath, deep in thought. "This lady isn't the one. I'm almost sure of it."

"I know. But…what do we do?"

"I say we stick to our plan. Especially now that Scarletti isn't going to be looking at anyone else until he rules this lady in or out."

"I agree."

Lyla watched curiously as Tate turned down a narrow, two-lane road, taking them further away from the Cleveland suburbs and into a less-developed area of rolling fields and small tracts of woods.

"It's pretty here," she told him.

"Home always is," he smiled back.

She'd be lying if she said that she wasn't really looking forward to seeing the place Tate had grown up. It was part of what made his new plan so attractive, given that it might be the only chance she ever got to find out more about what made him tick.

Tate wasn't quite done talking, however. With his window down and one hand loosely guiding the wheel, he turned to face her and asked, "Lyla, just out of curiosity, who do *you* think is doing this?"

"I've had this conversation with Scarletti several times," she told him. "I really can't think of anyone. As far as I know, there are no former colleagues who resent me. No mortal enemies. No bitter exes."

He laughed, "So, you're a good breaker-upper?"

"That's for me to know and you to find out, mister."

"What about someone who wanted the Red Devil gig? Did you compete with anyone over that?"

"Honestly, no one but Red and Piper even knew the imprint was going to exist. You can't want something you don't know is out there. And as far as the bigger authors go—Red Devil is brand new. Not too many people at that level would want to risk their career on an untested entity."

"But what does your gut tell you?" Tate prodded. "Is this just some random psycho? Or is this personal?"

"I…I really don't know. I'm sorry, Tate."

He stewed for a bit, watching the road. Then he muttered, "Well, this doesn't feel random to me, at all. It feels personal."

"I'm not sure if that makes me feel better, or worse."

"Me either."

AT THE END of a long lane, Tate pulled into the driveway of a tidy white farmhouse with a wraparound porch and planters of flowers hanging from its eaves.

The sun was just beginning to go down, and the whole place looked exactly like a scene from a jigsaw puzzle or a postcard.

Lyla's twisty imagination kicked right in, and she immediately wanted to make the idyllic spot the scene of a nefarious crime. That seemed like poor form, though.

Tate got out and gestured around, pulling her from her thoughts. "This is it. Home base."

"It's really nice."

"Thanks. We like it." He stood there with his hands on his hips and looked around. "Do you want to come in for a minute? Maybe have a snack and use the facilities before we return the rental?"

"Sure." Especially if it meant that she'd get to see a stray high school football photo of Tate on a wall or a shot of him in his dress uniform on the mantel. Lyla tried not to rub her hands together in glee at the prospect.

Tate led her up on the porch, then felt along the top of the doorframe for what Lyla assumed was the house key. While he searched, she pointed at the banner displayed in the front window, a starched flag with a blue background and a silver star at its center.

"So festive," she smiled.

Tate scratched his neck and looked uncomfortable, though. "Yeah, I've been trying to get them to take that down."

"Why? It's cute."

"It's embarrassing. And completely unnecessary."

That seemed a little severe for a simple holiday decoration. Lyla frowned. "I don't get it," she said, "What's wrong with it?"

Tate studied her face and sighed. "Lyla, what do you think that banner means?"

"That your parents are patriotic?"

"They are. For sure. But that's a service banner. It signifies that an immediate family member of the household has been wounded in action."

"Oh. I'm so sorry—I didn't know." Lyla was pretty sure she couldn't feel any more stupid at the moment.

Tate nodded, going over to tap on the glass. "Gold stars are for family killed in action, and blue stars are just for someone serving. They used to display that one," he told her. "The silver star is newer than the other two, but of course, my mom and dad were all over it."

Lyla smiled at him, trying to lighten his mood, "Your parents must be very proud of you."

"Well, I try not to let them down." Tate sighed, smoothed down his shirt, and brandished the key he'd retrieved. "Come on, let's see what Mom left in the pantry."

CREEPING THROUGH THE dim house after Tate, Lyla felt a little shady, like a burglar casing the joint when the owners were out.

She tried to surreptitiously look around without being too obvious, on the hunt for glimpses of Tate in his natural habitat, even though his parents weren't even home.

She was also trying not to trip over something and break her neck. Tate's mom appeared to have an affection for decorating with all kinds of antiquey-looking receptacles, since there was a variety of baskets, pottery jugs and wrought-iron *things* nestled in all the corners and sticking out into the hall.

Tate pointed out the main rooms of the downstairs before bringing Lyla to the kitchen in the back, then rummaged around in the refrigerator and walk-in pantry.

"Slim pickings, I'm afraid," he told her. "We've got cheese curls that are probably stale by now, since I'm pretty sure I bought this bag about a month ago—and some apple juice. Also…seltzer water."

Lyla laughed. "If you find any crayons, this could basically be kindergarten."

"Oh, God. You're right. What are we even doing here?"

"Don't worry. I can wait to eat. Just show me where the bathroom is, and maybe a couple of your baby pictures, and I'll be good to go."

"You're a cheap date, you know that?"

"I'll be sure to order heavy at the restaurant later if it will make you feel better."

"Nah. No one can eat *that* many portobello mushrooms," Tate snarked, then pointed back down the hall. "Bathroom's the first door on the left. If you turn on the hall light, you will also see every embarrassing school picture ever taken of Tom and me, from K through 12."

"Oh, goody," Lyla told him, twisting an imaginary mustache.

Tate rolled his eyes. "I'll see if there's any bottled water in the mudroom, and then we can get going."

BACK OUTSIDE IN the driveway, Lyla was still ticked off and bickering with Tate about those damned childhood photos of his.

"I mean, did you even have an awkward stage?" she accused. "Braces? A single pimple? Anything?"

"You don't have to sound so disappointed," he retorted.

"Maybe I wouldn't be, if you'd brought me to your actual home, instead of some perfect-family movie set."

"Knowing you, you'll probably try to kill one of us off in your next book, just to get back at me."

Well, that dig hit a little close to home. Lyla stood there sputtering, trying to come up with a suitable response, when she heard something very wrong, over near a big shed at the far side of the yard.

She motioned frantically to Tate. "*Shh.*"

Every nerve instantly on alert, he froze and whispered, "What?"

"I heard something weird."

He moved nearer, ready to shield her from the threat as he scanned the area and listened carefully to the sounds of the falling night. Lyla held still and inched closer, scared.

The big city, this was not. There could be any number of dangers she wasn't aware of out here, and unlike Manhattan, there wouldn't be a single soul to hear or see a thing.

Beside her, Tate abruptly chuckled and relaxed, however. "Lyla, stop—it's okay. I think you just heard the alpacas."

It was such an incongruent statement, that she completely forgot to keep her voice down. "Excuse me?"

"Alpacas," he reiterated. "Over there." He pointed at the big shed.

"Like…llamas?" Lyla wondered, utterly confounded. "*Here?*"

Tate laughed again. "They're way better than llamas. My mom sells their hair to some ladies who spin yarn to sell at farmer's markets. I'll show you."

Seventeen

W HEN LYLA SHUSHED him, Tate had tried to listen over the pounding of his heart in his chest—and the fear that he'd brought trouble to his parents' sleepy doorstep like a raw, jagged thing in his gut—but all he'd heard were the usual, comforting sounds of home.

Crickets in the dewy grass. Leaves rustling on the trees. The creak of old wood on the barn when the breeze blew, and the animals settling down for the night... *Oh.*

Thank heaven that had been all it was. He was still feeling some residual angst, however, when he pulled Tom's pickup truck out of the garage to park next to their rental.

"Listen, why don't you drive my brother's truck?" Tate told Lyla. "If someone really is looking for the SUV, you'll be safer in a vehicle they don't recognize. I'll lead the way on the drive to the rental agency, but you stay close behind."

Lyla nodded and snapped off a passable salute. "Aye, aye, Captain," she said.

"Call me and turn on your cell's speakerphone. If you set it on the seat beside you, you can tell me immediately if something goes wrong."

"Won't you be watching?" she wondered uncertainly.

"Of course, sweetheart." Tate took her into his arms and nuzzled her hair. "It's only a precaution, and only for a little while. We'll be back together before you know it."

"You promised me we wouldn't have to split up."

"To catch the villain," he smiled. "I won't ask you to split up *to catch the villain*. This is only to return a rental car."

"So you say," she muttered grudgingly.

AS TATE HAD hoped, the ride to Mentor was quick and the drop-off of the SUV reasonably easy. Mindful that they still hadn't eaten dinner, he and Lyla then headed to a tavern he knew nearby.

He'd heard from his parents that an old high school friend had bought it recently, and was serving some pretty decent gastropub fare, but he ought to have realized he wouldn't be the only former classmate stopping by to check things out and support the home team.

Mere moments after their arrival, Tate and Lyla ran smack into Kev Harris, the most irritating guy in the entire tenth grade, way back when. Figured it would be him.

Inwardly, Tate groaned. Kevin was drunk as usual, and exactly the kind of horse's ass that would think it was funny to share awkward, fifteen-year-old tidbits from Tate's adolescence with Lyla. There was no avoiding it, though—Kev had recognized Tate instantly.

After greeting him and leaning into a sloppy bro-hug, Tate made the introductions, and kept things general. Lyla must have caught on to his reservations because when she reached out to shake Kev's hand, her game face was firmly affixed.

Kevin didn't let go when he should have, though, instead keeping hold of Lyla and turning her hand so he could get a better look at the inside of her wrist.

"What's that?" he demanded.

"It's a—"

In seconds, Tate could see where this was going. Lyla would say it was a quill, and inevitably follow that up with the fact that she was an author.

From there, Kev would want to know how much money she made and whether she was famous—and then he'd slither right into taking selfies to post on social media.

Kevin would probably want to get Lyla's autograph, too, and Tate would bet good money that it would show up on all kinds of auction sites once he had it.

None of that boded well for Tate and Lyla's new, supposedly-low profile, however.

Kev could fuck this mission before it even got off the ground, so Tate cut Lyla off with a terse, "Dude, you have eyes. It's a feather." For good measure, he added, "Lyla likes birds."

Lyla stared at him, but Kevin only laughed.

"Oh, that's real classy." He turned to Tate, annoyingly superior as usual. "Bro, I've seen you bag all kinds of chicks, but tapping the biker broads is new, even for you."

In her neat cardigan, Lyla was about the furthest thing from a biker girl that Tate could imagine, but luckily, she seemed supremely unbothered by the comparison. She just cocked her head and announced, "Kevin, I suspect you wouldn't know class if it crawled up your nose and died there."

Tate tried like hell to hold in his stunned laugh, but it was impossible. Lyla was fucking amazing every time she opened her mouth, and he adored her.

Kev turned beet red, but she made a smooth escape before he could come up with a retort.

"Will you excuse me?" she asked Tate sweetly. "I'm going to find the ladies' room."

"I'll be here," he told her, then watched until she was securely closed inside.

From this vantage, Tate had a perfect view of the front and back doors of the tavern, as well as the bathrooms. He knew from experience that the bathrooms had no windows, either. No one was getting to Lyla without him seeing it.

Once she was safe, he turned back to Kev.

"May I?" he inquired, neatly separating the man's beer can from his sweaty hand and setting it aside. Then, Tate shoved him back against the wall and held the prick there.

"What the fuck, Monroe?" Kevin bleated. "You seriously mad over some ho you prolly just met?"

"Kev, Lyla is a truly decent human being and unlike you, one of my favorite people on this planet. If you so much as *think* another disrespectful word about her, I'm going to fillet you with my fucking pocketknife."

At least Kevin had retained enough sense not to fight back. He hung there, unresisting, while he sputtered, "So much for *bros before hos*, asshole."

"Kev, you're not my bro, and you're clearly too drunk to stay here any longer trolling for *hos*. Call a damn cab and go home."

Tate caught sight of the bouncer headed their way, and reluctantly let Kevin go.

The knucklehead found his feet and laughed. "Monroe, you've been in the desert too long. No one takes cabs anymore, you dickwad."

He wrenched his polo shirt into place with the kind of jacked-up dignity only lushes could muster, and then began weaving his unsteady way toward the front door. Tate gave the bouncer a nod, and the guy changed course to follow Kev out—hopefully, to make sure the tool didn't do something stupid, like get behind the wheel.

Lyla popped up at Tate's elbow a moment later, with only the scent of her seductive perfume as warning.

"What was all that about?"

"Let's just say, old Kev got even classier after you left. But don't worry—I set him straight."

"Yikes," she grimaced. "That only makes me more worried."

"Anyway, I'm sorry about what he said. Apparently, my tolerance for idiocy was much larger when I was sixteen."

"It's okay. I appreciate you sticking up for me."

Tate knew he ought to say something tough like, *It's my job*, but those weren't the words that exited his lips. Instead, he murmured, "Always," and watched, intrigued, as Lyla's eyes went soft as honey.

Before he could decide whether to kiss her or not, she spun toward the dance floor, though, jumpy as a jackrabbit at the sudden commotion out there. "What're they all doing?"

Tate glanced over. "Dancing, Lyla. That's called dancing. You may have heard of it."

"I know *that*!" she retorted, in annoyance. "But what kind is it?"

"Two-step. You wanna take a spin before we eat?"

"I don't know how to do that."

Tate grabbed her hand and dragged her toward the floor. "It's easy. Come on."

"Tate, I—"

He tucked Lyla into his arms and led her through a few steps, counting off the beat for her. Her nose crinkled up adorably as she concentrated on placing her feet, but the rigid set of her spine relaxed little by little as she got the hang of it.

Before long, Lyla was laughing and getting into it. "Hey, you're pretty good at this," she yelled above the music.

Tate shook his head. "I swear to God, you better not tell anyone—especially the guys from my team. I would never hear the end of it."

"Like I'm ever going to meet *them*," she scoffed.

Her certainty about that fact made Tate pause, but he went on, "Or Red and Luca. Definitely don't say anything to them, either."

"Tate, they're your best friends," Lyla argued. "They won't care."

"Lyla, those two got years of comedy out of the fact that I grew up in *Ohio*. What do you think they'd do with this information?"

"Okay, fine. You win," she relented. "But I want it on the record that I think boys are weird."

"We'll add you to the master list. Now—what do you say we get some food to go and head out of here? It's a nice night, and I know where we can see some stars before we head to Erie."

Lyla arched her perfect eyebrows at him, the epitome of feminine scorn. "I do not want to know how many women you've used that line on."

"No, you do not," Tate laughed, "But I am serious. Follow me to freedom. It's so quiet where we're going, you could even do your interview there."

NOT MUCH LATER, Tate found the turnoff he remembered and pulled his brother's old truck to the side of a dirt road that cut between two wide-open fields. He turned off the engine and looked around fondly.

In the summer, people brought picnic dinners here to watch the town set off fireworks. Other times, kids came here to play capture the flag, and teenaged couples came to find some privacy.

While Lyla called the reporter to do her interview over the phone, Tate got out and sat on the tailgate, remembering when he'd been something other than a blunt instrument of war.

He couldn't think about this kind of thing too much when he was overseas—it made him too homesick. But here, now…it was simply a joy to be home.

Muscle memory was strong, too. Once Lyla was done with her call, it took Tate all of five minutes to unroll his brother's sleeping bag in the truck bed and coax her into hopping up with him. True, he had to convince Lyla that he wasn't an ax murderer first, but that was a mystery writer for you—always suspicious.

They ate in companionable silence, sharing fries and trading bites of food like an old married couple, and Tate had to remember not to get ahead of himself. It wasn't his place to want more from her. He could only enjoy the here and now.

Once Lyla was done, she laid back, oohing and aahing at the inky expanse of sky dotted with glittering diamond stars. Tate stretched out beside her and marveled at how freaking beautiful she was, how smart and how...*saucy* she could be. She was, without a doubt, the perfect woman.

Teenage Tate's knees would've been knocking to be confronted with a female like her, but knowing him, he still would've gone for it, anyway. He chuckled, trying to picture how it might've gone.

"Why do I suspect you did this kind of thing a lot when you were eighteen?" Lyla murmured, turning to smile at him. It was like she could read his mind.

Tate laughed, "Whatever are you implying, Ms. Lawson?"

"Tell the truth." She poked him in the ribs. "This was totally your make-out spot, wasn't it?"

Well, she had him there. Tate cracked up. "Are you kidding? Of course, it was. I don't think I got laid in an actual bed until I was like twenty years old."

Lyla snorted. "Oh my God. Where did you go, then? Besides here, obviously."

Tate folded his arms behind his head and grinned up at the stars. "You name it. Parks, barns, cars, couches...the dorm stairwell a couple of times."

Her laugh was low and breathy, and for once he didn't mind getting called out for being a hound back in the day.

"And meanwhile," Lyla said, "I didn't sleep with anyone at all until I was 22."

"You serious?" That was interesting. Tate rolled to his side so he could see her better. "Why so late?"

"Is that late?"

Tate shrugged. To him, maybe—but to a woman like Lyla perhaps it was exactly right.

"There wasn't some big reason," she murmured. "Just super picky, I guess."

Tate turned back to the blanket of night arched over their heads, liking knowing that little detail about her. He had not been picky at all, but at least he'd been with some very nice girls over the years, and he had some fun memories of them, hazy as they were.

None were like Lyla, however. Not even close. And while it was entirely possible that this book tour was all he'd ever get the chance to have with her, he didn't think he would ever forget a single second of it. Didn't that just figure.

AX MURDERER CONCERNS aside, Lyla was not immune to the romance of a summer night in the country. She and Tate spent a couple of heated hours out there enjoying each other before he finally conceded that they ought to get moving again.

They took a roundabout route to Erie and were in the process of checking in to the hotel when Lyla got a phone call from her parents.

"Hi guys," she said, juggling her purse and the handle of her rolling suitcase. "We just got to the hotel in Erie. Can I call you back in a couple of minutes?"

She waited until Tate cleared their suite, then kicked off her shoes and dialed them back. In moments it turned testy, and Lyla was hanging up angry again.

She didn't seem like the type to have such a rocky relationship with her folks, and it had Tate wondering.

Once they'd showered and put on pajamas, he asked her, "What was the deal with that call, anyway?"

"It's nothing," she sighed. "My parents are good friends with their neighbors, but the couple is really annoying, that's all. I love my folks, but I just get tired of hearing about every little thing their buddies say and do. And I kid you not—their last name is even Jones. My mom and dad are *literally* keeping up with the Joneses."

"Hello, suburbia," Tate smiled.

"And, since I can't tell my parents that I've acquired a lunatic superfan," she complained, "those people are, like, all we have to talk about."

"First, you have a *stalker*, not a superfan. And second, why can't you tell them about your stalker?"

Lyla rolled her eyes. "Tate, much as you'd like the world to believe it, I know you did not simply spring from the earth one day in all your fabulous glory. You have parents. What would they say if you told them some weird freak had started sending you scary letters and might possibly be staking you out?"

"Okay, we clearly need to get a few things straight here. Yes, I did so spring from a very manly patch of ground, fully-formed and immediately magnificent. However, shortly after that I was taken in and raised by a kindly couple who taught me not to brag about it."

"Oh, my God. It never ends with you, does it?"

Tate barreled on, "Second, they are deeply aware of the fact that I chose a career in which people regularly want to shoot at me, and do. So…there's that."

"So, what you're saying is, your war games trump my superfan."

"He's a stalker, Lyla. A *stalker*." Her refusal to call the asshole by the correct noun was going to drive him insane. "And no, what I'm telling you is that—much like the lovely folks who fed and housed me until adulthood—your parents are grown-ups and can probably handle the truth from you."

"You haven't met them," she muttered.

"True. But I've met you, and I've got a sneaking suspicion you didn't turn out this way in a vacuum."

Lyla glared at him from behind her cute glasses, wrinkling up her nose and looking not the least bit mean. "What way is that?"

Tate smirked at her and tugged on a lock of her silky hair. "Oh, completely terrifying, of course."

She threw up her hands and stomped as far away as she could get—which, given the dimensions of the hotel suite's sitting area, wasn't more than about eight feet.

"What did I do to deserve you? Piss off some god out there in the ether, or what?"

"You act like I'm a punishment."

"Aren't you?"

"You wound me." Tate moved closer and snaked an arm loosely around her waist. "And here I thought I was your reward for good behavior." Lyla sniffed but she didn't pull away, so he pulled her in next to him.

"What makes you think I've been good?" she asked, a sexy, teasing tone creeping into her voice.

Tate's whole body warmed up real quick when he heard that. "Oh, I'm dead certain you've been good," he told her. "And I hope you'll be even better somewhere in my immediate vicinity. Any minute now."

Lyla closed her eyes in exasperation, but God love her, she couldn't resist him. She burst out laughing and finally hugged him back. "How in the world did your poor mother survive you? How does anyone?"

"I don't know what you mean. I get thank you notes for being awesome all the time. Every day, almost."

"Please shut up," Lyla said, and then planted a hearty incentive right on his puss.

When they came up for air again, Tate wondered, "No joke, though. Your folks have got to read your books. It's not like the concept of high-profile people with stalkers will be alien to them."

"I will grant that they probably know about stalkers. However, they do not read my books. They think they're too scary."

While Tate had also not read any of her books, he found that difficult to believe. "Well, what do they read, then?"

"Mom likes women's fiction with no sexy times. Dad just reads the paper and does crosswords."

"Hell, Lyla—the newspaper's way scarier than some crime thriller," Tate protested.

"Don't I know it. I get some of my best ideas from the news."

"I still think you should tell them," he urged her.

"Tate, you have your arms around a willing woman and you're two feet from a bed. Do you *really* want to keep talking about my parents with me?"

"You make an excellent point."

"I have others. Come here and let me tell them to you."

Eighteen

RATHER THAN LEAVE Erie right after Lyla's signing the following morning, as most people would expect them to do, Tate suggested to Lyla that they change things up and stay on at their current hotel.

And so, instead of checking out, they booked another night and left their things in the suite while they went to the bookstore hosting her event. Afterward, they lingered over lunch and decided to leave for her signing in Elmira the next day.

With the rush hour traffic to consider, it left them less time to get there than Lyla was generally comfortable with, but again— they were trying to behave unpredictably.

It wasn't that Lyla disagreed with Tate's plan, she thought, pushing the last few shreds of lettuce around her bowl—she just hoped that ditching Trident's publicized tour schedule worked, and that there wouldn't be another peep from her superfan for the next few weeks.

Once they got back to New York, Lyla would probably need to come up with a new plan, since Tate was going to be returning to his unit soon. She'd cross that unhappy bridge when she came to it, though, and hopefully, he'd help her figure something out before he left.

For now, all she needed to do was try to relax and get some words down on the new book. So they paid the check and drove back to their hotel, Tate alert for any hint of something amiss the whole time.

Lyla hadn't been herself the last couple of days, but simply hanging out in the room with him helped dispel enough of Lyla's anxiety that she was sure she could get in a solid evening of work.

It felt companionable, being near him. Parked at the hotel desk with her laptop, Lyla barely had to turn her head to see Tate sprawled on the tacky brocade sofa nearby. He had headphones on and was watching a movie on his tablet, but winked devilishly whenever he busted her looking.

Tate had plans for later, that much was clear.

Lyla watched him periodically as she wrote, and gradually his traits began to seep into her story. She didn't see the harm, since Tate rarely read fiction. He'd never even know that she'd co-opted parts of him for her character.

Eventually, Lyla's fingers slowed on the keys and she had to admit that she was doing more staring and yawning than actual writing. She caught Tate's eye.

"I'm hitting the wall," she told him. "Will it bother you if I turn in?"

The politeness came out automatically, but Lyla could tell it exasperated him.

"No, Lyla, it will not bother me if you're sleeping in the next room. Just like it hasn't bothered me any of the other times you've done it."

A pink flush was creeping up from his collar, though, so Lyla wondered, "You sure about that?"

He shrugged and smiled sheepishly. "Maybe we need to define bothered."

It'd bothered her, too. Having Tate sleeping mere feet away night after night had driven her slightly nuts—she'd tossed and turned for hours, picturing Tate spread across stark white hotel sheets, those thick biceps on display.

Now, she knew firsthand what he looked like with nothing on but a smile. Tate's tousled, sandy blond hair got even messier. His skin grew warm. His stomach was flat and taut, his thighs thick with muscles, his…

She snapped her laptop shut and jumped up. "Okay! Well, good night. Feel free to join me when your movie is over."

"Movie? What movie?" And then Tate commanded, "Hang on," stopping Lyla before she took more than two steps. "Let me check the other room one more time before you go in."

"Tate, we've been here all afternoon. I'm sure it's fine. We would have heard something if it wasn't."

"Even so. After what happened in Cleveland, I'd rather take another look. Stay here."

Lyla rolled her eyes and flopped back down, and Tate slipped into the attached bedroom.

"You know you just want to paw at my underwear in peace," she called.

"It's more fun when it's actually on you." He clicked on the light, then roared, "God *damn* it!"

Lyla shot out of her chair. "What?"

"*Fuck*. Fuck, fuck, *fuck*," Tate growled, stomping around next door.

"Tate?" She took a couple of steps toward the doorway, only to be met by his bristling body blocking the opening.

"You stay right there. Don't come a step closer, you hear me?"

"What's going on?"

"I'm not fucking around, Lyla. I don't want you to see this."

"There's something in there? How is there something in there!"

"I don't know, but I'm not fucking happy about it. Now sit down right there where I can see you and don't move."

"*Tate*," Lyla pleaded, hating how her voice shook. "You're scaring me."

He took a deep breath and shook his head, clearly trying to calm down. "I know. I'm sorry. Just…just try to stay put for a minute while I take some pictures and make a couple of calls. Do not come in here, no matter what, okay?"

"Can I do anything to help?"

"When, uh…when the cops get here, you can let them in. But make sure they show you their IDs first. Don't let them in if they won't."

Lyla sank to her knees on the carpet and watched his big frame move back and forth across the doorway, while Tate phoned the police, and then the hotel staff. He took photos with his phone from every possible angle, but she still couldn't see what had him so upset.

Maybe that was a good thing, though. Tate wasn't exactly prone to overreaction, and he hadn't even been this shaken when her fan had slipped those photos under the door in Cleveland.

Soon, Lyla heard sirens approaching outside, and a few minutes after that someone in the hall was shouting and pounding on the door. She got up and went to look out of the peephole.

However, Tate had apparently rethought the job he'd given her, because he cut her off and pointed her toward the couch, instead. "Stay there," he barked, with one hand on the knob. And then, more gently, "Please."

Any desire to argue flew right out of her when she saw the look on Tate's face. He was pale and grim, with two flags of color high on his cheekbones, and the tendons in his neck stretched tight as bows.

Lyla did as she was told and once she was in place, Tate let in the two uniformed officers, speaking rapidly as he led them to the other room.

While she watched and waited, they were joined by the hotel manager and staff security guards, and then by a second set of plainclothes police officers carrying a bunch of forensic equipment.

Apparently, the Erie PD had better staffing—or more time on their hands—than their counterparts in Manhattan. Or maybe it was just a slow night.

Lyla's breath was coming short and shallow in her chest. Her ears picked out Tate's voice from the crowd next door, seizing on the deep authority in it like a life raft amidst the turmoil swirling in the suite.

Two of the cops came over to squat next to her, wanting to know if she'd seen or heard anything unusual since she and Tate had returned to the room earlier.

"I was working," Lyla said. "And it was just the two of us in here. I didn't hear anything else."

"And did you…"

They trailed off when Tate walked over and stood next to the sofa, arms crossed across his chest as he stared down at them. Her bodyguard's face was stony. The only signs of life were the vein pulsing at his temple and the way his chest rose and fell like a bellows.

"Are we in danger right now?" she asked him.

Tate told the officers, "I hope you understand, but Ms. Lawson's safety is my top priority. I'd like to get her out of here as soon as possible. What can we take with us and how soon can we leave?"

"We have a few more questions for both of you before you can take off. If we need to follow up later, we'll call you," the cops replied, then got to their feet. "As for what you can take, we're looking at the whole suite as a crime scene—especially until we can determine how the perp got in here. So…"

The hotel manager walked up, waving his cell phone. "I can help there. One of my housekeepers has just reported that her master key is missing."

The officer nodded. "Okay, we'll need to talk to her as soon as possible." He turned back to Tate and Lyla. "You two can head out now, but give us your cell numbers before you go. Until we can process the scene, your luggage needs to stay here."

Tate clearly didn't like the sound of that. He immediately countered, "Ms. Lawson's purse, laptop, and briefcase were never out of our sight or possession all day today. Same for my tablet and go-bag over there."

The cop nodded. "Fine, you can take those. Don't go far, though, in case we need to see you again tonight."

Tate explained, "Ms. Lawson has scheduled events that she can't miss in Elmira tomorrow. But we can stay in town until then."

The hotel manager bowed slightly. "If I may, we'd be honored to offer you another, upgraded room at no charge—"

Tate's scowl was immediate and ferocious. "With all due respect, sir, you currently have a master key in the wind. We won't be staying anywhere under your roof tonight."

The man shrank back. "Of course. I understand."

Tate bustled over to the desk and began gathering Lyla's computer and notebooks into her briefcase, then jammed her cell phone and charger into her purse. He offered her his hand. "You ready, Slick?"

Lyla shrugged. She still had no idea what the hell was happening here, and wasn't entirely sure that leaving the protection of all these cops was the best course of action.

She trusted Tate more than any of them, though, so she said, "I guess."

"Alright, then let's roll."

Lyla stood up and was completely confused when her knees buckled.

"*Shit*," Tate muttered darkly. "Are you going into shock?"

"I don't know. I've never been in it before."

"Okay. Well…first let's get you out of here, and then we can get you all fixed up once we find a new place to crash. Sound good?"

Lyla nodded, so he slipped an arm around her waist, glared at the hotel security guards, and hustled her out the door.

IN THE ELEVATOR, Tate handed Lyla her purse and laptop so he could keep one hand wrapped around her arm once they reached the lobby, and the other—the one she abruptly realized was holding a gun—free to shoot.

He dragged her across the dark parking lot, scanning back and forth like someone in an action movie, while Lyla stumbled and tried to keep up with his longer strides. In seconds, Tate had her buckled in the truck and was peeling away like a bat out of hell.

They drove rapidly through neighborhoods and side streets for an hour or more, taking turn after turn while Tate watched his mirrors in dogged silence.

Lyla held out her hands and watched fine tremors quiver through her fingers. She couldn't seem to stop swallowing nervously, and her breathing sounded all wrong. She was freezing, too, despite the balmy weather.

Tate, on the other hand, was pissed as hell but otherwise looked fine—not a quiver or a whimper to be seen, of course. This little soiree, whatever it was, was probably small potatoes compared to what he normally did for a living.

Which only made Lyla more embarrassed that she couldn't control her own body's responses to the situation.

Considering all the dark books she'd written in her career, it seemed strange that this felt so much scarier. Maybe that was because Lyla was only used to bad things happening to made-up people, instead of to her.

Or perhaps her fear came from not knowing what all the characters were thinking, or how the story was going to end.

Lyla had been in *that* position before, however. Fortunately for her, writer's block never lasted long—at some point, all the pieces in play resolved themselves in her brain and became very clear. It was that knowledge, for whatever reason, that settled her now.

Soon they'd figure out who was targeting her, and why. And before long, the story's ending would reveal itself. Until then, she had Tate.

By the time he pulled into the quiet lot of another hotel across town, and turned to ask her if she was doing okay, Lyla was ready for him.

"Yep," she answered. "Though I wish they'd let us take our stuff. I could use a long-ass shower and my PJs."

Tate didn't look like he believed her, but he still answered, "Same here. But we can use the hotel toiletries tonight, and since none of our luggage was, uh…near what happened…I bet the cops will let us pick up our bags tomorrow morning."

"I hope they do. I have another signing to get to."

Tate's mouth was a hard, straight line. "Only if it's safe, Lyla."

She studied him for a moment, then asked, "Are you planning on telling me what happened back there?"

Tate looked away, staring into the dark clutch of trees crowding against the side of the lot. Eventually, he blew out a long breath and said, "I don't want to. But let's get you inside, and then we'll see if you can convince me it's a good idea."

HE BOOKED THE room under Mr. and Mrs. T. Assateague. Lyla tried not to react outwardly, but she couldn't deny the little thrill that small detail gave her, even under these circumstances.

Being the wife of a man like Tate would be something all right. If and when he was ever ready to cast that role, however, Lyla would be well out of the picture.

Tate had said himself he wasn't the type to keep up a long-distance relationship, and she knew he'd never give up his beloved career for a woman he'd only known for a matter of weeks.

Once Tate got cleared to return to duty and the cops caught the dumbass who kept bothering her, she'd probably never see him again.

It was just as well, Lyla supposed. It would kind of suck to have to rub shoulders with him all the time and know there was no chance for more. This way, they could both go on with their lives like their brief relationship was no big whoop.

And it wasn't—not really. Lyla and Tate were just a woman and her bodyguard, enjoying some sexy, but temporary, side benefits.

She tried to keep those benefits front and center in her mind while Tate secured the room, triple-checked it to make sure it was safe, and then accepted her offer to use the shower first.

He didn't act the least bit self-conscious when he emerged from the bathroom with only a small, threadbare towel wrapped around his waist. And Lyla wasn't terribly ashamed to be caught staring, either.

Still, she supposed they had some business to take care of first, so she put her sinful thoughts about GI Joe aside and went to soak her head under the scalding shower spray.

When Lyla got out, Tate was dressed in a pair of gym shorts he must've had stashed in his go-bag. He offered her a clean t-shirt he pulled from it, too—but he didn't make a single joke about them sharing clothes or Lyla's lack of pants.

Distracted as she was by all the tantalizing chest on display, it took her a little while to realize Tate was still fuming.

If there was any human being more reliably cheerful than Tate Monroe, then she hadn't met them yet. But Lyla hadn't realized how much she'd been counting on his indefatigable affability until it was gone.

"Dare I ask how many times you've masqueraded as—what was it? Mr. Assateague?" she asked, hoping to lighten his mood.

"Never had to before now. Let's just hope no one knows it's me."

"Why on earth would they ever connect it to you?"

Tate stared at her. "Because it's my middle name, Lyla. It was stupid of me to use it, but I choked and couldn't think of anything else."

"Really?" She sat down and cocked her head, examining him. "That is a very…interesting name."

He groaned and paced around. "Maybe a little too interesting. It'll stand out if someone takes a look at the guest list."

"Tate, no one knows we're here. And we'll be gone again before they could possibly check the lists of every hotel in town."

"That's the idea—but we also don't know who we're dealing with. They might have resources we aren't aware of."

The air was fresh with the clean fragrance of the hotel soap, but it seemed very sparse and hard to breathe with Tate prowling around in it. Tension crackled off his body and Lyla began to wonder…was he angry with *her*, for some reason? Did he think this was all her fault?

Lyla stood and moved to the bed against the wall, then pulled the covers over her legs. She felt like hiding, but forced herself to face him.

"Tate. Come on. Tell me what's going on."

"Christ. You're not really going to make me do this, are you?"

She couldn't take her eyes off all the coiled energy jumping under his skin. Only something big would have had this kind of effect on him.

"Do what? Make you talk to me?"

"Yeah. For starters."

"But this whole thing is *about* me. Don't you think I have a right to know what's going on?"

"Actually, no. Not this time, I don't."

Lyla stared at him. "You think this is all my fault, don't you? You think I did something to bring this on myself."

Tate whirled on her. "Jesus, Lyla, *no*. Of course not. I'm just so…goddamned…" He paced back and forth, then threw his hands wide. "…furious." At last, he stopped moving and sank down on the mattress opposite her.

"Well that's obvious," she whispered, despising how small her voice sounded.

His eyes were glued to her face. "I'm angry and I'm upset, it's true. I just can't figure out how that bastard got past me, and it's making me crazy."

"You're scaring me."

Tate blinked at that. "I'm really sorry," he started. "I don't know how your stalker got in there, but he was gone again by the time we came back. You know *that*, right?"

Lyla shook her head. "No, I didn't know that, because you haven't *told* me anything. And I'm afraid to ask more because it seems like you're mad at *me*."

Tate set his elbows on his knees and propped his head in his hands. He looked like the statue of an ancient warrior come to life.

"God, I'm terrible at this shit." He raised his head to look at her. "Sweetheart, I'm mad at myself and I'm mad at that freaking sociopath, but I am not mad at you. I swear."

"Tate, what happened?" Lyla pleaded. "You have to tell me, or my mind is going to concoct all kinds of crazy stuff."

"To be honest, I really don't want to upset you more. Maybe it's better for you not to know."

"I disagree. It feels worse not knowing, trust me."

Tate gazed at her, obstinately mute.

"You do realize I make up stories like this for a living, right? In all likelihood, I've come up with far worse things than whatever happened tonight." It was the truth, but Lyla wondered if she really knew what she was talking about.

"He left a message for you," Tate capitulated. "Let's put it that way. It was weird and frightening, and all over the wall and the bed. I know the cops are probably going to tell you everything at some point, but…"

"How do we know it was even meant for me?" Lyla interjected. "Maybe—"

Tate waved her off. "Because your picture was everywhere, okay? Can we leave it at that? He had copies of your face spread all over his little art installation, and a nice succinct message to go along with it. Is that enough for you, or do you need more?"

"I think that's enough," Lyla admitted softly. And even as amped-up as Tate looked, she still longed to cross the small divide between the beds and crawl into his lap so he could comfort her.

The way his super-human body was put together, she was awfully glad he was the one standing between her and whoever was out there.

She needed to let him off the hook, now. Lyla said, "So…Assateague, huh?"

Tate sighed and slumped back. "My mom loves horses, and my dad took her there one time when she was pregnant with me. Naturally, Tom's always enjoyed emphasizing the *Ass* part."

"Oh no."

"Not in front of Mom, though. She would've killed him."

"What's *his* middle name? Just for reference?" Lyla smiled.

Tate's face softened. "Tahoe." When Lyla frowned, he added, "We suspect that's where he was conceived, but I really don't want to think too much about it, obviously."

"Geez, all I got was *Katherine*. It seems really boring, all of a sudden."

Tate smiled at her, but for some reason, Lyla began shivering again. She was suddenly ice cold, despite the humidity pervading the air from their back-to-back showers, and then, inexplicably, she had to squeeze her eyes shut just to keep them from overflowing.

In an instant, Tate was next to her, wrapping Lyla in his arms and enveloping her in the comfort of his warmth.

"Hey," he murmured, "I'm not gonna let anything happen to you, sweetheart. I promise." His big hands stroked up and down her back.

A week ago, when Lyla kissed Tate for the first time, she'd wanted to chastise herself for her lapse. She was a professional, after all, not some lonely heart with dubious morals. But the heady combination of Tate's strength and sweetness were making her realize she was up against more than the usual kind of man.

Tate Monroe was a force of nature, and he checked every box she had.

Lyla tried to laugh at herself, but it came out watery and unsteady. "I'm sorry. I'm being a big baby," she told him.

She hadn't seen what Tate had seen—so instead of trying to get him to lighten up, she ought to be giving him credit for trying his best to protect her from something that worried even him.

"Give yourself a break," he murmured. "This whole thing is really stressful. Both of us are bound to feel it."

"I don't want to be scared anymore."

"I know."

"How did he find us, Tate? We changed out the truck and everything," Lyla sniffed.

"Christ, you're shaking like a leaf." Tate pulled back to study her face, then said, "Come here, Slick. Lay down with me."

"Okay." When Tate stretched out beside her and opened his arms, she snuggled in tight.

"I'm going to fix this, Lyla. I promise you."

Lyla held on and prayed he was right.

Nineteen

TATE LAID AWAKE for most of the night, stroking Lyla's hair whenever she stirred and trying to parse the problem. They had an information leak, obviously, and they had to plug it immediately.

It was difficult to imagine that Red hadn't personally vetted his employees as soon this issue had arisen, particularly since Tate's buddy had been concerned enough to take the step of hiring a bodyguard for Lyla.

Furthermore, Lyla considered the people at Trident her friends—she couldn't have known most of them for long, but he wasn't prepared to doubt her instincts about people just yet.

He had a hunch that the leak wasn't coming from her publisher, anyway.

He simply couldn't unravel how Lyla's stalker kept finding them, over and over, wherever they were. It was maddening. More than that, though, it was worrying.

Soon enough, Lyla was going to read that latest police report and learn what Tate already knew—her stalker had moved past merely gloating about the error of Lyla's ways.

The guy was truly incensed now, and it seemed likely it was because Tate had come on board and was standing in his way.

Not likely, he corrected himself—certain. Tate didn't think he'd ever be able to scrub the image of the stalker's last set-up from his brain, and that wing of the old memory banks was already chock-full of ghastliness.

Countless photos had been strewn around that hotel bed and stuck to the wall behind it, splattered with blood-red paint. Most of them had been some old promotional shot of Lyla, but they'd all been stabbed and gouged right between the eyes.

That was disturbing, to say the least.

However, some of the pictures had been of Tate. The photo looked like the one his parents' local paper had run, back when they'd written an article about him coming home wounded after his stay at Landstuhl.

Those copies weren't just stabbed—they'd been shredded into jagged, angry pieces, and Tate would have been lying if he said that didn't piss him off.

Lyla wouldn't have been infuriated by the sheer malice involved, though—she'd have been scared, and Tate didn't know which part of the scene would've upset her the most. She was just as likely to be disconcerted about the threat to him, as she'd be about the one to her.

The worst thing of all, however, had been the note finger-painted on the wall, in that same red paint. *Only the ignorant would keep ignoring me. Soon you'll suffer for your wrongs. Soon.*

BY THE TIME dawn sent pink streaks across the horizon, Tate had managed to formulate his next steps.

First, he had to call Red and get his friend up to speed. The guy needed to look through his organization one more time, to make absolutely sure the private details of Lyla's tour weren't getting out that way.

Tate also wanted to see about postponing—or even canceling altogether—the events that were left, to give Lyla some added protection.

Next up was getting back their stuff. He'd had a brief call from one of the Erie PD officers late last night, letting him know they could pick up their luggage from the station later this morning. Tate added that errand to his list and starred it. Lyla would want some fresh clothes as soon as possible.

As much as he'd enjoyed it, he could hardly expect her to go waltzing around in one of his t-shirts all day—not in public, anyway.

After that, Tate supposed he had to give Detective Scarletti a heads-up that the officers in Erie would be calling him. Scarletti would not be thrilled to discover that he had the wrong perp in custody, and knowing him, he'd probably try to blame Tate for it, somehow.

That was what happened when you rushed to judgment and didn't examine all the facts, however. Tate wasn't the least bit sorry the dude was about to get burned. If Scarletti had taken the threat to Lyla more seriously from the get-go, they might not be where they were now.

Lyla was beginning to shift restlessly in her sleep beside him. Tate kissed her awake then shooed her cutely groggy butt into the shower, in case Red couldn't do anything about moving her signing in a few hours.

Reluctantly, he also put aside the predictable desire to join Lyla under the hot spray, in favor of ordering them some breakfast from room service.

Crapping out on Lyla once had been plenty—and as exhausted as he was right now, Tate did not want to head out on an empty stomach and risk a reenactment.

While he waited for their food to be delivered and for Lyla to finish up in the bathroom, he wondered whether he'd have to prop his eyelids open with toothpicks later today. Insomnia sucked, and starting his day tired wasn't particularly helpful when he had to stay alert more than ever now.

Tate pulled his list in front of him once more. In the margin at the top, he added *FIND COFFEE*, then used his phone to search for the best place in town.

TATE AND LYLA were on the road and nearly to Elmira when they got word from Red's assistant that the morning's signing had been canceled, along with a few others scheduled for the next two weeks.

Tate had only gotten one cryptic text from Red that said, *On it,* though. While he was grateful his message had clearly been received and acted on, Tate wished he'd been able to confer with his friend in person.

Unfortunately, he and Lyla also hadn't heard a peep from Scarletti—they'd both left messages on the detective's voicemail, but he hadn't seen fit to return their calls, as yet.

Tate fervently hoped that was because Scarletti was too busy springing his hoarder lady and dealing with the Erie cops—and not because he was being a sore loser.

Tate had placed one other call that morning, however, while Lyla used the ladies' room at the coffee shop in Erie. That was the one eating at him the worst right now. Since he had other legitimate reasons to keep checking his phone, he didn't feel any need to mention it to Lyla.

But for crying out loud—how long were those Med Board fuckers going to make him wait before they deigned to share the results from his second evaluation? Amidst all the other crap going on with this stalker shithead, Tate was sick of privately climbing the walls, hoping for word.

It wasn't like he could just up and leave Lyla now—not when the danger to her appeared to be getting more serious, and more imminent. But it sure would be nice to at least have a date scheduled for his return to active duty, so Tate could prepare for it.

He peeked at Lyla over on the passenger side. She was alternating between frowning absently at the passing scenery and scribbling in her notebook, as she often did on the road.

If all went well, he might only have a few more weeks left with her, and the thought left an uncomfortable tightness in his chest. Tate took a hand off the wheel and scrubbed at it.

He was probably just hungry.

"Hey, you ready for some lunch?" he asked Lyla. "There's a rest stop coming up here in a few more miles."

"Sure, I could eat," she murmured, not bothering to look at him.

Hoping for some company, he said, "I wish one of those people would call us back."

Lyla gave him a distracted, "Hmm," wrote some more, and then looked back up like she was just returning to the world in front of her. "At least Trident got us the morning off, though, right?"

"Right."

Lyla still had a book club she'd arranged to meet with later on, but that had been done privately, outside the scope of the Trident tour.

Because of that, they'd decided she would keep that appointment, but Tate intended to stick to her side through the whole thing. He couldn't care less if it raised awkward questions, either.

AFTER TATE DOWNED a few cheeseburgers and Lyla demolished a salad the size of her head, she ducked into the rest stop women's room and he seized the opportunity to make one more personal call.

Tate grabbed a table a few steps from the ladies' room entrance, pulled a chair around so he could watch for Lyla, and crossed his fingers that she would take her usual sweet time in there.

Then he dialed his buddy Luca and hoped he'd catch him at a good time.

As world-reknowned physicians went, Luca was chill. He was zen, in that laid-back *life-is-short* way that Italians had a lock on. Tate was banking on him knowing what Tate should do about all of this simmering frustration crawling around under his skin, and he suspected Luca would be quicker about it than the therapist Tate was supposed to check in with periodically.

After only two rings, the good doctor answered with a delighted, "Tate! *Ciao!*"

"Hey, dude," Tate said. "You got a minute?" He'd need at least that long to complain about Red's disappearing act today.

Once Tate was finished whining, Luca explained, "I think he took Piper away for the weekend. That's probably why. What's going on?"

He updated him on the stalker and the book tour from hell, which, unfortunately, took quite a bit longer than his Red issue. Hopefully, Luca wouldn't wax poetic now, though, since Tate really needed to leave time for the Q and A session at the end.

In response, his friend only sighed and said, "Love makes a man do crazy things."

"That isn't love, *cazzo*—it's obsession. Lyla's really scared of this guy."

"What about you?" Luca asked.

For the sake of brevity, Tate was honest with him. "Dude, I'm freaking worried."

"Because you don't know who it is?"

"Not that so much, even though it would be nice to know. I'm more concerned that I won't be able to keep Lyla safe when the shit hits the fan. And it's going to, believe me."

Luca grunted. "I have always thought that was a disgusting phrase."

"Worse than *porca puttana?*"

Luca cleared his throat. "Anyway, do you really think it's going to come to that?"

Tate thought about it. "As of yesterday, the NYPD was convinced Lyla's stalker was some lady who collects too many books. But I think this thing has asshole-man written all over it. You, too, right?"

"Absolutely. Scorned women use scalpels—very sharp and patient scalpels. Scorned men, however, wield hammers."

"That's the truth," Tate said. "Which means I have a heavy hammer headed right for me, and I have no idea how I'm supposed to prepare for it."

"But you love her," Luca retorted. "You'll think of something."

"*Christ*, Luca—what is it with Italians and love? I only met Lyla a few weeks ago."

"So what? With love, sometimes it only takes seconds. For example, Daisy and I think that Lyla fell half in love with *you* before she even met you."

"That's..." Tate's breath lodged in his lungs. "*What?*"

"We were all out at this bar and we were talking about how you should've been there. Daisy drew the funniest cartoon about you. And Lyla kept it, you know. She was, uh...*incantare.*"

Tate hastily typed the unfamiliar word into his phone's translation app and stared down at the answer he got. *Bewitched.* No way.

"How in the hell..." he began, then refocused. "You know what, never mind. You're nuts. You're so drunk on Daisy, you don't even know what you're talking about."

"Oh, I do so," Luca retorted. "You forget I diagnose people for a living, *mio fratello.*"

"Why do I continue to call you? Why?" Tate wondered morosely.

"Because I myself am lovable, in addition to handsome and intelligent. You obviously admire me and want to learn all you can from me."

"Invariably, I hang up more agitated than when the call began," Tate muttered to himself.

"Tate, that's only because you're at the falling-in-love stage where you're still fighting the inevitable. But don't worry. We all go through it."

"Luca, I already told you—Lyla is my job, not my love interest."

"You'll feel so much better once you accept your fate," Luca countered.

"Will you knock it off?" Tate cried. "You sound like a fucking Jedi!"

His friend simply intoned, "Heed me. The doctor has spoken."

Tate groaned and seriously considered hanging up before Lyla could overhear even a word of this nonsense.

"Wait," Luca said suddenly. "Daisy says I did it wrong. I was supposed to say, *Spoken, the doctor has.*"

The combination of Luca's suave Italian accent and the worst Yoda impression Tate had ever heard released something that had been coiled tight in his chest all day. He let it go and laughed along.

"Dude, you've totally lost it."

"Strangely, I still feel fantastic."

Tate noticed Lyla making her way back out of the ladies' room, and told his friend, "Hey, I gotta run. I'll call soon, okay?"

"I look forward to it. Let's find a day when you and Lyla get back to town to all have dinner. Daisy is working her way through my family's cookbook and needs new taste-testers."

Tate stood up and returned Lyla's smile. "I'll let you know," he told Luca and hung up.

Lyla didn't *look* like she was bewitched by him. She looked exactly the same as she always did—gorgeous and completely out of reach for a guy who spent the majority of his time thousands of miles away from home.

It was a good sign the world had gone sideways, when the Army made more sense than civilian life did. Tate couldn't allow the idea of Lyla digging on him to gnaw at his focus, though, and that went double for the notion that Tate could love *her* eventually.

But even if it couldn't happen now…might it happen someday?

"I think I'm going to get some more tea before we head out," Lyla announced. "You want coffee?"

Tate peered at her face again. Still normal. "Yeah. Sure."

LYLA'S READING FOR the group of local book clubs was done in a wine bar late that afternoon. She stayed on for about an hour afterward, signing books, taking pictures, and socializing with the attendees.

Tate tried to stay close but out of her way, eventually stationing himself at the end of the bar, where he could keep an eye on Lyla, as well as the exits and bathrooms.

It was hard not to pick up on some of the conversational topics being bandied around, however. There were the usual inquiries about inspiration and real-life crimes, but there was also a long, disconcerting discussion with some of the folks about the intimate scenes in Lyla's books.

Tate hadn't known mysteries *had* sex scenes, but abruptly remembered Red telling him that was why Lyla was so perfect for Trident and its new Red Devil imprint—her books straddled a line between romance and mystery that made her the ideal crossover talent.

Tate was rabidly curious to hear more, of course, but couldn't risk coming off as too eager—so he ended up missing the bulk of Lyla's response when they asked if her real-life experiences had ever made it into any of her books.

He supposed he didn't need to know that, anyway. Tate could go on with his life, happily pretending like Lyla had never kissed another man but him, and that would be just fine, *thankyouverymuch.*

Sadly, now Tate never could read any of her books, either, because he'd probably spend every page wondering which ex of hers was about to get screwed by the heroine, then ambushed by the butler.

Regardless, by the time the event wrapped up, it was well past dinnertime, Tate was a horny mess, and Lyla wasn't the only one looking a little flushed from the merlot.

She was the only one he had to be concerned with, luckily.

Tate watched the way Lyla held herself as they walked to the car, that tell-tale combination of loose-limbed swagger and odd reticence acting like a neon sign that Lyla was a little tipsy but didn't want to show it.

Two or three glasses of wine on an empty stomach would do it to her, for sure. Even though she never swayed or stumbled, he knew Lyla would be mortified if Tate thought she couldn't hold her liquor—even if she couldn't, and he did.

Tate immediately snapped into solution mode—wracking his brain for the location of the restaurants and drive-throughs they'd passed on the way there. He had to be careful not to let on what he was doing, though.

"I'm getting hungry," he told her. "Feel like some burritos?"

"Hmm. I don't think so. Why don't we just see what they have at the hotel?"

More room service, which likely meant the usual sad selection of burgers, sandwiches, and salads. Tate figured if he never saw a chicken Caesar wrap again in his life, it would be too soon.

"We can. Or we can grab some take-out on the way," he tried again.

Lyla smiled sweetly at him, and it shot straight to his groin. "Whatever you want," she said. "You're the boss."

AND SO, BACK at the hotel, Tate let Lyla carry in the Thai food they'd ended up with, while he kept one hand on her back and the other free to grab for his weapon if he needed it. He guided her swiftly through the lobby and directly into an open elevator.

A conference looked to be underway in the ballrooms of the hotel and a horde of nerdy types followed them into the elevator car, laughing and chatting with each other about biometrics or some shit. It was crowded and stuffy, and the ride up to their suite felt eternally long.

Tate moved in front of Lyla and tried to hold some space open for her in the corner of the elevator. The crowd and the confined space were making him antsy, so when Lyla's perfect little body melted seductively against his back, he nearly jumped out of his skin.

Good thing he wasn't facing her, though. Tate only had so much control—and at this point, he was just unhinged enough that having a tipsy Lyla in a corner of an elevator made him liable to take her up against the wall, right there in front of everyone.

He glanced down at her over his shoulder, checking to make sure she was still okay—and was further undone by the mischievous, conspiratorial little smile she was shooting up at him.

Jesus.

Out in the hallway, Lyla snagged her heel on the carpet halfway to their room. She fumbled the food, Tate snatched her up, and a hop, skip, and a jump later—there he was, carrying her over the threshold like it was their freaking wedding night.

She was giggling. He was trying mightily not to kiss her senseless. But Tate had a job to do and a future she wouldn't be a part of, so he set his charge on her feet with a firm, "Stay here," and began sweeping the room.

Twenty

THE THRILL LYLA felt when Tate's eyes fell on her, during that racy discussion Lyla had with the book club ladies, was something she wouldn't have thought she was capable of, given what was going on with her superfan. But his gaze had been possessive and hot as the sun, and seared her from the inside out.

Combined with the slight buzz she was still sporting from all the wine, Lyla was eager to get Tate alone—and that was before she even got to the sexy little episode they'd had in the elevator.

Okay, so maybe her effort to settle her nerves had worked a little *too* well. Lyla wasn't going to lament where it might lead tonight—even if Tate was as sober as a judge.

As it turned out, however, watching him sift through the suite, serious and focused on his task, was even hotter than when he'd been mentally undressing her from his barstool.

Tate looked big and tough and ready to obliterate anything that tried to come between him and Lyla. *Huge turn on.*

And, while she knew she was supposed to hang out near the door so he could do his job, she couldn't help wandering closer so she could cop a feel of those arms.

"What are you up to, you little minx?" Tate muttered, slipping away to peer inside the closet.

"I'm *trying* to take your mind off the crappy day we've had," she said. "If you'd only stand still long enough."

"Hang tight, sweetheart. I'm almost done." He bent to search under the bed.

"That's what they all say."

Tate chuckled, gave the bedroom one last, searching look, then pulled her closer. "I'm surprised you're not exhausted. The last day or two have kind of sucked."

"I know. Are *you* tired?"

"A bit. I didn't exactly sleep through the night." Tate kissed the top of her head, then ran a hand down her back and smoothed it over the curve of her ass. "Mmmm, I like that," he growled.

Lyla let her hands do some exploring of their own.

"Well, this is very interesting. What do we have here?" she purred, palming him through his dress pants. "Hello, big boy."

Tate went still. "I hope you don't mind. I brought a friend along."

"Bit like bringing a cannon to a gunfight, isn't it?"

"Yeah, well—he's a male, Lyla, and you know how guys are," he gasped when she stroked him. "You give them one compliment and they're puffing out their chests and standing up straight, begging for more."

"I'm just a little surprised he's so tall, if you're as tired as you say."

"Have you ever even looked in a mirror?" he laughed breathlessly.

"Once or twice," Lyla grinned. "I don't suppose you brought anything for him to wear."

Tate extracted his wallet from his back pocket one-handed, flipped it open, and pulled out two condoms. He threw them on the bed with a huffy, "Always prepared, Slick."

She smirked at him and raised a finger. "I have a question."

"What a shocking turn of events."

"Were those condoms meant for me all along or had you been hoping for some different off-duty extracurriculars when we hired you?"

Tate rolled his eyes. "Lyla, I don't know how it couldn't be obvious by now—since I met you, there's been no room for anyone else."

"Because I'm your job."

"Because you're you."

But that wouldn't be the case for long, would it? Sometime soon, Tate would go back to his real life, and Lyla would be nothing more than a distant memory to him.

She shook off that disconcerting thought and said, "Second question."

"Have mercy. My nerves can't take all of these plot twists."

The thing Lyla really wanted to know was what came next for them, but she couldn't make herself ask it. Instead, she wondered, "Why are we still wearing pants again?"

"Lyla, you're kind of a dirty girl when you're drunk," Tate laughed. "You realize that?"

"Oh, and you aren't?"

"First off, I'm a dude. We're dirty every second of our lives. But you're nice—no one expects it from you."

"Oh, for the love."

"Seriously. It's like a science project for horny guys. Take one Betty Sue, mix with merlot, and *blammo*—cue the Bunsen burner."

Lyla shoved at his chest, but naturally, he didn't budge. "So what? Probably ninety-five percent of the women I know are like that. Why do you think people write so many country songs about it?"

Tate cocked his head and mused, "I might need to broaden my musical tastes."

"Among other things," she snorted. "And you're not fooling me, Tate Monroe. I've seen you two-step, remember?"

"Good. Now take off your pants," he fired back.

Lyla eyed him archly. "I don't understand why you think I'm so newsworthy, anyway. You might as well be the poster boy for the *stripper with the heart of gold.*"

"You got that right. *Lady in the streets, freak in the sheets*," he agreed with a smile. "Now, how about you ditch those jeans so we can actually get to the freak part?"

Lyla stared at him. For a long, laden pause, Tate stared right back. And then, they both broke at once, doubling over and laughing hysterically.

After a while, still wiping tears from the corners of his eyes, Tate tried to speak again. "Oh my God. You're…that's…that was…" He broke down into helpless giggles once more.

Lyla grinned at him. "You're fun."

He pulled himself together and lunged for her, taking Lyla down to the mattress in a way that was both rowdy and careful not to hurt her. "You take that back, you big bully," he said, nipping at her neck.

She squirmed, trying to slip out from under his bulky frame. "Never! I enjoy your company immensely and I'm not afraid who knows it!"

Tate wedged a hand under her ass and squeezed. "Damn it, Lyla," he chuckled. "Straighten up and fly right. I'm a hard-assed warrior, not some good-time Charlie. I eat things like fun for breakfast."

He blew a raspberry right on her sternum, making Lyla laugh so hard she could barely lob her next volley back at him. "That's so weird. All this time I thought it was oatmeal."

"Oatmeal! Shows what you know. That's the ground-up bones of my enemies." And then he started tickling her ribs.

Lyla screamed. "Wait! Wait, leave me alone! I—I have something that you want!"

"You're right about that, Slick."

"I'm serious! I'll trade you if you stop!"

He lifted his hands and narrowed his eyes, ready to dive back in if she was bluffing.

Lyla rolled away, digging into her pocket to find the slip of paper she'd stuck there earlier for luck. She pulled it free with a triumphant, "Ha! See this?"

Tate blinked in sudden confusion. "Is that my list?"

"Oh, so you admit this belongs to you?"

He scowled. "I admit nothing, you shrill little harpy."

Lyla unfolded the paper and read aloud, "*Buy snacks. Get gas. Call Mom.*"

"That could belong to anyone," he scoffed.

"*Tell Lyla she's beautiful,*" Lyla crowed, delivering her death blow.

Tate flopped on his back and covered his face with a groan, his neck turning a vivid shade of red.

"You think I'm pretty," she teased, "Don't you, Captain? And you wanted to make sure I knew it, too."

"I threw that list away," he mumbled from under his arm.

"It was in plain sight, on the floor next to my shoes," Lyla fired back. "And by the way—you're not supposed to throw away a list without completing all the tasks, Tate."

"I added it to the next day's list, okay?"

"And to the day after that, too? Because I found this one three days ago."

"And you *kept* it?" he protested, outraged. "What kind of psychopath are you?"

"One who wants to hear you say it."

Tate sat up and opened his mouth and suddenly, a duck began quacking somewhere in the other room.

They both froze, listening to the bizarrely incongruent sound. And then, in the time it took Lyla to inhale and ask what it was, Tate was up and off the bed, lunging for his cell phone.

"Hello?" he asked breathlessly. "This is Captain Monroe." He listened a moment, and his spine snapped ramrod straight. "Sir. Yes, sir."

Lyla sat up, too, and ran her hands over her hair and clothes even though no one but Tate was here with her. She trailed after him, curious.

When he saw her, Tate turned to the side and sat down on the couch.

"Yes, sir," he said. And then a tentative, "Right."

Lyla paced a couple of feet away, but it wasn't like that amount of space was going to give him any more privacy. It did give her a better view of Tate's face, though.

He held the phone to his ear and pinched the bridge of his nose as he listened for a while, then massaged his forehead. He dragged his hand down his face and glanced quickly at her.

Lyla smiled, then busied herself with unpacking the food they'd gotten for dinner. She laid out all the cartons on the hotel desk and fished around in the bag for the napkins and utensils.

When she checked on Tate again, he was staring at the ceiling with a look of frustrated disbelief. "Okay," he said at last. "I appreciate you letting me know." He paused, then replied, "No, let's set it up in Cleveland again, with Dr. Ross, if that's okay."

Lyla looked away, all traces of her former buzz completely extinguished by what was obviously a call from one of Tate's doctors. Maybe he'd be leaving for duty even sooner than she'd expected. If that wasn't a mood killer, then she didn't know what was.

Behind her, Tate murmured, "Yes. I understand. I will, thanks."

Lyla fumbled with one of the drinks in the take-out bag, the sweating can slipping out of her hand and dropping loudly on the desk.

She heard Tate stand up. He said, "Thank you. That's the plan," and then, "Okay, you too. Bye."

Lyla turned slowly around and met Tate's eyes. He didn't look frisky anymore—he looked wild. Almost…feral.

"Everything okay?" she asked, even though it was patently clear it wasn't.

"Yeah," he lied. "But you know what? I'm wiped out, and I'm only going to be more tired once I have a full stomach. Do you mind if I jump in the shower real quick now, just to get it out of the way?"

He wanted to get away from *her*, that much was clear. Unfortunately, their arrangement meant that Tate couldn't go very far.

Lyla choked back on all her other questions and told him, "Sure, go ahead. I'll probably shower in the morning, anyway."

"You don't have to wait if you're hungry. Eat without me if you want."

Lyla turned back to the food, stung that he wouldn't confide in her. "Okay. Thanks."

Tate plugged his phone into an outlet next to the TV, grabbed some things from his bag, and ducked into the bathroom without another word.

Lyla picked up her tofu pad Thai and sank into the ergonomic desk chair. Something was going on, but what? While she nibbled on her lukewarm noodles, she shuffled through possibilities.

The Army could have told Tate he was going back, or they could've said he wasn't ready yet. They could also have been calling Tate to tell him he was never going to return, and Lyla knew by now that he'd take that news the hardest.

But would he tell her which it was? She wanted to think they'd become friends, at least, if not something more than that. But maybe Tate could already sense that Lyla's feelings for him were crossing the line into something hard to manage.

Maybe keeping secrets was how he would keep her at arm's length until he was finally free to leave.

Over on the television console, Tate's cell began ringing again. Lyla wandered over and peered at the screen, and saw her boss's name flash before the call rolled into voicemail.

Shoot. They'd been waiting for that call—and Tate would be even more unhappy once he realized he'd missed it. Lyla bit her lip and tried to decide what to do.

A moment later, her phone began ringing, too. "Hey, Red," she said in relief. "You don't give up easily, do you?"

"Understatement of the year. Where's Tate?"

"He's in the shower. But his phone is next to mine, so I saw your call come in."

"Got it. Anyway, I'm sorry I couldn't get back to you guys earlier. Piper and I thought we'd check out the Catskills this weekend and cell service has been shitty, to say the least."

"It's okay. Did you listen to Tate's message?"

"I did. I'm sorry you're having to go through this, Lyla. Wayne's working with Trident PR to scrap as many of the remaining events as possible, okay? We might try to set up a few more back in town, but otherwise, we'll just shift the budget into alternative advertising for now. Oh, and Wayne's going to email you in the morning, so keep an eye out."

"Okay."

"I did leave him a voicemail, but will you reassure Tate that this stalker character isn't one of our people at Trident? We've looked at everyone, and so have the cops. They're all fine."

"That's good to hear. And Red, I do want to apologize for this whole mess," Lyla said. "I feel really bad that you took a chance on me, and now my weird fan could ruin the whole Red Devil launch."

"Lyla, it's not your fault, and it won't ruin a thing. We'll just pivot and attack it from a different angle."

"But if I don't do the last events, will my new series even have enough buzz to help you?"

"The book tour was a great idea, but it's not going to make or break the bigger picture. And we're not going to let your new books flop, Lyla. I promise."

"I'm not worried about myself. I just mean that—"

"I know what you meant. But the top priority right now is your safety. Everything else can be sorted out," her boss assured her. "How's it going with Tate?"

"Fine, so far. All things considered," Lyla told him a little guiltily. "We get along well, so there's that."

"I thought you might." Red paused for a minute, then asked, "How's Tate doing, otherwise? Does he seem like he's feeling okay?"

Lyla went on alert, wondering if Tate's friend was asking her to tattle on him. It felt disloyal, somehow, to report on Tate's continuing light sensitivity, or his dizzy spell from a few days back.

She said, "He seems to be good. I haven't noticed anything off at all."

She'd noticed other things, though—many handsome and enticing things, that Lyla wouldn't be allowed to keep.

"And he seems to be sleeping okay?" Red prompted.

Lyla squinted—it was a landmine question, obviously. If she and Tate were behaving themselves, she shouldn't know the answer to it.

"I assume so," she answered vaguely, and threw in a casual shrug that her boss couldn't even see. "You'd have to ask him that."

Red was quiet for a minute, then laughed loudly. "Nice save."

"What?"

"Hey, I gotta run. Piper says hi, and wants you to call her when you and Tate get back to town, okay?"

"Okay. Have fun on your trip."

"Will do. Call if you need anything else, and Lyla—stay safe. Let Tate help you."

"I will. Bye, Red."

Lyla disconnected the call and looked up to find Tate standing there studying her. His hair was damp, and he'd changed into a t-shirt and a pair of sweatpants, but his eyes still looked haunted.

"Feeling better?" she asked him.

He walked over and nodded but didn't quite meet her eyes. "Sure. Just…" he trailed off and poked at the food containers. "Which one of these is mine?"

"The one with the wide noodles, I think. It looks like it has beef in it."

Tate opened the lid, snapped apart a pair of disposable chopsticks, and crammed a big bite of food into his mouth. "I'm starved," he mumbled, chewing.

Lyla set her pad Thai aside. "That was Red. He called while you were in the shower."

"Really?"

"Yeah. He called you first, then tried me. He said he left you a message, and that my fan can't be anyone at Trident. They've all been cleared, supposedly. And they're working to cancel as many of the remaining events as they can, too."

"That's good," Tate said, swallowing. "So much for you getting out of New York being helpful, though—clearly, that was wishful thinking."

"Clearly."

Lyla watched Tate as he shoveled more food into his mouth, as industrious and efficient as a machine. She'd never seen him leave his food unfinished, and this time was no different. In minutes, he'd cleaned the container and was looking for more.

Tate was still restless and distracted, though. *Troubled.* Lyla was going to have to be the one to make the first move if she ever expected to draw him out of the shell he'd retreated into.

He grabbed the box of spring rolls, sat back on the sofa, and finally met her eye.

Lyla held his gaze, and then asked him softly, "What is it? What's going on?"

Twenty-One

TATE LOOKED INTO Lyla's sympathetic face and thought seriously about making something up, even knowing that she'd heard his half of that fucking conversation.

He simply couldn't do it, though.

"I got a call back from my PEBLO," he told her. At Lyla's look of confusion, he amended, "The Army caseworker assigned to me. I, uh…I left him a message this morning."

"And?"

Tate took a deep breath. Even though he should have expected something like this, it still felt like a punch in the gut. He'd had to go hide in the shower like a goddamn pussy, just so he could pull himself together enough to sit in the same room as Lyla without losing it.

"Well, I was expecting to be removed from the TDRL—essentially the disabled list, like they have in sports. I failed my first evaluation back at home, but I did another one in New York, right before we left."

"I see," she said, calm as can be.

"I failed again."

Lyla looked thoroughly aggrieved on his behalf. "What? *Why?* Look at you—you're fine."

"Apparently they disagree. They want to see me again in six to eight more weeks."

She picked up one of her chopsticks and poked grumpily at what was left of her dinner. "In Cleveland, right? I think I heard that at the end."

"Yeah," Tate agreed. It was hard to gauge her expression. He explained, "The doctors there know me a lot better than the ones who reviewed me in New York. I figure maybe they'll give me a fair shot. Fair-*er*, anyway."

Lyla's voice was laden with compassion when she spoke again. "Tate, I'm so sorry. Maybe this job was a bad idea. We've done so much driving and had some really late nights, and…hell, the stress alone has been a nightmare. If you still weren't feeling a hundred percent, I wish you would have said something."

Tate sighed. Her concern was sweet, but he couldn't let her think she was at fault in any way. "Okay, Slick—here's the deal. My head's *got* to be healed by now. I haven't had any major episodes, and as long as I avoid high-intensity exercise for the next few weeks, I should be good. I swear."

"But you had that bad dizzy spell. And it's obvious when the light is hurting your eyes."

Damn it—she wasn't supposed to mention that. "That's all better," Tate fibbed.

"Oh, really."

"And luckily, you're not in the Beatles, so we don't exactly need to hotfoot it out of your book signings, you know?"

"Not yet, anyway," Lyla said. "But you should know, this next book is going to be pretty awesome."

"And here I thought Trident was taking care of all your publicity."

"Every little bit helps, wiseass."

"*Now* you tell me."

Lyla dimpled over at him while she sucked on her soda straw. "I tell you everything. For example…"

Looking at the nervous expression that crept over her face, Tate couldn't help the flare of panic he felt. He also couldn't help what came out of his mouth next.

"There's more, though. Something no one else knows." That stopped whatever she was about to confess really quick.

"You know I love a good secret," she breathed, leaning in.

"I do. Which is why I'm going to tell you this, and then you are going to put it under super-spy lockdown, forever."

Lyla's eyes got wide behind her glasses, and she instantly mimed turning a key in front of her delectable peach-colored lips before throwing it over her shoulder.

"I don't think it's my head injury benching me anymore, Lyla." Tate could not believe he was telling her this. "I think it's my psychological evaluations."

Those perpetually kissable lips dropped open. "What?"

"I got a little too talkative when I was in the hospital in Germany. They've had me checking in with a shrink ever since. It's completely ridiculous."

"Is it? That doesn't seem like the kind of thing they'd do for no reason."

"Trust me, I'm fine. I said some stupid stuff and the Army overreacted, thinking I have survivor's guilt or some shit. That's why I don't want you to tell anyone. It's pointless—and my parents, and Red and Luca, are already acting like nervous nursemaids as it is."

Lyla studied him in that incisive way she had. Unfortunately, any vestiges of her earlier tipsiness appeared to be gone, so Tate couldn't count on her being inattentive or forgetful here.

In an even more depressing development, she'd also lost all traces of the silly affection she'd been lavishing on him when they'd entered this damn room.

"You're right. They all would be worried about that," Lyla mused. "But…what do the doctors in charge of your reviews think?"

This was the part that was utterly confounding him, because Tate didn't *know*. "I'm not sure," he admitted. "During both evaluations, they asked me a lot of questions, and it was obvious they were waiting for me to say something specific. I just can't seem to figure out what it is."

"I'm not sure that's how it's supposed to work."

"It's a game, Lyla," Tate explained irritably. "I take the right steps, and they let me move forward. But because it's the Army, they like to make the actual rules kind of murky. Keeps it interesting for them, I guess."

Lyla took a deep breath and held it, and Tate didn't like the look of that furrow in her brow. "Tate—" she began.

His cell phone went off again, bleating out the old-school reveille ringtone that signaled an unknown caller. Talk about being saved by the bell—Tate was pretty confident this counted as divine intervention.

He glanced at the screen but didn't recognize the digits. Just in case, he answered, "This is Captain Monroe."

"Tate the Great!" his teammate Tank yelled. "How the hell are you, buddy?"

"Tank?"

"You know it, baby."

"Oh my God, who was stupid enough to give you a phone, man?"

"Don't ask. They gave us a couple days of R&R, so I caught a ride to fucking Amman with a friend. I promised the other guys I'd try to catch you while I was here."

"I'm glad," Tate said. "How are they?"

"Oh, you know. The usual. Food sucks and the chicks all have guns. Monkeys running the zoo. Nothing's changed, believe me."

"*Jesus.*" Tate did not miss any of that, not at all.

"You know, we keep trying him, but the dude's stopped taking our calls. We'll keep at it, though."

"There ya go."

"How are *you*? Geez, Tate…it's been a while, you know?"

"I'm all right. I got sick of hanging around my parents' house like a waste of space, so I picked up a temp job working security."

"No shit? Like a mall cop?"

"No, more like a bodyguard gig."

"Anyone I know?"

Looking at Lyla in her demure cardigan and sexy heels, Tate not only didn't want to share her name with Tank, but he also didn't even want his teammate to know she was a woman.

So, he only said, "This mystery author that works with my college roommate."

The instinct to keep Lyla to himself for a while longer was powerful, and reminded Tate of the way some of the other guys used to absolutely refuse to share a single detail about their women back home.

He'd never understood what the big idea was before, but he sure got it now—the notion of tainting someone as fine as Lyla with the ugliness of war repulsed him.

"That's cool," Tank said, once it was clear Tate had nothing further to add. There was a long pause, and then he asked, "So…have you gotten any word on when they're gonna let you come back yet?"

"I'm still waiting," Tate lied. "I had a second evaluation a few weeks ago, but…no results yet." He couldn't bear to tell Tank he'd been turned down only moments ago, but it didn't help that Lyla was obviously listening to him to sit there and deceive his friend.

"Dude. What the fuck's the holdup, anymore? You said you're tight now, yeah?"

"I think so. I guess maybe they believe my brain's still healing? Who the hell knows."

"I mean…it's not like you need to do calculus here. You just need to be able to hump yourself across some sand and pull a trigger. How is that hard?"

"You think I don't know that? Tell them, Einstein."

"No, *you* tell them and then get yourself back here *fast*. We need you for the next…thing we're supposedly doing."

Tate's whole being perked up at that bait in the water. "What thing?"

"Nothing definite yet. But there's been some talk."

"Tank, don't be a cagey asshole. Just tell me."

"Hang on." There was some muffled whispering, an assurance to whoever Tank was with that he'd *be right back*, and then a door slammed and the background noises faded to silence. "You there?"

"Yeah."

"Word is, we might be moving on Asif Abd-el-Kadir, sooner rather than later," Tank said low and fast. "HQ got some fresh intel on his location, and people are saying we're the guys who are going to get him."

"No fucking way."

"Way."

"Tank—" Tate forced himself to take a deep breath. "*When?*"

"Soon. Maybe right after we all get back from leave."

"But you said you only got two days."

"Why do you think I'm trying to get you to hurry back? Just for shits and giggles?"

Tate had just flunked another evaluation, however, and his next one wasn't for six or eight more weeks. There was no way he could hurry back, no matter how much he wanted to be in on this mission.

They'd been hunting that freaking zealot for *years*. Tate wanted to scream and kick things knowing he would miss the man's possible capture, but all he could say to Tank was, "Trust me, I'm trying, man."

"Hell, I know that. I'm not looking to make you feel bad—I just wanted to give you a little incentive. You know, in case you hadn't already tried to beg, borrow, and steal your way back. Or whatever else you have to do."

"Roger that. Are the other guys…is everyone else doing okay? You think they're up to this?"

"Oh, they're ready. They've been chomping at the bit after what happened to you, Robinson, and…the rest." Tank choked on the names of the other men who hadn't been as lucky as Tate.

His voice cracked when he added, "You've never seen them all so murderous. Kadir won't know what hit him."

"Well, damn. Try not to get your asses shot off, would you please? You don't have anyone there to babysit you anymore."

Tank laughed, but it cut off fast. "You're not coming back in time, are you?"

"Not yet, Tank," Tate admitted. "I'm sorry. You know I want to."

"Don't worry about us, brother. You work on getting better, and we'll go out and show you how it's done, all right?"

"No mistakes, man. March in, do the job, march out."

"*Whatever.* You act like we're going to elementary school. You and I both know it's bound to be a complete shitshow if it's anything like the last few years. I just want to live through it so I can go home and meet my new niece one of these days."

"I'll hope for the best."

"And we'll prepare for the worst, you grim fuck. Call me if you hear anything in the next few days, though, okay? Maybe I can delay until you get here."

"You bet."

"*Ready and Deadly.*"

"Hooah."

Tate hung up the phone and didn't know what the hell to do with the overwhelming sense of helpless frustration brewing in his chest. He knew Tank hadn't meant anything snide by signing off with their unit's motto, but could it feel any less applicable than it did right now?

What the hell was he even doing in this fancy hotel room, sitting across from a smart, beautiful woman who—for some unknown reason—occasionally wanted to get in his pants? Hunting extremists, this was not.

Tate didn't belong here. He wasn't any good at civilian life and hadn't been for too long.

What had Becky called him all those years ago? *Easy to fuck, but hard to love?* God, that was the truth.

Sequestered in the Army with all the other knuckleheads was undeniably the best place for Tate to be. So, why couldn't anyone but him see that?

Lyla set aside her soda can and eyed him warily. "Let me guess—more bad news?" she asked. "And please don't turn this into some kind of joke."

Tate retorted, "Hey, did you hear the one about the badass soldier who had to sit out the fight of his life?"

Lyla's eyes went soft and her plump bottom lip stuck out in a pout. Understanding was written all over her face.

"No?" he demanded, forestalling whatever pity-party she was about to try selling him. "Yeah, me neither."

"*Tate*."

"That's because badasses don't sit out fights," he explained testily. "Right now, I'm *here*, and my team is *there*. So, what does that make me?"

"Human. It makes you human."

Tate talked right over her. "Not a badass, that's for damn sure. Christ, at this rate I might as well have joined the Chair Force, instead of the freaking Army."

"My grandpa was in the Air Force."

"Did he spend his tour sitting in hotel rooms thousands of miles away from the action?"

"No, he fought honorably in Korea and when his service was done, he came home to raise a family and be a productive member of society."

"Good for Gramps."

"Tate, don't be mean," Lyla said. "It's beneath you."

He swallowed back the bile trying to climb his throat and stared down the woman who was rapidly becoming one of the most important people in his life. He forced himself to calm down—to treat her like she deserved to be treated.

"I'm sorry. I shouldn't have spoken to you like that."

"Is there anything I can do?"

"Come here," Tate said and pulled her into his lap. "I feel so freaking helpless. I should be over there making sure none of them get killed, not eating takeout every night in ritzy hotels."

"It's not in your control, Tate. And not for nothing, but…you're doing something big here, too, in case you've forgotten. If it weren't for you, who knows what I'd be dealing with right now."

"Maybe things would be better. Maybe without me here, your stalker wouldn't have gotten so mad at you."

"Do you really believe that?"

Tate admitted, "No."

"Neither do I." She pressed a soft kiss to his lips and just that quickly, his body ignited.

"Lyla," he groaned. "You don't know what you're starting. You should stop."

"Is that what you want?"

"No. But you're biting off more than you can chew, sweetheart. I'm a little unbalanced right now."

"I don't care. I need this with you. I think you might need it, too."

She had no idea.

When Tate didn't respond, Lyla slid off his lap and knelt on the carpet between his legs.

"Let me make you feel good," she said, setting her glasses aside. "Can I?"

She was definitely not expecting to be refused, because Lyla reached for the waistband of Tate's sweatpants immediately. He'd already gone hard at the sight of her on her knees, but he got even harder now.

Still, Tate grabbed her hands and held them away from the family jewels.

"You don't have to do this," he told her. He sure wanted her to, though.

The sight of those perfect lips in such close proximity to his cock was nearly enough to push him over the edge completely.

Tate wouldn't be forgetting how Lyla looked right now, that was for damn sure. Not any time soon, anyway.

He couldn't pretend to understand all of Lyla's reasons for wanting to do this now, of all times, but what he did realize—albeit belatedly—was that once she'd reached for him, the path of retreat had ceased to be a viable option.

"I know I don't have to. I want to," she said. Her eyelashes flickered as she gazed up at him, her expression steady and composed. He didn't have the resistance to say no to her.

Tate let out his breath, helped her push down his pants, and moved his hands unsteadily out of her way.

There was only one way forward now, and he'd have to navigate it carefully. If he didn't, Lyla might beat herself up over this later—and Tate would forever be something she regretted when it was all said and done.

He had to make this time—and every other time they had left—good for her.

Lyla set her palms on his thighs and moved in. She took Tate deep into her hot, wet mouth in one stroke, her tongue molding to the sensitive underside of his cock, her lips tight against his skin.

He growled her name and wound his hands into all the shiny, silky mahogany hair flowing over her shoulders. Lyla smiled, then set a firm, fast pace. It felt so fucking good—sending electric shocks down his spine and sparks through his limbs. Tate couldn't have stopped her, even if he'd wanted to.

His balls drew tight far sooner than he wanted. He tried to warn her.

"Lyla, sweetheart, stop. I can't wait any longer."

She wasn't deterred, though. She gripped the base of his cock with her fist, moved her mouth up and down smoothly, and executed some crazy swirl with her tongue on the tip with every quick stroke. Tate was a goner, and then some.

He squeezed his eyes shut, grabbed her head to hold it still, and gave himself up to the shattering climax with a long, stunned groan.

This woman. She was everything.

He hauled Lyla up and shuffled her to the bed, then tipped her back onto the bed so he could climb over her. Lyla's eyes were watchful, but whether she was simply studying him for kicks or parsing Tate's state of mind remained to be seen.

If Tate had his way, she wouldn't be analytical for much longer. He contemplated her long, luscious body and tried to decide where to begin. It wasn't easy—as always, all of his choices looked equally enticing.

"God, you're beautiful," he told her, and registered the immediate flare of push-back in her eyes a split second before he leaned forward to brace his hands next to her shoulders.

Lyla opened her mouth, no doubt to school him on what a hot mess she was after such a crappy couple of days.

"Don't argue," Tate instructed.

She arched a brow at him but wisely pressed her lips together.

He brushed his own lips over the skin near Lyla's shoulder and cataloged her full-body shiver. She might not be good at losing herself in the moment, but he was not a man who was used to failure.

Tate had been determined since the day he was born. He would march or trudge—or even limp doggedly forward, if necessary—but come hell or high water, Tate got where he wanted to go.

And so, by the time he was through with Lyla tonight, she'd better have no doubt in her mind what Tate thought of her. He only hoped it would be enough to keep her from hating him once he was gone.

Tate pressed open-mouthed kisses to the delicate skin of Lyla's neck, and inhaled the warm fragrance near her ear. "So beautiful," he repeated, then went for her mouth before she could try to explain about long days or limp hair.

He must have been off his game, however, because Tate could tell, somewhere around the time he reached the tantalizing plain of Lyla's lovely stomach, that her brain had kicked into overdrive again. While he was busy marveling at the softness of her skin against his lips, he could almost hear the gears start turning in her never-dormant cranium.

Damn it. He wasn't about to concede defeat now. Tate narrowed his eyes, knelt between Lyla's knees, and ran his palms up the insides of her silky legs. His rough hands seemed like an affront to all that pretty female skin, but he used them to push her knees wider apart anyway, making room for himself.

No way was his woman going to feel one iota of doubt about him. *Fuck that.*

Quick on that thought's heels came a wave of possession that startled Tate. *His.* This extraordinary woman felt like *his*, as freaking unlikely as it seemed.

He was going to have to do something about that really goddamn soon. Not yet, though. First, he had to deliver what she wanted.

Twenty-Two

I'M AFRAID I'M going to be too rough," Tate murmured, pulling himself up Lyla's body to brush her hair away from her face.

He'd been working her into a frenzy for what felt like an eternity, coiling the want inside her tighter and tighter until she couldn't take another second of it. She'd had to pull on his shoulders and beg him to stop.

Or rather, beg him for more than his mouth.

"I just want to be with you, Tate—however it's going to be," she said.

His blue eyes went dark. "Then roll over," he told her, helping Lyla turn onto her stomach.

He arranged her on her hands and knees, until her ass was in the air and her forehead was resting on the bed.

"You okay?" he checked.

"Fabulous," she laughed.

Lyla heard him rip a foil packet open, and then Tate was dragging his fingers between her legs. "Fuck, you're so ready for me. Did you like getting me off, sweetheart? Were you thinking about how I'd feel buried deep inside you?"

"Oh God, yes," Lyla whimpered into the mattress.

"You're so beautiful like this," Tate continued. "Perfect ass, pretty legs…such soft skin." He stroked a hand up her spine and moved her hair to the side. "Look at me," he commanded.

Lyla peeked over her shoulder to find Tate on his knees behind her, his long, erect cock gripped in his hand. Impossibly, it looked even bigger than it had moments before.

"I can't go slow or soft," he warned her.

"I don't want it that way."

"But you do want it?"

Lyla dropped her head back down. "More than I want to sit here with my ass in the air debating it," she grumbled.

Tate chuckled and smacked her lightly on the butt. "Someone's feeling pretty full of herself right now."

"I'd rather be full of you."

He growled and grabbed onto her hips, driving into Lyla in one hard thrust. All the breath rushed out of her lungs. *So big. So full.*

"How's that, Slick?"

"More," she pleaded. She gripped the covers in her hands and pushed back against him.

Tate leaned forward, caging her in and surrounding her with his heady, masculine scent. He braced on one forearm and held her steady so he could pound into her, relentless and demanding.

Lyla wanted to sing with elation. It had never been like this with anyone else—never so good, so all-consuming, so earth-shattering. Tate was a tempest, wreaking havoc on her body and her heart.

"Can you still taste me, sweetheart?" he rumbled in her ear, "Because I still have the taste of you all over my tongue."

His hand dipped down and his fingers pressed against her, Tate's pounding pace never letting up as Lyla came apart under him, shattering into a million pieces and spinning out into the night.

He followed her moments later, his usual filthy commentary silenced, for once. Tate only collapsed beside her, speechless and spent and breathing hard.

Lyla's pulse hammered in her veins, a staccato drumbeat calling his name.

"There is no one as amazing as you," he whispered softly. Tate pressed his lips to the side of her neck and held them there for a long time before he finally rolled away and padded into the bathroom.

Lyla ducked in once he returned, tying her hair up and showering quickly, then brushing her teeth and slathering on a little moisturizer.

Sternly, she stared herself down in the mirror. She had to stop wishing for more than this was.

Tate was incredible—strong and steady, sweet and fun. However, despite the yearning washing through her, she was not allowed to keep him.

He had to go back to his real life, and his real job. Tate wanted that more than he wanted anything else, including her. If Lyla cared about him at all, she had to let him go.

Which meant absolutely no talking about *feelings*. She could enjoy what he was willing to give her now, and if she had half a brain, she would. But she could not tell Tate that she was falling head over heels for him, she could not use the L-word, and she could not tell him she hoped he'd stay.

Lyla especially couldn't say that she wouldn't be sorry if he never got cleared for active duty again. Tate would never forgive her for that.

She nodded to herself and tried hard to believe this was the right thing to do, even if the resolution sat like a stone in her chest.

Back in the room, Tate had fallen into an exhausted slumber in the short time that she'd been gone. Lyla crawled under the covers and curled up facing him, watching his eyelids twitch while he dreamed.

LYLA LURCHED SUDDENLY awake sometime later, when Tate bolted upright with an ungodly howl, chest heaving. *Damn.* Another nightmare.

"Tate?"

He shook his head fast and mumbled, *"Don't."*

Lyla scooted closer and tried to put her arm around him. Tate shied away, but not before she realized he was sitting there trembling, drenched in a cold sweat.

"Oh my God, Tate—you're soaked. Was it that bad?"

"Sorry," he muttered sullenly. His breath was still coming fast, like he'd just sprinted a mile in his sleep.

"Don't be sorry," Lyla told him. "Are you okay?"

"Fuck, no."

Tentatively, Lyla put a hand on his clammy shoulder and tried to gently kiss his cheek.

Tate turned suddenly at the last minute, devouring her mouth in a sudden, livid tangling of tongues. When Lyla tried to pull back, he nipped at her lip, a shade too hard to be comfortable.

He watched her blink and rub at her mouth, then stared contritely down at his hands.

"Tate, how can I help?" Lyla asked him.

"You can't."

"Okay. Then I—"

He cut her off with a scornful grunt. "You think *any* of this helps? Because it doesn't, Lyla. None of this is helping at all." He clutched his head in his hands.

Lyla couldn't help it—resolve or not, that hurt. But Tate wasn't done.

"How could this help?" he wanted to know, throwing his hands wide and narrowly missing her. "Even if, by some strange miracle, the Army decides to let me go back, I'm still going to be a wreck. Don't you get it? It will just be for a different reason now. I'm going to be freaking out every fucking minute, wondering if you're in danger—not knowing if some nutjob has gotten to you and is hurting you, without me here."

Lyla tried to keep calm in the face of Tate's bitter anger, but it was hard. He was intimidating like this, but at least his concern for her was coming through loud and clear.

"So, you dreamed about me," she said. Lyla paused, but he didn't deny it. "Tate…I care a lot about you, as well. And it'll be okay. We can keep in touch with each other. I'll be worried about whether you're doing alright, too, and whether—"

"Lyla, stop. *Worry* is not what I'm talking about. *Worry* is what you do when you can't remember where you left your fucking house *keys!*"

Lyla got out of the bed, pulled some clothes off the floor, and got dressed unsteadily. "I realize that you're upset, but please stop yelling at me. I'm not the enemy."

"Given what you're doing to me, I'm not so sure that's true," Tate muttered darkly.

Lyla gaped at him. "*Wow.* Okay. Thanks for that." Tears pricked at her eyes, and she swiped quickly at them before they could shame her and start falling.

Tate blinked and looked abashed. He scrubbed his hands over his cheeks, then got up, too, peeling off his sodden shirt and yanking on a pair of gym shorts before he faced off with her again.

"Okay, wait," he grumbled. "I didn't mean it like that. I…I'm sorry." He seemed a little disoriented.

"Are you sure about that? Because I'm not convinced. What's gotten into you, anyway?"

She wondered if she ought to call someone for him, or if this episode would pass quickly. In the dead of night, after such a sudden wake-up, it was hard to think straight.

Tate swung away, clenching and unclenching his fists and breathing hard. "I'm just…so…God *damn* it. What the hell am I going to do, Lyla?"

Lyla had no idea how Tate would react if she got too close. It set off an ache in her chest to stay where she was and not go to comfort him, but she did it anyway.

He'd never forgive himself if he lashed out and she got caught in the crossfire, even accidentally.

"Tate, just out of curiosity," she wondered quietly, "When was the last time you checked in with one of those therapists?"

He wheeled on her with a look of utter betrayal. "Are you fucking *kidding* me right now?"

"But maybe they can help. Talk through what you're feeling right now, and…"

Tate turned to the bed and punched a pillow so fast it surprised a ridiculous, high-pitched squeak out of her. Lyla swallowed the rest of her sentence and backed farther away.

"What's that for?" Tate demanded, eyeing her. "You can't possibly think I would ever lay a hand on *you*. I'm here to *protect* you!"

"It doesn't feel like that, at the moment."

Tate glared at her and Lyla stared right back, until all the air abruptly went out of him and he deflated like a popped balloon.

With shaking hands, he felt beside him for the edge of the bed and sank down. "Jesus, Slick. I'm…" he swallowed thickly, "I'm really sorry. All of that was totally uncalled for. I don't know why I'm being so…Please don't be afraid."

Lyla admitted, "I'm scared *for* you, not of you. And honestly, I think it's a good idea that we're scrapping the book tour and heading home. This whole thing has not been good for you—it's not what you should be doing during your recovery."

"Lyla," Tate said forlornly, "Right now, it's all I have."

"That's not even kind of true."

"But we can still finish the tour. I swear this won't happen again. I don't know what got into me, but I promise I won't—"

Lyla shook her head. "Wayne already emailed me. We're done with the Trident events. The only thing left is…no. Never mind. I'll do it some other time."

"No, tell me. What?"

"I thought we might stop by my parents' on the way back. But you're not up to that."

"I am," Tate insisted. "I will be on my best behavior. Cross my heart." He ran his fingers through his hair, trying to make it neat.

Lyla knew this was probably her only bargaining chip, but she still felt a little bad laying it down.

She looked at Tate as levelly as she could, and said, "Call your therapist first."

"Excuse me?"

"I'll consider it, *if* you call your therapist and talk to them about all of this, first thing in the morning."

"And if I say no?"

"Then we'll meet with Red as soon as we get back, so you can resign."

He gaped at her. "You're *firing* me?"

"No," Lyla explained, "You are acknowledging that you made a mistake when you agreed to act as my bodyguard, and you are taking yourself off the job."

"*No.* I'm no quitter. I'm going to see this through. You *need* me to see this through."

"Great. Then call your doctor as soon as their office opens."

Tate's mouth opened and closed as he sat blinking at her. When it seemed like he could make his voice work again, he told her, "Lyla, you've got goosebumps. Here, get back under the covers before you freeze."

"With you? I don't think so," she scoffed. As much as she wanted to hold Tate and be held by him, that was not going to be productive right now.

He looked wounded by her refusal. "It's okay. You take the bed. I'll just go in the other room."

Lyla thought about that. She'd never be able to get back to sleep now, anyway, no matter how hard she tried. "Actually," she told Tate, "You can stew in here while you make your decision. I'm going to go out there and try to get some work done."

Lyla was going to have to mask her stupid wish that Tate would leave the military by putting some distance between them. His retirement would give them the chance to have more, after all—but if Lyla ever told him that's what she wanted, she might really screw things up for good.

"At least take the blanket with you."

"I'll turn down the A/C. I'll be fine." As she rounded the bed and headed for the sitting area of their suite, Lyla peeked at Tate's face.

He looked miserable, but underneath that was the budding seed of tenacity she'd been hoping to draw out. Lyla hadn't been sure if it would show up as stubbornness or resolve, but so far, it seemed like she might have won this battle.

God, she hoped so. She might have to resign herself to losing Tate—but that didn't mean it had to happen today.

BY EIGHT O'CLOCK the next morning, Tate was murmuring quietly on his cell phone in the bedroom, and Lyla was nearly wilting from gratitude that he'd chosen to stay on as her bodyguard.

When he leaned against the doorjamb a full two hours later, he had dark circles under his eyes and his face was drawn—but he seemed lighter somehow. Unburdened.

That impression was confirmed when Tate gave her a sheepish little smile and simply said, "Thank you for pointing me in the right direction."

"Do you feel any better?"

"I do."

Lyla cocked her head and gave him a once-over. He looked as depleted as she felt. "Well enough to meet my crazy parents later?"

He snorted, "Are you kidding? Parents love me."

"Mine can be…special."

"I'm not afraid."

"Give it time."

Tate waved her off. "I'm done in the bathroom if you want to get in there. I also ordered you one of those yogurt and granola things you like from room service. I hope that's okay."

"It's perfect, thanks." Lyla shut down her computer and tried to crack her back.

Tate had turned to slip back into the bedroom, so she called out, "Hey Tate?"

He popped his head around the corner. "Yeah?"

"We're good, okay? You don't have to make anything up to me. I want you to know that."

"I appreciate that. I'm…I feel bad about last night, though. You shouldn't have had to deal with me in that condition."

"And yet, I survived. And look—so did you. So let's not give it more weight than it deserves."

He came closer and toyed with a piece of her hair. "I meant what I said, you know. They really broke the mold with you, Slick. You are one of a kind."

Lyla blinked back a sudden rush of tears. "I'm going to take that as a compliment."

"Oh, it is." Tate pecked her on the nose and then on the lips. "Now let's get moving. I've got some parents to charm the socks off later, and I have to formulate my plan of attack. You can't just walk into these things cold—you've got to train. Prepare. Be primed and ready."

Lyla shook her head, but she still got up and followed Tate into the other room.

"There is no preparing for my parents," she told him.

"Shows what you know. Leave this to a professional."

Lyla groaned. Tate would learn—sadly, it would probably be the hard way.

WHEN THEY LEFT the hotel a couple of hours later, Lyla cast one last look over her shoulder at the room, unsure if she was feeling sad or relieved that her book tour—and her time with Tate—was soon drawing to a close.

He'd left the room as meticulously tidy as he always did, but today it seemed to underline the finality of things. Lyla may have gotten a reprieve, but it was only a temporary one. Tate would still leave eventually.

She wanted something more with him—something deeper. He did not, though. Tate still had too many major things to figure out in his life before he could commit to another person long term, supposing he even wanted to.

That didn't make it any less disappointing, however. Tate might try to sell Lyla the whole *one-in-a-million* line, but she knew for a fact she'd never meet another man like him again.

Right man, wrong time. Didn't it just figure.

Twenty-Three

ABOUT THREE-QUARTERS OF the way to Lyla's parents' house, Tate's cell phone began chiming with Red's assigned ringtone—a deep reverberating gong.

Tate took a moment to appreciate how inspired that choice had been, and then put it on speakerphone.

"Hey, dude. You're on speaker. What's up?"

"Where are you two right now?"

"On Route 17. Just passed somewhere called Scotchtown," Tate told him.

"Where the hell is that?"

"Maybe three hours from Elmira," Lyla chimed in. "We're going to swing by my parents' place in Rye on the way back to the city."

Red was quiet for a minute. "So you checked out around…what? Eleven?"

Tate shared a quick glance with Lyla and said, "Yeah. Why?"

His buddy let out a long, pained sigh. "I don't suppose either of you had a raging party before you left?"

Another confused look passed between them—last night had been anything but a party. But their argument, if you could call it that, had also not been particularly loud, and Tate doubted anyone but the two of them was even aware it had happened.

"Red, spit it out," Tate barked, all the fine hairs on the back of his neck raising in warning.

"Look, guys—Trident got a call from the hotel about half an hour ago. Apparently, someone got in and trashed the suite you stayed in after you left. Housekeeping found it when they went in to clean."

"Are you serious?" Lyla squeaked. Tate did a double-take—her voice was way too high to be normal, but he could hardly blame her for freaking out.

"As a heart attack. We figured it wasn't you, and we explained to them what's been going on. But…by the time they called us, there wasn't a lot anyone could do. The scene was basically destroyed. They said housekeeping scrubbed up whatever they could and threw out the rest."

"Has anyone called the cops?" Tate wondered.

"Yes, but I'm not sure why we bothered. From what I hear, the only thing left is what they could pull from the trash and the hotel's list of chargeable damages."

"We…the room was pristine when we left," Lyla said, almost to herself.

Tate put a hand on her leg and squeezed. At least they'd gotten out of there before something worse had happened.

"I'm sure," his buddy reassured her. "Unfortunately, there's no way for us to prove it now."

"Well, how much are they charging you? I'll reimburse you for it."

Red laughed. "No need. We took care of it."

"But you shouldn't have to—" Lyla began.

He cut in, "Lyla, it's done. Just go have a nice visit with your parents and check in with me when you guys get back to town."

She looked over at Tate, concern etched into every feature. Tate gave her what he hoped was a reassuring nod, then asked his friend, "You need anything from me?"

"Check your email, but otherwise no. I'll give you a call tonight."

"Roger that."

"Listen, Lyla," Red said, his voice dripping with authority. "I don't want you to worry. The important thing is that you both are safe, and the officers are looking into it."

If Red could see the expression on Lyla's face, he'd know how little she believed him, and it would drive him absolutely crazy. Tate knew the feeling.

"Thanks," she replied weakly. Tate tapped his phone and cut off the call.

"Tate, *how?*" she cried, as soon as he'd hung up. "How does this person always know where we are?"

"I have no fucking idea." He was furious at the lack of progress he'd made in figuring this out. He had no ideas. *None.*

"Is there anyone at all that you've spoken to?" Tate asked her. "Anyone?"

Lyla shook her head. "No one."

"Look at the call list on your phone. Maybe there's someone you're forgetting."

She pulled it out of her purse and began scrolling. "No, really. The only people here are you, Red, some people in Trident's PR department, and my parents. There's literally no one else."

Shit. That wasn't helpful.

"I don't get it, Slick," Tate admitted. "I just don't get it."

"What about you?" Lyla wondered. "Who have you talked to?"

"Red and Luca are the only ones. I talked to the Med Board doctors, Tank, and the therapist, too—but I never said a word about where we were."

They rode in silence for a while. When their exit came up on the right, he merged onto it.

"Maybe…" Lyla frowned out the windshield. "Maybe he's been following us all along?"

Tate wanted to think he'd know if that was the case, but he hadn't exactly been in the zone with this thing. "Maybe," he conceded, "But I don't think so."

"Then he could be tracking us. Like…with one of those little GPS things they use in spy movies—he could've stuck one in my stuff at a signing, right?"

Tate clutched the wheel with a scowl and turned that idea over in his mind. "Could be, but again—it doesn't feel right."

Lyla wrapped her arms around herself and tucked in her chin, the picture of stubbornness. "I'm going to go through my things anyway," she announced. "I just wish I'd thought of it before we left for my parents' house. If there is a bug, I'm about to bring it right to them."

"Want me to pull over somewhere?" he asked.

"Don't bother," she sighed, defeated. "We're almost there. Their street is up ahead." She pointed down the road, "First turn after the light."

Moments later, Tate came to a stop in the long, steep driveway of a tidy little bungalow, and put his brother's truck in park. Lyla eyed the house with obvious apprehension.

He didn't want to make it worse, so he pasted a chipper smile on his grill and elbowed her. "Let's do this. I don't know about you, but I'm excited. Are you excited? I'm excited."

"No, Tate," she moaned, dropping her head into her hands. "I am not excited."

"Why not?"

"Because I never bring guys home," she muttered. "And you're…" Lyla looked up, gestured emphatically to him, and added, "And we're…"

Then she flapped both her hands spastically between them.

"It's because I'm a stone-cold fox, right?" Tate joked. "You're afraid your folks might collapse in the face of all this hotness?"

Lyla rolled her eyes so hard she was lucky they didn't pop out and trundle right on down the road. "I will never understand how you are able to rebound so fast. It's a total offense to the natural order of things."

"Defying the laws of nature is a learnable life hack," Tate told her with a grin. "I can teach you some time if you'd like."

"Maybe later," Lyla said. "For now…don't be offended, but I am going to introduce you as my security guy, and *only* my security guy. Okay? There's no need for this to be complicated by my parents thinking you're son-in-law material."

Well, that took the wind out of his sails. Tate's smile fell away. "Ouch."

Lyla looked chagrined. "No—oh my God, *no*. I didn't mean it like that. Tate, you would be spectacular son-in-law material, but you're…you know. Come on."

"I'm what?" He wasn't entirely sure he wanted to know, however. The choices were ruthlessly endless.

Lyla emitted a startled little peep, then said under her breath, "You're about to meet my crazy parents. *Shit*, here they come. Brace yourself."

Tate looked toward the front walk, and sure enough, a genial couple was hot-footing it down the front walk, their faces wreathed in excited smiles.

His masochistic need to learn all the ways he was unsuited to be Lyla's future husband would have to wait.

"On three," he told Lyla.

Dutifully, she murmured, "One, two, three," like they were learning the steps to a new dance, and it was the cutest thing he'd ever seen.

In perfect synchrony, they popped their doors and stepped out. Her parents stopped and looked between them, genuinely conflicted about which person to tackle first.

Tate made things easy for them by rounding the hood and falling into formation two steps behind Lyla.

Mrs. Lawson hugged her kid first, but her eyes stayed on Tate over her daughter's shoulder the whole time. When she was done, she shoved Lyla toward her father, then bee-lined for Tate.

"Now, Lyla—who's this hunk of cuteness here?" she demanded.

"Mom! I told you I was bringing him. Tate's my security guy. Do *not* flirt with him!"

Mrs. Lawson's brows shot up, impressed. "Nice perk of doing business," she said drily.

"It's standard on book tours," Lyla lied. "For insurance purposes."

Tate shot her a look and stuck out his hand. "Captain Tate Monroe, ma'am," he said. Then, when Lyla's father approached, he did the same with him. "Sir."

Lyla announced, "Tate, these are my well-meaning but clueless parents, Jim and Peg."

"Pleasure to meet you both." Lyla's mom was hovering at his shoulder, nearly vibrating from excitement. Out of the corner of his mouth, he told her, "I don't mind if you want to flirt. It's kind of a hobby of mine."

Mrs. Lawson slapped playfully at his arm and crowed, "Oh you...I like you!" She told her daughter, "Lyla, I like Captain Monroe!"

Lyla sent him a baleful glare. "Okay, Mom? Settle down. Why don't we all just..." she looked around desperately. "Let's go inside for a bit. Tate and I have to be back in town later tonight, and I'd like to be able to visit for a bit before we have to leave."

"Right this way," her father sang, and led them into the house.

ONCE THEY WERE seated in a front parlor that was clearly reserved for guests and guests alone, Tate held to the whole bodyguard-without-benefits routine like he was trying to stay on top of a bucking bronco. As in—yes, he was still vertical, and no, it wasn't fucking easy.

On its back burner, his brain was chewing on the fact that Lyla's stalker seemed to have ESP about where they were going to be at any moment—and not liking how it tasted.

Tate was also fairly worried that the call he'd made to the therapist this morning might make it into his files and back to the Med Board assholes—thereby screwing up any chance he had of passing his next evaluation. Even though it'd been the only possible choice to make, it'd still been an agonizing risk.

Tate had been really careful to sound as sane and balanced as possible, but would it be enough? God only knew.

Last but not least, he was getting pretty angsty about what Lyla could've meant by him not being son-in-law material. Tate *wanted* to bond with these people—he wanted to get to know them and prove that he was a worthy candidate for their daughter, as if he had a snowball's chance in hell of ever winning her.

And, he was having the devil's own time trying to keep his grubby mitts to himself, as it turned out. Seeing Lyla with her parents, in the snug and cozy house she'd grown up in, had the unexpected effect of making him want to get up-close-and-personal with all of her nooks and crannies.

If you got his drift.

With all of that nonsense frying his circuits, Tate was, quite frankly, barely tracking the conversation they were having. He prayed his anxiety wasn't apparent to anyone else.

It didn't help that the room they were sitting in, while tasteful and tidy, was also faintly uncomfortable in the way that all unused rooms tended to be. It wasn't helping him relax one bit.

Tate only hoped that the Lawsons would take his reticence as some kind of tough-guy professional reserve—and not a simmering pot of *I'm a mental case that wants to screw your daughter.*

They seemed to be unaware of his roiling thoughts. When he tuned back in, the topic wasn't *why are you wasting time with this moron,* thank fuck. Instead, Lyla's parents seemed to be happily recounting a recent lunch date with their pals next door.

That was normal enough. What wasn't, was Lyla's reaction to the news. Tate sat up straight and squinted at her.

Lyla scowled darkly and said, "I will never understand what you guys see in those people. They're horrible. Truly."

That was a bit extreme. Tate blinked at her, then turned to look at her parents on the opposite sofa.

By way of explanation, Lyla's mom leaned in and confided, "It's not their fault. The Jones's have never been the same since their son got sick."

Lyla snorted, clearly taking exception.

Curious. Tate inquired politely, "Really? That's a shame. What happened?"

Lyla's dad tapped his head and made eyes at him. "Touched in the head, poor kid. Needs round-the-clock supervision." It wasn't much in the way of an explanation, but it got across Jim's feelings on the subject quite handily.

Tate sat back and tried to mask his immediate, defensive need to react. The bum brain insinuation hit a little too close to home. Neighbor Jones, after all, wasn't the only one short a few cards in his deck. Tate could relate rather intimately, at the moment.

Lyla's mom took advantage of his silence to grind an ax that sounded as if it had been pulled out a time or ten before. "You'd think Lyla would be more understanding, given how long we've all lived here. But no—she's just as touchy about them as she's ever been." She folded her hands in her lap and eyed her daughter critically.

Christ, if this was what a casual visitor got? Tate could only imagine what a potential suitor might hear. He was nearly slavering with the desire to find out, though. He wanted all of Lyla's dirty secrets, *stat.*

Lyla was a tense bundle of nerves beside him. She spat out, "Brett is a jackass, mom. He was a jackass before, and he is still a jackass now. Come *on.*"

"You haven't been very nice to him over the years," her mom countered. "You guys were friends. You shouldn't say things like that."

"We weren't friends!" Lyla cried. "Why should I start now?"

Her dad jumped in quietly, but with authority. "Bill and Midge would be very sad to hear you say that."

She had a ready answer for that too, though. "Luckily, they won't have to, will they?"

Tate didn't have to be a rocket scientist to see how this was spiraling.

"Lyla," her mom squawked, "I don't understand—"

He jumped up and clapped his hands loudly, and all three Lawsons fell into stunned silence.

Tate turned and stared down at Lyla, so there'd be no doubt who he was talking to. "Hey, Lyla—I just remembered. Didn't you say you had some old trophies up in your room that you wanted to rub my nose in?" He kept his voice bright and easy and hoped she'd play along.

Her dad grumbled, "Trophies? Lyla didn't play sports. She doesn't have any—"

Lyla popped right off that loveseat, though, and mimicked Tate's pose perfectly. "Oh, just you wait, Mister. I'm going to blow your stupid football letters right out of the water."

Her parents lapsed into a confused, hushed discussion down on their sofa.

"Peg, what's she talking about? Lyla doesn't have any trophies."

"Maybe she means those old ribbons from art class?"

"Well, she did get those certificates—Honor Society, wasn't it?"

"Yes, you might be right."

Tate raised his eyebrows at Lyla, giving her an unequivocal get-moving stare.

"Right this way," she chirped and dragged him to the stairs.

Twenty-Four

O N THE WHOLE, Lyla generally thought her mom and dad were wonderful people—kind and generous, and happily engaged in the world around them in a way that her friends' parents never seemed to be.

Her folks made friends with all kinds of people, all over town—but their lack of innate suspicion meant that they rarely saw the bad in any of them.

Since Lyla spent most of her time in the city, where things could get a bit more fraught on a day-to-day basis, she generally viewed her parents' attitude as sort-of refreshing and sweet. Naïve, maybe, but still nice.

But—and this was a huge *but*, all things considered—the way her folks had taken to Bill and Midge Jones was beyond her comprehension. Lyla had never met a more oblivious couple in her life.

Case in point: while their son had bullied his way through his adolescence, they'd blithely continued to sing his praises to one and all.

Talk about your blind spots. The one they had for Brett was like a black hole, devouring the galaxy of the neighborhood in its complete cluelessness.

It just figured that Lyla's mom and dad would trot out their tired old routine about the Joneses in front of Tate, too. Lyla had wanted to scream and rage in protest, but the whole thing was so unutterably stupid that she figured it would only make her look petulant to him.

Thank God Tate had the presence of mind to cut things off before she and her parents really got going. Lyla had never been so grateful to be handed a reprieve—a lifeline from the feeling that she'd gone back in time to her dorky fifteenth year, when she'd been frustrated by every inexplicable thing her mom and dad had said.

"Thanks for getting me out of there," Lyla told Tate now. "We've had that fight so many times, I could probably recite everyone's lines in my sleep."

"No biggie," he smiled. "Every family does it."

"That's kind of depressing."

"Call me crazy, but the neighbors seem like a bit of a sore spot for you guys."

Lyla snorted, "You think?"

"Have they lived here long?"

"Yup. Nearly as long as we have."

Away from the fray, up here in her childhood bedroom, Lyla realized that it was going to take a lot more than a change of scenery to erase her irritation with the subject.

Why had she thought that bringing Tate here was a good idea? Now, instead of only him being grouchy, they both would be. *Fun times.*

He looked around her old room curiously. "This is cute," he told her.

Lyla shrugged. "Hasn't changed much since I went off to college."

None of it had. Most times, that was a comfort—but right now, the lack of evolution felt like a restless itch under her skin that she'd never be able to scratch.

Lyla couldn't wait to get home—her real home in the city, where she could be herself and *breathe.*

At least there in town, she and Tate wouldn't have so much forced proximity to contend with. Except…that hadn't turned out so bad, had it? Sharing rooms—and then beds—had worked out just fine until Tate had gotten all angsty on her.

He walked over to look out her window, then pulled the sheer curtain aside so he could see better. Lyla went over to see what had caught his attention.

Next door, Brett was in his back yard, pacing rapidly around the lawn and muttering to himself, as he sometimes did. He kept glancing quickly at Lyla's house, then taking another agitated loop around the grass.

"That the boy wonder?"

"Yup."

Tate pointed and asked, "Who's that guy?"

On closer inspection, Lyla realized that Brett's sourpuss father was out there, too, perched on the back stoop. So, it was a conversation, then, instead of a monologue. *Not that it mattered.*

"Meet Mr. Jones," she said.

Lyla kept back by the wall, out of sight. If they spotted her up here, the whole crew would be over in a hot minute, wanting to grill her about her life.

She was too spent to go through *that* routine today, and she'd certainly never willingly subject Tate to it, either.

"Did you go through school with that dude?" he asked.

"Sure did."

"Why does he keep looking over here?" Tate muttered. "He looks like a freaking tiger at the zoo."

"Brett's always like that," Lyla told him. "He's probably riled up because he saw the strange truck in the driveway. The entire family is nosy, though. I'll bet you ten bucks that the minute we leave, Midge will be on the phone, wanting to know who was here."

"And they say the city is crowded. At least people ignore you there."

"Tell me about it. Why do you think I moved?"

Tate let the curtain fall back into place and went to sit on the edge of Lyla's bed. He pulled one of her old yearbooks off the bookshelf nearby and absently began flipping through it.

"What's your deal with those people anyway?" he asked. "I've never seen you react like that before, and you've had some pretty nutty fans come to your signings."

Lyla sighed and flopped down next to him on her old patchwork quilt. "Honestly, it's all so dumb. Brett was one of those stereotypical jocks in high school, lording it over everyone younger and weaker than him. He was straight out of a 1980s teen movie, trust me. Had the letterman jacket and everything."

"Sounds like me, too," Tate smiled, pointing at himself. "You're looking at the Homecoming king, co-captain of the football team, and an Eagle scout. The works, baby."

Lyla could see it, clear as day. He must have been irresistible. "Yeah, except you were probably the good guy, not the jerk," she pointed out.

"True. I tried not to be an asshole. I was carrying groceries for grandmas all over town."

"I believe it," Lyla told him. And those old biddies had probably adored Tate as much as everyone else.

"So…what happened to that punk next door, anyway? Your dad kind of hinted, but he never actually said." Tate shifted around and met her eyes, and Lyla was surprised to see a thread of discomfort there.

Of course he'd wonder, she realized. Lyla had seen the flash of uneasiness on his face when her dad had dismissed Brett's condition so cavalierly, and though Tate might try to bluster about it, she knew he saw himself as damaged goods, too.

Why else would he feel the need to constantly reassure her that he wouldn't fail her?

"I don't know," Lyla shrugged. Whatever it'd been, the Joneses no doubt would've found a way to spin it in Brett's favor. "I heard he went off to college and joined a fraternity, and then next thing I knew, he came home again. I wouldn't be surprised if he partied too much and flunked out, but he's been living with his parents ever since."

"How predictable of him. But what I meant was—"

"I know," Lyla interjected. "But it's never been clear what made him like…*that*. Knowing Brett, he probably OD'd or crashed into a tree while drunk or something. You'll never hear that from Bill and Midge, though. They still think he's the best thing since sliced bread."

Tate huffed, "What is wrong with people? I swear I will never be that parent."

"I hope I won't be either," Lyla sighed, staring at a hairline crack in her ceiling that had been there for twenty years. "But my mom always says that parenting throws you for loops that you never see coming. So…I guess I'd better keep my options open. Maybe I *will* be that parent."

"Doubtful," he smiled.

Tate set her yearbook aside and looked around once more. "I don't suppose you've got any cheerleading uniforms you'd like to model for me, as long as we're here?"

"Sorry, dude," Lyla told him. "You're barking up the wrong tree, there."

"Lacrosse, then?"

"Nope."

"Tennis."

"Too much running. *Pass.*"

"*Golf?* How about golf?" he pleaded.

"Tate, if you want me to wear a short skirt for you, all you need to do is ask."

He blew out a long, disgruntled breath. "Where's the fun in that?"

"Buck up, chief. Grown women have terrific tricks up their sleeves—ones that'll make your head spin."

Tate nodded avidly, "I believe you, and I am one-hundred-percent down for that. Just…not here in this little pink bedroom. Feels weird. Sorry, not sorry."

"Agreed," Lyla laughed. "How about I meet you in the big city later, and we'll see what we can get up to?"

"That's a date. Now, on to more important items. When's dinner, and what are we having?"

"My guess? Meatloaf at 6:30 sharp. It's my mother's go-to for guests she doesn't know well. Congratulations."

"And I'm assuming you want to hit the road after that?"

"Oh God, yes. I'd be burning rubber right now if I thought I could get away with it."

"You can't, Slick. Didn't you notice how happy your folks were to see you?"

"On that note, I suppose we've been hiding up here long enough. If we stay here any longer, they're bound to think we're doing something indecent."

He looked her over. "Which would be bad, because..."

"Tate, you *just* met my dad. Surely you don't want him to deck you already?"

"He wouldn't dare. I'm a decorated member of this country's armed forces!" Tate protested, feigning outrage.

"Oh, he'd dare, alright. Now shine up that charm you keep telling me about, and maybe we'll all get through the next two hours without coming to blows."

Lyla pulled open her bedroom door and held her arm wide like a gameshow hostess.

Tate peeked into the hallway, then crowded up close to her when he saw that the coast was clear. "Yeah, the only word I heard there was *blow*. Why didn't we want to get busy up here, again?"

"Because it's completely inappropriate," Lyla groaned. "Now come on. If you're a good boy, I'll get my dad to make you one of his famous martinis."

Tate pecked her quickly on the lips and stepped away. "I'm driving, remember? No booze for me. Sorry, sweetheart."

"That's okay," Lyla said airily. "I'll drink yours, too. Maybe it will numb my pain."

"Right, because that's worked so well for you, so far," he commented, dry as dust.

She scowled at him, then led Tate down the steps—and hoped like hell their remaining time here would pass quickly.

IN THE DINING room, Lyla's mother had indeed served up meatloaf for dinner, along with the expected side dishes of mashed potatoes and creamed spinach. Basically, what every health-conscious vegetarian longed to eat for a light summer repast.

Lyla stifled her exasperation that her parents had made no allowances whatsoever for her food preferences, loaded up on the spinach and potatoes, and slid into the seat next to Tate.

Her mom was primed and ready to make conversation, it seemed.

"So, Mr. Monroe," she said brightly, "You're Delilah's bodyguard."

"That's right," he nodded, digging into his food like he hadn't eaten in weeks.

Lyla's father asked, "How'd you get into that line of work?"

Tate grinned, not the least bit bothered by their blatant prying. "Would you believe I knew a guy? He made me an offer I couldn't refuse."

Her dad arched a dubious eyebrow, but at least he laughed along.

Lyla explained, "Dad, Tate is close friends with my new boss. That's how he heard about the job."

"I see. So there was cronyism at play, then."

Tate, bless his heart, was still smiling amiably. "Or networking. It's also called networking."

Lyla's dad humphed and took a bite of spinach. Her mom dove in with her next question. "Now Tate, you said you're a captain. Do I have that right?"

"Yes, ma'am."

"What branch of the military are you in?"

"Army, ma'am."

Lyla shook her head. Her mother did love manners in a man, and she was beaming at Tate like she wanted to award him a medal. She settled for offering him more meatloaf.

Lyla was certain she was never going to hear the end of this tomorrow.

While Tate piled two more slabs of meatloaf on his plate, Lyla's dad asked him, "Why aren't you on a base somewhere? You retired?"

"Actually, I'm on temporary leave at the moment."

"I see. And why's that?"

Lyla knew that look on her father's face. He was going to keep trying to figure out the man his daughter had brought home, even if it took all night.

"Dad," she warned, "let's not—"

Tate patted her arm, though. "No, it's okay." He told her folks, "I caught a bomb upside the head a few months ago, actually. I'm on medical leave while I recover."

Right. Like it was NBD. Lyla's dad sat back in his chair and looked him over with new eyes.

Her mom's hand flew up to flutter at her chest. "Oh no!" she gasped.

"No worries," Tate continued blithely. "It took a while, but I'm right as rain now. I should be redeploying soon."

Her father asked, "Great. Where you headed?"

Lyla tried again. "Dad, he's—"

"I'm not at liberty to say, sir," Tate interrupted gently. "I'm sorry."

Both of her parents took breaths and opened their mouths, but Lyla had no desire to hear what snooping questions they'd come up with next.

She dropped her napkin next to her plate and begged, "Guys, can we please table the inquisition for now? Let's talk about something else."

"All right," her mother said, clearly unhappy to be thwarted and drawing out the syllables. "What about…have you seen any good movies lately?"

Lyla blinked at her tart tone. "No, I can't say that I have. Have you?"

Tate's eyes ping-ponged between them as he chewed. He was no dummy—he knew this was a tentative truce, at best.

"Oh, yes," her mom said. "We saw a lovely film last weekend with Bill and Midge. It was about this laundrywoman during World War I."

"*Really.*"

It never ended with these two. Never. And if Tate weren't here, Lyla would tell them so.

Her father warned, "Peggy…"

"Midge said—"

"*Mom!*" she squawked. "You promised not to bring them up again!"

"Maybe not the best story, Peg," her dad murmured.

Beside her, Tate was gripping his fork with wide eyes and a faintly amused look, ready for more fireworks. Thankfully, though, Lyla's mom backed down and resumed picking at her meatloaf.

Lyla met Tate's inquiring gaze and looked pointedly down at her watch. "Oh, man. How did it get so late already?" she announced.

He was right on it, the big handsome stud. "What time is it, Lyla?"

"It's already 7:30. We've got to get going!"

"*Shoot.* You're right." Tate set down his fork and looked expectantly at her parents.

"You're leaving? So soon?" Lyla's mom bleated.

"I'm sorry." Lyla stood and yanked Tate up with her. "I promise I'll come visit again soon, okay?"

"You say that all the time, lately."

"Come on, Mom. That's not true."

Her dad murmured, "Peg, leave her alone. Lyla has her own life. Besides, nothing's stopping us from going into town to visit her, too, you know. We can make a day of it."

Lyla agreed, "That's right. You guys should. We can see a show or visit a museum…whatever you want."

"Okay!" Her mother perked up at the promise of a fun outing. "I'll call you tomorrow and we can set something up." She stood and began gathering plates. "Do you want to take any leftovers home? Tate? Want some meatloaf?"

Lyla waved her off. "No thanks, Mom. Tate doesn't have a fridge. We're good. You want us to help clean up before we go?"

"No, your father helps me. Just leave everything where it is."

Lyla's dad pushed up from his chair and smoothed the wrinkles out of his pants. "I got some ice cream at the store today. Take some with you."

"Dad, it's okay. It will just melt in the car," Lyla said. "Besides, I can buy ice cream two blocks from my apartment. I don't need to get it here."

This could go on all night, and probably would. She shot a pleading look at Tate, who immediately took her arm and steered her toward the front of the house. "Thank you so much for having me," he called over his shoulder. "Dinner was terrific."

"You're welcome anytime," Lyla's mother said grandly. She picked up the stack of dishes, blew Lyla a kiss, and headed for the kitchen. "Drive safe, honey!"

At the door, Tate reached out to clasp her father's hand. "Pleasure meeting you, sir."

"Likewise. You keep our girl safe, all right?"

"Sure thing."

"And Lyla, don't forget to touch base with your mom tomorrow. She misses you, you know."

"I know, Dad. I will."

She grabbed her purse off the floor, hugged her father goodbye, and soon she and Tate were back in the truck and on their way.

"*Sweet baby Moses*," Lyla groaned, massaging her forehead as they headed for the highway. "I am so sorry about that. My parents were acting even loonier than usual tonight."

Tate just laughed. "Nah, they were all right."

"They were cross-examining you!"

"Yeah, they were, weren't they? I don't think they bought the whole *we're just coworkers* line."

"Oh, no. Please don't say that. I will never hear the end of it if those two caught even a whiff of potential coming off of us."

Tate's grin got wider. "What's wrong, Lyla? Embarrassed of me already?"

"You know what I mean," she fumbled. "I just don't want to get their hopes up." Or her own, for that matter.

Tate's smile faded a little in the face of her distress. "I guess we'll see, won't we?" he muttered, leaving her with yet another thing to worry about, on top of all the others.

Twenty-Five

THEY WERE TEN minutes outside of town when Tate got a call from Luca. He grabbed his phone from the cup holder and held it to his ear, not wanting to risk the speakerphone after the way their last conversation had gone.

"Hey, man. What's up?"

"I heard you and Lyla were coming back tonight, so I wanted to make sure you knew that Daisy has our guest room all set up for you. When do you get in?"

"We're about half an hour away," Tate hedged, buying himself some time, "But listen, you don't have to worry about me. I don't want to intrude on your little love nest."

"No intrusion," Luca protested. "You're family. You shouldn't have to stay in some hotel with no one to feed you. Come here. Stay as long as you want."

"I appreciate the offer. But let's wait and see, okay?"

"Wait for what? Where are you going to sleep tonight?"

"TBD."

There was a brief silence, during which Luca clearly attempted to read between the lines. "Okay, so if you hate the thought of staying here, Red said you could stay at their place on the North Fork. It's beautiful out there. You should see it. Maybe take Lyla."

"To Long *Island?*"

"Why not? He also told me if you really needed to be in town, you could take their loft and they'll go out there. Either one works for them. Whatever you want, he said."

"You two need to stop worrying about me. I'm a big boy. I can figure it out," Tate laughed. He did relax a little, though, knowing he had a few more backup plans if what he really wanted to do didn't pan out.

"I realize that. We just want to help," Luca said. "And please remember, Tate…we deserve to be a little bit selfish, here. It's been a long time since we've seen you."

"It's been three months!"

"That didn't count. You weren't yourself. We want to spend *quality* time together before you leave again."

"You will, dude. We have some leeway still. Don't worry."

"How much leeway?"

"That's a subject for another conversation." Tate peeked at Lyla, and sure enough, she was listening in curiously. "I'll call soon, okay?"

"We'll be up late if you change your mind. Just give the doorman your name and he'll buzz you in."

"Thanks, brother, but don't wait up." Tate disconnected the call and darted another look at Lyla.

"What was that about?" she wondered immediately.

"It was Luca. He wanted to know if he and Daisy should expect me to stay over tonight."

"Oh." Lyla seemed taken aback. "Why?"

"Well…I guess because you and I didn't exactly hash out what we were going to do once we got back to town. My status is a little bit up in the air."

"What do you mean?"

"Well, for starters—where do you envision me staying at night?" Tate held his breath, waiting to see how Lyla would respond.

She frowned. "I guess I assumed you'd go back to your hotel."

"I gave up the suite when you and I left for your tour. It seemed like a waste, since I was going to be gone for so long. Red and Luca were agitating for me to stay with one of them once we got back, anyway," Tate explained. "Now, it seems that the Trident folks were so busy canceling your last events, that no one thought to book me something new."

"*Ah*. That is a bit of an oversight."

"The problem, as I see it," Tate told her, "Is that Red's place is down in Chelsea and Luca's is over on the east side. If I stay with one of them—"

Lyla picked up his train of thought instantly. "You won't be close to me."

Tate nodded. "Exactly, which rules them out as crash pads, as far as I'm concerned. So, let's think this through—what *is* close to you? Where can I get a room nearby? It doesn't have to be anything fancy."

Lyla's frown deepened, and she nibbled uncertainly on her lush lower lip. "Tate, I'm not sure how you'll feel about this, but what if…"

His heart dipped and leaped with hope. There was only one thing he wanted to happen here, but he couldn't ask for it. It had to come from her.

"What?" he prompted.

"What if you stayed with me?" Lyla asked in a nervous rush. She added, "I mean, it makes the most sense, and we've been handling it well, so far. I think. And even though my apartment is smaller than some of those suites we had, I do have a comfortable pull-out couch. And working A/C. And indoor plumbing. It's not very neat, though. I should mention that."

"It'd be a lot safer," Tate acknowledged happily, "But are you sure you don't mind having me underfoot?" He really, really wanted to be, though. Under any part of her, really—Tate wasn't particular.

"I'd feel better not being alone, to be honest. At least until they catch my superfan, anyway."

He tried not to let his relief and triumph show too obviously. "Okay. Well, if that's what you want, then that's what we'll do."

Lyla brightened. "Do you have anything you need to pick up anywhere?"

"Nope. I travel light. I have everything I need right here in this truck."

That was putting it lightly. He may have won this small victory, but what the hell was Tate going to do when he finally got cleared to head back to his unit? How was he supposed to walk away and just leave this incredible woman behind?

They'd essentially been living together for weeks, and now he knew that was going to continue. Tate had met Lyla's *parents* tonight, for crying out loud. True, it'd been a bit like having discount seats at a low-rent boxing match, but come on—Tate hadn't met a woman's parents in a decade or more.

It felt important. *Meaningful.*

He dwelled on why that was for the rest of their drive, and for the whole time Lyla was getting him settled into her cozy little apartment.

None of this could end well for him at all, but Tate simply couldn't resist squeezing out every last second of time with her. Someday soon, it was going to come to an end.

WHILE LYLA BUSTLED around, unpacking and attempting to rearrange some of her larger piles of clutter, Tate parked himself on her couch and took a stab at writing out a list for tomorrow. He ought to pick her up some groceries, for one thing, and they needed to check in with Lyla's PR people, too.

He probably ought to find a place where he could get in a few workouts, Tate thought, so he didn't turn into a total bump on a log while he was here.

He'd also have to figure out a better place to park his brother's truck than the expensive garage they'd stashed it in tonight—or come up with a plan to get it back to his parents' house soon.

He should probably coordinate that trip with his next Med Board evaluation. They hadn't given him a specific date yet, but by the time they got around to it, Tank and the rest of the team would no doubt have already snatched up el-Kadir and taken him in to answer for his crimes.

Assuming they got him alive, that was. Tate sort of hoped they didn't—that the bastard fought the inevitable and had to be put down where he stood, like the rabid animal he was.

Lyla poked her head out of her bedroom, startling Tate from that gruesome daydream. "You may as well get your laundry together, too," she said. "I've got a ton to do, and you can throw yours in with mine."

Tate ambled over to find Lyla standing with her hands on her hips, contemplating a towering mound of silky clothes on her bed.

He hooked a finger through a skimpy blue thong and dangled it in front of her with a grin. "So *that's* what's going on with Mount Mischief, here."

"Of course. What else would it be?"

"I don't know, Slick. Maybe where you come from, girls pile all their best lingerie on their beds to entice innocent men into naughty deeds. Like sea sirens."

Tate nearly choked on the word *innocent*, but somehow managed to keep a straight face.

As he'd expected, Lyla almost choked, too. But, after sputtering for a minute or so, she came back at him with, "If you think that's my best lingerie, you are woefully misinformed."

He chuckled. "Nice job. You're getting really good at the whole sexy banter thing."

"Thank you," Lyla said primly. "Now go grab your stuff. The laundry room is dead at this time of night, but this pile is going to look a lot more daunting once you see how small the machines are."

Tate went and rifled through his bag, then came back with an armload of t-shirts, gym shorts, and boxer briefs to toss into the mix. "If you know of a drycleaner close by, I should drop my dress shirts off tomorrow. And I might do a separate load of whites in the morning, too, if that's okay."

"Sounds good."

Tate eyed her as Lyla loaded half the pile into a large plastic hamper she pulled from her closet. "I'll say this," he told her, "You sure know how to seduce a guy."

Lyla ignored him, naturally, and Tate didn't even know why he'd tried—it was virtually impossible to flirt with a woman when she was trying to do chores.

He couldn't seem to help himself around her, though.

"You carry the basket." Lyla instructed. "I'll grab the detergent and the quarters. The laundry room is down at the end of the hall, opposite the elevators."

Tate hefted the load and jerked his chin at her. "Lead the way." The whole situation was ridiculously domestic, and he had to admit—he kind of loved it.

Only one machine was in use, so Tate walked to the washer at the end of the row and tipped the basket over the well, so Lyla could scoop their clothes in. She hadn't been kidding about the size of these things—barely a quarter of their stuff fit. They had to repeat the process three more times before they had their laundry all divvied up, and this was only half of what needed to get washed.

While Lyla messed with the quarters and the soap, Tate set down the hamper and pulled tomorrow's list from his back pocket again. He added *drop off dry cleaning*, and then, for good measure, included *get rolls of quarters.*

Lyla was a good sport to put him up—but there was no need for her to have to foot the bill for everything, on top of it.

When Tate was done, he tucked the paper away and saw that Lyla was watching him with a little smile. "So…" she drawled, "you think I'm seducing you, huh? How do you figure?"

So, she *had* heard. "Oh, you know," Tate smirked back. "Your sexy little scraps of lace taking a hot soapy swim with all my boys.

Who knows what could happen in there?" Tate lounged back against one of the dryers and winked at her.

Lyla pushed up her glasses and blinked rapidly. "Tate, they're clothes. *Dirty* clothes."

He waggled his eyebrows. "Real dirty. And about to get dirtier."

She gave up trying to make sense of it and just laughed, "You truly are incorrigible."

"Flatterer."

"Come on, frat boy," Lyla groaned, shaking her head. "These won't be done for at least forty minutes. Let's go eat popcorn and watch TV while we wait."

"Is that what they're calling it these days?" Tate asked, trailing after her with the empty basket. "Last I heard it was *Netflix and chill.*"

"Does it matter? Besides, it wasn't meant to be a euphemism. I really do want to put my feet up and veg out. We can do *other stuff* later. Once the clothes are out of the dryer."

"You're the boss," Tate told her, and the boss had a schedule.

He didn't have the heart to break it to her that they could manage all kinds of *other stuff* during the rinse cycle alone.

THEY DIDN'T EVEN get through one goddamn movie or the whole bag of popcorn before real life intruded again. Lyla's phone started ringing pretty much the second their asses hit that sofa, and it didn't let up.

"Who is it?" Tate asked for the tenth time, when Lyla came back from the kitchen with the receiver and a deep scowl.

"I don't know. The caller ID still just says *Unknown Number.*"

"Don't answer it."

"But what if—"

"Just turn off the ringer," Tate told her. He'd been begging her to for an hour now, at least.

Lyla hesitated, and it was obvious she was thinking the same thing he was. She cradled that phone in her hands like it was a live grenade. "*Tate...*"

"I know," he said. "But it might not even be him. Maybe it's only a telemarketer or something."

The sound stopped, then started up again a second later. Fed up, Tate took the phone from Lyla and turned off the ringer. "We don't have to worry about it tonight," he said. "Anyone important can reach you on your cell." He walked into the kitchen and replaced the handset in its charging station.

Lyla sagged into the couch cushions, her previous good mood seeping away like rain into a sewer.

"Come on, Slick. We can fold the laundry in the morning. Let's just hit the hay."

Lyla straggled after him and slumped down on her bed, her eyes vacant and glazed over while Tate moved around the room and the bathroom—triple-checking windows, drawers, closets, and what-not, one last time for the night.

When he finally came and sat beside her, she didn't even react. "Lyla?"

"Hm?

"How you holding up, sweetheart?"

When she raised her eyes to his, they were bleak and threatening to spill over. Tate's heart clenched a little to see her so distraught.

"What's going on?" he asked softly.

"Why?" Lyla wondered. "Why...*me?*"

He tucked a lock of her hair behind her ear, studying her face. "You really have no idea, do you? No clue whatsoever how you come off to other people?"

Lyla shook her head. Hell, maybe it was just Tate who felt this way about her. He doubted it, though.

"You know, I actually believe that. But, God—Lyla, I don't even know if I can explain it in a way you'll get."

"Try." Her voice was wooden, and Tate wondered how much she'd even be able to listen.

"Sure, I can try," he said. "But you know that out of the two of us, you're the one who's good with words."

Lyla snorted in derision. "I think you do all right, Fast Talker dot com."

Tate hiked one knee up on the bed so he could face her. If he simply blurted out the truth, he had to think that his true feelings for her were going to be more than a little obvious. Lyla would have to be a fool not to understand, and that couldn't lead anywhere good.

Still, the defeated look on her face made him blunder ahead anyway. "The thing is," he said, "You're gorgeous, and so sexy. That's really the first thing that hits people when they lay eyes on you. But the problem is, when people see a woman like you, they kind of assume she's going to act a certain way, you know? They figure you know you're amazing, and you're going to try to manipulate them with it."

"Oh, for crying out loud," Lyla huffed.

Tate motioned for her to wait. "So then, when you open your mouth and you're not that way at all—not stuck up, but warm and friendly and kind—it throws folks for a loop. I mean, you're totally oblivious that you're enchanting them, and then, the more you talk, the clearer it becomes how smart and funny and charming and sweet you are. Any average-Joe faced with that kind of sensory onslaught is bound to fall just a little crazy in love with you, in only the time it takes for you to sign his book."

"Tate—" she sighed.

"But if you get some nutbar who obsesses over things like the subliminal messages in fast food commercials, and you throw—" Tate tried to gesture at her, but ended up bracketing Lyla in his arms, instead, "—all *this* at him…Lord. He won't have a prayer of resisting you."

Lyla shook her head. This close, he could still smell the cinnamon tea she'd been drinking in front of the TV. "You can't be serious."

"Of course, I am."

She contemplated that. "How am I supposed to do anything about it, then? I am who I am. If I tried to be different, I'd just seem fake—and trust me when I say, readers can spot a phony from a mile away."

"Lyla, you're wonderful and you should stay that way. I'm here now, and I'm not going to let anything happen to you. If you believe anything at all, believe in that."

"Okay," she whispered.

Tate leaned forward and kissed her, but what was intended to be an encouraging peck rapidly grew wings and took flight. Lyla ended up in his lap, with Tate's hands groping the goods.

"Sorry," he muttered sheepishly. Christ, the poor woman was upset. The last thing she needed was to be mauled on top of it.

Lyla smiled, however. "Don't be."

Her busy little paws snuck around him and quickly encountered the gun he'd stuck in the back of his waistband a minute ago, intending to stash it in here so he could have it close by during the night. Lyla froze, hazel eyes wide behind her glasses.

Tate smirked, set the gun within easy reach on the nightstand, and then shucked off his button-down and tossed it on the chair.

Lyla rolled her shoulders and tried again, this time running her palms up his sides while he kissed her. In seconds, though, she ran into Tate's shoulder holster, and was clearing her throat and raising her eyebrows in mock annoyance again.

With an apologetic grin, he shrugged out of the holster and placed it beside the pistol on the nightstand. Tate got rid of his undershirt for good measure, too, but Lyla still eyed him carefully, hands hovering over his chest and not making contact.

"It does add a certain element to things when you have to disarm the other party before you jump them," she said.

"It's so arousing, right?" Tate teased. "Next time, I'll strap on some knives for you. Maybe hide some throwing stars where you least expect them."

Lyla groaned, "Oh, come on." She flushed and tried to wriggle off him.

Tate locked his arms around her like a vise. "Where do you think you're going?"

"Wouldn't want to attack you when you're so full of yourself. You might go and sprain something." She rolled her pretty eyes, and Tate decided it was one of his favorite expressions.

"Like my ego?" he suggested, poking Lyla in the ribs.

"That is a good example."

"Don't worry, I can take it. Besides, I understood this to be something of a mutual attack. You ride me. I wrestle you. That kind of deal."

"You do know how to sweet talk a girl, don't you?"

"I mean—*yeah*," Tate said. "I've got a decade-old rep I need to protect now that I'm back on home soil. All these dudes are coming up, trying to dent my swagger. I gotta stay sharp."

Lyla sighed and shook her head forlornly. "And they say romance is dead."

"Who says that? Cause if it's Piper, I'll know the world's over once and for all."

"No, definitely not her," Lyla laughed.

"Thank God," Tate smiled back and dropped one very chaste kiss on the tip of her nose.

The shadows were still there, lurking behind her eyes. Those calls tonight had scared Lyla. And, as much as he'd like to lay her out on this bed and rock her world till dawn, he couldn't make himself do it if Lyla wasn't in it for the same reasons as he was.

He wanted her to adore him the same way he adored her— and not just use him for stress relief when she'd had a bad day.

Right now, it seemed as if Lyla wanted to use sex with him to forget all the things bothering her, and not to connect to Tate on a deeper emotional level.

It felt wrong—and that was a first for him. Tate held Lyla at bay as best as he could, and desperately tried to decide what the hell to do about it.

Twenty-Six

L YLA PERCHED ON Tate's lap and waited for a spark to finally ignite in him. She was straddling him, for crying out loud, trying to make it clear with each kiss she planted on his lips where she wanted this to go.

Tate's hands stayed resolutely parked on her hips, however, and wouldn't migrate an inch.

His kisses remained light and teasing and didn't get the slightest bit deeper or more intense.

Hell, Tate's tongue hadn't even breached her lips yet, and that wasn't his usual speed at all.

After several minutes of futile encouragement, Lyla realized she wasn't getting anywhere. She was so frustrated she wanted to scream, but given how much Tate enjoyed tormenting her, she refused to give him the satisfaction.

Instead, Lyla swallowed her disappointment, called a halt to all the going-nowhere kissy-facing, and tried to climb off him.

Damn, Tate's arms were strong—they caged her in with barely a flex to show for it. Evilly, Lyla wondered if biting him might do the trick, might surprise Tate enough that he'd let down his guard and allow her to get away.

"Again, with the retreating?" Tate wondered. "Where to now, sweetheart?"

Lyla felt her face get hot. Could he *be* any more confusing? "Well, since it's obvious you're not interested in much more than sharing air with me, I figured I'd retreat with my dignity intact."

"Pardon me?"

"Don't play dumb. You obviously don't want me tonight, and I'm done trying to convince you. So let me go, already."

That gave him pause, but Tate still didn't relax his grip. "Oh, I want you, Lyla," he drawled softly. "I want you with every bone in my body. But," he swallowed nervously, "you and I both know those phone calls scared the daylights out of you tonight. And…I'm a hell of a lot bigger than you are. I don't want to overpower you and end up scaring you worse."

Lyla stared at him. "But I'm not scared of *you*."

"You might feel differently once I've got you pinned beneath me," Tate retorted.

"Even then, you won't scare me. I want this, Tate. I want you."

He looked oddly wan, however. "I don't want to frighten you," he said again, like he was reminding himself instead of her.

Lyla thought about how dangerous he'd seemed when she first met him, how that threatening edge had clung to him, despite all of his wisecracking.

And yet, Lyla had known right from the start that Tate would never unleash it on her, even on that horrible night when he'd woken from his nightmare.

"You don't. I feel safe with you," she told him, "Always." She ran her hands over his big biceps. "I like your strength."

To emphasize that point, Lyla wrapped her arms around Tate's neck and arched against him one more time, then brushed her lips over the side of his neck.

"I want to make you feel so good," she murmured. She felt him shiver.

"Trust me, sweetheart. You do."

Suddenly, Tate was there with her again—not as some remote bodyguard keeping his distance, but as Tate, *her Tate*, once more.

One big hand palmed her ass and pressed her against his now-obvious arousal. The other gripped the back of Lyla's head to hold her in place while Tate's tongue invaded her mouth and took immediate possession.

"Why are you doing this?" he murmured against her lips. "Tell me."

Lyla told him the truth. "Because I can't be here with you and *not* do this. I need you, Tate. I need you like I need to breathe."

In moments, he yanked her shirt up, tossing it aside so he could dive lower to nip and suck at the tops of her breasts. Lyla pushed off her shorts and shimmied out of them, hoping that would encourage him some more.

And then Tate was scooting back, holding Lyla tight against him as he braced his back against the headboard of her bed. He teased her nipples through her bra until they were tight, hard peaks against the damp lace, and Lyla was moaning for more.

Tate pulled back suddenly, gasping for air and spreading Lyla's legs wider so he could pull her even closer against him.

He looked down and hooked a finger under the string of her panties at the side of her hip. "These are nice," he commented.

"Thank you."

He pulled the string tighter and gave a sudden, sharp yank, snapping it handily before doing the same thing to the other side. In seconds, he'd tossed the useless scrap on the floor and sat smiling at her smugly.

"*Okay*," Lyla laughed breathlessly. "That's going to throw off the laundry schedule."

"You're resourceful," he commented. "I'm sure you can figure something out."

Tate dipped her way back on his thighs and ran the tip of his tongue lightly along the crease of Lyla's leg. A faint red line was just visible there, from the elastic of her panties pressing into her skin.

She yelped and dug her fingers into his arms, bracing against the tickling sensation.

Tate laughed and pulled her up again, urging Lyla into a grinding rhythm against his cock while he kissed her deeply.

"Like this?" she gasped, when she came up for air.

"Love it, sweetheart. Just like that."

Lyla worked her hand between them so she could undo Tate's pants. She wanted to feel him against her without all the layers of material between them. But once she had him free of his khakis and briefs, he took her hand and wrapped it around himself, stroking up and down a few times.

His lips devoured hers hungrily. Why did it feel like Tate was cherishing her? That was definitely an illusion—another talent in his varied bag of tricks—since a man like him would obviously never do such a thing.

The other women he knew probably ate it up, too. Lyla couldn't be the only one who was such a sucker for his charms.

It wasn't like she could take exception, though, since she'd started this whole shindig to begin with. What was she supposed to say? *Stop acting like you care so much—it's throwing me off my sexy-times game?*

As Tate's lips and hands progressed down her body, Lyla decided he was way, way too good at this. She was losing sight of what they were doing here, and beginning to have some inconvenient worries about what was going to happen to her heart once Tate left for good.

She had to remember that he was being paid to be here and that he'd made it very clear he couldn't wait to leave. Lyla could not tell him that with every day and every kiss, she was falling harder for him, because the instant they caught whoever was bothering her—or the minute Tate got cleared to return to active duty—he'd leave.

He'd go back to doing what he'd been trained for, and what he loved. Tate would resume his regular life, fighting in places Lyla never wanted to visit. He would continue saving the world every day, and he'd probably act like it was no big deal.

And then, when he wasn't busy being a hero, Tate would no doubt manage a succession of flings with a bevy of beautiful women—and in all likelihood, he would kiss them like he was kissing Lyla. Stupidly, they would most likely fall for him, too.

Lyla couldn't have any illusions that she'd see Tate again, once his job as her bodyguard was over. He might have friends in New York, but his family was in Ohio. If Tate ever got leave, he would go see *them*, not come to visit her.

Pining away waiting for him would be foolish and completely useless.

Lyla had to be prepared to return to her regular, everyday self—solitary, hardworking, and bookish. She'd probably have to adopt a cat or two, just to keep the theme going.

Abruptly, Tate's careful touches felt like sandpaper against her nerves. She needed something harder from him—something forceful enough to wipe her pointless anxieties from her brain.

She didn't count on the aces Tate had stashed up his sleeve, though—or in his fingers, as it were. A stray nudge here, a focused caress there, and soon he was laying down cards that had Lyla invoking deities and forgetting all about future heartaches.

There'd be time enough for worry later, Lyla conceded. For now, this man was here, and he was hers.

When she floated back to earth, Tate hauled her body close and nuzzled into her hair. "I want to love you all night long," he murmured. "I never want to stop holding you tight and breathing you in."

Foolishly, Lyla blurted out, "You do know when you say things like that, women can't help falling for you. Right?"

Tate froze, holding still for an excruciatingly long moment while Lyla's heart leapfrogged around behind her ribs. "How about we agree that if you're the one doing the falling," he finally said, "I'll do the catching?"

He *had* to know he was different. Had to know he was special to her.

Lyla laughed, suddenly and awkwardly, and wondered if it even mattered. "Is that some veiled reference to me being clumsy?" she bluffed.

That squashed whatever moment they'd been having pretty expediently. Tate nipped her on the tender part of her shoulder and barked out an unsteady laugh, too. "No need to be coy. Everyone already knows you're a klutz."

"Good thing you're here to remind me."

"Agreed. Just to be safe, though, you'd better let me do all the work on this next part. You know, so you don't hurt yourself."

Lyla feared it was already far too late for that.

THE FOLLOWING MORNING, Tate stood at her bathroom sink like he'd been doing it for years, a towel wrapped snugly around his waist while he finished shaving. His skin was still warm and damp from his shower, and Lyla thought she'd never seen a sexier sight.

She wrapped her arms around him from behind and laid her cheek against Tate's back, wishing she could hold on to him in other ways as easily. His muscles rippled under the surface as he rinsed off his razor and laid it down.

A moment later, Lyla heard the unmistakable sound of pills rattling out of a bottle. She peeked around Tate's shoulder, wondering if he had another headache—but that wasn't garden-variety ibuprofen he was holding. It was a prescription bottle.

Tate met her eyes in the mirror a little guiltily, and Lyla looked quickly away. Curiosity was all fine and well, but it wasn't her business what medications he was taking. She should leave and give him some privacy.

But Tate tapped Lyla's hand, still resting against his stomach, to get her attention. When their gazes connected again, he showed her the bottle.

"Anti-convulsant," he said. "To prevent seizures." Then he fished around in his kit, held up a second prescription, and added,

"And this one is an anti-depressant, since I was a little unhinged at first, when I managed to squeak through and so many other people didn't."

"Oh. Okay."

"Hopefully, I'll be off both of them really soon. That's what they've told me, anyway. I'd really love to have a freaking beer one of these days, and not have to worry about what's interacting with what."

And here Lyla had been assuming he never drank around her because of the job. "I appreciate you telling me," she said, "But you really didn't have to. You don't owe me an explanation just because I'm nosy."

"Yes, I do," he told her. "I don't want you to worry about me. I am okay, I swear. I won't crap out on you."

"I'm not concerned about that in the least."

"Good." Tate paused, then said, "But Lyla, listen—I'm still not…a good long-term bet. You should know—"

Lyla turned him around and laid her fingers against his lips. "Please don't."

Tate kissed her hand. "Don't what?"

"Don't wave me off before anything's decided. Okay? Can't we just enjoy what we have together now, and worry about the rest later?" It was a risk, she knew, but Lyla longed for him to agree.

Tate looked troubled. "I want to. But maybe that's not the best idea. I don't want you to get hurt."

She noticed he didn't seem worried about himself in the least. "Whatever happens," Lyla told him, more confidently than she felt, "I know you will never be hurtful intentionally." She'd be devastated enough by the unintentional part.

Tate didn't respond. He only bent to rest his forehead against hers.

He smelled like toothpaste and shaving cream, and Lyla would've given anything right then to have him smiling and cracking jokes again.

"I'm not going to beg you," she said. She wanted to, though—God, she really wanted to.

Stay with me. Don't leave.

Tate pulled back and framed her face in his hands, then kissed her softly. His eyes searched hers, wide and uneasy.

"We'll figure something out," he conceded at last. "But please promise me you won't make me into something I'm not. Don't put the cart before the horse, here."

Lyla smiled. "Now you're a horse?"

Finally, finally, Tate's shoulders relaxed, and he cracked a wide, cocky grin. "It's *stallion*, sweetheart. The word you want is *stallion*."

As he sauntered away, Tate whipped off his towel, spun it around, and snapped Lyla in the ass with it—like they were a couple of dudes in a locker room, instead of a man and a woman having a serious discussion, sort of, about their future.

"Ow!" Lyla complained.

Tate bestowed his most devilish wink on her, then turned to his duffel bag to get dressed.

Had they decided anything just now? Lyla didn't have the faintest idea.

Twenty-Seven

THE PHONE WAS ringing again.

It had been for a while, Tate thought. Ringing, falling silent, then kicking back on again at least two or three times now. At first, Tate had assumed he was dreaming it.

He scrubbed at his eyes. It must be a wakeup call that Lyla had scheduled without telling him.

Once he cracked his lids, it would undoubtedly be morning, and *yeah*, who was surprised that he didn't feel rested in the least?

However, even with his eyeballs peeled wide, the room stayed just as dark as before. The bathroom door was still cracked, emitting its quarter-inch sliver of light, but beyond the windows, the sky was inky black. A quick glance at the bedside clock confused Tate even more—it was only 3 a.m, not six or seven.

They'd been asleep for four hours, at most. And, Tate remembered abruptly, he and Lyla were back at her apartment, now, not in a hotel.

Ergo, this was not a wakeup call. It had to be her fucking stalker again, ruining their sleep for the second night in a row. But when had Lyla turned the ringer back on?

She hadn't even budged next to him, courtesy of the industrial-grade earplugs she'd started wearing once they'd returned to town. So, Tate rolled over and did the honors himself, grabbing the receiver and trying to calm the instinctual uptick in his heartrate.

Middle of the night calls were never good news. Literally everyone on the planet knew that. Frankly, it'd be better if this was the stalker—then, at least it wouldn't be someone they knew, calling to say they were in the hospital or something.

"Hello?" Tate's voice came out gravelly, and not a little breathless.

He hoped to hell the caller wasn't one of Lyla's parents—or Red, for that matter. There'd be a shit ton of explaining to do, if so, because even Tate had to admit he sounded like he was mid-fuck.

If only.

The line was silent for a long moment, but then a reedy kind of chuckle filtered over it. "Well, look at that," the voice cackled. "I'm right again."

The stalker. It was the first time Tate had talked to the asshole himself, and his brain was spinning, trying to gather any and every detail he could from the sound of the guy's voice.

It was definitely the same person from the recording he'd heard. Definitely a man.

It was also hard not to lay into the freak—to chew him out for tormenting Lyla the way he'd been doing. But Tate reined in his inner caveman and merely inquired, "Right about what?"

He had no idea if Scarletti had a tracer on Lyla's landline, but it sure would come in handy right about now.

"I guess Lyla's not the only one who's always getting things wrong," her stalker said. "You're wrong, too, if you think you'll ever get to keep her."

Indeterminate age. No noticeable accent, but maybe he was altering his voice to hide it?

"Why's that?" Tate wanted to keep him talking, but he saw no need to point out all the reasons why the prick was probably right.

"Because..." Another chuckle, some rustling, but no other sounds that could be used as clues, like you saw in the movies—not a train whistle, foghorn, or car alarm to be had. "Delilah's going to have to pay for her mistakes, now. It's time."

Tate frowned. No one but Lyla's mom called her Delilah. Most people didn't even know it was her real name. She'd said so herself.

"What mistakes?" Tate asked. He needed the dude to say more, to give him something to go on here, to make a mistake. Something. *Anything.*

There was a small click and line went dead.

"*Shit,*" he muttered. What was he supposed to do with that?

As gently as he could, he set the phone in its cradle and felt around for his cell. He had to enter the time and details in the log they'd been keeping, before he forgot anything.

When Tate was finished, he laid back down, but he knew he wouldn't fall asleep again. His nerves were jumping under his skin like live wires, itching for the chance to pummel something.

There was a soft touch on his arm, and he nearly jumped out of his skin.

"*Jesus,*" he gasped, pulse galloping even faster, now.

Lyla's voice was small in the dark. "Sorry."

"No, it's just—"

"Was that him?"

Tate *really* wanted to punch something, now. "Yeah, Slick. It was."

She cuddled closer. "What did he say?"

"Bunch of crap. Barely made any sense, the psycho fuck."

Lyla sighed, "You can tell me, Tate. I've heard it all before. What was it this time? More stuff about being wrong?"

"Yeah." He blew out a frustrated breath. "He's a one-trick pony, all right."

"Could you tell anything else?"

No, he could not, and the fact was making him crazy. Tate shook his head, running through every word her stalker had uttered.

Hold on.

"Does he always call you Delilah?" he asked.

"Yes, and it's so creepy. How did he even find that out?"

"Could be a lucky guess," Tate mused, "but you know how the internet is. People can find all kinds of crap out there."

"I suppose."

He rolled to his side and stroked her arm. "I'm sorry it woke you up. I was hoping you wouldn't hear anything."

"I didn't hear the phone—I felt you move. I always feel it when you get up."

"Damn, Lyla. I get up a lot. I'm sorry."

"Don't be. I'm still sleeping better than I did before you arrived."

Not Tate. He was sleeping worse, knowing there was a second body to protect besides his own—and one that was a heck of a lot more important in the general scheme of things.

Lyla didn't have to know that, however.

"I'm glad," he told her. "And listen—now that he's gotten some attention, I bet he won't call back tonight. Let's try to catch a few more Zs while we can."

Good little soldier that she was, Lyla agreed readily, even though she probably knew, as Tate did, that sleeping was going to be impossible.

And they were right. That asshole kept up his campaign of harassment for the next hour—calling and letting it ring once or twice, then hanging up again. He waited longer and longer between calls, letting them think he was done before starting all over, once more.

Turning off the ringer did nothing, now that they were both awake. The way the handset lit up with each call was like having a strobe light on the ceiling.

When he couldn't stand it anymore, Tate finally ripped the cord from the wall and threw Lyla's stupid phone in the tub. They stood shoulder-to-shoulder in her tiny bathroom, watching it for a long time—like they both expected the device to come to life, even without any juice.

Eventually, Lyla turned on every light in the place and made some tea. Then she sat on her couch until dawn, watching cartoons and clutching her arms around herself like she could keep from disintegrating that way.

Tate kept her company, but his thoughts were going in circles.

There was something nagging at him—some small detail that his subconscious had picked up on in the last couple of days—that related to that fucker's call. It was out there, teasing at the edges of his brain, but kept eluding him.

He didn't think he'd ever felt so helpless.

AFTER THEY'D DOWNED enough caffeine between them to power a nuclear reactor, Tate shooed Lyla into the shower and went into her kitchen to fix them some breakfast.

When Lyla wandered out of her bedroom a while later, she had a towel wrapped around her hair and her eyes were bleary. Tate pecked her cheek and handed her a plate, then pointed to the sheet of paper he'd noticed on her refrigerator.

"Hey, Lyla? I keep seeing this thing on your fridge. What is it?"

"Daisy drew that," she smiled. "It's supposed to be you, Red, and Luca. See?" She pointed each of them out, and Tate smiled at how well his buddy's fiancée had captured their likenesses with just a handful of lines.

"We're in a bar?"

"Yeah. Piper told the joke and Daisy drew it as she talked. You know, like—a CEO, a doctor, and a soldier walk into a bar?"

"Go on," he chuckled, enjoying the visual.

"See, the CEO ordered a whiskey. The doctor ordered wine…"

"—and got kissed by someone, apparently." Luca's image had small lip prints drawn all over his cheek and collar.

"As I said, Daisy was doing the drawing."

Tate was happy his buddy had found someone so totally devoted to him. "Looks like I got a…bomb. Not a drink?"

"Because you like to 'end the week with a bang.' That was my contribution." Lyla bit her lip like she wasn't sure whether to laugh or flee. "Look—there are your hordes of admirers, off to the side. Get it? Because 'bang' can mean two things, and…"

"Yeah, I got that," Tate told her, amused but also *not*. "That's how my friends still see me, huh?"

"We were just screwing around, Tate. Being silly."

"I see how it is. Pick on the guy who's not there to defend himself." He tried like hell to keep his voice light, but apparently, it didn't work.

Lyla asked, "Are you offended? Most men wouldn't care if their buddies thought they were players." She set her plate down and put her arms around him.

"Except, why does it feel like they've been allowed to grow up and move on, and I haven't?" Tate hadn't intended to blurt that out, but now that he had, it felt so true.

"I'm sure no one meant it like that."

Tate shrugged, unconvinced. "When did you guys do this, anyway?"

"Maybe…four or five months ago?"

"We hadn't met yet."

"No."

"But you kept the cartoon. Why?"

"Ummm…I don't know." Lyla's face turned red. "Maybe out of curiosity? Or maybe for good luck. It's hard to say. They talked about you sometimes when we all got together, and I always sort of wondered what you were like. But *this* happened the night your mom called Luca to tell him you'd been injured. It was all so horrifying, but Daisy told me to keep it until it was funny again."

"Oh." Tate could imagine what that call must have been like. His eyes swung back to the drawing, and the whole thing took on new shades of meaning.

"You should have seen the way your friends swung into action, Tate. They really do love you."

"They're good people," he conceded. "The best."

"You, too, Tate. You are, too."

"I don't know. I try, but…anyway. Our food's getting cold. Let's eat."

AFTER BREAKFAST, HE and Lyla were going over her calendar for the next few weeks, when Tate's cell began chiming with an unfamiliar local number.

He and Lyla watched it for a long moment before Tate snatched it up and answered, "This is Captain Monroe."

"Captain, Detective Scarletti here. I got your message. Good thing, too, since I was hoping to catch a word with you today."

"So, what do you think?" Tate asked him. "Can you guys get something on Lyla's phone to trace who keeps calling?"

"We'll look into it. In the meantime, I'd appreciate it if you could do me a favor."

"What's that?"

"I'd like to have a timeline of your injury and subsequent recovery, to stick in Ms. Lawson's file. Where you were, what you were doing, and when. You can drop it by the station whenever you have it ready for me."

Tate held still for a long beat, immediately on guard. "And why would you want that?"

"Crossing all my t's, chief." A pause, then, "Unless there's some reason you don't *want* to share."

What an asshole. "Detective, I have absolutely nothing to hide."

"Great. Then I'll look for you this afternoon. How's three sound?"

"Fine. Three sounds fine," Tate gritted out. He stabbed at the screen, infuriated. What was the officer trying to pull? Was he trying to *intimidate* him?

"What was that about?" Lyla wondered.

"Hang on," he told her, then dialed Red. When he answered on the second ring, Tate barked, "Dude, why the *fuck* is Detective

Scarletti asking me to give him a timeline of my injury? How is that remotely applicable to Lyla's case?"

Red wasn't surprised. "Yeah, I've been trying to get a second to call you all morning, but I've been stuck in meetings. That bastard showed up at Trident first thing, supposedly to pick up an updated chronology of Lyla's run-ins with her stalker. But he was really sniffing around asking questions about you. I'm just happy I was there to run interference."

"What did he say?"

"Well, let's see. One highlight was when he asked if you read a lot of mysteries, and I told him he was a shithead for implying anything. He gave me the whole, *What? Convalescents read* bit."

"Not this one," Tate muttered.

"I might have mentioned the difficulties you had with focus at that time," Red admitted.

"Terrific. I'm sure that will improve his opinion of me dramatically."

His friend said, "Tate, Scarletti's on the wrong track, and he will figure that out sooner or later. There's no way he can tie you to Lyla's problems, even if he wants to."

"Dude, don't you watch TV?" Tate complained. "Cops can prove whatever they want to prove."

"Don't get paranoid. Now, what's the deal with the timeline he wants?"

"He said to bring it by the station at three."

"You do not go there alone. Do you hear me?" Red demanded. "Scarletti may be trying to get a rise out of you, but you are not going to give him any more ammunition than absolutely necessary. I'm going to call my lawyer right now. He'll meet you at the precinct house. Listen to him and do exactly what he says."

"Oh. come on. Is that really necessary?"

"Yes. Now quit being a baby and follow orders. You remember how that works, right?"

"I hate you."

"What else is new?"

"Also, thank you."

"Don't mention it. Call me later and let me know how it goes, okay?"

When Tate hung up and looked back at Lyla, it was clear she'd heard everything. No surprise there—Red had a tendency to speak a bit...*forcefully* when he got agitated. But it seemed Tate had bigger problems than one misled cop and a loud talker.

"I'm going, too," Lyla announced firmly.

"The fuck you are," he fired back.

"Well, I'm not staying here by myself," she countered calmly. "We're supposed to stick together, remember?"

She had him there. "*Shit.*"

"I'm sure they won't let me sit in with you and the lawyer, but maybe I'll get a chance to tell Detective Scarletti what a jerk he's being."

"Lyla, we want this guy helping you, not pissed at you. I would not do that."

"I can't make any promises," she huffed, and stomped off.

AT A QUARTER to three, the lawyer met Tate and Lyla on the sidewalk outside the station, looking precisely the way Tate had expected one of Red's attorneys to appear—polished. Rich. Loaded for bear.

He introduced himself as John Davidson, shook both their hands, and marched them inside.

Detective Scarletti separated them immediately, installing Lyla in a waiting room with a gnarly old coffee pot and a TV playing the news, and ushering Tate and the lawyer into a shabby conference room.

The lawyer handed over the timeline that Tate had emailed him an hour earlier. Scarletti smiled and leaned back in his chair, like they were a few old pals shooting the breeze in a pub.

The conversation itself could've been lifted from a late-night cop show.

"Thanks for coming in."

"Happy to help," Tate said.

"Mind if I ask you a couple of questions?"

"Nope."

"Mind if I record it?"

"Also no." He'd talked about all of this on the phone with Davidson not half an hour ago, and so far it was going exactly according to the expected script.

"You ever hear of Ms. Lawson before your buddy hooked you up as her bodyguard?"

"No, I did not," Tate answered.

What would he have thought, he wondered, if he'd seen Lyla's photo all those months ago? Would he have even realized what she'd become for him?

Scarletti prodded, "You do much reading in your free time?"

"Not really. It's kind of hard to lug around a book when you have an M16 in your hand."

Abruptly, Tate realized it probably wasn't smart to remind the cop that he was trained to kill. Scarletti had already leaped to enough stupid conclusions as it was.

The detective scribbled something on his notepad, then asked, "Any violent impulses from the PTSD?"

Oh, Christ. Tate gritted out, "I have not been diagnosed with PTSD." *Specifically, anyway.*

The lawyer had been taking breaths and holding up his hand with each rapid-fire salvo, but now he gripped Tate's forearm and squeezed it hard. Tate zipped his lips and sat sullenly, letting the man do his thing.

Mr. Davidson said, "Detective Scarletti, it is our understanding that my client is not a suspect in this case. Is that correct?"

"Yeah. For now."

"Then we are done here. You have your timeline. If you need anything else, you can request it through my office." Davidson slapped a business card on the table and yanked Tate out of his seat.

"Catch you later, Captain Monroe," the cop smirked.

"In your dreams."

Out in the hallway, the lawyer told Tate, "Please, shut up. Why would you even engage with him? A pissing match does not do you any favors."

"Because Scarletti's an asshole, that's why. Some psycho is out there threatening Lyla, and he's going to come at *me*?"

The lawyer rolled his eyes. "Just…let me handle him, okay?"

They came up to the waiting room and looked in. Lyla's face brightened up immediately and she popped out of her seat. "Hey guys, how'd it go?"

Twenty-Eight

Y OUR BODYGUARD HAS a big mouth," Davidson said drily, "but I think I can work around it. Call me if they reach out to you again, okay? I've got to take off now."

Tate clapped him on the back. "Hey, man, thanks a lot for coming. I really appreciate it."

Tate and Lyla followed the man out and let him take the first cab that came by. While they strolled down the block watching for another, Lyla leaned in and purred, "His mouth's not the only thing that's big."

Tate grinned, "You got that right, Slick," then slung his arm around her and walked a few more paces.

His smile faded quickly, however, and soon Tate was staring off down the street, deep in thought again.

"Are you worried about what happened at police headquarters?" Lyla asked him. She hadn't liked being told to wait in that dingy little room, but she'd despised not giving Scarletti a piece of her mind.

Red's lawyer had insisted she hold her tongue, however.

Tate shrugged, remarkably sanguine given that his character and honesty were being called into question. "Scarletti's just grasping at straws."

"Then what's wrong?"

"I don't know. Something's bothering me about that phone call last night."

He dropped his arm from her shoulders and stepped to the curb, hailing the taxi that was barreling down the avenue. When it squealed to a stop, Tate opened the door for Lyla, then slipped in beside her.

"I know what's bothering me," she said. He arched a brow at her, so she explained, "What time he called. I feel like I could sleep for three days. Let's go home and take a nap."

"Good plan." Tate watched the leafy streets of the Upper West Side go by for a minute or two, then asked suddenly, "Why does that fucker call you Delilah?"

"I don't know," Lyla answered. It was a detail that had truthfully always bothered her. The weirdo's use of her real name had always felt invasive, somehow, like a secret he shouldn't know about her.

"But you said no one calls you that except your mom. Right?"

"And even she doesn't do it all the time," Lyla agreed.

Tate had a strange expression on his face. She laced her fingers through his and squeezed a little. "Hey. What's going on?"

He murmured, "I'm wondering…your mom…" Then Tate shook his head. "When we were at your parents' house, maybe…"

He fell silent, long enough for Lyla to ask, "Tate?"

He blinked and met her eyes, frowning mightily. "We need to go back there."

"To my *parents'* house?"

"Yeah." With every word he uttered, Tate got more confident. "There's something…I'm missing something. But…I think it's there. Did you call your mom to set up your get-together yet?"

"No," Lyla said. "I tried to call her while I was waiting for you just now, but there was no reception."

Tate poked at her purse. "Call her and ask if we can go back there today."

"You're serious, aren't you?" she asked him. "I don't get it. What could my parents have to do with this?"

"I'm not sure, but I'm going to figure it out," Tate said ominously.

"WOW, AREN'T WE lucky?" Lyla's mother cried a few hours later. "Two visits in one week? It feels like winning the lottery, doesn't it, Jim?"

But Lyla's father was studying Tate's drawn face and seemed to have already picked up on the fact that this wasn't a social call.

"I'm not sure they're here to visit, Peg," he said, waiting for confirmation from her bodyguard.

And Tate *was* Lyla's bodyguard at that moment. His eyes were darting restlessly around, cataloging everything, and his muscles twitched under his skin. Lyla didn't worry a bit that her folks would suspect there was more to their relationship this time.

"I'm afraid you're right, sir," he told her dad. "There is something I need to remember from our visit the other day. It's right at the edge of my memory, but I can't quite pull it up. I thought if we came by again, I might be able to figure it out."

"Seems like sound reasoning."

"Let's hope so."

"Well, maybe we can help," Lyla's mom offered. "Was it something about that fun veggie dip we had? I got the recipe out of my magazine. I could show you if you like."

"No…I don't think it was that," Tate smiled.

"How about the car? You looked at our new Buick," her father reminded him.

Tate shook his head and frowned, looking away. Evidently, the barrage of helpful suggestions was muddying the terrain for him.

"You two are going to stay for dinner, right?" Lyla's mother asked. "I'm sure whatever it is will pop right into your head any minute. We can sit and have a cocktail until it happens."

"I make a mean martini," her dad offered.

Tate grunted.

Lyla held up her hands. "Guys, maybe we can give Tate a little space for a minute, so he can decide if he's even on the right track. We can probably stay for dinner, but..."

She caught Tate's eye where he was fidgeting in the foyer, and he gave her a quick, distracted nod.

"Yeah, we'll stay for dinner," she said. "But let's go in the kitchen and leave Tate be. I can help you put something together."

"No, not you," Tate barked. "You stay here with me."

Everyone froze. Then Lyla's mother, clearly impressed, whispered, "*So professional,*" to her husband.

Lyla's father gave Tate another apprehensive once-over, then stuck his hands in his pockets. "Something going on?" he asked.

"Nope!" Lyla chirped. "Tate's just being his usual thorough self."

Tate ignored them. His eyes were roaming around, taking in every detail of the entryway and the adjacent sitting room.

Her dad didn't seem convinced, but he still herded his wife toward the kitchen at the back of the house. "We'll be in here," he said over his shoulder. "Let us know if you need anything."

NOW THAT HE was free to rove, Tate was like a bloodhound let off his leash, retracing all their steps from their visit a few days ago.

It was mildly alarming, watching him go from room to room, announcing what they'd done and what had been said, before shaking his head and moving on.

"Hey, Lyla," he said finally, once he'd stopped in the front parlor. "A few days ago, when we were looking at our phones, you said you'd talked to your parents."

"During the book tour, you mean?"

"Yeah. How often did that happen, would you say?"

"Maybe...every other day? Sometimes more."

Tate stared hard at her. Lyla rushed to explain, "I know that seems like a lot, but I've been really busy with this whole Red Devil thing. I haven't been getting out to see them much, so…"

"You told them where we were, didn't you?"

"I…don't remember. Maybe?"

Tate nodded, lost in thought, and moved on.

Lyla tried to hang back so Tate would have space to do his thing, but the more he muttered, the more her nervousness grew. His brow was furrowed and he kept picking up little knickknacks and then putting them back down again.

It didn't take long before he led her to her bedroom upstairs. Moments after that, Tate was hunched on her little twin bed with its patchwork quilt, leafing slowly through her old yearbook page by page.

"It's here. I know it's here," he told her.

When he got to all the signatures Lyla's friends had left on the back pages, Tate stopped and read each one out loud.

Hearing the childish sentiments spoken without a hint of his usual teasing tone made Lyla wince. She considered hiding in her closet until all the *keep in touch*s and *you've always been there for me*s were over.

Tate was so serious and intent on his task, though, and she wanted to see where he was going with this.

He reached Brett Jones's inscription about halfway through. "*Delilah. Guess you got it wrong, Twerp,*" Tate read, "*I am special. I'm everything—you'll see.*"

Tate stopped and stared up at her, his finger tapping on the fifteen-year-old scrawl impatiently. "This. What is this about?" he demanded.

Lyla sighed and rolled her eyes. "*Ugh.* I'd forgotten about that."

"Why'd he write this?"

"Because Brett was a bully. When I was a freshman, he was a senior. He wouldn't leave me and my friends alone. One day I just snapped. I told him he was nothing but a punk and was never going to amount to jack shit in life. Brett was so pissed, and guess what—somehow he got his hands on my yearbook and managed to write that in there for me to find."

"What a dick," Tate said.

"Tell me about it. I wish either my parents or his would move away from here, so I'd never have to hear a word about him again."

Tate stared down at the page, nodding. He obviously wasn't ready to move on yet, however. "Except…look at the *words*. Don't they remind you of anyone?"

Lyla's eyes tripped over that coincidental string of syllables. *You got it wrong.* "No way," she scoffed.

"Why not?" Tate wondered. "He lives close enough to Manhattan. Why not?"

Lyla sank down beside him. "Tate, Brett was an ass a long time ago. But you saw the way he is now—I don't even think he can drive anymore. How would he get anywhere?"

Tate was undeterred. "So? He could take an Uber."

Lyla rolled her eyes. "What is it with you and Uber?"

"Okay, well…someone could have driven him around. Like…what about his kooky parents?"

"They wouldn't."

"Wouldn't they? You yourself said they think he can do no wrong. Even now, you said."

Lyla *had* said that, but still—it was too far-fetched to make any sense whatsoever. The cops were looking for a disgruntled fan, not some annoying guy she'd known in high school.

"Tate, I don't know about this," she said.

"Well, I'm bringing this with us," Tate told her, brandishing her yearbook. "Maybe Scarletti can analyze the writing or something."

"Feel free," Lyla shrugged. "But I swear to God—if my freshman year picture makes it into the gossip rags, I'm coming for you, Buster."

At last, Tate managed a small smile. "Sounds fair," he told her, relaxing a bit. "Now let's go eat whatever that delicious food is I'm smelling."

Lyla flopped onto her back. "It's pork chops. I'd know that smell anywhere. It's one of the primary reasons I stopped eating meat."

His eyebrows shot up in surprise.

"Seriously. I still have bad dreams about that smell," Lyla groaned. "It makes me gag."

"I'm sorry I dragged you back here," Tate commiserated. "Especially after the way things went the last time. Thanks for being a good sport."

"I don't mind, as long as you got what you need."

"I think I may have. It feels right. I just need to ask your folks a couple of questions, so try to play along."

TATE LIKED HER mother's pork chops nearly as much as he'd enjoyed the meatloaf. Of course, he did. He was so irritatingly wholesome he probably would've raved about tuna casserole, if Peg Lawson had given it to him.

But, while Tate shoveled her mom's dinner into his face and complimented the woman on her cooking skills, he was also trying to subtly interrogate her about the Jones family.

Lyla felt a little embarrassed, listening to him. Try as he might to keep her oblivious mother on topic, Tate just couldn't. He was far too polite, for one thing, and her mother was way too eager to impress him.

But it was the way her mom studiously avoided any mention of the neighbors that made Lyla suspect she was still smarting from their last visit. Undoubtedly, her mother blamed herself for the way they'd bickered, and for the way Lyla and Tate had booked it out of there a few days ago. Lyla would have to find a moment to apologize to her before they left tonight.

Lyla's dad wasn't saying much—he merely watched and listened, his face an unreadable mask as he moved his food around his plate.

Lyla suspected she and her father would be having a heart-to-heart about Tate before long, but she didn't have the first idea what she could possibly say to him when it happened.

She had to think that *I'm crazy about him, Daddy* wouldn't quite fit the bill. He could already tell there was more to it than that.

There were bigger things to worry about first, however. Dinner was winding down, and Tate was clearly getting frustrated by his lack of progress.

Unless Lyla could come up with some pressing excuse to linger longer, she and Tate would be saying their goodbyes without him having learned anything he wanted to know.

Twenty-Nine

THE LAWSONS WERE proving to be a tougher nut to crack than Tate had anticipated. The last time he and Lyla had visited here, they'd been downright verbose about the neighbors, so he couldn't fathom why—now that he actually needed to know more—they were shying away from the subject like cats from water.

He'd spent the entire meal attempting to steer them in a helpful direction, to no avail. Now, Lyla's mother was endeavoring to move them from the dining room to the front parlor for *after-dinner drinks*. Tate could only assume that was a precursor to showing them the door.

Besides, the parlor was uncomfortable, and he couldn't drink alcohol, anyway. Fortunately, Lyla seemed to be on the same page as him.

"Oh, come on, Mom," she was groaning, "We can sit in the family room. It's fine."

Her father was a step ahead of them, settling into a dingy blue recliner in there, and clicking through the sports channels with a full belly and a contented sigh.

"Don't be silly," Mrs. Lawson argued. "Your friend doesn't want to get lint on his nice pants. The front room is much nicer for talking."

Tate disagreed, but he'd make the concession if it meant that Peg would actually talk about what he wanted. It was time to stop pussy-footing around and get to the point.

So, once he, Lyla, and her mom were parked on the stiff sofas, Tate took a deep breath and dove in.

"Mrs. Lawson, Lyla and I were talking about the neighbors earlier and it got me to wondering. What specifically happened to the kid next door, anyway?"

She glanced nervously at Lyla, but her daughter only sat there studying her fingernails, as if she was bored to death instead of driven to insanity like she'd been the last time.

Mrs. Lawson confirmed, "You mean to Brett?"

Tate nodded.

Lyla's mother explained sadly, "Midge told me once that it was schizophrenia. Came on out of nowhere when Brett was only twenty." She looked pointedly at Lyla, and added, "But even though his circumstances changed, he still stayed loyal to his old friends. He didn't abandon them, like Lyla and the other kids in the neighborhood did to him. I've always thought it was very mean of them to ignore Brett, just because he's got some issues now."

"So, Brett considers himself one of Lyla's friends?" Tate inquired carefully.

Lyla snorted loudly next to him, rousing herself to gripe, "Mom, that's complete BS, you know. The Joneses always, *always* exaggerated our relationship. Brett was a jerk from day one. We aren't friends—we've never been friends."

Tate put a hand on Lyla's leg and squeezed, hoping to forestall any more outbursts. If Mrs. Lawson saw anything out of the ordinary in the gesture, she didn't comment on it, though.

Peg told him, "Brett is a big fan of Lyla's. He reads her books over and over."

"Is that so." Tate ran his hand over his jaw. Something was rotten here. *Big time.*

Her mom continued, "Bill and Midge told us he watches the cop shows on TV, so he'll understand what Lyla is writing about in her stories. He always asks what she's up to, they say."

Lyla muttered something under her breath but fortunately managed to restrain herself this time.

Tate had to be careful, here. This was going somewhere—somewhere important—but his hosts were not going to like where that was one bit.

"Midge said that Brett even keeps a scrapbook of all Lyla's articles and interviews and whatnot. Isn't that nice?"

Lyla sat bolt upright beside Tate. "*Mom.* You never told me that."

"Well, you said you didn't want to hear about them. You specifically instructed us to stop talking about them with you. Don't you remember?"

Tate couldn't let this devolve into another bout of bickering. He'd never get what he needed if it did. So, he interjected with the most interested voice he could muster and pressed his fingers into Lyla's leg as firmly as he dared.

"Do you talk ever about Lyla's upcoming events with the neighbors? Like what book signing she's doing next, that sort of thing?"

"Oh, sure. But Brett usually already knows. You should see him—he hangs on every word when she comes up in conversation. He doesn't have much else to occupy him, you know. He can't work or anything, and Midge gets tired of the TV being on too much. So, he keeps up with the other neighborhood kids on the computer, I guess. That's what they tell me, anyway."

Perched beside him on the fancy couch, Lyla swallowed loudly. "Mom—"

"Delilah, maybe you could try to keep up with Brett more," her mom suggested. "He's got to be lonely with only his parents to see all day. Midge said they tried to buy him one of those silly prepaid phones, so he could feel like all the other people your age, but he got bored with it."

So, the dude had a computer and a burner phone, Tate thought. *The hits just kept coming.*

He wrestled the floor back from the combatants once again. "Ma'am, has Brett Jones ever *been* to any of Lyla's events? Maybe to a signing or a reading or something?"

Tate's mind was already racing toward the end zone. Even if Jones wasn't allowed to drive, he could be taking cabs or buses or fucking *Ubers* to get to Lyla. And if he was, there would probably be records somewhere that they could subpoena.

Of course, it was also possible that the asshole was just stealing his parents' car to get where he needed to go. If that was the case, Jones could be crossing toll booths and bridges and tunnels with that car, and Red's investigator could almost certainly find that trail, too.

They could catch the fucker. They were *going* to.

Across from Tate, Mrs. Lawson had switched gears easily. "Of course he has. Brett wouldn't miss Lyla's appearances for the world. In fact, I believe he makes Bill take him to every last one. They drive all over together."

"Mom, that can't be right," Lyla protested. Her voice shook only the tiniest amount, but it still made Tate want to wrap his arms around her and shield her from this mess. "I've never once seen any of the Joneses anywhere."

"Well, they did say they try to keep out of sight. Brett gets embarrassed for people to see him like he is now." Mrs. Lawson folded her hands in her lap primly, and then—lest there be any doubt of what she was implying—she added, "He's afraid you'll act snooty."

Tate was absolutely certain that Lyla had swallowed her own tongue. It was the only explanation for the odd choking noise that was coming from her throat, and for the fact that no new invective was spewing from her mouth. He patted her knee in sympathy.

She whacked him on the arm. At least tongue-swallowing didn't appear to be fatal.

Her father strolled in and leaned against the doorjamb, picking up the thread of conversation amiably. "Bill spends a fortune on gas. He's been joking that he ought to start charging you mileage, Lyla—especially with that new gig of yours."

That posed a few new questions, as far as Tate was concerned. Could the father be in on it? Was Bill Jones her stalker, instead of his son Brett? Or, God help them, were both of the Jones men working together?

"I think we have a real lead for once," he murmured to Lyla. "Don't you?"

Lyla's eyes were huge and worried. She whispered, "Brett's really weird and a total jerk. But this is a whole other thing, Tate. My parents are going to freak out."

"I know. We have to be positive before we start accusing people."

"So, what do we do?"

Her mother piped up, "What are you two talking about?"

At that moment, Tate was acutely aware of two things: Lyla's parents had no idea that their neighbors and friends might be harboring a very dark secret, and the Lawsons definitely did not know that their own daughter was being threatened by a stalker.

They had no clue that the secret and the stalker could be one and the same.

Tate didn't know what to say to these people, and he had to talk to Lyla alone, *right now.*

He defaulted to that old standby, "Nothing much," then immediately regretted it when Peg's voice got sharp.

"Is this about Brett? Did I say something wrong?"

Lyla had recovered herself enough to jump back in, thank fuck. "No, Mom, of course not. We just realized how late it's getting, that's all."

Tate was more than happy to board that train. "Do you mind if we have a couple of minutes? We need to work out some scheduling details before we take off."

Lyla's father frowned in the doorway. "You're not hitting the road yet, are you? Mom got apple pie today. You remember, Lyla? From the orchard out by Aunt Helen's?"

Lyla looked pained. "Mm-hm," she whimpered.

"You don't want to miss this," he confided to Tate. "Come into the den where it's comfortable. We can watch the Yankees beat up on Tampa Bay while the girls dish out dessert."

Mrs. Lawson pushed up from her seat with a shake of her head. "Sometimes, it's like the Fifties never ended," she muttered, then bustled toward the kitchen.

Lyla's dad stood there expectantly, and Tate was engulfed by a wave of homesickness and longing for the sheer normalcy of it all.

Well, except for the "girl" bristling angrily beside him, and the little neighbor/stalker problem they might be having.

"We'll join you in a second," he said. "We just have to discuss a couple of things."

The man gave them a knowing smirk. "All right, well, don't take too long. Don't want that hot pie to melt all your ice cream."

Tate turned to stare at Lyla, wondering if she thought that sounded as hilariously dirty as he did—but she just sat there with a stiff, plastic smile aimed resolutely at her father. When he finally turned and ambled out, she leaned in close.

"So, what do you think?" Tate asked. "Doesn't it sound like we might have our guy?"

"Not here," she hissed back. "Let's go out front where they can't hear us."

"But your mom has pie," he teased.

"Are you freaking kidding me right now?" Lyla glared daggers at him.

"Yes, I'm kidding," Tate relented. "Come on."

They slipped out the front door and huddled together in a dark corner of the porch, shielded from the street and the neighbors' yard by a stand of tall holly bushes. Tate tried really hard not to let the arousing combination of furtiveness and hot, melting things take over his higher reasoning.

This was clearly not the time for his over-sexed, long-deprived libido to befriend the general populace. And by general, he meant *Lyla.*

She snapped his errant thoughts back into place fast, though. "Tate, this is really bad," she whimpered in his ear. "I don't know what to do."

"So, you agree? You think it could be him?"

"You heard her," she fired back. "Brett's condition is a lot more serious than I knew. And all that scrapbook stuff is kind of scary."

"You're worried about the scrapbook?" Tate marveled. "Because I'm a hundred-percent focused on that fucker coming to all your gigs, Slick."

She moaned. "*Ugggghhh.* It's so creepy. What are his folks thinking?"

"They think you two are buddies, obviously."

"Tate, what are we going to do?"

The curtain in the front room shifted, so he wrapped an arm around her and pulled her close. Let her parents think what they would—at this point, Tate didn't care about who he was or wasn't supposed to be.

"Listen, I'm not going to lie," he murmured into her ear. "Brett sounds sketchy as all get out. But the fact that his father is bringing him to all your events makes me wonder about him, too."

"*No,*" she gasped.

"Never say never. Parents will do all kinds of crazy stuff for their kids. We have to consider every angle, okay?"

"But how do we figure it out?"

Tate had been considering that. "Here's what I think. You know that investigator that Red has?"

"Um, *no.*"

He took a deep breath and started over. "Red knows a private investigator. He's used him for a couple of things over the years. Why don't we call him when we get back to the city and see if he can look for some evidence for us? Maybe he can find proof that Jones was in the area whenever the stalker left you stuff. Or maybe he can tail him and see if he does anything hinky."

Lyla pressed her fingers against her mouth, then wrenched them away again. "*Oh my God.* My parents are going to flip out. *His* parents are going to flip out."

"We don't have to tell them yet," Tate assured her. "Let's wait and see if the PI comes up with anything first."

"Okay."

"Now, can I have pie? I promise I'll eat fast."

"Are you nuts? How can you even eat right now?"

"I'm a growing boy," Tate shrugged. He'd been woefully far away from kinky-sounding pie a la mode for a very long time, and he refused to apologize for it.

"Tate! Wait," Lyla insisted, when he reached for the doorknob. She stood there wringing her hands.

"What?"

"Brett's scrapbook. Do you think Red's guy could…" She trailed off uncomfortably. The poor thing looked so freaked out, Tate wanted to kiss her just to take her mind off this whole mess.

"Oh, believe me. I'm going to get eyes on that scrapbook if I have to go over there and get it myself."

And that's when he heard it—a tortured, stifled little moan just on the other side of the hollies.

"*Shh.* Did you hear that?" he asked.

Lyla nodded, looking scared in the dim porch light. In the yard next to them, a screen door banged and Mrs. Jones called out, "Brett? Honey, are you out here?"

Tate spun and peered into the darkness, scanning the space between the two properties as best as he could through the landscaping. A flurry sprung up suddenly near the bottom corner of the Lawsons' porch, and a big dark shape darted across the lawn.

The door banged again, and then the yard fell silent.

"What was…was that…?" Lyla stammered.

"You're right," Tate said, crowding her toward the front door. "Fuck the pie. We gotta get moving."

Thirty

H ER PARENTS WERE looking at them like she and Tate had gone insane. Lyla wasn't so sure they were wrong.

"Mom," she said, as calmly as she could, "If I told you where I was during my book tour…that was supposed to be kept between us."

"But it was! The Joneses don't count. They're like family to your father and me."

Lyla thought her head might explode. "I have to get out of here."

"Lyla, what about the pie? Why are you two leaving? What's going on?"

"What's going on, Mother, is that you completely neglected to tell me that a deranged man has been tailing me all this time. That's what's going on," Lyla blurted out, fumbling to get her purse strap up over her shoulder.

"I simply didn't think it was pertinent, honey. Not in light of how mad you get."

"You didn't think it was *pertinent*? Those people over there have been following me around for how long now, and you simply never thought to mention it?" she cried.

"Lyla, the boy has so little to keep him occupied. I didn't see what the harm was. And honestly, given Brett's lifelong devotion to you, I'm appalled that you don't feel just a little bad about the way you talk about him."

"That *boy* is thirty-four years old, Mom. And it's not devotion—it's fixation."

"Lyla—"

"Mom! For the love of God!" Lyla cried, before Tate put a hand on her shoulder and squeezed.

"Ma'am, I know you said they go to all of Lyla's appearances, but you only meant the local ones, right?" he confirmed. "They wouldn't have driven as far as, say, Cleveland, would they have? Or Erie?"

Lyla's mother blinked rapidly, trying to keep up with the change in direction. "Oh, that's not so far away. I'm sure they would've."

Her dad cleared his throat. "Well…"

"You don't think so?" she wondered.

"Maybe not with Bill's foot, these days," he said.

Her mother gasped and nodded. "Oh, of course. You're right." To Tate, she explained, "Bill had surgery on his foot a few weeks ago. Poor man's been hobbling around in a walking boot over there ever since."

"So, he's not driving," Tate said.

"No, not for another couple of weeks, I'd say."

Lyla stared desperately at Tate. "Now what?"

Tate asked her father, "Does Brett drive, do you know?"

A guilty look passed between her parents, and Lyla demanded, "Guys? What?"

Her dad explained, "He's not supposed to."

Tate pinched the bridge of his nose to keep his cool. "But he does?"

"Only once in a while," Peg rushed to explain. "Midge doesn't like to drive at night, and with Bill's foot the way it is…well, sometimes I think they're in a bind. But they only let Brett do it when they're with him, so I'm sure it's okay."

Lyla couldn't believe what she was hearing. "Mom, are you *serious*?"

"You don't have children, honey. You can't imagine what it's like for Bill and Midge. They try to help Brett feel like he's as capable as he always was, but it's hard sometimes."

Lyla threw up her hands and stared up at the ceiling. "I don't even know what to say you guys right now."

Her father murmured, "Lyla, it's not our call to make. He's their kid."

She gaped at him. "Would *you* do something like that?"

"Of course not," he told her.

"Who can say what we'd do?" her mother speculated. "If it were you."

"*Mother.*"

Tate said gently, "Lyla. Lyla, stop and think."

She rounded on him furiously. "Tate, I swear—this is *not* the time."

"Lyla, she doesn't know," he retorted, calm and quiet as a spring breeze.

Her dad frowned at them. "Know what?"

Tate held Lyla's gaze and enunciated each syllable clearly and distinctly. "They. Don't. *Know.*"

Now her mother was the one throwing up her hands in exasperation. "I'm so confused. Lyla, what is he talking about? What is Tate saying?"

Lyla belted out, "Nothing."

At the same time Tate turned to them and explained, "Mr. and Mrs. Lawson, the truth is, Lyla has had a stalker for many months now. That's why her publisher hired me—to keep her safe on her book tour. The NYPD is involved, and they thought they'd arrested the right woman, but unfortunately, the threats to Lyla haven't stopped."

"So, what are *you* doing about it?" her father wanted to know.

"Everything I can. And, to be perfectly honest, Lyla and I think that Brett Jones might be involved. We're going to head back to the city right now and hand over some evidence to the detective in charge of her case."

"Evidence? What evidence?" her mom squawked.

"Brett wrote something in my old yearbook that sounds a lot like things the stalker says to me," Lyla told her. "And we're hoping my boss's private investigator can tie him to some other…" She paused.

Too many details would only scare her mom, and she didn't want anything to get back to the wrong ears.

Tate picked up the mantle, though. "…other things," he said vaguely. "I'm sorry. I know this can't be good news to hear."

Lyla's dad had flipped smoothly into crisis-control mode, though, which was a welcome relief given the storm brewing in her mother's expression.

He said only, "What can we do?"

"Jim!" her mom cried. "They're obviously *wrong*! Brett isn't capable of something like that—tell them."

"Peg, we'll talk about it later. Tell me what we can do to help you, Monroe."

"I would very much appreciate it if you would not share any details whatsoever about Lyla with other people, but particularly not any member of the Jones family. We need a little time to figure this out before one of them catches wind of what we suspect."

"We can do that."

"We can *not* do that!" Lyla's mother protested. "Those people are our friends!"

Jim spun on his wife so fast, they all took a step or two back. "And Lyla is our *daughter*, Peg! If she's in danger, she comes first. Think about what you're saying for one goddamn minute, would you please?"

Lyla's mom blinked like an owl, then sat slowly and carefully down on the sofa. "Oh my God. Oh my *God*." She looked shocked and horrified.

"What else?" her father asked Tate.

"I could really use a recent photo of the Jones family," he replied. "Brett in particular. Could you text one to Lyla?"

"Sure thing," her father told him. "You guys go do what you have to do. I'll take care of Mom, here."

Lyla darted forward to peck him on the cheek. "Thanks, Dad."

"Call me if you need me."

Tate said, "We will, Mr. Lawson. Thanks."

"Hey. You—you keep my girl safe, you hear me?"

"I'll do my best, sir."

"You'd better."

ON THE DRIVE back to Manhattan, Lyla dropped her head in her hands and moaned, "Oh God, Tate. What the hell is happening right now?"

"Sweetheart, we can do this. Take a deep breath and let's talk this thing through. We agree that Brett Jones could be your stalker, yes?"

"Yes!" she wailed. "And he just heard us talking about him. What was he even doing out there?"

"I don't know."

"Well, how do we know he isn't following us right now?"

"Because I'm watching for that," Tate told her. Lyla realized it was true—his eyes had been flicking between the road and the rearview mirrors with more than a little laser-like focus.

"Are we…is he…"

Tate shook his head. "So far, no one on the road but us and a thousand other anonymous New Yorkers," he smiled.

"Okay."

"Here's what I think we need to do. We have to get your yearbook to Detective Scarletti and see if the NYPD can link Brett's handwriting to any of the other evidence."

Lyla nodded. "Maybe this will convince Scarletti to stop bothering you."

"Maybe, maybe not. Which is why I think we should also get in touch with Red's investigator. We need to see if we can place Brett in any of the cities on your tour where stuff happened. See if we can find his parents' car on traffic cameras or something. Show his picture around at the hotels."

"Are we even allowed to do that?"

"Let's leave that up to the PI."

"But, Tate—" Lyla gnawed on her lip, thinking about it. "How long is that all going to take? Brett just heard us talking about him *now*. He's upset, *now*. What's to say he won't try something before we have a chance to link him to everything?"

Tate made a low sound, deep in his throat. "If that fucker wants to get to you, he's welcome to try," he growled. "But he's gonna have to get past me first."

"Uh, that's kind of hot," she told him with a shaky laugh.

Tate shook his head. "You're insane." He reached over to squeeze her thigh but got right back to business again. "We have a few more minutes before we get you home. Why don't you try Detective Scarletti now? You can fill him in, since I seem to be rubbing him the wrong way this week."

"Okay." Lyla found the officer's contact in her phone but hesitated, her finger hovering over the icon uncertainly.

Tate noticed, and rushed to explain, "You don't have to. I only thought, since we had the time—"

"It's not that. I just…" She winced. "*Damn it.*"

He glanced between her and the road. "What?"

"Well…are we really one-thousand-percent sure about this? Because once we call the cops, it becomes *real*—not just you and me with an idea, you know? We'll be making suspects out of my parents' best friends."

"I doubt the parents are involved, Slick. At worst, Bill and Midge are only aiding and abetting their son."

"Fine, then we're making a suspect out of their son. How is that any better?"

"It's not," Tate agreed. "But a minute ago you were terrified of this character. Why the cold feet now?"

"I don't like Brett, but that doesn't mean I'm in a rush to ruin his life. If anything, it means I need to be more careful, to make sure my emotions aren't coloring my judgment."

"That's very kind of you," he said gently. "But what about the part where your life is being ruined? Where you're frightened and on edge and worried that your stalker's messages are getting more threatening by the day? Those things factor in too, Lyla."

She nodded. "I know."

"If it makes you feel any better," Tate said, "I don't believe the cops will pursue this guy without cause. They won't go after Brett if the evidence doesn't support our theory."

"Said the innocent guy who got called in to the station just the other day."

"As much as it pisses me off to say this, I think Scarletti was only being thorough." When Lyla snorted, he conceded, "Fine, territorial, as well. But he's not the kind of guy who's going to railroad someone just because it's convenient."

"So, you think I can trust him to do this right?"

"I do."

Lyla made the call. When she got a message at his office, she tried Scarletti's cell, but had to leave a message there, as well.

"Hey, Detective," she said. *"This is Lyla Lawson. I found something today that makes me think I might know who's been bothering me. I'd love to show it to you and get your opinion. Would you give me a call when you get a chance? Thanks."*

"Well, that's that," she sighed.

Tate looked so confident and strong behind the wheel, making his way across town to her apartment. More than anything, she trusted *him.*

After a couple of minutes, he pulled into the public garage near her apartment and circled the levels, looking for a free spot.

"I have a hunch about this, Lyla," he said. "I really think that yearbook might be the clue we've been hoping for."

He locked up the truck and they walked to her building. Tate's hand was tight around hers as his head swiveled back and forth, watchful and wary.

Lyla shivered. "I hope Detective Scarletti calls back soon."

"If he doesn't call tonight, we'll drop by the station in the morning. Maybe they can get someone to keep an eye on your apartment until everything is settled."

They crossed her lobby and headed for the elevator at the back. Once the doors closed them in, Lyla stepped close to Tate and ran her hands up his broad, hard chest. "And you can keep an eye on me," she murmured.

"I can," he agreed, his voice low and dark. "And I intend to do a very, very good job."

Thirty-One

"WELL DAMN, CAPTAIN," Lyla breathed up at him. "Look who gets all sexy when he's being tough."

Tate's heart ticked into a higher gear, the stress of the day abruptly mutating into something hungrier—needier—like it always did when Lyla was near.

He put his arms around her as the elevator chugged upward. "Is that right?"

"Yes," she whispered, leaning in for a kiss. They'd reached her floor, though, and the doors cranked open. He wished he could bring her somewhere more secure—some safe little hidey-hole that no one knew about, instead of the apartment she'd lived in for years.

Lyla had insisted, however, and she was effectively his boss.

Tate glanced up and down the hall, then hustled her to her door. While she dug around for her keys, he asked her, "Lyla…are you feeling okay? You haven't lost your marbles from the stress or anything, have you?"

Because he really shouldn't get ahead of himself here. No less than half an hour ago, she'd been completely terrified that her strange, scary "superfan" wasn't a fan at all, but someone she knew well.

Now she was coming on to him?

It was as crazy-making a situation as any writer could cook up, including Lyla—so her emotions were bound to be all over the place.

She might not be in a seductive mood at all. She could just be in shock.

Which was exactly why Tate ought to pump the brakes here, instead of letting his below-the-belt wingman do the deciding.

The last thing Lyla needed tonight was for Tate to come in hot and hard for a landing, while her ground crew was frantically trying to wave him off at the last minute.

She got her door open and stumbled over the threshold, letting out a slightly manic giggle on the way.

"You know, maybe I have," she said. "How could I not have seen this coming? I *should* have seen this coming. It's so ridiculously obvious. I can't believe no one figured it out before."

Tate raked a hand back through his hair. "Let's not get too far ahead of ourselves. No one had all the information. That's always how things slip through the cracks."

Lyla wasn't listening to him any longer. She was staring morosely at the top of his head. "Is the Army going to make you cut your hair when you go back?" she asked.

The non sequitur threw him off. "I…will probably do it either way," Tate said.

It *had* gotten a little shaggy, he supposed, but he'd had other things on his mind. He could add a haircut to his list, though. Maybe next week, if he remembered.

Lyla advanced on him, reaching up to thread her fingers into his hair and tugging gently. "It's so soft," she murmured. "I'll hate to see it go."

"Thanks." But Lyla wouldn't have to, would she? Now that her case was on the verge of being closed, she'd have no more need of him, and Tate was going to be sent packing.

Soon. Too soon. By the time he was getting his hair cut and shipping out, he'd have been jettisoned from her orbit and then some.

Tate stared down into her beautiful face, and Lyla stared right back—like she could hear his sorry thoughts loud and clear.

She launched herself at him with sudden desperation, gasping, "Kiss me," a split second before her mouth hit his.

"Now?" Tate pulled away. Everything was spinning so fast. He needed to make some sense of it. "Wait."

"Please, Tate," she begged, pressing her lush, curvy body against his.

It was impossible to think when everything he wanted was right there in his grasp. At some point, this thing with Lyla had zipped way past desire and hurtled straight into bigger, more treacherous things.

Things that spelled out picket fences and forever.

"What happened to you being scared?" he asked, trying to buy time.

It was okay to care about her, it was the decent thing to care about her—but this wasn't caring. This felt unnervingly like…

No. *Shit*, Tate could *not* go there. He had no business going *there*.

"I don't really know," Lyla admitted, her hands busily tugging on his shirt buttons. "I'm out on a ledge somewhere, and it feels like you're the only thing left to hang on to."

And just like that, she snuck under all Tate's armor and made a home in his chest. This woman destroyed him.

"Then do it, sweetheart," Tate told her. "Hold on tight to me."

"If you don't want to—"

"Let's get one thing straight. There will never come a time when I don't want to. Not with you."

This time, when Lyla's lips met his, he didn't fight her. Tate's tongue tangled with hers in a kiss that consumed him, body and soul.

He wondered what she'd do if he handed her his heart right now. If he handed her a ring.

In fits and starts, she tried to give him another out. "We don't have to…" Lyla gasped, "We can just…"

"*Fuck that.*" Tate lifted her up and wrapped her legs around his waist. "Come here and love me, sweetheart," he demanded, then immediately wanted to cringe at his word choice.

Lyla didn't notice his slip, though, so he took the three steps over to the breakfast bar leading into her kitchen and set her ass on one of the stools there. Tate worked her soft skirt up over her hips, then let her shimmy out of her panties while he went for his wallet, and the condom stuck inside.

Lyla didn't want to relinquish his lips. "Tate, please. I'm on the pill, and I'm clean. Could we just…do you want to…you know?"

Jesus—she was going to be the death of him. He laughed unsteadily, and told her, "I'm clean, too. I promise."

The thought of having Lyla skin-to-skin would've deranged him if he'd ever allowed himself to think about it—and now, with the prospect at hand, it had Tate's fingers shaking so badly, he could barely get his pants undone.

Finally, he freed his cock from his briefs, and Lyla batted his hands away so she could take over. She looked down at her prize and her eyebrows arched higher, even as she stroked him and palmed his balls.

"Really?" she wondered. "What's gotten into *him*?"

Tate chuckled darkly. "Locked and loaded and always ready for action around you, sweetheart. Haven't you figured that out by now?"

"Even now?"

"Of course. Now shush—you're going to hurt his feelings."

"You can't be serious."

"Well, you're not being very welcoming."

"Probably because I assumed I'd have to do some convincing, after the night we've had."

"Consider me convinced, Lyla." Tate spread her thighs wider, making room for himself to step between them. He ran his lips along her jaw, and bit down on her earlobe, just as he pressed his thumb against her swollen little nub.

She jerked like a live wire. "*Tate.*"

"Hmm?" She was so wet, and he couldn't wait to sink inside her—to feel all that slick heat with nothing between them.

"It's not going to work," she moaned, every bit of her body language pointing to the exact opposite conclusion.

Tate stepped back and regarded her wryly, unable to resist teasing her a little. "Oh, really. If that's how you feel, maybe I should take my toy and go home."

Lyla held up her palms immediately, like he'd gone and fired off a rocket launcher in a shopping mall. "Whoa, whoa, whoa," she said, in her best hostage negotiator voice. "Let's not be hasty, here."

He was aware that smugness was generally frowned upon in these situations, but sometimes it couldn't be helped. He smirked at her and sidled closer. "So, you *do* want him here."

"I never said I didn't."

Tate crowded up against Lyla and gripped the counter behind her, nuzzling into the delicious space between her neck and shoulder and inhaling her sweet perfume. "You kind of did."

"He just took me by surprise, that's all." She tilted her head to give him better access.

He murmured against her skin, "He's enthusiastic. Give him a break already."

Lyla responded as she always did to his tongue, almost purring when she pointed out, "He's a very nice boy."

"That's because he likes you," Tate explained. "A lot." And then he took possession of that ripe, sexy pout of hers. She tasted like cinnamon. Always like cinnamon.

He took himself in hand and guided his cock to her entrance, pressing in while Lyla wound her arms around his neck. "Bed's in there, Captain," she said.

"Beds are for suckers." He snaked his hands around Lyla's thighs and hitched her legs up around his hips, then drove home.

Lyla moaned, long and loud. Tate thrust into her mind-melting heat, and almost lost it right then. He grappled behind her for something to hang on to and ended up knocking her phone and some mail off the counter in the process.

"I'm going to fall."

"I got you," he assured her. "Hold on."

Lyla clung to him like the best, sexiest kind of vine, and Tate knew he wasn't going to be able to take this slow. While he kissed her, he freed one hand and wedged it between them so he could work her up faster. No way was he going to finish without her.

He couldn't help noticing a couple of pertinent facts, however. One, Lyla had been so fucking ready for him, he wanted to drop down on his knees and give thanks.

And two, she didn't need a single bit of help from him. "Geez, sweetheart—could you at least *pretend* you're into me?" Tate joked.

Lyla was chasing her own pleasure like a wild, wanton goddess. Not that he minded. This Lyla could come out and play whenever the fuck she wanted, and he'd be here for it.

"Maybe next time," she fired back breathlessly.

Tate drove in again and kissed that sass right out of her, until Lyla was whimpering and writhing against him once more.

The slide of all that wet, wonderful heat against his cock nearly made Tate's knees buckle, but the sight of Lyla's open, uninhibited pleasure made him determined to hold his ground.

"Want you so much, gorgeous girl."

"Yes, yes, yes," Lyla chanted in his ear with each deep stroke. "Coming fast."

What *was* it about her? The way things ignited between them, in the space of a heartbeat, ought to be unnerving. Instead, it had him hooked.

Tate shook his head and tried to reason through the next couple of steps. He pulled back to look into Lyla's face and spotted a glow in her eyes he hadn't noticed before. Trust? Or more?

"*Lyla*," he whispered, unable to believe what he was seeing.

"Come with me," Lyla commanded. "Now."

Tate didn't argue. He powered into her in one strong stroke, and her body clamped around him like a silky, searing glove. He growled and squeezed his eyes shut so he wouldn't beat her home.

Lyla swiveled her hips and did some truly diabolical thing with her internal muscles that had her moaning and him on the verge of losing his mind once and for all.

"What the fuck was that," he gasped.

She did it again, and it was *Hi-ho Silver, away*—Tate pounded into her, hard and fast against her kitchen bar, until every breath that left Lyla's lungs emerged in a high-pitched cry that made him twice as hard and three times as ready to cross the finish line.

Except, he didn't want it to end. Dear God, Tate couldn't take his eyes off Lyla's blissed-out face as they came together like a summer thunderstorm, and he never wanted this to end.

TATE'S HEART WAS pounding. His throat was tight like he'd been yelling for hours. Lyla was a warm, sweet bundle against his chest.

"Damn, girl," he laughed, when he could make his voice work again. "I'm beginning to think you're an adrenaline junkie. What got into you?"

Lyla tipped her head back and smiled sadly at the ceiling. "You really want to know?"

"Yeah." Tate pulled her up so the edge of the counter wouldn't dig into her back, and Lyla met his eyes again.

"You solved the case, Sherlock. You're going to pass your next evaluation. That means you're going to leave soon. The party's almost over."

Tate stared into her pretty hazel eyes and swore they had a sheen that hadn't been there a minute before. "I don't know what to—"

Lyla talked over him, "If the clock's ticking on us, I guess I don't want to miss a single minute that's left," she told him. Her kiss-swollen lips were inches from his.

Her pulse ticked against the delicate skin of her throat. Tate touched a finger to it and heard the hitch in Lyla's breathing.

Well, hell. When she put it that way—

Tate crashed his mouth against hers, devouring her with abandon. He was on fire for her, an inferno of want, and it consumed him from the inside out. It burned away every woman who'd come before her, leaving only ash in its wake—and Lyla.

Always Lyla. Forever Lyla.

Lyla, who was his in this moment, and who he'd have to walk away from any day now.

Tate loved her and hated her for turning him into this complicated mess of feeling and need. She hadn't even tried, and he'd fallen anyway. He couldn't stand the thought that she might be unaffected, while he was a wreck.

But what was he supposed to do? Make her fall in love with him, just so he could break both their hearts when he left?

"Do it again," Lyla said next to his ear.

"What?" And now he was hearing things.

"I'm serious, Tate. I want to obliterate everything else— everything except what's real and true, here and now."

"You and me," he whispered, though that probably wasn't what she'd meant.

"You and me. That's it—that's everything."

Lyla couldn't possibly know how true those words were to him. He couldn't say all the things he wanted to say back, not without leaving a crater-sized hole in his wake when he was gone. But Tate could show Lyla how he felt and let her draw her own conclusions.

He lifted her up and carried her straight into her bedroom and did his best to lay bare what was in his heart.

Thirty-Two

S HE COULDN'T KEEP this up much longer. Sooner or later, Lyla was going to have to confess to Tate how she felt about him, but her window for doing that was getting smaller every day.

If she never said anything, though, how could she expect to win him over? She had to be brave if she wanted the chance to keep him once this job had ended.

The only problem was, every time Lyla planned to talk to Tate about their future, something else seemed to get in the way. Tonight, for instance, there'd been that wild, flashfire hookup on her kitchen stool, followed by a second, longer interlude in her bedroom.

Lyla tried not to worry about it. It'd been a long day, and neither of them had been sleeping particularly well lately. They needed to rest more than she needed to expose her soul.

There'd be plenty of time to talk come morning, especially since Tate would be staying with her for the time being.

And here in her own bed, Tate had cuddled up to her the same way he'd done in the hotels, wrapping a heavy arm around Lyla's waist and nestling her snug against his chest as he dropped off to sleep. He'd done it as easily as if they'd been sleeping together for years, not weeks.

Lyla probably shouldn't read as much into that as she did. Physical compatibility would only get them so far, after all. If she really wanted to hold onto Tate for the long term, she had to convince him that they were compatible in other ways, too.

Coward that she was, though, Lyla was hoping to have that discussion when Tate was in a happy, affectionate mood. Unfortunately, recent events were not exactly working in her favor.

She'd been somewhat busy freaking out, and that had tended to put Tate in a bit of a mood.

His usually-sunny disposition completely evaporated when he was stressed out, but the fact didn't bother her like it once had. Now that Lyla knew his full story, she felt only sympathy for the ordeal Tate had gone through in the last several months. He'd earned the right to be grouchy now and then.

Not just because of his own injuries, either, but also for what he must be feeling about his teammates who weren't so lucky. Tate never admitted how much it bothered him, even now, but Lyla hoped that he'd learn to deal with those demons in time. For his sake, and for hers.

She kissed his arm lightly. Maybe it was a good thing that she hadn't gotten a chance to tell him how she felt about him yet. Until Tate handled the rest of what was keeping him in limbo right now, he shouldn't have to worry about a lovelorn woman, too.

Lyla turned to face him and watched his eyelids flutter as he dreamed. She could wait a while more for Tate. He was worth it, and so was what she felt for him. What was developing between them was rare and sweet—magic that didn't come along every day.

Lyla knew it like she knew her own name. So why was she so troubled? She'd woken up only an hour after falling asleep, antsy and restless. Her mind simply wouldn't settle down, looping over and over on how to eventually tell Tate what she wanted, and what they could do about the distance problem once he returned to active duty.

Lyla laid there in the dark and thought about her parents, as well. She hoped, for their sake, that she and Tate were somehow wrong about Brett. She couldn't decide what would devastate them more—that someone they trusted had terrorized their daughter, or that they might have been inadvertently responsible for supplying her stalker with a stream of information about Lyla's whereabouts and activities.

After a while, it became clear she wasn't going to be falling back asleep anytime soon, so with a quiet sigh, Lyla carefully extracted herself from Tate's protective embrace and padded out to her kitchen.

In the weak street light coming in through the window, she got a cup from the cabinet and poured herself some milk. Maybe it would give her stomach something to do besides tie itself in knots.

She thought about getting a little work in, but suspected the words wouldn't flow, given how out-of-sorts she felt.

Maybe she could just turn off the sound and watch some television.

Lyla leaned against the counter while she drank, watching the kitchen curtain furl hypnotically in the breeze, ethereally, like a ghost. It had gotten cooler once the sun went down, and the early summer air smelled fresh and clean.

Tomorrow, no doubt, she'd smell the trash bins in the alley mixed with the exhaust of a million cars, even if she closed up the apartment and turned on the air. For now, though, this was nice.

Lyla jerked upright. *Wait.*

Why was the window open? Neither she nor Tate had come in here since they'd been home, and he never would've let her leave it open when they left for her parents' house.

On the heels of that thought, came the memory that Tate had never gone through the apartment once they'd returned. They'd made love, twice, and then they'd gone to sleep.

Lyla had set down her cup, thinking that Tate was going to be absolutely furious with himself in the morning about this, when she heard her bedroom door slam closed.

She spun around, and a huge black shadow loomed up in front of her. Lyla didn't think—it was simply base instinct that made her duck out of the way and dart for the living room.

The shadow resolved into the outline of a man, who crashed into the counter, cursing.

Lyla yelled, "Tate!"

The intruder let out a strangled growl and stumbled after her. "No! That's wrong. You're wrong, wrong, *wrong*, Delilah."

Like that, Lyla realized who it must be. "*Tate!*" she screamed louder.

Brett was holding something strange in his hands as he came toward her. He lunged suddenly, trying to get it over her head, and Lyla barely had time to wheel out of the way again.

Behind her bedroom door, there was a sudden crash and an unholy roar. Lyla spotted the chair Brett had wedged under the knob and called out, "It's blocked! Tate, he blocked the door out here!"

There was no time to free him, though, because Brett was lumbering after her again, his movements broad and uncoordinated, and made doubly frightening by his size.

It'd been a long time since Lyla had been this close to her old classmate and neighbor. Brett had been a big kid back then, but he seemed to have doubled in size since she'd moved away. Maybe it was the tight confines of her apartment, or maybe it was just his deranged frustration, but either way, it was scary as hell.

Lyla wasn't sure she could evade him for long. With the way Brett kept charging her, she'd never have time to unlock the deadbolts on her front door or do anything about the chair penning Tate in the bedroom.

She trained her eyes on Brett and backed away, keeping as much distance between them as she could. Even in the dark, she could see that his gaze was wild, and his movements unfocused. She wondered if he was drunk.

However, if there'd been any remaining doubt that he was her stalker, it was gone now. Brett kept muttering the word *wrong* as he tossed Lyla's things aside, trying to get to her—just like he'd written in her old yearbook, and just like in all the notes and calls since.

Off to the side, Tate sounded like he was throwing his entire body weight against the bedroom door, and Lyla hoped he managed to get himself out soon. God only knew whether any of her neighbors would hear a thing, or even think twice about it.

Brett charged her again, holding what seemed to be a fabric bag that he tried to jam over her head. Lyla held out her arms and fought like hell to keep it off, but Brett had managed to pin her between his body and the couch, and it was tough.

"No! Brett, stop!" she cried.

"Delilah, *you* stop," he sputtered, struggling with her. "Stop fighting. It's wrong to fight me."

"Tate!" she called again, but her bodyguard had gone eerily silent. Lyla refused to believe that meant she was on her own. He'd never desert her when she needed him.

Brett leaned his full weight against her, bearing down with all his bulk to keep her from getting away again. But the effort didn't quite give him the leverage he needed to get her head covered with that material.

Lyla shoved and wriggled as much as she could, trying to fight him off or slip away, but Brett was so damn heavy and strong. She couldn't get a leg up to knee him, and she couldn't get her arms or hands into position to poke him in the eye or jab him in the throat. What good would cracking her knuckles do now?

It was suffocating and terrifying and happening so fast, and all at once, true panic set in. Tate couldn't see their secret signal and he couldn't help her in time. Lyla couldn't help herself.

Brett was going to get his way, and she was suddenly extremely scared about what that might entail.

"Why are you always so *wrong*, Delilah?" Brett demanded, his breath fetid and hot in her face. "I keep explaining to you, and you just *won't*—" he reared back and sneered, "—*listen.*"

Brett slammed his forehead hard against hers. Lyla saw stars. Her whole body went slack and the room took a couple of sluggish spins around her head, and her attacker took the opportunity to slip that bag right over her skull.

"No!" she screamed, horrified at the sudden absence of sight and air, and the claustrophobic feel of the cloth against her face.

Incomprehensibly, Brett gurgled in response. In slow increments, he backed away from her until Lyla's body slumped to the floor. The sudden movement made her retch, and she curled into a ball until the feeling passed.

When nothing else happened, Lyla scrabbled at the edges of the hood, wrenching it off and looking frantically around.

Brett was on his heels and sagging weirdly backward, choking and clawing at a thick forearm wrapped around his throat. She didn't know how, though, because her bedroom door was still closed behind that chair.

"Tate…?"

"Lyla, call the cops," Tate grunted from behind Brett. "And hurry. This fucker is big."

"How did you…?"

"Used the window," he forced out. "Now *call.*"

There was no fire escape outside her window. Tate would've had to shimmy along a ledge three stories up to get to her.

Holy crap.

Brett was still writhing and kicking, trying to get free. Lyla snapped out of her haze and dove for her purse near the front door, then pawed around inside, looking for her cell phone.

"No," Brett was howling. "This is wrong. *Wrong!*" He flung his arms and fists backward, trying to land a shot on Tate.

"*Lyla,*" Tate warned. "Come on, sweetheart."

The endearment seemed to enrage Brett, who redoubled his efforts to get free with a croaky bellow. Crouched beside the sofa,

Lyla got her hands on her phone and tapped the screen alive right as her stalker broke free of Tate.

He made a move for her, but the unmistakable click of a cocking gun froze him in place.

"Go ahead and touch her again, you crazy fuck," Tate said. "I've been dying for a chance to shoot your ass for weeks."

Brett stared into Lyla's eyes and wavered, moaning with indecision and frustration.

"*Do it*," Tate muttered.

Lyla was afraid to move a muscle. If Tate missed Brett by even a millimeter, that bullet would head straight for her.

As she contemplated that outcome, Brett burst into sudden motion, feinting sideways to get around her sofa and barreling toward her front door. Somehow, he managed to get the locks free before Tate reached him, and in seconds the two men were stumbling into the hallway, then racing full-tilt down the hall.

Lyla scrambled off the floor and ducked out the door just in time to see Tate hit the stairwell at the end, in hot pursuit of Brett despite the fact that he was only wearing a t-shirt, a loose pair of gym shorts and had bare feet.

Tate had said he wasn't supposed to do any vigorous exercise yet, Lyla thought. Between fighting a man as big as Brett, then chasing him down, though...*oh, God*. This was bad.

She fumbled the phone clutched in her hand a couple of times, her shaking fingers refusing to cooperate for excruciatingly long moments before she was able to place the emergency call.

And then Lyla grabbed her keys and locked her door behind her.

No way was she going to wait in there alone like some sitting duck. If she could find the men downstairs, she could try to help Tate—or at least give directions to the cops.

Lyla took off running and prayed she'd be in time.

Thirty-Three

B RETT JONES MUST have been a pretty decent ballplayer back in the day, Tate thought, as he charged down the hall after him. Even now, the fucker still had some legs on him.

He booked it down three flights of stairs to the ground floor and across the small lobby of Lyla's building, then hit the street with a stupid burst of speed that could only have been fueled by total mania—or three seconds left on the championship clock.

Tate barreled after him and felt every single second of his four-month recuperation in the burning of his thigh muscles and the ragged breaths sawing in and out of his lungs.

He kept up with the bastard, though, because *fuck that*. If Tate let Brett get away now, he'd never be able to look at Lyla—or in the mirror—ever again. Every day after this one would suck worse than the one before, knowing that he'd failed her.

Luckily, there weren't a ton of people on the street at this hour, so even though Brett did his level best to lose him, Tate had no trouble hitting a sprint and following along.

He'd run for a few touchdowns himself, once upon a time.

The difficulty now was that, once the other man decided to bang a hard right down a dark alley, Tate was reasonably confident that no one in Lyla's quiet Upper West Side neighborhood would be sticking around to see what happened next.

Tate slowed to a stop at the mouth of the narrow gap between two brick residential buildings, then quickly peeked around the corner to determine if it was a dead-end or not.

Small mercy—it was. About a block deep, at most, and dark as an abyss at its far end. No one short of Spiderman was getting out of there any way but the way they'd gone in.

That meant that if Tate wanted to get his hands on the asshole who'd been tormenting Lyla for the last several months, he was going to have to go in there, too.

He shook off the wave of dizziness that washed over him, resolving then and there to step up his workouts, no matter what the doctors said. This being out-of-shape thing was for the birds.

Tate took a deep breath and edged around the corner. As his eyes adjusted, it became clear there were only so many places Jones could be hiding.

Only two, in fact—dumpster A, or dumpster B.

Tate backed out and looked around, spotting a couple of kids hunched into their hoodies and trying to hustle by on the sidewalk. He pointed at them.

"Hey, you guys have phones?" There was no telling whether Lyla had managed to make that call or not, and Tate didn't want to take any chances.

The kids were smarter than they looked, not answering him and picking up their pace—probably thinking Tate was trying to jack them, or some shit.

Come to think of it, he *did* happen to have a weapon in his hand. He felt a little bad pointing it at them.

"You heard me," he said.

"We don't want any trouble."

"Me, either. Just call 911 and get them here fast. That's all I want."

"Can't do no cops, man," they told him, shifting around in their sneakers. Out for a late-night weed run, no doubt.

"Make the call." Tate shrugged, "Then take off if you want. Makes no difference to me."

They looked at each other, and then at Tate's weapon. And then, painfully slowly, one of them pulled a phone out of his front pocket and tapped the screen.

Tate didn't really listen to what the kid said, but he did hope the little shit had a better sense of where they were than he did at the moment. He'd kind of lost track of which block Jones had headed down once they'd exited Lyla's building.

And now, he was getting the oddest feeling that his mind was somehow detaching from his body—as if one was standing on the sidewalk, and the other was kicking back on a window ledge up high, waiting to see how stuff would shake out.

Even weirder? Tate smelled flowers, and there wasn't a single planter around here anywhere.

The kid ended his call, grabbed his buddy's arm, and slowly backed away. Tate nodded and turned to the task at hand, raising his pistol from his thigh and rounding the corner into the alley once more.

If he'd been worried about being able to find Brett in all that darkness, he didn't have long to dwell on it. Three steps into the gloom and the fucker was on him like a cheap suit, lunging out of nowhere in a flurry of grappling hands and wicked fury.

"Wrong move, wrong move," Jones growled, going for Tate's throat.

They tussled sloppily, crashing into the stinking metal trash bins and the jagged brick walls—but try as Tate might, he couldn't seem to herd the dude out of the alley and back onto the sidewalk, where the light was better and other people *might* be inclined to lend a hand.

Tate was going to have to raise a ruckus in here if he expected the cops to find them. He suspected Brett might've realized that as well, given the way the man was trying to either strangle Tate or smother him with his bare hands.

It was a smarter play than Tate had expected of him, frankly. And damn if the bastard wasn't strong—Tate was doing a hell of a lot of feinting and blocking, and not nearly enough offensive attacking.

There just wasn't a lot of space to neutralize the guy in the close quarters of the alley, and it was hard to catch his breath when Jones kept coming at him like some kind of ferocious, grasping octopus. Brett was relentless, and Tate was feeling troublingly…fuzzy. Not like himself, at all.

When he could work his arm free, Tate didn't bother trying to get a shot off—he just cracked Brett on the side of the skull as hard as he could and hoped it would do the job.

The blow would've dropped most men in their tracks, but Jones only groaned and stumbled against the wall of the alley. *Bad luck.*

Tate thought he heard running feet, and maybe a far-off siren—but who was kidding who, here? Those sounds could mean just about anything in the city at this time of night. It seemed ambitious to hope they signaled reinforcements for him.

Tate growled and bit back at the fog that wanted to settle over him, and refused to wonder if he really was out of his depth here. He reapplied himself to backing Jones out toward the street, where hopefully…where…

Shit. Lyla was there, standing in the weak glow of the streetlight. Why the hell was Lyla there? She should be safe at home, not in spitting distance of her deranged stalker again.

Only…she hadn't been safe at home, not even with Tate there to guard her. And now she had her phone to her ear, talking fast and looking from side to side, too agitated for Tate to catch her eye amidst the chaos.

Brett seized on Tate's distraction immediately, of course, finding an opening to knee Tate in the balls and lunge for his gun, somehow knocking it clear out of his sweating hand and across the ground.

Tate stopped and tilted his head, choking back on the wave of pain and nausea trying to take hold. The fucker wanted to play dirty, did he? Tate could do that, too.

He launched himself at the other man's burly frame, just like his old football coaches had taught him. If Jones wanted to get to Lyla, he was going to have to do it over Tate's cold, dead body.

They tumbled to the filthy ground of the alley in a tangle of limbs, each one of them frustrated and determined to get the upper hand.

Tate heard Lyla scream, "Over here!" and then she was creeping forward, into the alley. Her eyes were fixed on the ground, and not paying the slightest attention to Brett.

"Lyla, stay back," Tate barked.

Through clenched teeth, Brett grunted, "Wrong, wrong, *wrong.*" His eyes were fixed on Lyla, not Tate—which was probably why Tate didn't see his next move coming.

Jones reared back and cracked his forehead against Tate's.

The world swam sickeningly around, but all Tate could think of was how much it had to have hurt when Brett had done it to Lyla. This punk come too close to getting his hands on her tonight.

And he was *still* too close.

With everything in him, Tate fought to keep the other man on the ground and to stop the guy's arms from flailing everywhere. Inches away, Brett's jaws were snapping like he'd like to bite Tate's face off—but somehow, he managed to roll on top of the fucker and pin him with his body.

Jones *really* hated that. He writhed and bucked, and Tate knew he couldn't chance taking a hand off the guy or he'd lose his tenuous advantage.

The truth was, he had one tool left to end this fight now—and it was the one part of his body that Tate was supposed to protect come hell or high water.

His head. Brett's signature move, as it were.

Tate winced, dreading the impact, but it had to be done.

He steeled himself, then smashed his skull against the face of Lyla's stalker, once, twice…three times. Until the other man went slack underneath him and wasn't moving anymore.

Tate collapsed on top of him, letting himself rest for a long minute. The alley was getting darker, instead of brighter, and the sounds of the street were growing as garbled as if they were being filtered through a fish tank.

Much as he'd like to believe he was only having an out-of-body experience—brought on by what a beast he clearly was—this was something more. Something bad.

WHEN BRETT CAME to, he groaned like a goddamn animal and rolled to the side, pushing Tate away so he could get to his knees, and then his feet.

The sudden change in position jarred Tate's eyes open, but that appeared to be the extent of what he was capable of.

He sprawled there on the filthy concrete, disoriented but willing himself to stand up, too—except his limbs weren't getting the message. They lay still and unresponsive, ignoring the frantic commands he was sending them like useless lumps of clay, or the arms and legs of a mannequin. Pretty, but not accomplishing much.

Tate swiveled his eyeballs around wildly, finding Lyla standing nearby—holding her ground despite the fact that Brett was advancing on her step by lumbering step.

She had Tate's gun trained on her stalker with shaking hands. *So that's what she'd been looking at.* Tate was preposterously proud of her for her bravery and quick thinking, but also terrified. She needed to get the hell out of here—to get as far away from Jones as possible.

Why wasn't she running?

For that matter, why wasn't Tate? He had the weirdest feeling that he'd lost a few minutes somewhere in there, and though he couldn't he make himself move, his concern about it felt…remote. Like something he was reading about, rather than experiencing directly.

Tate's heart skittered around in his chest like a panicked rat, but it stopped completely when Brett lunged for Lyla, and the gun went off with a sudden, deafening crack that echoed around the alley.

Jones fell down with an inhuman shriek, but as best as Tate could tell, Lyla had only managed to shoot him in the leg. At least she'd hit the fucker, though. That was good.

A flash of motion in his peripheral vision caught Tate's attention. A beat cop out on the street seemed to have heard the gunshot and come running, because she had her gun out, and was talking fast into the walkie-talkie clipped to her vest.

Tate blinked and looked for Lyla again, but the strange darkness was creeping back, squeezing in from the edges of his sight like the ending of his own personal cartoon episode.

"TATE? TATE CAN you hear me?" Lyla was bending over him now, her face a mask of worry.

Tate wanted to squeeze her hand, to reassure her, but he had that same disconnect between his brain and his fingers again.

There were a lot more cops milling around the alley now, along with some paramedics. A few were several feet away, dealing with Brett. And a few were loitering around Tate, taking his vitals and talking too fast for him to make out what the problem was.

He felt like he was sitting on the bottom of a well. Little by little, some feeling was returning to his hands and feet, but unfortunately, it was coming in the form of pain.

His knuckles were throbbing, and his feet were—Tate frowned. His feet were pretty chewed up. Why wasn't he wearing any shoes?

The EMTs were attempting to shift him onto a stretcher, and Tate tried to wave them off. He didn't need to take a ride in the ambulance.

He just needed a minute or two to recalibrate himself, and…Tate gagged. A tidal wave of nausea barreled through him, and he curled into himself, unable to push it back.

His ears came back online with a slow but steady ramping up of sound, like someone had found the volume button on the remote and given it several upward clicks.

One of the EMTs was telling Lyla, "Mount Sinai is closest."

Next thing Tate knew, though, Lyla was asking them to take him to Weill Cornell, where Luca worked.

Damn it, the last thing Tate needed right now was an overwrought Italian getting all up in his business. It had been bad enough when Tate had been injured, and Luca and Red had flown to Landstuhl with his parents to bring him home.

Whatever was wrong with Tate now was bound to throw his friend into even bigger fits—and if Tate ended up at Luca's hospital, maybe even under his care, there's be no reasoning with the man.

He wanted to protest, but his tongue felt like it was three times as big as usual, and he still couldn't make his stupid mouth work right. So, Tate glared at Lyla for all he was worth, and silently begged her to read his mind.

Thirty-Four

L YLA KEPT TATE'S gun trained on Brett's head, even though the weapon was heavier than she'd expected, and her arms and legs were trembling with fear.

The two men laid still in the alley for a long time, though—long enough for her to wonder if Tate had knocked himself out, along with Brett.

But then Brett began pinwheeling his limbs, wriggling to get free. Before long, he had pushed Tate aside and gotten unsteadily to his feet. He wobbled a bit, and Lyla tried to keep her aim—but she was distracted by what could be wrong with Tate.

He was just *lying* there in an ungainly heap, staring at Lyla like he'd blacked out with his eyes open. And then, as she watched, Tate started shuddering, his limbs jerking in bizarre, uncoordinated movements, his head tossing around on the dirty concrete.

"Tate? Tate!" Lyla yelled, horrified by what she was seeing.

He'd fought Brett off like a man possessed but was clearly paying the price now. Lyla looked from him to Brett and back again, paralyzed with indecision. What was she supposed to do?

Could someone hurt themselves during a seizure? What if the cops didn't get to them fast enough? What if she couldn't remember how to work Tate's gun?

In front of her, Brett was inching closer, feinting right and left and beginning to grin like a ghoulish boxer, looking for her weak spot. Lyla felt for the safety on the pistol, but it was already off.

Brett told her, "You got it wrong again, my, my, my Delilah. I'm still the one on top. Not you. Never, ever you."

And then Brett charged, arms out, right for her.

Lyla pulled the trigger, and he dropped in his tracks with an otherworldly wail. Tate had gone quiet again.

Everything happened fast after that. Police officers swarmed the alley, stomping around the scene and shouting to each other and into their radios.

The street near the alley flooded with flashing lights and emergency vehicles.

An officer got up in her face, demanding, "Drop the gun."

Oh. Lyla hadn't even realized she was still white-knuckling Tate's handgun, but she uncurled her fingers and let it fall to the ground with a heavy crack.

Then she collapsed, too, landing on her knees like a puppet with its strings cut. Some of the cops dragged Brett aside, but he fought and cursed so much, they had to cuff him and hold him down so they could check out his leg.

Lyla only wanted to help Tate—to pull his head into her lap so it wouldn't loll on the concrete like it was—but an EMT was already kneeling next to him, taking his pulse while her partner set up a stretcher nearby.

At the touch of a hand on her shoulder, Lyla jolted. "Lady, you wanna tell me what the hell is going on here? We must've gotten four different phone calls about a fight in this alley," one of the officers said.

"He broke into my apartment and attacked us," she said, gesturing at Brett. "I called it in, but then he ran, and Tate chased him here—so I followed, but…"

"Who is he? Do you know him?"

"You have to call Detective Scarletti," Lyla whispered. "Tell him you have Lyla Lawson and Tate Monroe here. And tell him…tell him…"

Lyla couldn't take her eyes off Tate, though. Why wasn't he moving? She pointed. "What's wrong with him?"

"He's out cold," the cop told her. "Don't worry. What do you want me to tell Scarletti?"

"Tell him Captain Monroe caught my weird fan…I mean, my stalker. Tell him Tate caught the stalker."

"That character you just popped in the leg? Seems to me like you were the one who caught him, Miss."

Lyla shook her head. "No, I just finished him off. Tate's the one who saved me."

If it hadn't been for Tate, Brett would've had her trapped all alone in her apartment, and Lyla had the sickening feeling things might've ended up a whole lot worse than this.

"Still. Nice job getting him in the leg. Dropped him like a bad habit, didn't you?"

She blew out a breath. "I was aiming for his chest."

The officer just chuckled. "Okay, so who is he? You know him, or what?"

"His name is Brett Jones. He lives with his parents in Rye, on Maple Avenue. I bet they're wondering where he is right about now, too."

Across the way, Tate had opened his eyes and was batting ineffectively at the EMT's hands as she tried to strap him onto the stretcher. Without warning, though, he doubled over and fell to the side, coughing and retching up bile.

"Tate?" Lyla scrambled toward him on her hands and knees. "Oh my God, Tate!"

The paramedic barked, "Keep her back!"

"What's wrong with him?"

The officer who'd been talking with Lyla hooked an arm around her and hauled her backward, sitting her on her ass and holding her in place. "It's okay. They've got him. Let them help."

The paramedics got Tate settled again and onto the stretcher, and then they were lifting him up and carrying him carefully toward the ambulance parked on the street.

Another set of EMTs were guiding Brett into a second vehicle, surrounded by a knot of grumpy-looking cops. Lyla could still hear her old neighbor complaining, but his words were indistinct.

Nearby, one of the paramedics attending Tate was repeating, "12-alpha-2," into the radio set clipped to his vest.

"12-alpha-2?" Lyla asked the cop. "What's that mean?"

"Seizure with an unknown cause. Your boy overdosing, by any chance?"

"Oh my God, *no*."

"What about epilepsy?"

"No," Lyla said. "He's in the Army. He's been recovering from a TBI for months. But he takes an anti-convulsant. He showed it to me."

The officer jogged over to the EMTs to relate what she'd said. Lyla followed, trying to get closer to Tate so she could see for herself if he was okay.

"Where are you taking him?" she asked.

"Mount Sinai is closest."

But Tate didn't know a soul at Mount Sinai, and he should have people who loved him taking care of him now. On impulse, Lyla blurted out, "I don't suppose there's any chance you could bring him to Weill Cornell, instead?"

They all peered at her in annoyance, so she bluffed, "I think that's where his insurance is." But then she felt guilty for lying to the people trying to help him, so she added sheepishly, "Also, his best friend works there."

Tate met her gaze and blinked up at her, his eyes hazy and confused.

"Don't worry," Lyla told him. "Luca will get you all fixed up."

They rolled him into the back of the ambulance and hopped in after him.

"Can I come with you?" she called, but the EMT didn't hear her over all the commotion on the sidewalk. His partner climbed behind the wheel and he reached to pull the doors closed.

"Wait!" Lyla said, "Can I—"

The patient compartment slammed shut, and a moment later the vehicle was pulling away with its lights flashing, but sirens eerily quiet.

Lyla spun around and met the eyes of the officer who'd been sticking by her side. "I need to go to the hospital," she told him. "I have to call a cab or something."

He nodded but gestured her away from the curb. "We'll get you there in a little while. First, why don't you walk back to your apartment with me, so we can start processing the scene. Detective Scarletti is on his way in. He said he'll meet us there."

Lyla cast a look over her shoulder, where the ambulance was just turning down Amsterdam Avenue, on its way to cut across town to the East Side. She'd need to stop at home before following Tate anyway, to pick up her purse and his wallet.

He'd need ID and his insurance card. He would want his phone, too, so someone could call his parents and let them know he was okay, and, for crying out loud, Lyla probably ought to bring him some *shoes*, too.

She reached into the pocket of her pajama bottoms and pulled out her own cell, staring at the dark screen blankly. She should call Red. Lyla should warn Luca that Tate was on his way.

"Ms. Lawson?" the cop asked. "Let's get moving."

"Okay. It's…" she murmured, blinking and looking around at the thinning crowd. "…right. My building's this way."

FOR THE NEXT few hours, Detective Scarletti and the officer from the alley—who Lyla learned was named Malloy—presided over the investigation unfolding in her apartment like a pair of grumpy choir directors.

Members of the NYPD strung crime scene tape, bagged evidence, and combed over her home with stark efficiency, all under the terse direction of Scarletti and Malloy.

It was daunting, given how tired and overwhelmed Lyla felt. They'd planted her on one of her kitchen stools and instructed her to stay put, but all the while, the need to get to the hospital, and Tate, beat like a pulse under her skin.

Eventually, however, the officers began to pack up their equipment and depart, and the detective came over to stand beside her.

He jammed his hands in the pockets of his rumpled dress pants and rocked on his toes, looking at Lyla quizzically.

"Sorry you had to get dragged out of bed for this," she told him.

"Eh, no biggie. Comes with the job," he shrugged. "I sleep like shit most of the time, anyway."

"There's a lot of that going around."

"So I gather."

They stood there in silence for a few awkward moments, and then Scarletti said, "So…Brett Jones, huh? Former classmate of the victim."

"Who would've thunk it?" Lyla retorted wryly. "I hope this means you'll stop looking at Tate as a suspect."

"Well, you know—it might've been nice if someone had told me that the mentally-ill neighbor kid hated you. At the *beginning* of this whole thing."

"First of all, I had no idea that was the case. And secondly, it honestly never occurred to me. Besides," Lyla grouched, "You can't make this my fault. You didn't think of him, either."

A small smile flitted around the detective's lips, making him seem almost friendly. "Touché," he said. "And for the record, I wasn't laying blame. I'm just annoyed that your little boyfriend beat me to the punch, that's all."

"Tate's not my boyfriend," Lyla blurted automatically.

"Does he know that?"

Lyla sighed heavily. "Detective, do you need anything else from me?"

"As a matter of fact, I do. You've got a goose egg the size of Queens on your forehead. Has anyone looked at that yet?"

"No. Bigger things to worry about, I guess."

"Not anymore, Ms. Lawson. Let's get you to the hospital and make sure that asshole didn't give you a concussion, all right?"

"How convenient," Lyla said. "I was just heading that way."

Scarletti's brows drew together in surprise. He clearly hadn't expected her to agree with him so easily. "You were?"

"I happen to have a friend being treated there, at the moment. I need to check on him."

The detective dropped his head back and groaned, "*Ah, Christ.* I should've known. Need I remind you that Sinai is five minutes away, and Cornell is clear across town?"

Like Lyla cared about that. "I can find my own way there," she said.

"Yeah, right. And I'll bet my last nickel you won't mention the fact that you got cracked in the skull to a single soul once you get there. You're going to head straight for Captain Monroe and sit vigil next to him like your life depends on it."

Well, Scarletti had her there. Lyla crossed her fingers in her lap and countered with, "I promise I will have someone check me out. *After* I make sure Tate is okay."

He only shook his head and laughed, though. "No deal. Come on, put on some real pants and grab your stuff. I'll take you over there, now. And, not a word about the good captain until the ER staff gives you the all-clear. You hear me?"

SCARLETTI LEFT LYLA in the care of a well-meaning clutch of emergency room nurses, and he must've warned them about her intentions in advance.

They kept her for a full two hours before Lyla was able to break free of them, and find her way to the room upstairs where Tate had been moved.

He'd been kept overnight for tests and observation. He was still being treated for a migraine and the doctors were consulting with his regular physicians back home in Ohio about the reasons for his seizure.

At least, that's what Red told her when he found Lyla dozing on a waiting room bench later that morning.

She had not been able to learn a single thing from Tate himself, because once he was allowed visitors, he had stoutly refused to see her.

Learning that, Red had brought Lyla a cup of scorched and bitter coffee, and then had sat and chatted with her for a while.

His face was sympathetic when he told her, "Listen, I think Tate is just embarrassed. He thinks he failed you, but he's all turned around in his head right now. He'll come around."

Her boss was obviously full of it, and not doing a very good job of hiding it. "Now that you've delivered the party line," Lyla said, "what's really going on?"

"Honest to God. Let Luca and me try to talk some sense into him. You go home and get some rest, and we'll call you and let you know when to come back."

"You guys are circling the wagons, aren't you?" she accused.

"Only temporarily," Red admitted. "My car's downstairs. I'll call down and tell my driver to bring you home, okay?" He looked her over in concern. "You need to eat, and rest."

And take a long, hot bath, Lyla realized, registering her own appearance for the first time.

"You'll tell Tate I was here?" she asked.

"He knows. I'm sure he just doesn't want you to see him hooked up to all the machines and stuff. It's emasculating."

Lyla wasn't so sure. Still, she got dutifully to her feet and followed her boss out of the waiting room.

There was no doubt in her mind that Tate Monroe had saved her life last night. However, Lyla was beginning to suspect he didn't see it that way.

Thirty-Five

L AYING IN A hospital bed for the second time that year, Tate realized that he was perhaps even worse off than he'd been the last time—at least then, he'd had the hope of recovery on his side.

Now, he had nothing. No prayer of getting his career back, no excuse to speak to his woman ever again, and hang-ups galore.

It was possible that his brain might never be the same again, and his nightmares were back, so there was that.

Red and Luca had both come to see him repeatedly, trying to reassure Tate that all was not lost and that he only needed to call Lyla and tell her how he felt.

It was exactly the kind of advice he ought to have expected from two lovelorn idiots, but given their longstanding friendship, Tate at least expected them to extend just a tiny bit of understanding.

But no—here Red was again, settling into the chair beside Tate's bed and giving him the same old song and dance.

As long as his buddy was determined to visit, though, Tate figured he may as well get a few questions answered. He couldn't face Lyla after the way he'd failed her at the most critical moment—but maybe Tate could make sure she didn't need anything.

"So, how's, um…how's Lyla?" he asked. "Is she doing okay?"

Red sat back, folded his hands on his stomach, and rolled his eyes. "You're really a piece of work, you know that?"

"Not the time, Red. *Christ*," Tate slammed his fist on the bed, yanking his fucking IV in the process and wincing at the sting before he could think better of it.

Red's face went from mocking to concerned in the blink of an eye. "You okay?"

"Fine. Just tell me." Tate gently rearranged the tubing snaking across his arm then looked across the room, focusing on the quiet television up in the corner.

Let Red think he was watching the sports highlights—then maybe he wouldn't read too much into Tate's inquiry.

His buddy sighed, but he gave up the goods. "She was banged up pretty good, but otherwise seems to be doing okay. She'd be better if you let her come see you, though."

"Not gonna happen, bro."

"Because you…failed her somehow?" Red arched an imperious auburn brow at him, and Tate gritted his teeth.

"Exactly. It's better this way."

"But you caught the guy."

They'd been over this before. "*Again* with that shit? Having a seizure and blacking out on the fucker does not count as *catching him*. When I think of what Jones could have done to Lyla if she hadn't gotten ahold of my gun…or if the cops couldn't find her…"

"That didn't happen, though," Red said reasonably. "You sacrificed your own well-being to neutralize her stalker, giving Lyla a chance to defend herself and the police plenty of time to get there and keep her safe. Tate, you seem to be giving yourself demerits for what-ifs that never even took place."

Tate knew it was going to be impossible to reason with his old friend. When Red got it into his head that he was right, he was as obstinate as they came—logic be damned. And frankly, Tate was in no shape at the moment to put up much of a fight.

"Look, I told you how it had to be, and nothing you say is going to change my mind."

Tate didn't even know how Lyla felt about him anymore. For a while there, he'd wondered if maybe she cared about him as much as he did her, but Brett's attack had changed everything.

For all Tate knew, Lyla had only viewed him as a convenient fuck buddy, anyway—and now that the danger to her was past, she was more than happy to move on.

Red leaned in to catch his eye, and said, "You know you're my brother, Tate."

"But?"

"But you're being an unreasonable ass about this. Just talk to the woman. How is that so hard?"

"Says the man who didn't collapse at the worst possible moment, putting the person he was supposed to protect in grave danger."

"It all worked out," Red insisted.

"If you say so." Tate crossed his arms over his chest, then immediately uncrossed them when he realized it probably made him look like a sullen kindergartener.

"Tate, Brett Jones is on psychiatric lockdown, and he's staying there indefinitely. NYPD is charging him with all kinds of crap. Seems he's been flushing his meds and stealing his parents' car, and mommy and daddy had no fucking idea."

"He'll beat it," Tate said grimly. "You'll see. They'll transfer him to a hospital, and before long he'll be allowed out to visit his parents, and next thing you know, it will be like nothing ever happened."

Red frowned at him. "When did you become such an unrelenting pessimist?"

"When I went to war, dickhead, and instead of it making sense, it turned out to be a big cesspool of *what the fuck.*"

Red shook his head, and Tate wanted to beat the look of pity right off his handsome face. They weren't a couple of hotheaded college kids anymore, however. Red had a billion-dollar business to run and a woman at home that he was scheduled to marry in a matter of weeks.

So, Tate kept his hands to himself and concentrated on not saying something foul to the man who was supposed to be his best friend.

Red was as unrelenting as ever and tried another track. He commented, "If Jones ever does get out, Lyla will need you again."

"Wrong. She will need an actual bodyguard who is trained and qualified to do the job without fucking it up," Tate corrected.

"She won't want that."

"Then make her want it."

"You, of all people, ought to recognize the futility of that."

"Red, if you are half the friend you claim to be, you will find the deadliest motherfucker on the planet to guard that woman, and you will make her agree to it. Do you understand me?" Tate growled. "That is not negotiable."

Red blew out a long breath and shook his head.

"Promise me, MacLellan. If you do nothing else, at least give me that."

"Fine, dumbass. But this conversation isn't over."

"Oh yes, it is."

NEXT UP WAS Luca, who strolled into Tate's room in his starched white lab coat that afternoon, carrying a clipboard and sporting a suave grin.

"So," he drawled, "Red tells me you are still being a stubborn little *idiota*. Am I going to have to keep you in here, eating terrible food for another week, just to get you to be reasonable?"

Tate glared at him. "For your information, Red has already played the bad cop, today. Aren't you supposed to be the nice one, now?"

"*Me ne frego*," Luca said. "I don't give a damn. I never get to be the bad cop, and besides—if there was ever a situation that called for two bad cops, this is it."

"This is *not* it," Tate argued. "And everything would be fine, asshole, if you two would only leave me the hell alone."

Luca chuckled darkly. "And here I thought it was the Italians who were supposed to be inept. But look at you, trying to speed on the JFK Expressway with a little thirty-year-old Vespa."

"All right, Dirty Harry," Tate groaned. "Would you please cool your jets?"

"No, really. You're being even more intractable than usual."

"Why do I have the feeling you're going to use this as an excuse to take out ten years of unaired frustrations on me?"

"Because that's what you or Red would do." Luca settled into the green armchair next to Tate's bed, and sighed, "Listen, Tate. Do you remember all those years ago, when we first started school? I was such a fish outside the water, just like you used to say. You and Red were my only American friends—the only ones who took the time, at first, to find out anything about who I was as a person."

"Dude, we had to," Tate blustered, growing uncomfortable with the direction Luca was taking. "We lived together."

"You didn't have to," his buddy argued softly, "And you and I both know it."

"Okay, fine. So, you were mildly entertaining. What does that have to do with me now?"

"Okay, well—how about last year? Don't you think I was nervous to come back here?" Luca inquired. "To all of the uncertainty about what was the proper thing to do, and whether I was saying words correctly or acting strange to Americans?"

"I have to tell you, bud, I was knee-deep in fringe-group fuckfaces at the time. I wasn't spending a whole lot of time noodling about your emotions," Tate said.

"I have no doubt. But I guess the point I'd like to make is that both times, I might have been out of my element, but at least I had you and Red. You two gave me a push when I needed one, and look at me now. Happy as a mollusk."

Tate snorted. "I hate to say this, but for some unknown reason, clams are the only specific mollusks known for being happy."

"Be that as it may," Luca fired back, getting testy now, "if it weren't for your unwavering loyalty, I might not be here. Therefore, I intend to repay the favor, and I will do it using any and every means I find suitable. Even doubling up on the Bad Cop routine, to get you out of your comfort zone."

"Damn it, Luca—the least you could do is throw a punch or two. How the hell am I supposed to fight romance like that?"

"You could try some romance yourself, *Tater Tot*."

"Okay, A—you know I don't play for that team. And B—I'm pretty sure we determined about ten years ago that neither Red nor you would be calling me that ever again. You might recall the chokeholds."

Luca tilted his head. "That's strange, I don't. But I recently ate one of those little potatoes in the hospital cafeteria and I think the name might suit you, after all."

"Do I even want to know how you came to that bizarre conclusion?"

"Well, let's see. They're a bit salty. They can take the abuse of blisteringly hot oil and disgusting ketchup and still remain perfectly fine. And, as long as we're remembering things today, I have a distinct memory of a young lady referring to you as *delicious* in junior year. And...a different one senior year, come to think of it."

Tate groaned, "Luca, this is officially the worst pep talk in the history of pep talks."

"Good, because it isn't meant to be a pep talk. It's supposed to be a *stop screwing around, you idiot cazzo, and get your ass in gear* talk. Now, then. You fell for the woman of your dreams, correct?"

"Sure." As long as everyone was going to assume it anyway, Tate figured there was no harm in copping to it.

"You basically saved her life when she needed it, yes?"

"Barely. Lyla still had to shoot the dude."

"Even so, you got the job done. And now, though the obstacles to you two being together have been disposed of, you are still dithering about riding up on your white horse and declaring yourself to her. Do I have this correct?"

"No, asswipe, you don't. I am still in the Army until they tell me otherwise. And even if that Jones fucker is out of commission right now, it doesn't mean I'm any good for Lyla. *Christ*, I'm not just geographically undesirable now," Tate cried. "I'm probably about to be unemployed. What am I supposed to do? Wait tables while she swans around being amazing all day?"

Tate scrubbed his hands over his face and added glumly, "Not to mention the fact that I'm basically a mental case."

"Seriously?" Luca shook his head at him. "We're back to that again, are we? You're completely sane, Tate. All of your fears and reactions and triggers are perfectly normal and rational manifestations of the life you've been living for many years. Sane. Normal. Rational. *Really*."

Yeah, right. Easy for Luca to say—he didn't see the faces of dead men in his dreams every night. Tate wasn't going to be a shit and point that out, however.

Instead, he asked, "Luca, have you stopped for one minute to consider what I'd be offering Lyla? Forget about all the other stuff—just focus on the fact that I used to play football in school. Now I've had a TBI, and whatever else I've done to myself *this* time. I'm, like, a sure bet for getting CTE, dude."

Luca threw his clipboard onto the nightstand and steepled his fingers, instantly flipping into physician mode. "Tate—"

Tate didn't want to hear statistics, though. "No, really. I'll probably end up a drooling zombie long before my time. So, what kind of ogre would I be, to knowingly saddle Lyla with that? She'd have to take care of me, instead of the other way around. It wouldn't be fair to her."

Luca was frowning thoughtfully. "Have you had any other concussions besides the one?"

"No, dude. I was too quick to get tackled back in the day," Tate boasted. "Probably still am." But then he sobered. "That hardly matters when you've been blown clear out of your boots like I have, though."

"There are a lot of research studies on this. You could—"

"Luca, seriously? What the fuck?"

"I'm sorry. We can talk about all that later." His friend sat back and contemplated him. "For now, please know that you can't decide for Lyla whether that risk is one she doesn't want to take. It's her decision to make, so you have to present her with the facts and go from there."

Tate exploded in utter exasperation, "I don't even know if she loves me back!"

Dead silence. Like a fucking tomb.

"And now we come to the real problem," Luca said softly.

"Oh, it's a problem all right," Tate muttered bitterly. "With fangs and claws and a whole army of orcs to help it on its way."

"I am not going to ask you what an *orc* is right now. But let's say, just for the sake of argument, that Lyla *might* feel the same way. Are you going to be happy with yourself five years from now, knowing that you missed your chance? Knowing that both of you sat around for ages, wishing the other one knew how they felt? That's awfully morose, even for this new version of you."

Tate sagged into his pillow and realized he had no answer for that.

Sure, he and Lyla had shared some fun times in and out of the sack, but that didn't mean she wanted anything more from him. It didn't automatically translate into happily-ever-after.

It had just been for kicks. Something to cut the ever-present tension hanging over them while they waited for her stalker to make a move, or slip up. Tate didn't count for more than his muscle in Lyla's eyes.

Only—it had never once felt like that with her. It'd felt real, every minute.

"But…"

Luca jumped right in. "What?"

"Not that the odds are high or anything, but if I were curious, how would I even find out how she really feels?" It wasn't like Tate could simply *ask* her—he'd spent days avoiding the woman for crying out loud. By now, she probably wanted to shoot him, too.

"Well, that's where things get tricky," his friend admitted. "I can't tell you the words to say, because that has to be something between you and her. I can tell you this, however—you're going to have to take a risk. You'll have to stick your neck out."

"That's some a-plus advice, coming from a fucker who supposedly saves lives for a living."

"Yes, well—I feel confident that grave injury will not result."

"Pollyanna? Party of one? Your table is now available."

Luca smirked. "Look, you're a natural at waiting tables, already."

"You haven't seen me in an apron," Tate groused.

"Nor do I intend to. But at least think about this. If we agree to release you, you're planning to go home and see your parents this weekend, right?"

"Yeah." Tate had to show his face in Ohio, or his mom would never stop worrying.

"Then, take the time to clear your head and figure out what you really want," Luca told him. "If it's Lyla, then come up with a way to tell her. The rest will sort itself out. I promise you."

"That's what Red says, too."

His buddy nodded sagely, "Yes, well—we both have very recent experience in this area."

Tate laid there and considered it, but it wasn't like he had anything left to lose by agreeing to do some thinking—hell, the last remaining shreds of his dignity had flown the coop days ago.

"All right, bro. I'll do it," he said. "But I wouldn't expect any miracles or anything."

Luca just chuckled. As blissed-out and in love as he was, the dude probably walked around expecting miracles every day of his life, these days. *Bastard.*

"And maybe, as long as you're contemplating things, give some thought to this."

Luca set a thick pamphlet down, and Tate felt all the acid in his gut curdle when he read the cover.

"What's this supposed to be?"

"It's a guide to assist wounded veterans reintegrating into civilian life. I have a couple of contacts that I can introduce you to—"

"*Luca.* For fuck's sake," Tate complained. "Could you please back the fuck off for one goddamn minute?"

"Well, I'm trying to segue into Good Cop now."

"No, thank you."

"Listen, I know you think you aren't good for anything, but there is a lot you could do if the Army ends up discharging you. You could be a police officer or a private investigator. You could be a bouncer or a bodyguard or even a teacher. There are many military contractors around, too. Any of them would be thrilled to have you."

Tate groaned. It was like talking to his dad all over again. "Please, please stop talking," he begged.

Besides, if it wasn't going to be Lyla's sweet body Tate was guarding, then it wasn't going to be anyone's.

"Or you could even go home and farm like your parents." Luca paused and frowned. "Do I have that right? They are farmers?"

Tate had to laugh at the poor guy's confusion. "They raise alpacas. Close enough."

"Alpacas? Like llamas?" It was obvious that was news to Luca.

Tate explained, "Alpacas are smaller and have way better hair."

"I am certain I did not know this about you."

"Moving on," Tate said pointedly, "you maybe remember that I have a degree in poly sci, not agriculture. I will not be opening my own alpaca farm. Okay?"

"Fine," Luca conceded. "Just promise me you will evaluate *all* your options. You have many."

"Sure. If it will get you to shut up and leave, then I promise."

"And come stay with me and Daisy when you get back."

"Not on your life."

If Tate hadn't wanted to intrude on Love Street before, he sure as hell wasn't going to do it now that he was riding the Bachelor Express again. Three minutes with Luca and his lady love, and Tate was bound to be pounding on Lyla's door, begging for her to take him back.

He couldn't do that, even if he already felt the absence of her like a phantom limb. *Painful. Chronic. No freaking cure.*

Tate had to get out of this town before he did something stupid that they'd both regret.

Thirty-Six

LYLA GAVE HERSELF one week—a mere seven days—to wallow in the misery that consumed her once she finally accepted that Tate was gone for good.

She would let herself feel all the hurt and disappointment, the sadness and the worry, and then she'd force herself to move on.

It wasn't like she hadn't seen any of this coming, after all. She'd known very well how hard it would be to let Tate go, once the time came. Lyla simply hadn't factored in how much worse it would feel for him to leave the way he had.

Tate hadn't given her some passionate, movie-worthy kiss on a street corner to bid her a fond farewell. Instead, he'd skulked out of town like a fugitive, without a single word of goodbye.

He was there, fighting off Lyla's attacker with every ounce of determination in his body, and then he was gone.

And by gone, Lyla meant really, *really* gone, too—Tate didn't call, he didn't write, and he didn't send apologetic flowers. It was as if her former bodyguard had been nothing more than a fantastic-looking mirage. An erotic dream, haunting her for weeks.

But even if Lyla could acknowledge how much his departure stung, she couldn't fathom why Tate had chosen to do it the way he had.

What they'd shared in their time together had seemed so real—so right. How could a person simply walk away, without feeling a thing?

Lyla couldn't prove that part for sure, though, could she? Maybe Tate felt all kinds of things right now. A sense of freedom. Happiness. *Relief.*

All she felt was heartbroken.

HER *CRY IT out, then forget him* campaign might've gone swimmingly, if everyone Lyla knew hadn't come out of the woodwork partway through, wanting to discuss what she was going to do about Tate.

First up was Piper, the romance author she'd been friendly with for years, who'd gotten engaged to Lyla's boss recently.

She'd wheedled Lyla into meeting her at a new coffee shop in Midtown, then casually commented, "So, Red heard from Tate. Sounds like he went back to Ohio for a bit."

"Not my business," Lyla said.

She was only on day four of her Tate-withdrawal program, and things weren't exactly proceeding smoothly. The less she had to talk about him, the better her chances of holding herself together in public.

"He told Red he had another medical board evaluation coming up, and that he wanted to return his brother's truck."

"Again—Tate has made it eminently clear that his life and mine don't overlap anymore, Piper." Lyla tried to say it gently, so her friend wouldn't take offense.

Piper was determined to say her piece, however, and continued doggedly, "Supposedly Tate refused to leave New York until Red confirmed that your old neighbor was locked up for the long haul, and that you were doing okay. Those were his exact words, Red said—*Is Lyla okay, or not?*"

Lyla frowned. Why should Tate care? "I hope Red told him that I am as okay as 'okay' can possibly be."

"I assume so," Piper said. "But…are you really?"

"Sure. Why wouldn't I be?" Lyla had even put on extra eye makeup today, just to make that eminently clear.

Piper peered at her over the rim of her latte. "Oh, I don't know—maybe because Tate's being a complete dolt by ghosting you?"

"Is he, though?" Lyla sat back and contemplated that. "He took a job, performed the job, and when the job was over, he returned to his regular life. I don't think we can fault him for that. He did exactly what he promised to do."

She dunked her tea bag in the little pot of water a few more times, but it was obviously not hot enough to brew anymore. Lyla sighed.

Story of her life.

"Except…you're kind of glossing over some of the important middle parts, aren't you?" Piper prodded.

"Not really. We got along great, but we both knew he was intending to return to active duty at some point. It's not like we had a whole future planned out together, or anything."

"Even so, that doesn't mean you can't be hurt by what he's doing."

Trust another author to be inconveniently nosy. Unfortunately, as Lyla studied Piper, she couldn't remember anymore why it was so important for her to put up a good front today.

She might as well admit that life wasn't entirely fine and dandy. It wasn't like other people didn't get their hearts broken all the time, too.

"I know, and it does hurt," she confessed. "But giving in to it will get me exactly nowhere. Tate doesn't want to talk to me. He doesn't want anything to do with me, apparently. That narrows my options considerably."

Piper pressed her lips together unhappily, then went with, "Red thinks he'll come around eventually. I do, too."

"I hope you will both understand if I don't sit here holding my breath, waiting for it to happen," Lyla told her.

"I do. And maybe I'm not reading the situation well. I had the impression that you cared a lot about Tate, but if you don't..." Piper's eyebrows knitted together, and she examined Lyla with a worried frown. "Maybe I shouldn't have said anything."

"No, it's okay. You aren't wrong. Tate's a really good guy— the best, actually. I wish...I wish..." What *did* Lyla wish for? She had a sinking suspicion it was still *everything*—all of him, forever.

"I wish Tate had stuck around a little longer," she told Piper sadly.

"Me, too," her friend said. "And we really do think he's crazy about you, Lyla. Maybe don't write him off just yet. If you can manage it."

"Don't worry. I have no desire to run out and hook up with someone new this week."

"Okay, good," Piper smiled.

Lyla took a sip of her weak, tepid Earl Grey. "Next week, though..."

Her friend laughed. "You can't keep a good woman down. We'll just have to hope that Tate comes to his senses fast."

Lyla wanted to believe her, she really did—but odds were, Tate wasn't ever coming back.

MERE HOURS AFTER her outing with Piper, Lyla's parents called—ostensibly to check on her welfare, but really wanting to discuss the current candidate in the Future Son-in-Law rodeo.

It didn't take them long to get to the point, either. With both parents on the line, they only required half as much time to bring the conversation around to the topic of the day.

Her dad led with, "I still feel awful about what happened, kiddo. If you had only told us what was going on, right from the beginning..."

"I didn't want to worry you."

"We know. But hiding it from us made us unwittingly endanger you—how is that any better? And now, I'm always going to worry that you're secretly in trouble and not telling us."

"You can relax," Lyla sighed. "It's not like that."

"Well, at least you have Captain Monroe there with you," her mother interjected. "That's a consolation, at least."

Lyla winced. She should've been prepared for that. "Actually…Tate's not here anymore. He went home to Ohio to stay with his family."

Her mother huffed, "But he'll be back, right?"

"No, Mom. After that, he's probably going back to his unit, if the Army lets him. They might not."

"Not that I wish him ill, but that would be good, wouldn't it? If Tate gets discharged, then he could stay in New York with you."

Lyla groaned. "I wouldn't count on it."

"I would," her father stated firmly. "That boy shook my hand and promised to take care of you. A man doesn't do that with a woman's father unless he means it."

"Dad, come on," Lyla complained. "Guys say that kind of thing all the time."

"No, they don't. Not like that."

"Well, nothing's going to get solved right now." Or ever, but they'd have to realize that in their own time, just like Lyla had. Someday, there'd be other men for them to focus on, other prospects to dream about.

"As long as you're fine," her father said dubiously.

"I am, I promise. But how are you guys doing? Everything okay on the home front?"

Her mom chirped, "Oh, we're fine, too. We're always fine. Don't worry about us."

Lyla bit her lip, uncertain if she should broach a touchy subject, but she *was* really curious. "Have you…talked to the Joneses lately?"

"No, they've been laying low," her mother said. "I think they're probably mortified by what happened."

"I'll bet they are. They should be, anyway." *And then some.*

How could those people not have known what was going on under their own roof?

"Brett had been stable for so long," Lyla's mom told her. "I think Bill and Midge probably let down their guard and stopped believing he would ever backslide. They want him to be well so badly, I think they let their longing blind them."

Lyla was angry, but she also felt a little sorry for the couple. "I'm sorry," she said. "I know you guys were close."

"And maybe we will be again someday. But you should never doubt that you come first for us. Always," her father said.

"Thanks, guys."

LAST BUT NOT least came Detective Scarletti, stopping by that evening to share news about Lyla's case, and his thoughts about certain bodyguards.

He began by telling Lyla that the Joneses had admitted to periodically letting their son use the car on his own, even though he would sometimes "get lost" for hours on end.

Because Bill hadn't been able to drive while he healed from his foot surgery, and Midge didn't drive on highways, Brett had skipped his last doctor's appointment and blood work—and no one had realized that he'd stopped taking his medication.

The detective explained that the preponderance of evidence against Brett—including the scrapbook Lyla and Tate had told him about—had convinced the family to admit guilt and take the plea deal they'd been offered.

Lyla wouldn't have to testify, thankfully. She hadn't been looking forward to sitting in a courtroom, facing off with her parents' best friends while she damned their only child.

Scarletti explained that because Brett's gunshot wound was healing up, he'd soon be transferred from Mount Sinai to a high-security psychiatric facility upstate.

He wasn't expecting her to have any more trouble, but as the detective nursed the cup of coffee she'd given him, he said, "Maybe keep that bodyguard of yours around for a while, just in case."

"Too late," Lyla told him. "Captain Monroe has already gone back to Ohio."

For some reason, it wasn't getting any easier to tell people that, even though it felt like she'd had to do it over and over today.

The cop eyed her speculatively. "Is he going back to his unit soon?"

"Maybe. Last I heard, Tate was still trying to get cleared by his doctors, but I suspect this latest incident isn't going to help his chances."

"Well…I wouldn't worry about it," Scarletti said, scratching at the five o'clock shadow coming in on his jaw. "I'm pretty sure a pretty girl wins out over getting shot at every day of the week."

Lyla rolled her eyes. "That's nice of you to say, but I don't think it applies in this instance."

The officer set down his mug and grinned at her, for perhaps the first time in their entire acquaintance. "Ms. Lawson, did you, by any chance, happen to see the way that guy looked at you?"

She lied and didn't even care that he'd see right through her. "No, Detective, I did not."

"Might wanna get that eyeglass prescription updated, then. That fella is in deep."

Lyla blew out a beleaguered breath, wondering which other unlikely suspects might try to ply her with relationship advice before this all was over. Maybe her super could get in on the act—or even Mrs. Meecham down the hall.

"Detective, did you have anything else you needed to tell me?" she asked, picking up his mug and walking it to the sink. "It's been a really long day."

Scarletti smirked at her as he stood up and brushed at his pants, amused by Lyla's resignation. "No, we're good. You might hear from the district attorney's office in a few days about the restraining order, but otherwise, I think you're all set."

Lyla smiled back. The truth was, he wasn't *such* a bad guy—he'd just been stuck with a really crappy case. "Thanks again. I really appreciate everything you did for me."

"No sweat. Don't hesitate to call if you have any questions, or you ever hear from that punk again, okay?"

"Okay."

As he stepped to her front door, Scarletti had a very uncharacteristic twinkle in his wry brown eyes. "And, when you're putting together the guestlist for your wedding in a few months, be sure to put me on it."

With that, he walked out, strolling down the hall whistling tunelessly.

IF LYLA WAS going to have to talk about Tate with everyone she knew, she thought sometime later, it was going to take a hell of a lot longer than seven days to get over him. It could take a month, or maybe even a whole year.

Perhaps even the rest of her sorry, empty life.

Tate had clearly had the right idea about this whole debacle. It was obvious that the less said about him and Lyla's brief relationship, the better.

It appeared to be the only way to move on with her dignity intact. What Lyla was doing now was only keeping the wound fresh.

Maybe she ought to follow his lead in other ways, as well. Just like Tate, Lyla could not only go dark but get out of town. The idea intrigued her enough that she cracked open her laptop and started clicking, investigating trips and cruises she'd probably never get to go on.

In reality, Lyla had to stay here in New York for a while, at least. The untested Red Devil imprint was launching her new series *now*, and by the time their big marketing push had passed, Lyla doubted she would miss New York's favorite bodyguard as much anymore.

With a heavy heart, Lyla switched over from images of tropical islands to her final edits on the unplanned book she'd managed to whip out over the last several weeks. Trident's team was ecstatic that she was delivering her next title way ahead of schedule, but Lyla was conflicted.

While she'd been writing it, she'd loved every word. But now that it was close to passing out of her hands, she couldn't help feeling a little sad, too. Tate would never know that it had turned into a love letter to him because he'd never read it and she wouldn't tell him.

In the harsh light of his departure, it only seemed pathetic, these days—the daydreams of a foolish, lovestruck introvert. But life kept moving on, and so would Lyla.

She squared her shoulders, sent the file to her editor, and snapped her laptop shut. Someday, the way she felt right now would be a distant memory. *Tate* would be a distant memory.

That was, by far, the most depressing thought of all.

Thirty-Seven

ONCE TATE RECEIVED the all-clear from his doctors to get out of Dodge, the first thing he did was arrange to go home.

His long-suffering parents had been tying themselves into knots ever since they'd returned from their cruise to discover their oldest son was in the hospital again. Since Tate had refused to let them come see him in New York, he figured he'd better show his face in Ohio to prove he really meant what he'd said—he was *fine*.

Thankfully, Luca and Daisy had already retrieved his stuff from Lyla's apartment, so all he needed to do was get a ride to the garage where he'd stashed Tom's truck and then he could be on his way.

Just to underscore how capable he was, Tate made that ride an Uber. His first one. *How about that, world?*

However, as he rolled along the roads between Manhattan and Cleveland, Tate's confidence began to waver a bit. He couldn't help feeling like he was leaving in disgrace, even if everyone else told him he was full of shit.

Honestly, though—he'd been hired to protect Lyla, and she'd still had to take care of things herself in the end. That made Tate the city's biggest waste of space, as far as he was concerned.

Honor was honor, though, so he'd attempted to return the money he'd been paid to act as her bodyguard. To the surprise of no one, Red had shut him down, and even though it hadn't been terribly hard to predict, it had made Tate feel exponentially worse.

And that was before he let himself consider what Lyla must think of him right now.

Funny thing how, four months ago, Tate had truly believed his life had gone to shit. In comparison, his mood now made that guy look like a hopeless romantic.

ABOUT FIVE MILES from his folks' place, Tate stopped at a gas station to fill Tom's tank. He called his mom to see if she needed him to get her anything on the way, and when he hung up, Tate noticed that he had a new email from Red.

That, no doubt, could wait.

Tate went into the minimart to grab his father some chips and his mother the requested coffee creamer. As he stood in line waiting to pay, he scanned the rack of paperbacks off to the side with an unsettling combination of dread and hope.

Romances. Books of daily devotions. Atlases. And there, smack dab in the center of everything, was the new mystery by Lyla Lawson. *Damn it.*

Tate swallowed and looked away, bouncing on his toes with a sudden, desperate impatience. He needed to get away from that book—almost as much as he needed to buy what might be his last and only piece of her.

He held out for two whole minutes, then caved and grabbed the only copy just in time to pay.

Tate felt like a pathetic, grade-A ass, but he clutched that stupid paperback to his chest all the way to the truck like he'd scored the winning lottery ticket. Then he stashed it on the passenger seat to deal with later.

Lyla's headshot on the back made her look smart and sexy, and made Tate's chest ache with longing. God, he missed her.

However, in three days he was going to be evaluated yet again by the Army Medical Board, and his future in the service would be decided, for better or worse. By next week, Tate would either find himself on his way back to the desert, or he'd find himself with the rug pulled out from under him.

Either way, Lyla was better off without him.

TATE STAYED UP all night that first night reading her book, then slept late the next day, trying to compensate. Nearly twenty-four hours passed before he remembered that email from Red.

When he finally cracked it open, Tate was stunned to see that his friend had sent him a file containing Lyla's newest, as-yet-unpublished manuscript, with the terse command to *Read This*.

He didn't pause to consider the source, or whether he should actually be reading something that wasn't in the public arena yet. Tate didn't stop to wonder why Red had thought it was so necessary to share it or to ask whether his buddy had Lyla's permission to pass along the advance copy.

He simply closed himself in his childhood bedroom, kicked back on his bed, and began reading *The Last Man Standing*.

It didn't take long to realize Lyla had written a fictionalized version of their relationship, and a hot one. If Red had thought this would help Tate pass the time while he licked his wounds, his friend had been dead wrong.

Tate's wounds were now officially worse. In fact, by the end of the book, he was nearly out of his mind, trying to figure out why the cop in the story would spend two hundred pages longing for the chick he was protecting, and then not tell her—thereby driving her right into the arms of the bad guy.

Was Lyla trying to send him some kind of message? She must be, Tate decided. Why else write the story that way—even if Tate shouldn't have been able to read it for months yet?

What the message was, however, was escaping him. It wasn't like Lyla had gone and fallen for Brett Jones since he'd last seen her.

He sat for a while and toyed with just calling and asking, but this didn't strike him as a phone call kind of conversation. Tate needed to see Lyla's face if he confronted her—to see what those eyes looked like, and what that sexy, pouty mouth of hers would do.

He knew that even if Lyla tried to dance around the subject with her fancy author words, her expression would tell him the truth. She might be able to spin wild tales on paper, but in real life, the girl couldn't lie worth shit.

If only he wasn't so confused about what all this *meant*. Was Lyla in love with him or the exact opposite? Was she just a vulture, snatching at snippets of real life to make a buck? God only knew.

After days of hanging out with his parents and secretly obsessing about it, though, Tate had a bit of an epiphany. Whether Lyla loved him back or not didn't change the fact that he was head over heels in love with *her*.

He was all kinds of wrong for the woman, but he wanted her badly. He didn't want to wait for her, either.

For years, Tate had been living every breath as a soldier, but somehow, without intending to, he'd broken himself of the habit.

His desire to get back to active duty had suffered a quiet death sometime in the last few days, killed off by the accumulation of all those normal meals and comfortable beds, and by Tate's reluctance to give up any lingering hope he had of being with Lyla long term.

Now, he could actually see that there might be more in store for him than war and deprivation. Tate could have more holidays with family, with actual seasons and gifts to give. He could share more laughs with friends, with beers and cards and Monday Night football on the television.

Tate could have a real life, with kids and pets and a home of his own. A picket fence and a warm woman in his bed at night, as long as that woman was Lyla.

He would convince her, even if he had to die trying.

So, Tate pulled out a fresh notepad and began writing a new list. Any mission was possible, he'd learned, if you did the right recon and planning—and Tate wasn't the best at what he did for no reason.

By the time he was done, Lyla was going to be his.

THE AFTERNOON BEFORE his Med Board review, Tate sat in Dr. Ross's office to review the CT and MRI results that Weill Cornell had sent him, as well as to discuss what he could expect from the Army doctors the following day.

Given what had happened after only a little hand-to-hand and a quick sprint down the block, Tate could guess they wouldn't be too excited about green-lighting him.

But, while Tate listened to Dr. Ross yammer on about the need to keep him on the anticonvulsant for a while longer, he was also thinking about Lyla's book.

He thought about the way she looked at him, and about how much his parents and his brother would love her. Tate daydreamed about what it would be like to roll into his hometown with Lyla in tow—to show her off at weddings and introduce her to his former teachers and coaches on the Fourth of July.

A future with her rolled out in front of him like an unspooling ribbon, and Tate *wanted it*. He wanted all of it like he'd never wanted anything before…and that definitely explained what happened next.

He hadn't planned out this part, per se, but suddenly it felt *right*.

First, Dr. Ross said, "The psychiatrist gave you your best review yet, so that's good. I feel comfortable going ahead with our plan to wean you off the antidepressants now. But I'd still love to hear it from you. So, tell me—besides that one crazy episode in New York, how are you feeling about your recovery?"

"I'm good," Tate replied. And that was all thanks to Lyla, the woman he'd never expected to meet and couldn't, as it turned out, let go.

"But…to be honest," he continued, "I'm not sure I'm ever going to get to the point where I'd want to be, in order to be active again."

Dr. Ross froze in the act of flipping Tate's chart closed, his eyebrows climbing sky-high. "What do you mean?"

"I'm no expert, but I think I'm as good as I'm going to get now. I don't feel like things are improving anymore. I'm…I've plateaued." Tate held his breath and watched to see what the other man would do.

"Interesting," Ross murmured, blinking fast. "This is quite a switch for you. What makes you think you've leveled out at a competency lower than desirable?"

Tate tried to think of the best way to explain himself. "I mean…I'm functional, for the most part, in civilian life, but going back to my unit is another story. I won't be able to make adjustments to my days if I don't get enough rest, or if I feel dizzy or whatever. And frankly, Doc, I'm liable to get myself killed if I drop with another seizure when the bombs start going off."

Dr. Ross took a deep breath, picked up his pen, then put it down again. "Well, as they told you in New York, we believe the seizure you had was an anomaly, brought on by the strenuous burst of activity you experienced."

"Except…those are kind of the norm in my job," Tate pointed out.

"Right. Of course." The doctor pushed up his glasses and looked down at Tate's file again. "So…let's talk about your symptoms. Have you seen any improvement in the motion sickness?"

Tate's crazy idea was beginning to gather steam, forming into an engine that wanted to barrel down the tracks of his suddenly-tantalizing future.

He told the man, "No, if anything it's gotten worse."

"*Worse?*"

"Yeah. Hell, sometimes even a quick drive to the store gets me green around the gills." If the store was clear across town, that was, and an over-caffeinated cabbie was doing the driving. Anyone would get sick from that.

"Wow. Okay," Dr. Ross said. "What about the migraines? How often are you getting those now?"

Rarely, unless Tate had just collared a demented stalker. Still, he figured it was sensible to round up, so he estimated, "Around seven…no, ten. Ten a month, give or take."

"That many?" Ross was incredulous, and no wonder. At their last meeting, Tate had reported fewer than four a month, but then he'd definitely been rounding down.

"Yep." Just thinking about the ribbing Red and Luca were likely to dish out about this was almost giving Tate a headache now, for crying out loud.

"And the nightmares? How many of those?"

"I'd say most nights," Tate bluffed. He neglected to mention that his bad dreams were now of the *Is Lyla Safe* variety, rather than the *My Convoy's Getting Blown to Smithereens* type…but really—that disconnect was on Dr. Ross. He didn't ask.

Tate's heart beat faster as he met the eyes of the man who, all these months, had been as focused on getting him back into fighting form as Tate had been. Dr. Ross clearly smelled a rat now, but couldn't seem to figure out where it was.

"What about the dizziness and nausea?"

"Definitely. Both of those." Especially if Tate actually went through with his plan to confront Lyla about that freaking book of hers—but honestly, stronger men than him had been stymied by conversations like that.

The doctor sat back with a snort, looking Tate up and down. "So, you've given up, then? Is that it?"

"I wouldn't go that far," Tate huffed. There was no need to be insulting.

"But you're done."

He swallowed. It sounded so final when he put it that way. "Yeah. I am, Doc. I really need this to be over, once and for all."

More raised brows. "And by *this* you mean…"

"The Med Board mess, not my life," Tate smiled.

Dr. Ross smiled slightly, too. "By any chance, does this change of heart have to do with the woman you nearly killed yourself trying to protect?"

Tate pasted an innocent expression on his mug, but it went over about as well as a lead balloon. Rather than retreat, though, he just leaned into it. "Why, Doctor—whatever do you mean?"

The man chuckled, but pointed out, "Tate, be sure of what you're doing here. There's no going back from this. As long as the Med Board is still in process, you have a chance of returning to active duty. But once it ends, that's it. It's all over—and you're out for good. Do you understand that?"

"I do, sir."

"And you are telling me that you are fine with that."

"Believe it or not, yes. I really am."

"All right, then. I'll support you." The doctor sat back in his chair with a long sigh. "But tomorrow should be very interesting."

"Let's hope so," Tate said.

AS IT HAPPENED, the Army turned out to be just as sick of Captain Monroe, as he was of them. Tate endured two days of semi-polite tests and interviews, then had to wait another thirty-six hours before he had his answer.

Honorable medical discharge with full benefits. His parents didn't know whether to laugh or cry, and frankly, neither did Tate.

Still, with phase one in the bag, it was time to set the next part of his plan in motion, so Tate texted Red and asked his friend to call him when he had a chance.

Fifteen minutes later, he did just that. "Hey man, glad I caught you," Red said. Like Tate had anything better to do at the moment than sit around waiting.

He rolled his eyes. "And, to the surprise of no one, here I am."

"Listen, I need to give you a heads up. Luca's going to be calling you—"

"Already heard from him, bro."

"*Huh*. He works fast. So, do you think you can make it?"

"To your bachelor party?" Tate laughed, "Of course, I can. Wild horses couldn't keep me away."

Red muttered, "Oh, thank fuck." And then added, "I thought we'd go to a pool hall, but Luca seems to be heading in the opposite direction. He's talking fancy wine bars and shit."

"Seriously?" Their friend had neglected to mention that part during Tate's call with him.

"*Yes*. Tate, you need to rein him in. He's getting all creative, which means he's probably enlisting Daisy's help."

"Not for nothing, but I thought you liked wine."

"I do," Red said, "in certain circumstances. This is not one of them. You need to get back here and bring some fucking balance to this shitshow. I don't want to sip chardonnay for my bachelor party. I want to beat both your asses in a three-hour drunken game of billiards."

Tate laughed. "All right, brother, slow your roll. Order will be restored forthwith. I'm good to go here, so I can come back there as soon as I get a ticket or a rental."

"I'll send you the ticket in an hour," Red barked immediately.

"The hell you will." Tate might be at loose ends for the foreseeable future, but he wasn't a charity case.

Red, fortunately, knew a losing argument when he heard one. He sighed, "Fine, but at least let me arrange a hotel for you."

"No need, big shot. Daisy's already badgered me into staying with them."

"*Jesus*, I hope you're prepared to gain ten pounds. That woman is becoming a formidable cook."

"Looking forward to it, actually."

Red let out another, bigger sigh. "Okay, good. This is good. I feel better already."

"Do you?" Tate asked. "Because you sound even tenser than usual. Don't tell me you're getting cold feet, big man."

"Not even close. I just want this wedding to be perfect for Piper, but my mother's been driving us nuts with a ton of last-minute crap. She's a basket case."

"Red, if I know you, you've had every last possible contingency taken care of for weeks."

His buddy grunted in agreement.

"So, don't sweat it," Tate told him. "Piper only wants you."

"God only knows why. Anyway, enough about me. You said you're good to go there. Does that mean you've gotten word on your status already?"

"Let's just say…my schedule's loosened up a bit," Tate said. "I can make your stag party and your rehearsal and your wedding. Hell, if you want to throw a baby shower in a couple of years, I can make that, too."

There was a beat of silence over the phone line that stretched on and on, and Tate bit back his grin as he pictured Red's expression.

"They didn't approve you again?" his friend finally asked.

"No, they did not."

"When's your next—"

"No *next*, dude. I'm done."

More silence. Tate waited him out.

"Tell me they didn't fuck you over," Red growled at last. "Did they at least throw you a bone and give you the benefits?"

"Shockingly, they did," Tate assured him. "But now your boy's unemployed, so maybe don't fill that mailroom position before checking with me first."

"Whatever you want," Red said quickly. "Seriously. Luca and I are both here to help."

"I appreciate that, but I hope not to need it."

"Do you know what you want to do?"

"Not yet. Let's get you hitched first, then I'll come up with something." Something that included Lyla, front and center, if all went well.

Red considered that for a bit, then groaned, "*Christ*. I feel like you getting booted out is my fault, Tate. If I hadn't dragged you into the mess with Lyla, you probably would've been good to go."

"First of all, I suspect getting discharged was inevitable, I just didn't want to face it. Secondly, no one drags me anywhere."

"Typical."

"Last, but not least, don't you dare apologize for hooking me up with Lyla."

"Shouldn't I?" Red wondered.

"Come on, dude—don't be an ass."

"Oh, now *I'm* the ass? After the fucking disappearing act you pulled on her?"

"I did not enjoy it, I just did what I thought was necessary. But now things have evolved, so to speak, so…"

"Oh, really."

"I could use a hand if I'm going to…you know."

"I am not going to help you get back with that poor woman, just so you can jerk her around some more," Red fired back.

Tate argued, "I'm not going to do that."

"She deserves better than what you did, you bonehead."

"I'm aware."

"Lyla cared about you. A *lot*. You get that, right?"

"Shut the fuck up, would you please?" He was so done. Red could try to block his efforts, but Tate would only find a way around him.

"Then convince me you know what you're doing this time," his buddy said.

"I don't need to convince you of jack shit," Tate bristled. "Lyla is the one I have to convince. So if you don't want to help me win back the woman I love, then at least stay the hell out of my way."

Red chuckled. "Well, look who's finally joined the party. Took you long enough, Tater Tot, but I suppose you always were the slow one. I take it you read the book I sent you?"

"Bite me."

"No thanks. What else do you have in mind?"

Tate grabbed his list and outlined his plan.

Thirty-Eight

AS LYLA DARTED around her bedroom, trying to get ready for Red and Piper's rehearsal dinner, she realized she was losing it, big time.

However, sometime earlier that day it had suddenly occurred to her that Tate would, in all likelihood, be there tonight—not to mention at the wedding tomorrow.

The wedding would be big enough that she might be able to avoid him. The rehearsal dinner, however, promised to be intimate and awkward as all get out. What was more, Lyla could not risk screwing up or Tate was bound to realize what she'd been going through these last few weeks.

She could not let that happen.

Consequently, she needed to be sharp and completely on her game, just as if she was going to a book signing or a conference meet-and-greet with her fans.

The only problem was, she didn't seem to own a single shred of clothing that communicated the perfect *I-don't-care* ethos she was hoping for.

The retro burgundy party dress she was currently sporting, for example, might as well be screaming *trying-too-hard*—even if Lyla had gotten it for a song in a consignment shop last winter.

Out in the main room, the buzzer sounded next to her front door, jarring her from her thoughts. She spun around to check her clock, but her ride wasn't due to arrive for almost two more hours. Unless she'd gotten the time wrong.

Oh, crud—had she gotten the time wrong?

On the bed, her cell phone rang with a call from the doorman. "Hello?"

"Ms. Lawson? It's Joe, downstairs. I have Captain Monroe here. He said you're not answering your buzzer. Should I send him up?"

Lyla sank down on the corner of the mattress. "I'm sorry— did you say Captain Monroe?"

"Sure did. He says he has something for you." Her heart seemed to be doing some very unhealthy things inside her chest.

"*The* Captain Monroe?"

Joe paused. "Are there others?"

Lyla shook her head. There were none that mattered as much as hers did. It took a few tries to clear the frog from her throat, but eventually, she was able to croak out, "Uh, no. Go ahead and send him up."

Holy crap, Tate was here. Why in the world was Tate here?

She raced around the room, grabbing cast-off outfits from the floor and the bed and tossing them into her closet. She wasn't a particularly neat person, but why did her usual clutter suddenly seem to be proclaiming loud and clear what an emotional mess she'd been lately?

For good measure, Lyla kicked some random shoes under her bed, then went to stand near her front door. In a matter of minutes, she was going to be face to face with the man she loved with all her soul—the same man who'd broken her heart into a million jagged pieces.

There was absolutely no way to prepare for that, but she took a few deep breaths anyway.

At least she could count on Tate not knowing about the new book, since it would be months before it was released and he didn't read fiction, anyway. And, after this weekend, he would no doubt be getting on some military transport or other and heading back to his real job of protecting the country.

Lyla only had to fake her way through the next few minutes, and she'd be in the clear.

If Tate didn't care about her—as his actions had rather definitively declared—then she couldn't have him thinking that she cared, either. She *had* to project the perfect illusion of a confident woman, one who could walk away from him just as easily as he'd left her. This was only happening a bit sooner than she'd anticipated, that was all.

No hard feelings, right? Lyla laughed. She was so doomed.

MOMENTS LATER, LYLA heard Tate march up to her door, and the sharp rap of his knuckles on the other side made her jump like a damn cricket.

She took a couple more deep breaths and crept to the peephole, finding Tate impeccably turned out in a familiar suit and brandishing something on his cell phone that looked an awful lot like the title page of her new book.

Lyla narrowed her eyes, wondering which rotten, interfering Judas had given it to him. She'd bet a million dollars it was Red.

She swung open the door with what she hoped was an air of indifference—or, at minimum, not a greedy devouring of the man with her eyes.

"Tate? What are you doing here?" *There. Super casual.*

He puffed out his chest, standing at attention. "Hey, Lyla. I'm putting myself back on the job."

She stepped aside to let him in, then scoffed, "Why? Brett is on lockdown in a high-security psychiatric facility right now. And I doubt I'll be in danger at Red and Piper's wedding. Half of Manhattan is going to be there."

Tate was undeterred, though. At her words, he merely planted his feet and announced, "Before you know it, the Joneses will be trying to arrange a transfer to a local joint, and if they're successful, home visits are the next step. I don't feel comfortable leaving you unprotected with that on the horizon."

"Tate, honestly. Listen to yourself," Lyla said. "You're being paranoid for no reason. Besides, you'll be on your way back to your unit by then, anyway, and I'm fine. This is completely unnecessary."

"It's very necessary. And for the record, I'm not going back to my team."

"Wh—what?" She took a step back. That was news.

"You heard me. I'm not going back. I'm out. For good."

Lyla held still. No one had mentioned that to her, but of course, she'd made a herculean effort not to ask. "But…but your evaluation…"

Tate shrugged, like he hadn't been gung-ho to get back to fighting only weeks before. "Honorable medical discharge. I'm still going to wear my dress uniform tomorrow, though. I didn't have a tux for this shindig, so monkey suit, it is."

"It's…" Lyla faltered in the face of his sheer serenity about such an earth-shattering development. This beautiful man would undoubtedly look twice as delicious in his uniform, too—but she couldn't forget that he was still so far out of her reach.

For example, neither of them had even mentioned yet that this was the first time she'd laid eyes on him since the EMTs had carted him off after his seizure in that alley. That was a problem.

But Tate looked good. *So, so good.*

Lyla swallowed, and managed to say evenly, "I'm sure you'll look very nice in the uniform. And I'm sorry you didn't pass your evaluation. I know how much it meant to you."

"Don't be sorry," Tate replied cheerfully. "I flunked it on purpose."

What on earth? "But why would you do that?"

"For a lot of reasons. It was time, for one thing, and there was you to consider. There was *this.*" He gestured between them.

Lyla was obviously hearing things, so it was probably time to make a break for it here.

"Tate, as nice as it is to see you looking well again, I don't have time for whatever *this* is. I have to finish getting ready for Red and Piper's rehearsal dinner."

"You're ready. You look great," he said, stepping closer and cupping her cheeks before Lyla even had a chance to evade him. He pecked her softly on the lips, then murmured, "You look like a dream come true, as always."

Lyla pulled back and spun away, flustered by his unexpected show of affection. "My ride's going to be here in an hour and a half. I have to—"

Tate laughed, "I hate to break it to you, but I'm your ride, Slick."

"*Red*," Lyla growled.

"Yes. But don't be too mad at him. He let me borrow his new car for the weekend, so I could pick you up."

Lyla's eyes flew wide and she turned back to Tate, stunned. "The Alfa Romeo?"

He held out his fist to bump hers. "You know it, sweetheart. You're going to love it, too. Rides way smoother than my brother's truck."

Lyla shook her head, trying to clear it of everything that *did not matter* in the grand scheme of things. "Be that as it may—" she began.

Tate just waved her off. "Don't worry. This shouldn't take long."

She frowned at him. "I'd ask what you meant by that, but I already saw your little visual aid through the peephole. Do I even want to know where you got a copy of *The Last Man Standing*? It's not even out of editing yet."

"Where do you think?"

"Red." Lyla groaned. "Again."

"I'm sorry, Lyla," Tate said. "He may be big, but his bark is worse than his bite these days. Piper's turning him into a regular romantic down there."

"It's like her freaking superpower," Lyla muttered with a scowl. She'd hate the woman if she weren't so damn likable.

"I mean, hey—she's gotta go with her strengths, right?"

"I would like her to not be so strong at that."

Tate straightened up, suddenly saying, "Speaking of strengths, I meant to tell you the security in this building is pretty weak. You know that doorman, Joe? He just let me stroll on by, before— didn't even want to know why I was here. We should talk to him about that."

"Tate, he *remembers* you. You've only been gone for a month," Lyla retorted in exasperation. One month—and it had felt like a year.

"That's plenty of time to turn bad if you ask me."

She groaned, "Okay, *enough*. I don't believe for one second that you've turned bad, so *why* are you *here?*"

"I've come to make peace, Lyla. If you'll let me." Tate took a couple of steps toward her and held out his hand.

Lyla stared at his handsome face and felt her heart throb painfully in her chest at his words. She wanted to have him back like she wanted to keep breathing, but if Tate thought he could simply roll in here and shake hands, then live happily ever after as *friends*, he was about to get a real education in scorned women.

Still, like a lovesick floozy, she put her palm in his. As long as he was standing there, she couldn't resist the impulse to touch him again.

Tate smiled tentatively at her, and that's when the angry red scratch on his cheek finally registered. Lyla reached out to touch it gently, asking him, "Is this from your fight with Brett? It still hasn't healed?"

"Uh, *no*," Tate sneered. "You think I'd let that fucker have a go at my face? Come on, Lyla—my smile may as well be my livelihood."

She rolled her eyes. "I see your ego is still intact. But if it's not from then, what happened to you?"

"Would you believe a fraternity reunion gone awry?"

"You were in a fraternity? I'm surprised." Fraternity boys would forever be linked with the likes of Brett Jones in her mind, so it was hard to picture Tate as one, too.

"Small group, only three members," he grinned.

Oh, brother. "Let me guess," she said, catching on. "Red, Luca, and—"

"Me. Correct."

"And what did you name yourselves?"

"We didn't pick it, but people called us TDH. Have you heard of us?"

"Can't say that I have," Lyla said wryly. "And I am very afraid to ask what it stands for."

Tate chuckled. "Nothing skanky. Only, *Tall, Dark,* and..." he waggled his eyebrows knowingly at her.

"Heroic?" Lyla guessed.

"No. Handsome," Tate corrected her. "Obviously."

Obviously. She asked him, "And the flesh wound?"

"So...fun fact—Red is kind of amazing at darts when he's tanked," Tate explained. "And, some Wall Street dickheads took exception to it during his bachelor party the other night."

Lyla gaped at him. "By throwing a dart at you?"

"Well, to be fair, they threw it at Red. But Piper would've killed us if we'd returned her groom looking like Scarface. I had to leap on the grenade, so to speak."

Tate looked a little sheepish as he told the story, and his expression was so familiar and so charming, it almost made her melt into a vaguely Lyla-shaped puddle at his feet.

She pulled herself together, slipped a hand around his waist to get closer, and was instantly rewarded by the feel of Tate's arms closing warmly around her.

"You're making it a bit of a habit lately, getting in the way of trouble. Aren't you?" she asked softly.

Tate picked right up on her hint. "About that—Lyla, I'm really sorry about what happened. You shouldn't have had to shoot a dude to protect yourself like that. I should've been the one doing it. I should've gotten the job done for you."

"That's a lot of *shoulds*, Tate."

"I have others if you'd like to hear them."

"I'll pass, thanks. The few you used were lame enough."

"*Lame?*" he squawked, but his gorgeous blue eyes were dancing.

"Yes, lame, you dope." Lyla ought to have known he'd be blaming himself. "You're recovering from a traumatic brain injury, Tate. You had to exert yourself in exactly the way you weren't supposed to, but you did it trying to keep me safe. There's no *should* or *shouldn't* at that point. Your brain simply hated it, and it told you so."

"But—"

"But, nothing. You were amazing and you probably saved my life. What you *should* be apologizing for is what you did next," Lyla told him.

Tate dropped his forehead gently against hers. "I was getting to that part."

"Was it going to be anytime this century?"

He grinned and pressed a hard kiss against her lips. "Lyla, I have missed your sassy mouth so much. And I am very, very sorry that I left without saying a word. It was shitty of me."

"And for not letting me come see you in the hospital, too, I should hope. Because that was extra humiliating."

"For that, too. Incidentally, did I bend your screen when I pulled it in through the window? If so, I'm happy to replace it."

"Tate, the screen works fine. But most people would've just popped it out and let it fall into the alley. No—scratch that. *Most* people would've kept pounding on the *door* to get out, instead of tiptoeing along a ledge three stories up. What were you thinking?"

He looked perplexed. "I was thinking that Brett must've gotten in through the kitchen, and if he'd done it, then so could I," he said.

"Except Brett only had to climb up the fire escape. You had to act like a freaking cat burglar to get to that window," Lyla complained.

Tate shook his head. "It was only a few feet," he said earnestly, "and then I jumped on the fire escape, too."

"You could've plummeted to your death, you big lunkhead."

"I don't think it was quite that death-defying, but I'm sorry for that, too," Tate smiled.

"I suppose your contrition is acceptable," Lyla said grudgingly, even though her bruised heart was beginning to sing. "Why did you go, though? Why did you leave that way?"

Tate sighed deeply. "I didn't think I'd be able to, otherwise. And I was laboring under a series of misconceptions that, in retrospect, seem excruciatingly dumb now that I'm here with you."

She could only imagine. "Like what?" Lyla smiled.

"Like, I'm not good enough for you, you're better off without me, and I have nothing to offer you. Especially now."

Now that her world was unexpectedly righting itself into a framework that made some logical sense, Lyla couldn't resist the softball Tate was tossing over home plate to her.

"I don't know," she hummed, "those reasons don't sound *so* farfetched."

"*Ha, ha.* Very funny," he griped.

"I hope you realize how completely ridiculous that all is. You do, right?"

"Whether it is, or it isn't, Lyla—the fact remains that once I read your new book, I couldn't stay away without knowing why you did it."

And here they were. Tate had come back, and he was actually opening up to her, but that was only the first step. If Lyla wanted to keep him here, she was going to have to be honest with him in return.

Thirty-Nine

TATE REALLY HAD been annoyed when Lyla's doorman waved him inside without hesitating, mainly because he couldn't believe he'd never noticed how lax the guy was before.

But everything around him felt clearer now that he was officially out of limbo and moving forward again. Tate was noticing details he hadn't before. He felt sharp. *Ready*.

However, when he'd knocked on Lyla's door and then nothing happened—he began to doubt the wisdom of his plan. What if he'd botched things up between them irreparably? What if the measly words he'd prepared weren't enough?

What if he couldn't even get her to open the door?

Impatient and frustrated and conscious of the fact that they had a rehearsal dinner to get to and a lot to talk about before then, Tate had waved Lyla's book at the peephole and shot her a look through the tiny piece of glass that could only be interpreted as *what the fuck is this?*

She'd opened the door. She'd looked perplexed. She hadn't bothered with *hello, how are you*—and Lyla hadn't said a word about her new book. She'd only wanted to know why Tate was there.

He was there because he'd been a fool to walk away from her. He'd been torturing himself for twenty-nine days with the dire outcomes that might result from him leaving, not the least of which was the fear that Lyla might meet some new man in this city of millions.

That she might fall for him, and he for her.

And, while the thought of any harm coming to her without Tate there as her first line of defense was enough to make his head explode, the notion of Lyla cuddling up to some other dude every night was a special, DEFCON-4 level of horrifying.

He'd realized, nearly too late, that Lyla was his—but more than that, Tate had figured out that he was hers, body and soul. He loved the woman standing expectantly in front of him like nothing else in this world, and it was about time he told her.

Before he could do that, though, they had to talk about her little story, and what she'd been thinking when she wrote it.

Tate pulled his phone from his pocket and once again cued up the pdf file that Red had sent him. Lyla eyed it warily, but she didn't look terribly guilty. If anything, she only seemed resigned.

She said, "I didn't think you would ever know about that."

"Know? I've relived our time together a million times. But to read it…read it like this?" Tate sputtered, searching for clarity. "Either I talk in my sleep, or you read minds, because that is the only way this book makes sense to me."

Lyla looked confused by his consternation. "I'm sorry—what?"

"God, you must've felt like you had a wolf slavering over you all that time. How did you stand it?"

"I don't really think…"

"You did yourself a real disservice, by the way," Tate told her. "You are far more beautiful, and clever, than this broad." He waved his phone again half-heartedly.

Lyla peered at his clenched hand and then at his face, sporting a puzzled frown behind her cute tortoiseshell glasses. "If you don't mind me asking, what exactly has you so worked up right now? Is it because you feel violated? Like I took something private and made it public?"

Tate paused. He hadn't considered *that* aspect of this whole conundrum for even one second. He'd been too busy feeling embarrassed over his pathetic puppy routine and wondering how to overcome it in order to get her back.

"You do know that I'm the only person who has any idea that book isn't complete fiction, right? Well, me and whoever gave that to you, anyway."

Lyla held an arm out and stood aside, gesturing him further into her apartment so they could go sit on her couch.

Right. Because Tate had been so keyed up when he arrived, they'd hadn't made it more than three feet past her front door.

He followed her and struggled to articulate what was so unnerving about *The Last Man Standing.* He had assumed he'd know what to say about it once he got here, but words were not his forte like they were Lyla's, and Tate was faltering.

Plus, when Lyla didn't even bother to deny it was really about them, it threw him even more off-balance.

He laughed at himself in contempt. "All that time we were together, I thought I was this impenetrable. I figured not even you could see through me—but I was transparent as hell, wasn't I? Mooning around like a lovesick middle-schooler with his first crush?"

"Tate—"

"What?" he complained. "It's humiliating. I might not be a real bodyguard, but I do have *some* training. I should've been able to conduct myself a little more professionally. But I couldn't resist you. I couldn't hold out for long at all before I was all over you like a cheap suit."

Lyla studied him in astonishment, her eyes like saucers and her lips hanging open.

Tate's eyes dipped to that mouth he adored so much, and he abruptly realized what he'd blurted out moments ago. Lovesick. *Love.* Oh, Lord. This was not the way he'd intended to tell her.

He had rushed back to New York because he was in love with this woman, and yet here he was, freaking *arguing* with her about some book, instead of falling to his knees and telling her what she meant to him.

Tate was supposed to be telling Lyla why he was still so hung up on her every minute of every day. He ought to be saying he was here—despite deciding in very definite and unwavering terms that he was going to move on with his life and let Lyla do the same—because he couldn't *not* be.

For heaven's sake, he'd been an irritable bastard to all and sundry for a month, pretending like he was hunky-dory when in fact he'd been dying without her. The whole time, he'd been low-key scouring the internet for any little mention of Lyla Lawson to get him through.

He'd yearned for his girl so much.

My, my, my Delilah. There'd clearly been a part of Tate clinging to the hope that he'd get to have her again someday, maybe even permanently.

And yet, Tate was finally in Lyla's apartment with her, and he was debating things that were so unimportant. All the wind went out of him just like that, and he slumped onto her couch.

He stared down at the phone in his hands in defeat. Yes, he was in love with her, but this was never going to work with a dunce like him at the helm.

Lyla was still watching him, Tate realized, but he couldn't make himself meet her eyes. Not yet, anyway. Not until he figured out what to do next.

She stood firm and cleared her throat to get his attention. "Can we go back to the beginning for a minute?" she inquired gently. "I think I might need to clear a few things up."

Tate nodded bleakly.

"You don't talk in your sleep," she stated matter-of-factly, "And I can't read your mind."

She studied him for a few moments longer, then continued, "I wrote that book very quickly, while we were together and in the first week or so after Brett's attack. It was like…like a souvenir—a picture of a place we'd been, so I wouldn't forget it."

Tate made himself focus on her, finally seeing past his own anxiety and noticing how nervous Lyla seemed, despite the determination in her voice. Didn't she realize that she was the one holding all the cards here?

She said, "I thought…I wanted to hold onto *us* for a while longer. I wasn't sure I should even be writing a book that personal, you know? But with Red Devil's launch and Trident so eager to get my new series off the ground…I ended up taking the leap of faith anyway."

Then she perched beside him gingerly, explaining, "The book tour—the part we got to, anyway—went really well, and people were getting excited about Red Devil because of it. The folks at Trident thought that if we could get this title ready to release quickly, having a second book published so soon would cement the series. They're rushing it out, Tate."

Surprise, surprise—Tate's protective instincts kicked right in. He sat up and wondered, "You mean *Red's* rushing it out? When you aren't ready. Do I need to hurt him for bullying you, or what?"

"He's not bullying me," she assured him. "He's simply…very persuasive. But that's not important. What I want you to consider is this: if you are about as easy to see through as a piece of granite and I have no telepathic ability, then where did this story come from?"

For emphasis, Lyla reached down and tapped Tate's phone screen.

She waited and waited, while Tate floundered and wilted under her scrutiny. When he couldn't come up with a response that didn't sound cocky as hell and he couldn't stand the quiet a second longer, he grudgingly asked, "I don't know, where?"

Sitting there like a dimwit student being grilled by his hot teacher, it dawned on him rather abruptly what Lyla was implying, though. Tate's head snapped up and he searched her face.

"If you were sticking to the *friends-with-benefits* rules," she asked, "Then which one of us, do you suppose, was the one who ended up too deep? Who was the one spinning unrealistic fantasies about an object of attraction who'd made their position on the subject exceptionally clear?"

Tate was, for one of the only times in his life, utterly speechless. He *hadn't* stuck to the rules. Lyla Lawson could not have gotten his viewpoint more wrong, and she couldn't possibly be telling him that she had fallen for him, too. It was inconceivable.

"Tate, whose brain works that way—so much so, that she's made a career out of it?" Lyla wondered softly. Then she raised her hands and pointedly cracked her knuckles.

It was their secret signal. She hadn't mentioned love, though, had she? Only…attraction?

Tate had already known that Lyla was attracted to him, of course, and it was a weak excuse for love, but suddenly it felt like something he could work with. If Lyla still wanted him to make love to her, then maybe Tate could make her love him, as well.

Eventually.

He stared at Lyla as his mind spun. His sluggish synapses were finally starting to drop pieces into the larger puzzle, and Lyla must have seen the glimmer of sense returning to his eyes.

She nodded. It was hesitant, almost imperceptible—but Tate had spent weeks learning how to interpret her every move. To him, that nod was clear as a bell.

Slowly, he leaned toward her, giving her plenty of time to reject him. He made a show of swiping past a few pages on the phone gripped in his hand and even glanced at a page, but he couldn't focus on a word. Tate could only see Lyla's beautiful eyes looking back at him.

She was beginning to look faintly alarmed, however. He'd better make this quick.

"Let's see," Tate murmured. "I think I know what comes next, here." He tossed his phone on the end table and edged closer still. "Probably had it memorized before you even wrote it."

Lyla wrung her hands together. "Are you afraid I made you look bad in the book? I didn't intend to."

He had to laugh at that. "Sweetheart, you made me look like a damn hero. Larger than life, even though I don't deserve it. You only shortchanged yourself."

Tate was inches away now, crowding Lyla toward the armrest behind her. When her back hit the pillows, she swallowed and whispered, "You don't see what I see."

How could his heart not go soft at that? He'd wanted to be a hero for her, and he'd blown it, but Lyla didn't seem to care. She was still looking at him like he hung the moon, and that meant maybe Tate would get another chance to show her he could be what she needed.

Tate would be anything and everything Lyla needed if she'd let him.

"All I can see is you," he said.

He rested one arm on the couch next to her and trailed his other hand through her slightly-damp, mahogany hair. It felt like silk, cool and smooth.

"How come you never called?" she asked him. "It hurt, Tate."

He was a big, asinine dunderhead, but he still nuzzled under the sweep of her hair to find the warmth of Lyla's neck, exposed so delectably by her pretty gown. When his lips met her skin, Lyla shivered, just like she'd always done before.

"How come you never told me how you felt?" he countered.

"Are you joking?" she laughed, but it was a sound without much humor. "It would've been pointless. I couldn't exactly ask you to carry on some long-distance thing with me when you were so anxious to leave, and besides—you'd already told me you didn't do that. What about me—"

Lyla gestured wildly to herself, narrowly missing Tate but managing to crack her knuckles against a nearby lamp in the process.

She winced, but finished, "—would convince a guy like you to stay *here*?" She blurted it out as if that one sentence encompassed a myriad of unsuitable things about her.

Tate smiled. Lord, she was even cute when she was klutzy, and Lyla's vulnerability at that moment made this whole undertaking seem crazily possible, all of a sudden.

He moved his lips up her throat and came to stop near her ear. "*Everything.* Everything I always wanted in a woman and could never find. Everything I didn't even know I needed. But I still tried to make myself walk away. I tried to make myself leave you because you deserve so much more than some washed-up soldier with no future."

Tate exhaled heavily, the weight of that statement bearing down on him. Lovey-dovey feelings were all fine and dandy, but if he couldn't take care of his woman…then what good was he going to be to her?

Lyla's expression was sympathetic, though. Her hand crept along his waist and slipped up his back, and Tate pressed closer, a sucker for her touch every time.

What he actually needed, of course, was to be kissing her, and beyond that, to be buried deep inside her, so far that neither of them knew where one ended and the other began.

Tate's throat closed. He lost his train of thought. He went instantly hard, remembering how good those things were between them.

However, he had to push distractions like that aside for now, or he was liable to find himself tossed right back out into that soulless hallway before he won this battle. Tate couldn't bear that so soon after reuniting with her again.

Lyla's hands framed his face, and he looked down at her. Her voice only quavered a little when she said, "What I deserve is you."

She took in a big lungful of air that pressed her breasts against his chest, then dropped her hands to his shoulders. Tate tried mightily not to get sidetracked by all the enticing sensations winding around him.

Lyla went on, "I never thought you'd see that book. That was why I agreed to let them release it so soon. You told me you never read fiction. I thought it would be safe."

Tate examined her closely. Lyla seemed embarrassed that he'd discovered her secret, but was she ashamed because she'd taken the skeleton of their relationship and dressed it up to sell some books—or because she'd meant every lovelorn word and thought he was here to give her a hard time about it?

In some dusty corner of his brain, he recognized that he ought to give the poor woman some space until they sorted this out. However, now that he had her in his arms again, he couldn't seem to let her go. *So much for self-control.* Where Lyla was concerned, Tate had none.

She said softly, "The only way I could be brave enough to give us a happily-ever-after, was because I thought I wouldn't ever have to face your…" she chuckled that same, oddly mirthless laugh, "…I don't know. Amusement? Teasing? I can't believe you actually read it, Tate! I'm going to kill Red."

For some reason, Lyla's dismay tickled the hell out of him, so Tate planted a happy little kiss on the tip of her nose. He scooped her up in his arms and pulled her back into his lap, smiling widely. His plan was actually going to work.

Lyla's face looked as dejected as his must have earlier, but she still wrapped her arms around his neck and rested her head on his shoulder. So sweet, but so put-out that she'd had to admit she wanted Tate for more than his horizontal boogie skills.

They were both complete numskulls, but strangely, the fact gave him hope.

"Slick, why exactly do you think I'm here?" he asked her.

"Pride?" she guessed. "Your enormous ego? Because I took your huge freaking *ego* and turned it into a book?" Her jaw jutted out sullenly.

Now, Tate was definitely amused. "Say I'm huge again," he told her.

Lyla whacked him on the arm.

"You're not even close, Einstein," he explained. "Review, if you will, everything I've said since I got here, and see if *you* can figure this out." It sure had taken him long enough to catch on, but Tate was confident she'd get it faster.

Lyla scowled darkly at him. "What are you talking about?"

"It's okay, take your time. I'll wait here."

She blinked at him. A furrow dug in between her brows, her nose crinkled right over the bridge, and she nibbled on her bottom lip. Lyla was a sexy study in piqued concentration, and Tate wanted to kiss her senseless even more than he had before.

"You…" she accused finally. "You…"

"All caught up now?" he inquired cheerfully. "Good."

Lyla rolled her eyes, but she was smiling, and that was a start.

"Lest there be any misunderstanding," he said, "I'm in love with you, Lyla. Wholly and completely."

"You are?"

"I really am. You are warm and sweet and beautiful, and I want to hold you close every day for the rest of our lives, even if you make me eat a lot of those big portobello mushrooms."

"Oh, thank God," Lyla breathed, burying her face in his neck and jabbing him in the throat with the corner of her glasses. She did it again when she raised her head a second later. "Tate—I am wildly, crazily, totally in love with you, too."

"I am very, very happy to hear that."

"But how do we do this? You told me yourself that you hate long-distance relationships. Are you going to stay in Ohio? Or move here?"

"For you, I would make long-distance work. But you don't have to worry, sweetheart. There will be nothing long-distance about you and me."

Lyla looked cautious but hopeful. "How do you figure?"

"Well, there's good news and bad news. Which would you like first?"

"The good. *Duh.*"

"You're looking at Manhattan's newest resident."

She gaped at him. "That's awesome. And the bad?"

"I might be a teensy bit homeless and unemployed for a bit. But who cares, right?" Tate laughed shakily. "Jobs have got to be a dime a dozen in this town." At least, he prayed they would be— if he had to, he'd fucking wash dishes, though, just to be close to her.

Lyla squealed and hugged him tightly. "You're moving here? You're really moving here?"

"I really am."

"But what about the Army? Are they going to put you on desk work until your discharge goes through?" She slapped a hand over her mouth. "Oh my God. They better have given you benefits. I forgot to ask."

"Lyla, it's all good. I'm done, and the separation feels like it was on my terms. I'll have medical benefits and a retirement stipend that will hold me over until I find something more permanent."

"Still, I am so sorry you couldn't help your friends with that mission they called about."

"Don't be. They can do it. And even though I didn't want to admit it, it was time for me to get out and try something new. Meeting you just helped me see that it wasn't such a bad thing, after all."

Lyla's eyes filled up, and she asked him, "Hey, did you hear the one about the badass who was in the right place at the right time?"

Damn, he couldn't love this woman more. "It's my favorite story," Tate grinned.

"Mine, too."

"You know what would make it even better?"

"Uh-uh."

He gave her a long, leisurely kiss, then set her beside him on the sofa and slipped down onto one knee. "If the badass got to keep the girl forever."

Lyla's face went slack with shock, so Tate hurried to explain, "Hey, I know it's soon, and we have a lot to figure out in the meantime. All you have to tell me now is whether, someday in the near future, you'd be okay with me getting into this position again, and doing it the right way—with the proper bling, and all the romantic trimmings."

"Wait, wait, wait, Mr. Always Prepared," she protested. "Do you really expect me to believe you didn't have this mapped out down to the second?"

"What can I say? I get carried away around you."

"*Yeah, right.*"

Tate laughed up at her. "And now, we welcome Lyla Lawson, killer of book characters…and apparently moods, too. Welcome, Ms. Lawson."

"Thank you," she said primly, "It's a pleasure to be here."

"So…what do you say?"

Lyla bit her lip, then grinned from ear to ear. "I would be very okay with you doing this again someday." She wrapped Tate in her arms, and murmured into his ear, "As long as it's not *too* far in the future."

"You have my word," Tate said—and this time, nothing on earth would stop him from keeping it.

Epilogue

TATE KICKED BACK at Red and Piper's reception, watching the women in colorful dresses swirl around the dance floor with their partners. Big band tunes were being played by the musicians tucked in the corner, and soon, he intended to get Lyla out there to take a turn or two with him.

They'd managed to get the happy couple hitched without any major snafus, but as Tate sat there with his arm around his woman, it didn't feel as if Red was the king of the world tonight. It felt like Tate was.

Lyla was a vision in her sparkly, bronze-colored gown, and she'd been getting an abhorrent amount of appreciative male attention all damn day. But she was in love with *him*, and it felt like a lightning strike of the first order—as rare and stupendous as they came.

Now that Tate had found the kind of love he'd only ever heard about before, he never wanted to let a day go by without it. Therefore, he needed to get his shit together fast, so he could deserve this extraordinary woman, and keep her.

She'd already convinced him to move in with her and they were on the hunt for a bigger place, but Tate still needed a real job to keep him busy, and to lay the groundwork for their future together.

To that end, he'd had a crazy idea in the middle of the night last night.

Now was as good a time as any to see what Lyla thought of it. It would impact her life as much as his and getting a new business off the ground could be hard. Tate might have to work some long hours in the beginning, and some really weird hours if it was actually successful.

"Hey, Slick?" he asked her. "What if, instead of looking for the perfect job for months on end, I just…created my own?"

"What do you mean?"

"Well, I've been thinking. I'm not the only guy getting out of the service with an interesting skill set. There are probably a lot of other veterans in the same position. Unfortunately, there are probably also a lot of people out there who could use our services."

"You mean as bodyguards?" Lyla wondered.

Tate had considered that, but he thought he could reach higher. "I was thinking more…high-level security."

She eyed him suspiciously. "Why do I get the impression you're not talking about mall cops?"

"Because I meant things like hostage rescues and stuff. Government contracting, maybe."

"Tate—that sounds dangerous."

"You're right. It would be. But I'd be really selective about what kind of jobs we took, and I'd take every possible precaution to keep the team safe."

"Wouldn't you need to outfit them? You'd need…what, like guns and ammunition, and gear and stuff, right?"

"All that. And ideally, I'd like to set up a home base of sorts, too. I have some cash socked away, so if I find a big enough piece of land somewhere out of the way, I could potentially do it there."

"Wow," Lyla breathed. "That's a big deal."

Tate agreed. "It is, which is why I want to make sure we're both completely on board before I do anything. I might already have a couple of early investors in Red and Luca. I mentioned it in passing to them at Red's stag party and they wanted to help. But I won't take any steps until I know you're okay with it."

"And if I'm not?" she asked.

"Then I'll find something else."

Lyla's eyes narrowed as she studied him. "*Something else* means the same kind of work with another security firm, clearly. So, you'd be in danger, either way."

"I'm sorry, sweetheart," Tate told her. "Right now, it feels like a good fit for me. The best of both worlds—a home life, plus the parts I enjoyed about the military."

"But what about your head?" Lyla spread her napkin on the table and began pleating it into a fan.

"Well, that's the beauty of this, I think. If it's my firm, I don't necessarily have to go out on all the jobs. I can stay or go depending on how I feel."

"Hmm."

"You were prepared to make it work if I stayed in the service, weren't you?" he asked, picking up her hand and lacing his fingers through hers. "This is no worse than that. In fact, it's better, because I'd be calling the shots. I won't have to wait on some egghead in D.C. to tell me whether to stay or go or pull the trigger."

Lyla chewed on her lip. "I know you'd be terrific at it, Tate. I just don't want to lose you."

"You won't. Not for a long time." He held her gaze, trying to communicate how much he meant it.

"Bold promises," she muttered, rolling her eyes. "Tempt fate much?"

"Listen, life's a long string of unpredictability. I could get CTE, or you could get hit by a car. One of us could get cancer. We could have a kid who gets cancer." Tate hated saying those words, but he had to put it out there.

"Or how about none of that."

"Or none of that, God willing. It's impossible for us to know what the future holds."

"True enough. I sure as hell never saw *you* coming," Lyla said, winking saucily at him.

"You can see me coming whenever you want," Tate growled into her ear. "And we'll deal with whatever else comes our way, too, I promise. But this thing—this could be a great thing for me, Slick. For us."

"I know," she conceded, then straightened her shoulders. "So, do it. We shouldn't decide based on things that might not happen. We'll hope for the best, and prepare for the worst, just like you said."

"Will you help me?"

"Of course. So, let's start at the beginning. Do you have a name picked out yet?"

As a matter of fact, he did. "How does Black Watch sound?"

"Like hell's a-coming."

"You better believe it."

Review

Did you enjoy **The Hero Was Handsome**? If so, please consider leaving a review at the retailer where you purchased this title.

Book reviews can be as simple or as detailed as you wish, but all of them help authors sell more books, and assist other readers in finding the stories they want to read.

Almost any book can be reviewed by simply logging into the website where you purchased the title, then scrolling to the bottom of the title's product page to find an area called "Leave a Review."

Up Next

Black Watch

A heart-pounding new romantic suspense series, full of deadly, sexy heroes and the capable women who steal their hearts.

Book One is coming your way soon!

FREE BOOK

Get a glimpse of Morgan, Meg, Molly and Mina—*before* their happily ever afters take place!

Sign up for the author's Reader's List and get a free copy of the Lost & Found prequel novella "Girls Night Out."

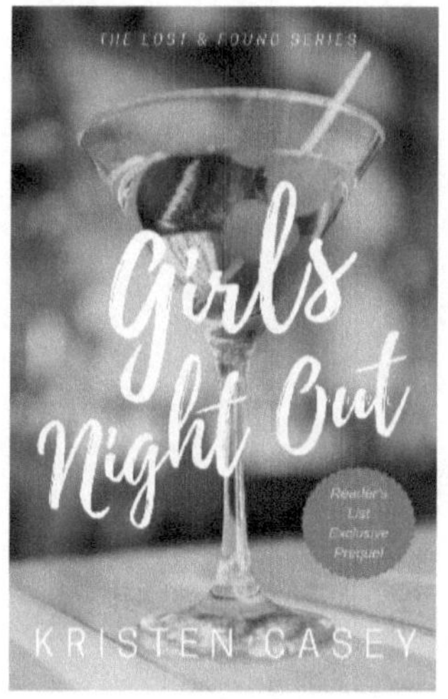

Visit Here to Get Started:

http://eepurl.com/ctGk1j

Also by Kristen Casey

The Lost & Found Series

Girls Night Out
Finding Home
Finding Love
Lost in Love
Lucky in Love
Christmas in Cambridge
The Flynn Sisters Box Set
Finding a Husband
Heroes & Husbands
Finding Forever
Forever and a Day
Forever Starts Now
The O'Connell Sisters Box Set

The Black Watch Security Series

False Flag
Heat Seeking Missile
Brothers in Arms
Fight or Flight
Search and Destroy
Squared Away

Acknowledgments

This book was hard to write—oh man, so hard—yet not in the sense of "what is it even about?" The novel was there all along, in my head and in my heart, but life got busy while Tate and Lyla's story was being developed, and there never seemed to be enough hours in the day to get everything done.

I had to shoehorn in the writing wherever I could—had to dig to find the time needed to sit and focus, get it out, and make it the best it could be. It wasn't easy, but eventually it all came together in a way that I love.

So, first and foremost, I want to thank my family for their patience, their understanding, and their willingness to stay flexible when Mom was trying to get it done. They gave me a pep talk when I needed it, they celebrated big and small victories, and they always let me finish that one last thought, paragraph, or page—so I'd be free to give them my full attention once more.

Plus, they pretended to be interested when I talked about all the minutiae of the plot and the characters, *and* the vagaries of the publishing industry—so I'm grateful for what good fakers they've all become, too.

Thanks also go to Deborah at Tugboat Design who, once again, has perfectly captured the feel of Hero's story with her beautiful book cover. She's so creative and resourceful, and always gracious about my odd, nitpicky requests. Basically, a dream to work with every time.

I also want to thank Helen Snay, my proofreader extraordinaire, who's been waiting semi-patiently for Tate's story from the very beginning. She's cheered me on, begged and pleaded with me to *finish it already*, and occasionally even encouraged me to get up and move around a bit—all so she could get Hero in her hot little hands faster. Here you go, friend: enjoy your new book boyfriend! I hope you love him as much as I do.

Last but never least, thank you to my readers: Your support means the world to me. Never change.

About the Author

Kristen Casey writes the kind of heartfelt, steamy books she loves to read—full of relatable characters and snarky dialogue. She lives in Maryland with her husband, two kids, and assorted cats, and in her free time enjoys all things crafty—especially projects she finds on Pinterest.

Sign up for her newsletter to receive exclusive content, sales, and new releases emailed right to your inbox.

Follow her on social media, for even more fun stuff!

Goodreads: Kristen_Casey

Facebook: AuthorKCasey

Twitter: @AuthorKCasey

Pinterest: KristenCase0461

Instagram: Kristen.Casey.Books

BookBub: Kristen Casey

TikTok: KristenWritesRomance

Reading Order of Kristen's Books

The Lost & Found Series

Girls Night Out (Prequel exclusive to subscribers)

Finding Home (Book 1)

Finding Love (Book 2)

Lost in Love (Book 2.5 – Includes *Lucky in Love*)

The Flynn Sisters Box Set (Includes *Christmas in Cambridge*)

Finding a Husband (Book 3)

Finding Forever (Book 4)

Forever and a Day (Book 4.5 – Includes *Forever Starts Now*)

The O'Connell Sisters Box Set (Includes *Heroes & Husbands*)

The Triple Threat Series

The Titan was Tall (Book 1)

The Doctor was Dark (Book 2)

The Hero was Handsome (Book 3)

The Triple Threat Box Set (Includes *The Masquerade was Magic* and *The Hero's Brother*)

The Black Watch Security Series

False Flag (Book 1)

Heat Seeking Missile (Book 2)

Brothers in Arms (Book 3)

Fight or Flight (Book 4)

Search and Destroy (Book 5)

Squared Away (Book 6)